WELCOME TO THE FAE WORLD

HELL FAE WARDEN

USA TODAY BESTSELLING AUTHORS

LEXI C. FOSS   J.R. THORN

Editing by: Outthink Editing, LLC

Proofreading by: Katie Schmahl & Jean Bachen

Cover Design: Covers by Juan

Cover Photography: Wander Aguiar

Cover Models: Sophie, Alex, Philippe, Forrest & Camden

Hell Fae Realms Illustration: Tomasz Madej of Fictive Designs

Chapter Header Art: Nathan Hansen Illustration

Ornamental Chapter Art: Ricky Gunawan

Chapter Watermark for Ajax, Cami, Az, and Typhos: Claire Holt

Chapter Watermark for Melek: Covers by Aura

Published by: Ninja Newt Publishing, LLC

Physical Edition

ISBN: 978-1-68530-242-9

To all those who love the "D." We have four of them for you to enjoy. Cheers.

A NOTE FROM LEXI & JEN

Thank you for picking up *Hell Fae Warden*! We hope you enjoy this dark world as much as we do.

For those new to the series, we strongly recommend starting with *Hell Fae Captive*, as this book picks up the same story to carry forward.

Just a note of caution: This series contains strong sexual undertones, violent scenes, and themes of dubious consent. There are also several strong male-on-male relationships in this world, and these men absolutely love to fuck each other. But they'll be inviting Cami to join them... once she proves her worth. ;)

However, Cami isn't the type of heroine to bend over and take it. She'll fight until the bitter end.

Her mates have a lot of work ahead of them.

As well as some groveling to do along the way.

Their journey won't be easy. But it'll be deliciously sinful.

So continue your trek through the Hell Fae world. Be careful who you trust. And watch out for the infamous mirages.

Nothing is what it seems.
Just like our Hell Fae mates...

ABOUT HELL FAE WARDEN

"Why am I naked and tied to a chair?"
Because you're in Hell, little rebel. *My* hell.

Camillia De la Croix isn't human.
She's a Halfling Hell Fae with a fiery spirit and a will that
refuses to break.

The rebellious beauty escaped my dungeon.
Fled Hell.
Then fucked off to fae only knows where.

Now I'm paying the price for her little jaunt around the fae
realms.
Because her antics earned us both the wrath of the Hell
Fae King.
He blames *me* for allowing her escape.

If I don't find out how she managed her little field trip, I'll
probably be shipped off to the Netherworld Kingdom to
play with the Corpse Fae.

Fortunately, Hell Fae Commander Az wants the answer to this riddle just as badly as I do.
Prince Melek, too.
The three of us will break Camillia's resolve.
Then we'll throw her back into the Hell Fae trials where she belongs.

You took advantage of my hospitality once, sweetheart.
It won't be happening again.
Now start talking, or I'll turn up the heat.
And this time, you won't be allowed to come.

INTRODUCTION

Welcome to the land of nightmares
where monsters are real,
seeing isn't always believing,
and fate is for the weak.
—Ajax

HELL FAE REALM

A REVEALED PAGE FROM LUCIFER'S BOOK, VITA

Once upon a time, an angel Fell. His feathers were stripped, his light was extinguished, and he landed in the fires of a broken land.

But this was no ordinary angel.

He knew his world was about to end before the ultimate betrayal arose, and inside him, he hid the source of his light. His true power. His ultimate revenge.

From that fiery ember of energy, he created a new world—the Hell Fae Realm. And within it, he accepted all the creatures every other fae realm rejected.

Nightmare Fae. Abominations. *Monsters*.

As his new court grew, various kingdoms were established. Each one is ruled by a protective Mythos Fae, and beneath them, various Fae Kings.

This entry is considered to be an index of those kingdoms and known species within. It changes and grows daily, but I am Vita, Lucifer's prized book. I know all. I document all. And now, I'll share that knowledge with you, dear reader...

Barren Lands: Desertlike dry areas with rocky landscapes and little to no water sources. Centaurs, Manticores, Minotaurs, Air Dragons, Griffins, and Boggarts make these lands their home. It has also recently been used to house the Hell Fae Bridal Candidates within a unique paradigm.

Hell Fae Kingdom: A centralized kingdom that Typhos Lucifer calls home. All non–Nightmare Fae creatures reside here, as do Lucifer's infamous Hellhounds.

Marsh Lands: Murky waters and swampy plant life make this an ideal home for Nagas and Unseelie.

Morpheus Kingdom: This is the land of dreams, where Nightmare Fae feed on terror and fear. Ghouls and Stigori call this place home, but one of Lucifer's personal creations lives here, too—the Kuntilanak Fae.

Netherworld Kingdom: Darkness and wisps of dull moonlight haunt the graveyards of this kingdom, making it an optimal home for Corpse Fae and Death Fae.

Underwater Kingdom: Vast oceans and coral-like castles paint this kingdom in a sea of unique colors. Kelpies and Water Dragons call this kingdom home, but some of Lucifer's personal creations, like Sirens, reside here, too.

HELL FAE REALM

Marsh Lands

Hell Fae Kingdom

Morpheus Kingdom

Underwater Kingdom

Barren Lands

Netherworld Kingdom

PROLOGUE: TYPHOS

Pain etched across my back, shredding through my feathers as I fell.

She betrayed me, I thought, whirling through a cloud of fiery intensity. *She used me. Vivaxia—*

A blast ricocheted through my being, the source ripping apart in response to my agony. My anger. My *need* for vengeance.

She'll pay. They'll all fucking pay.

I roared, my wings billowing in the fire, attempting to pull me to freedom, to face my aggressors, to slaughter them all.

But I was too weak. It didn't matter that Azazel had warned me. There hadn't been enough time, the plan too close to completion for me to properly prepare for this fight.

Oh, but Melek… I swallowed. *My precious Melek.*

Would it be enough?

Or would he perish with me in this fall? Tossed from the Virtuous planes. *Down… down… down…*

"Typhos," Melek whispered into my ear. "I'm here."

I glanced around the burning clouds, searching for my prince. My love. My *heart. Where?* I wanted to ask, unable to see him. *It's too bright. Too hot. Too—*

My eyes narrowed, a strand of gray light curling up into my vision with a tainted black edge. *What is that?* I wondered, suddenly distracted from the intense power eating away at my spirit. *Is the source... dying?*

No, that's not right. I frowned. *None of this is right.*

Where am I?

"Typhos," Melek repeated. "Look at me."

I blinked, then searched for him to obey, his voice an anchor in my world that I would forever latch on to. But I couldn't see him. Just more fire. *And that strange strand again.*

Something was... fracturing. *The source,* I recalled. *Yes. The reason I'm falling.*

Except... no. That wasn't right. I'd fallen eons ago.

What is happening to me?

"*Typhos.*" Melek's voice held a renewed urgency to it that pierced right through my heart. "Wake. Up."

Wake up? I repeated, delirious all over again. *I'm not...*

My lips curled down, that tendril turning completely black in my peripheral vision and forming a jagged edge in the white flames.

"*Typhos!*" Melek shouted.

But I was too consumed by that strange fissure in the otherwise flawless surface. I reached out to touch it and hissed at the sharp edge. *A fracture in the source,* I realized. *But that... that isn't possible.*

Nor was any of this around me.

This... this nightmare of my past melting into my present.

I'd fallen.

I'd created a new source.

And now, I *protected.*

Only, something was happening to those beneath my invisible wings. Something nefarious. *A breach in the Hell Fae Realm.*

My eyes flew open to find a worried Melek staring down at me, his multicolored eyes holding a white streak that only appeared when he was emotionally distraught.

"Melek?" My voice came out in a rasp, making me wonder how long I'd been asleep. It almost felt as though I'd been yanked out of a watery grave, my lungs having lost the will to draw in air.

"You wouldn't wake up," he whispered, his palm on my cheek. "And I felt... something. Something strange."

"The source," I told him, swallowing. "A breach."

His full lips curled down, turning his beautiful features into a frown that was so very unlike my little prince. "A breach?"

"In our realm." I cleared my throat and grabbed the back of his nape, mostly because I needed his support, but also because I needed to sit up. To think. To *focus*. He allowed me to move him, his palm going to my chest, right over my heart, as I searched my mind for my links to the source.

It responded immediately, granting me access to the heart of my power—a power I'd created—and showing me everything I needed to see.

Including that rotten strand.

Growling, I shoved my essence at the intruding energy and narrowed my eyes when it remained. *What are you?* I wondered. *You don't belong here.*

I gathered more strength to blast it again, when an alarm split through the air, a sound that could only be initiated by one of my Nightmare Kings.

My eyes flew open as Melek slid out of our bed to meander toward the source of the alarm. He didn't bother with clothes, my prince too concerned—or perhaps too confident—to care about his nude state.

I followed him to the screen, grabbing both my robe and his along the way. He took it from me without his usual side commentary, his jaw set tight as he selected a barely visible button in the air.

A hologram appeared with Onyx, the Corpse Fae King. "My liege," he greeted, his dark head bowing slightly. "We have a problem."

"Yes, I assumed that from the alarm. What's wrong?" I demanded.

He hesitated, then cleared his throat. "I... I'm not sure how to say this, but a portal has been created. One that traverses realms."

"What?" Melek asked, his gaze meeting mine. *Is this the breach you felt?* His mental voice was uncharacteristically soft, his concern hidden beneath a mask of stoicism for the Corpse Fae King.

It could be, I replied. *Or it's a result of the breach I sense in the source.*

Which meant someone was toying with Hell Fae magic, which shouldn't have been possible. Because only I could manipulate and control the Hell Fae Source.

"A portal." Melek returned his focus to Onyx. "To which realm, exactly?"

It was a wise question—not that I was surprised; my prince was a strategic genius when he wanted to be. The answer might confirm the motive behind the intrusion.

And that would lead us to the culprit.

Onyx cleared his throat. "It appears several Corpse Fae from the Netherworld, as well as a dozen or so Baku and Ghouls from the Morpheus Kingdom, have run off to some sort of human world. But it doesn't appear to be *our* human world."

"An alternate reality?" Melek translated, his brow furrowing. "That's not possible."

"I agree," I said. Except that dark little strand taunted my mind, suggesting that someone—or some *thing*—had fucked with my source. "Is the portal still open, Onyx?"

"Yes, my liege."

"Where is it located?" I demanded.

He provided the location, causing me to nod. "We'll be there in a moment to review and close it." I turned off the call before he could reply, my focus going to Melek. "There's a black strand in the source."

His eyes widened. "As in dark magic?"

I shook my head. "No. Like a light that's burned out." Just thinking about it had my jaw clenching. "Someone is fucking with the Hell Fae Source, Melek." And I had no idea how that could even happen. It was *my* source. I'd created it. Groomed it. Guarded it. *Lived* for it. "We—"

Another sort of alarm sounded, this one internal rather than external, and it hit me like a jolt from the heart. Because it'd come from Azazel. *What is it?* I asked him. *What's happened?*

Camillia De la Croix has escaped, he hissed. *And we have no idea how.*

"What is it?" Melek murmured.

"It's about your pet," I growled. "Apparently, she's escaped."

Find her, I snapped at Azazel, not having time to discuss an errant Hell Fae Bride. *Find her and bring her to me. I'll handle her once and for all.*

Because I wasn't in the mood for silly games. If she'd found a way to escape—likely by taking advantage of whatever the fuck was going on with my source—then she deserved to be punished.

Her parents had given her soul to me. I owned her.

5

Which meant I could either choose to keep her as a bride in the games or remove her.

"Ty," Melek started.

"Don't." We didn't have time to discuss his infatuation with his pet. We had Nightmare Fae to protect.

And a source to repair, I thought, furious at this turn of events.

Those two items took precedence over an infuriating little Hell Fae Bride.

Besides, my Commander and Warden could handle her.

Meanwhile, I'd fix this mess. Search for the culprit. And *end them*.

CHAPTER 1

CAMI

I'm naked and tied to a chair.

Because Az and Ajax have lost their fucking minds.

Mere hours ago, I'd awoken from a sea of perpetual orgasmic bliss. And I'd been eager to engage in more pleasurable fun, especially when Az's beautiful violet eyes were the first things I'd seen upon stirring.

But now? No. No, I did not want to engage in anything other than a bloodbath.

And I conveyed that by glaring at the males in question.

"You evaded my Phoenix for thirty fucking days, and you're going to tell me how you did it. Right fucking now."

Az's words from sixty minutes ago fluttered around in my mind, leaving me in a befuddled state. I hadn't been able to answer him, too confused by his accusation.

"Thirty days?" I'd repeated. "What are you talking about?"

"Don't play with us, little rebel," Ajax had growled. "Tell us where the fuck you've been."

I'd blinked at his too-beautiful face mere inches from mine, incapable of a reply. What was I supposed to say?

The last thing I remember is you going to take a shower—which I very much wanted to join in on, but Az said you would need some space. So I started reading from my magic law book, and then I somehow ended up in my old apartment-like dorm room. Oh, and only a few hours have passed.

His expression had told me that explanation wouldn't have been very welcome, and Az's dangerous blade had kept me from trying.

So I'd remained silent. And their solution had been to whisk me off in a cloud of smoke and tie me to this very uncomfortable chair.

I stared up into Az's pitch-black irises—a very different color from the violet I'd seen earlier, or whenever that had been—and swallowed.

His arousal had been fierce, but it was nothing compared to this.

Every muscle in his body was coiled as if he were about to strike.

The air distorted around him and wavered in submission. Even his dark hair softly flared out on the ends like feathers.

Or daggers, I thought, shivering.

It wasn't just the tension in the room that made it feel like I couldn't breathe. It was Az's magic, too. It plucked at me as if he had a molten hook inside my soul that he somehow controlled. Each movement left an ache inside of my chest, making me feel as though it wasn't just the rope bindings holding me down.

Tears burned at the edges of my eyes, but I didn't dare shed them. Crying solved nothing. And something told me it wouldn't sway the male before me in the slightest.

This was Az the Commander, not Az the lover. Not

that I knew either side of him well. But I much preferred the latter to the former.

He circled me, that deadly-looking blade still in his hand. Twirling. Repeatedly. Just inches away from my skin.

I swallowed. That was the same knife he'd used on me during sex. Well, not sex, technically. But our... *playtime*.

Only now I suspected he wanted to cut me for entirely different reasons—reasons that had nothing to do with sating Ajax's vampire-like hunger.

The Az from just a few hours ago was long gone. Replaced with a beast that seemed to think I had proved to be more trouble than I was worth.

Because apparently I've been gone for thirty days.

How is that even possible?

And how do I do it again?

Because if their accusations were true, I'd somehow escaped the Hell Fae Bride Trials. Which had been my goal from the beginning.

Lucifer had made a deal with my parents for my soul, forcing me into a battle I wanted no part of—the battle for a Hell Fae husband.

No, thanks.

I'd been holding my own, though. Mostly. All the while trying to find a way to break Lucifer's deal with my parents, or flee.

That made my statement of innocence unlikely to be believed, considering I'd vowed to Ajax that I would find a way to leave.

"I'll survive this," I'd told him. "I'll find a way out."

"You won't," he'd replied.

Apparently, I'd been right. I just had no idea how I'd managed it—something he was never going to believe, as evidenced by the way he lurked near the door to this windowless room and stared at me with unblinking blue-black eyes.

I could barely see him in the darkness of the room, his power seeming to blend into the shadows around him. Only a single torch lit the small space, and even its flame appeared to struggle against the deep chill in the air.

"How long can we stay here?" Az asked, his intense gaze on me despite speaking to Ajax.

Where is here, *by the way?* I wanted to inquire, but I didn't. Wherever *here* was, it was cold. Or I told myself that was the cause for the goose bumps pebbling across my skin. It certainly had nothing to do with the two handsome men holding me captive.

Ajax's dark cloak neatly shielded his body as he pulled a wand from the inner pocket. It flared with purple magic, suddenly brightening his perfect face.

A shiver traversed my spine as I took in his raw, unhidden emotions.

Fury.

Savagery.

Barely restrained rage.

"As long as we need," Ajax said as his magic scented the stale air with fresh pine. The purple glow swept around the four walls of the room, lighting up each brick until it was everywhere.

My nostrils flared and my lungs expanded on instinct as I drew in the familiar essence. Ajax's magic was like nectar to me after our shared experience.

Dizziness swarmed over me in the next beat, suggesting I hadn't been breathing properly. Given that the two powerful males had a chokehold on the oxygen in the room, that wasn't surprising.

It took effort to draw another agonizing gulp of air once the pine started to wear off.

This room was suffocating. Everything about it felt wrong. As did this entire situation.

Not just the windowless walls caging me in or the splintered ropes that dug into my skin, but the cold energy that radiated from everywhere.

We definitely weren't in the Human Realm.

And we weren't in Lucifer's territory, either.

My best guess? Ajax had taken us somewhere familiar to him. Which explained why Az had asked him how long we could stay here.

So we must be in the Midnight Fae Realm, I decided. Because that would be a familiar area to Ajax that he would know more about than Az.

And if we were in Ajax's home territory, then we were likely near other Death Bloods.

Which would also explain the deadly chill.

Although, based on the pungent smell that Ajax's pine-scented magic had finally expelled from my nose, it could also be a tomb.

Because this place reeked of death.

It wasn't exactly a scent like one that came from flowers or incense, but rather a secondary sense that my instincts picked up on. Courtesy of my fae side, not my human one.

Regardless of the source, my instincts fired with wrongness. *I shouldn't be here. We* shouldn't *be here.*

Az moved forward, returning my focus to his obsidian gaze and frying every thought in my mind. Because I was definitely staring at his beast more than the man.

He grazed the point of his knife up my exposed abdomen—not hard enough to bleed, just a subtle taunt to remind me how sharp it could be—and brought it up to rest at the knot directly over my heart.

I stopped breathing again.

"All right, little warrior. Now that you've had some time to think, how about you try answering my question again?" He ticked his head to the side in a birdlike gesture.

"I would if I could," I admitted. "But I don't know. Only a few hours have passed for me, not thirty days."

He grunted and shook his head. "Is that the story you're going with?"

"It's not a story; it's the truth." Alas, there wasn't a chance in Hell that these two would believe me. I could see it in their expressions.

Sure, we'd played around, shared a few orgasms. But that had changed nothing between us.

I was still a prisoner. A Hell Fae Bridal Candidate. Property of the Hell Fae King. And these two were his minions.

His Commander and his Warden.

The truth of my situation had me gritting my teeth.

I'd let these two males hypnotize me with their power and their sensuality. So much so that for a brief moment in time, I'd lost sight of what they really were—*my captors.* Quite possibly they'd also end up being my killers.

Which meant I needed to focus on *escaping.*

Oh, the irony. I'd been able to run away from the Hell Fae prison without actually meaning to, thus leading to this current predicament that I truly needed to get away from.

I would have laughed if I had enough oxygen in my lungs.

Instead, I opted to save my strength and focused on the ropes binding my wrists behind my back. If I could keep these two talking, I might be able to free myself.

Not that I could stand up against both Ajax and Az.

Hmm, unless I can somehow make them focus on each other instead of me.

They clearly had a history together, one that radiated

tension and hot sex. And a hint of anger. Or perhaps that was just both men in general. Ajax was always brooding, and Az... he just seemed *violent*.

Especially right now as he continued to study me with those obsidian orbs. He appeared to be thinking, perhaps about what to say or do next since I hadn't given him a good enough response.

His hand twitched, causing the blade to shift subtly against my skin. He immediately pulled back a little, his eyes flickering between violet and black.

That's interesting, I thought, studying him. *It's almost like he doesn't want to hurt me.*

Which was strange, considering he had a knife poised over my heart.

I leaned forward, curious to see how he would react, and felt a pinch against my delicate skin. Az's pupils flared, and Ajax made a noise that sounded a little bit like a growl. *A hungry growl.*

Midnight Fae were vampiric in nature, making blood their weakness. Especially my blood, which was empowered by fae magic.

"I didn't escape," I reiterated, pressing even more into the blade. "But let's say I did. Why would I go to such an obvious place to be found?"

Az pulled the dagger away, his eyes still flickering between violet and black, almost as though he was losing control over his inner Phoenix. *Odd.* The Commander was feared by the Hellbeasts, yet he seemed to be having trouble taming his own creature.

Because of me? I wondered. *Or because he's just so angry that he's struggling to tame his predatory instincts?*

Az whispered a command that dismissed the blade. Then his thumb replaced the empty space as he pressed down on the wound, disrupting my thoughts.

A hiss escaped through my teeth, my jaw clenching in pain. While the cut had been superficial, the pressure still hurt. Mostly because he wasn't holding back his strength.

Which I supposed answered my mental question. *He's angry. Very fucking angry.* Something I already knew. But it was even more evident in the way his Phoenix appeared to be taking charge.

"You don't know what I'm capable of, little warrior." His silky smooth voice wrapped around my neck like a noose, tightening with each word. "I suggest you cooperate if you don't want to find out."

"Az," Ajax interjected. "We need to remember the rules. She's a *bridal candidate* and therefore Lucifer's property. Not ours."

Az leaned back as soon as the Warden used my title.

Not my name, but my worth as a piece of property to be used for the Hell Fae King's bridal games.

Despite the threat of violence surrounding me, I rolled my eyes. "A bridal candidate. But not *your* candidate. Right, Ajax?" I asked, recalling his words from earlier—*or thirty days ago,* I corrected myself.

Az glanced at him with an arched brow, but Ajax just shook his head. "Have you told Lucifer that we found her?" he asked, changing the subject.

Az released me, leaving the sting of a future bruise behind. *Asshole,* I thought, glaring at his back. "No," he replied. "Our orders were to bring her to him directly, but given everything that's happened in the Netherworld Kingdom, I'm not sure if that's still his desire."

"Do you want to check with him?" Ajax asked, a hint of something in his tone that I couldn't decipher. Some hidden meaning that seemed to resonate between the two old friends.

Az considered him for a long moment. "Yes." Then he

vanished into a puff of ash, leaving me alone with the Warden.

I blinked, surprised by his abrupt departure. He'd seemed rather keen on tormenting answers from me. Or killing me. Perhaps both.

But this certainly presented me with an opportunity. If I could find a way to free myself, I might be able to get away from Ajax.

Maybe.

Probably not very likely.

However, it beat just sitting here and taking this treatment.

Leaning back, I rounded my shoulders and allowed the ropes to squeeze my breasts. The cold air had already turned my nipples into peaks, something Ajax seemed to be trying to ignore as he kept his chin lifted.

Half of my distraction tactic was already done for me.

Men are idiots.

"So what's going on in the Netherworld Kingdom?" I asked, searching for distraction as I continued loosening the knot behind my back. It was making a soft sound against the chair that I hoped our voices would mask.

He snorted. "Nothing to concern your rebellious little head about," he drawled, his gaze still on mine as purple magic weaved around the room, the source of it coming from his wand.

Does that mean his spell isn't done yet? Or is he just radiating power?

I glanced at the walls shimmering with violet smoke and tried to make sense of it, but there wasn't much to go off of. There wasn't much at all, actually. Just black bricks and dark stone with no furnishings or windows. Although, the door was a heavy panel that locked from both sides.

"I think I liked your dungeon better," I murmured, again trying to cover up the motions of my hands.

Stretch.

Scratch.

The rope twisted the wrong way, cutting off the circulation to my left wrist. I bit off a curse and swallowed the pain. *This isn't a great plan,* I told myself. *But what else can I do?*

"I'm sure you did," Ajax deadpanned, not giving me anything.

Right. "At least I had clothes," I hedged. "Sort of, anyway." They were practical outfits, but ones meant to showcase my feminine assets. Still, I hadn't been forced to sit naked before an audience.

Unlike now.

Granted, they'd found me without clothes on, so it wasn't entirely their doing. They'd just chosen not to offer me anything to cover up.

Ajax shoved away from the wall, making me flinch. But he didn't come toward me. He simply whispered a command and disappeared, just without all the black ash.

The temperature dropped—which was something I hadn't even thought was possible in the already chilled room.

Electricity zapped over my skin, leaving me with an ominous sense of dread.

And a subtle cloak of fear choked off my air as I struggled to determine where Ajax had gone.

"Ajax?" I called. When the shadows seemed to close in, I pulled the rope harder. The motion sent needles zipping down my fingers. Panic threatened to seize me as I raised my voice higher. "*Ajax?*"

Some sort of magic activated when I hit the louder decibel, tickling the hair against the back of my neck.

Then the echo of my voice evaporated as if the sound had hit a cotton wall.

Oh God.

It's soundproofing.

That was the point of Ajax's spell. He had created a chamber where no one could hear me scream.

The scent of pine engulfed me as Ajax's muted voice seemed to come at me from all directions.

"Welcome to Hell, little rebel. *My* Hell."

A whispered series of words sent another burst of pine rolling through the room. The ropes binding me turned into hissing snakes, making me screech.

"Now, let's try this again. *How. Did. You. Escape?*"

CHAPTER 2

A Z

MY CHEST HEAVED as I stormed down the hall in Lucifer's domain.

I could have simply reached out to him via our mental connection.

Just as I could have ashed straight to his door, not a thousand steps away in one of the nearby wings. But I needed to get my shit together before I talked to Typhos.

More accurately, I needed to harness my Phoenix before it clawed straight through my chest. The tattoo that marked my animal's spirit itched over my skin and burned as if I'd spread Manticore acid all over it.

It fucking hurt.

And it was all because of *her*.

"Stop this," I commanded my errant beast. "Camillia is not ours."

My Phoenix replied with a hiss across my skin, once again threatening to force me to shift.

I leaned against a stone wall with a wince and stared at my reflection in a nearby mirror. The silvery decor in this corridor offered me a broken view of my face, but I could clearly see the black flames of my Phoenix dancing dangerously in my gaze.

My irises were supposed to be violet. But when my Phoenix came out to play, my true nature seeped through.

And right now, he was pissed off.

Not at *her*, like he should be.

But at *me*.

I wasn't sure if anyone else could see him like I could. As a Black Phoenix, I shared my spirit with the beast. He was me, and I was him, but sometimes we maintained different opinions.

Such as our opinion on a certain little bridal candidate that had overstayed her welcome.

As if to remind me why I had once found the girl interesting, my Phoenix inspired a series of memories behind my eyes.

Admittedly, Camillia was beautiful with her warrior-like tendencies and athletic form. And fuck, the way she'd arched while coming in Ajax's mouth had been a repeat in my nightly fantasies for weeks. My Phoenix was salivating for another taste, determined to mark her, *breed* her, make her *his*.

It made no sense.

She wasn't our fated mate, something I'd adamantly told him a thousand times. But the damn beast had a mind of his own, clawing at my insides and demanding that we sink our teeth into her pretty flesh.

Fuck.

My hands curled into fists as I clenched my jaw. "*Enough*," I told my Phoenix.

It was almost as though he'd imprinted on Camillia, which was impossible. But he refused to listen to reason, leaving me with no choice but to bind him.

He hissed angrily in response, the echo of it fracturing

my heart as I tugged him back into the recesses of my soul. *Heel,* I commanded. *And stay.*

I'd pay for this later, likely in blood. However, I needed him under control so I could properly focus.

While my Phoenix could apparently forget that we'd spent the past thirty fucking days hunting Camillia, I could not. It reminded me of her elusive father. They were perhaps the only fae in history who had ever been able to evade my Phoenix.

But we'd found her.

A victory, I thought, my celebratory instincts warming my veins. Only, it wasn't a party or a drink that I craved in celebration so much as Camillia's blood.

Because I wanted to punish her for escaping. For running. *For being so damn good at hiding.*

The female would learn her place. She was nothing to me. Sure, we had played, but that was over. The moment she'd disappeared without a trace, she'd proved she couldn't be trusted.

That she'd hurt Ajax was all the more reason to punish her. He'd suffered enough for one lifetime. He didn't deserve her adding to his already overflowing plate of death and betrayal.

More so, if she'd had *anything* to do with the current issues plaguing the Hell Fae Realm, then she was a threat to Typhos. And that alone couldn't be tolerated.

That was why we needed to know how she'd escaped and what she'd been doing. I'd hoped to have those answers for Typhos before announcing that we'd captured her, but she'd been less than cooperative.

Of course, I'd barely interrogated her.

However, that was because my Phoenix hadn't allowed me to do what I needed to in order to acquire responses. He hadn't even let me hypnotize her. *Fucking beast.*

But you're quiet now, I taunted him. *Because I'm in charge. Not you.*

And I would rip the answers out of Camillia if I had to. I didn't care if it damaged her beyond repair.

I suspected Typhos would agree with my intentions, but it wouldn't hurt to ensure he approved before I truly interrogated her.

Of course, Camillia had run from his trials at the most inopportune time—or perhaps at the most opportune time, assuming she'd somehow taken advantage of the portal distraction.

Or she's the one who caused it, I thought, my teeth grinding together at the possibility.

Once I had Typhos's permission to unleash my dark side, Camillia would face the full wrath of my beast.

Except, my animal spirit clearly disagreed. My Phoenix had all but burst out of me to stop me from even scratching the female, and now he thrashed against his restraints, threatening to hurt himself. My ribs ached and my muscles burned with the effects of my animal's rage.

"What's wrong with you?" I growled as the fractal wall of mirrors around me filled with the image of black flames. "Why are you acting all territorial over a little blood? I barely nicked her, and you know I can do a hell of a lot more than that."

I mentally reinforced the binds to the point of breaking his wings.

Betrayal ran through my spirit, followed by a cold silence that sent a chill through my soul. *Fuck.* I'd done it now. Rage was an emotion I could handle, especially from my Phoenix. But this... this felt... *deeper.*

I swallowed. *It's for the best,* I promised him. *You'll see.*

Silence.

Not even a ruffle.

I closed my eyes and counted to ten, needing to right myself before I moved on. *She's not ours,* I kept saying to my animal. *Our mate is somewhere out there. We'll find her or him someday. But it isn't her.*

Still no reply.

Sighing, I opened my eyes again and noted that the striking violet had returned to my irises. Not even a hint of black flame remained.

Because I'd shackled it.

Only temporarily, I thought. *Until I do what needs to be done.*

But first, I had to talk to Typhos.

Huffing, I stormed down the remainder of the corridor with my feathers all in a mental twist.

You'll forgive me once I prove she's not ours, I told my Phoenix. *I promise.*

When I reached Typhos's door, I sensed the King of the Hell Fae Realm on the other side.

Just as he likely sensed me, perhaps even well before I'd arrived. My raging emotions probably served as a beacon to his senses. But he wouldn't press me to explain. That wasn't Typhos's way.

Besides, he had enough on his mind at present, what with his Nightmare Fae having thrown a mate-hunting party in another realm.

That fucking portal, I thought, shaking my head. *That* was a true problem. Unlike the one my Phoenix and I were debating.

My animal erroneously thought we'd found our mate. Meanwhile, Typhos was dealing with a potential threat to the Hell Fae Source, which put his entire realm at risk. Very different issues.

One minute, Typhos murmured into my mind. I hadn't needed the warning to know to wait. I could hear his agitated tone through the door, suggesting he was in the middle of talking to someone. Likely another Nightmare Fae King. They were all disgruntled and out of sorts over the delay in the bridal trials, but Typhos was just being cautious.

Of course, he'd phrased it as a punishment for his ungrateful Nightmare Fae.

"My bridal trials are clearly not good enough for you all," he'd said when addressing the Netherworld Kingdom and Morpheus Kingdom two weeks ago. "Why else would you find it necessary to engage in a *Monsters Night* in an alternate reality's realm?"

Apparently, that was a dangerous holiday in the alternate reality—*Monsters Night*. A night where monsters of various origins ventured into the alternate reality's Human Realm to kidnap and claim potential mates. And somehow, the portal created in the Netherworld Kingdom had accessed this infamous occasion.

Several dozen Nightmare Fae had escaped through the illegal breach to find themselves potential brides, thereby defrauding and negating everything Typhos had been trying to accomplish.

So far, only one of them had been taken into custody.
Maliki.
My fucking half brother.

Evidently, he'd manned the portal that had allowed a myriad of Nightmare Fae to slip through the Netherworld and into the Human Realm. And he was completely unapologetic about it.

If he were anyone else, Typhos would probably have killed him by now.

Alas, he was my kin. Therefore, he'd been spared. He was another problem for me to deal with at a later point in time.

Camillia had been priority number one, and still was.

The door opened to reveal Melek's angelic features, his multicolored irises flickering with secrets as he arched a brow at me. "You've found her?" A note of concern underlined those words.

A concern I ignored.

"She's tied up in the Midnight Fae Realm with Ajax," I replied.

"Oh?" That concern was immediately replaced by intrigue. "With rope?"

"With magic rope." Ajax had chosen it in case Camillia tried to escape again. I sort of hoped she would try, just so she could see what happened when she loosened the binds too far.

Snake vines were deadly and vicious and not to be trifled with.

And they *hated* betrayal.

A fitting punishment, I mused. My Phoenix had adamantly disagreed at the time, but he didn't so much as whisper now.

"Hmm." Melek's eyes lit up with amusement. "Good practice, then."

My brow furrowed. "Practice?"

"I assume she's unharmed?" he asked, ignoring my question. Typical Melek.

"Barely even a scratch," I replied.

"Hmm, well, rope can leave a mark when not affixed properly." With that piece of unnecessary advice, he stepped away from the door and led me inside.

Typhos glanced up from his chair in the corner, his legs spread lazily as he drummed his fingers against the table before him. A holographic screen hovered there, the image facing him and resembling a cloud on my side.

Despite his leisurely posture, his aggression practically sent heat waves throughout the room. My Phoenix—if it weren't locked up in a cage—would probably preen beneath the heat. Whereas I, the man outside of the feathers, found it uncomfortable.

I preferred my own black flames to Typhos's all-consuming fire.

His raw power was why I respected him, though. And his ruthlessness to make sure those under his protection remained safe.

Something I wished to mirror in myself. Especially right now. Because if I failed to harness my Phoenix's craving for Camillia, I might endanger those who really mattered.

Typhos.

Ajax.

Melek.

They had all earned my allegiance. Camillia De La Croix had not.

"Then I suggest you remind them who their king is," Typhos said before ending the call and removing an item from his ear.

That would explain why I hadn't heard any audio coming from the screen.

"Nagas tend to value their mates more than their kings," Melek murmured as he prepared a drink at the bar. "I'm not surprised that they're giving Viper a hard time."

Ah, that explained the reason for the headphones. King Viper tended to speak in low tones, making him often hard to understand. The stoic Naga wasn't one for speaking, choosing to whisper only when forced to. He was a Nightmare Fae who preferred action over words.

Very unlike the female of his kind—which were the most deadly and notorious of the Naga species. However, they were a dying race, thanks to the Hell Fae Source rejecting most of them. I assumed that was why his

Nightmare Fae were rioting now, furious that their trials had been put on hold. They needed more women to help repopulate their species. Hence their need for optimal brides.

Viper required one perhaps most of all.

The Nagas were nothing without a queen, but Viper had yet to find his fated mate.

"He needs to remind his constituents why he's king." Typhos sounded tired yet stern.

"While carrying out your order to delay their mating game with the potential candidates," Melek returned as he brought a glass over to Typhos and pressed the rim to the Hell Fae King's lips. "Drink."

Typhos's sapphire irises glittered as he met the Hell Fae Prince's gaze, but he didn't argue, choosing to accept the drink and swallow.

"None of the Nagas participated in Monsters Night," Melek said softly. "They feel they're being unduly punished for another kingdom's bad behavior. That's why they're acting out."

"Just like the Sirens." I didn't mean to interject, but I was aware of their protests as well. "And the Banshees."

"As well as the various dragon breeds." Melek took the drink away from Typhos to set it on the table. "So far it seems that only those who reside in the Netherworld Kingdom and the Morpheus Kingdom participated, making the punishment suitable for them. But the others..." He trailed off and gave Typhos a meaningful look.

"Might not deserve this punishment," Typhos finished, sighing deeply. "I already know that, little prince. But I'm trying to protect them."

"From a threat that may or may not exist," Melek replied, his fingers gently combing through Typhos's long, dark hair. "The source is clear, the portal is closed, and there have been no further incidents."

"That doesn't mean there won't be more," Typhos pointed out. And I was inclined to agree with him.

Just because everything seemed fine now didn't mean there wouldn't be another problem soon. We didn't know how the portal had been created. Or how a strand had been damaged in the source.

Just like we don't know how Camillia escaped or where she hid, I thought, clearing my throat and drawing Typhos's attention to me. "I don't mean to intrude. I know you have a lot going on right now."

"You never *intrude*, Azazel." He gave me a searching look, his brow furrowing as he studied me.

He no doubt could sense something was off, likely because my Phoenix was being abnormally subdued. But he didn't ask questions, allowing me to keep my secret, at least for now.

"You have news," he said, giving me a safe subject to discuss.

"I do." I cleared my throat. "We found Camillia De la Croix in the Human Realm. Ajax has her locked up in an old Midnight Fae Council dungeon for questioning."

Of course, that hadn't been what Typhos had demanded we do with her. He'd wanted her brought to him instead. But...

"We thought it might be worth knowing how she got out and where she's been before bringing her back here, just in case she's able to somehow use her escape tricks again," I explained.

Typhos nodded thoughtfully. "I suspect she simply took advantage of the breach somehow, but I agree it would be worth our while to know for sure. Unless she's already provided you with details and that's why you're here?"

"They tied her up with rope, my king," Melek inserted, a smile tainting his tone. "I doubt much talking has been done."

"Not all of us use rope the way you do, little prince." Typhos kept his steady gaze on me while he spoke, but I didn't miss the hint of indulgence in his response to Melek.

I ignored the rope commentary and instead replied to Typhos's question. "She's not being very forthcoming. She's instead pretending to be shocked that thirty days have passed."

"Pretending?" Melek didn't hide the skepticism in that parroted reply. "What if she means it?"

I snorted at that. "It's a ruse meant to hide her true whereabouts. Which I'll prove once I thoroughly interrogate her."

"Yet you're here instead of doing that," Melek said. "That's interesting."

I met his multicolored gaze. "I'm here to inform Typhos that we found Camillia, and to let him know why we took her to the Midnight Fae Realm instead of directly to him as he asked."

Okay, that wasn't entirely true.

I was also here because Ajax had recognized my need to blow off some steam. He'd probably thought it was just anger and my Phoenix's need to punish Camillia for her antics.

But that hadn't been the source of my contention with my animal at all.

Quite the opposite, in fact.

My Phoenix had wanted to embrace her and protect her, which was not going to happen. *Ever.*

"I agree with keeping her away from here until we have more answers." Typhos closed the hologram on his table and stood. "But I'm only giving you three days to break her, Azazel. This has already taken too long, and I really need your help within our world here."

I nodded. "I understand."

"The sooner we can restart the trials, the better," he went on. "However, the Netherworld trials and Morpheus trials are canceled indefinitely. They chose to acquire mates outside of the process. Therefore, they can test them on their own."

"A worthy punishment," Melek praised, referring to the way Typhos had chosen to handle the aftermath of Monsters Night.

He'd told the Netherworld Kings and Morpheus Kings to organize their own set of trials to determine the true worthiness of the females acquired during the illegal raid on the alternate realm. The edict forced the kings to take on some of the leadership burdens that Typhos often carried, thus providing a necessary lesson in respect.

It was a lesson that traveled down through the ranks to the very fae who had used that portal, too. Because most of the females weren't claimed yet, and as there weren't many of them, the various types of Netherworld Fae and Morpheus Fae had to be careful with their vetting of the potential mates.

Or they'd risk losing them all.

And Typhos wasn't going to give them any others after the stunt they'd pulled with that portal.

"If the Netherworld Fae and Morpheus Fae want to regulate themselves, then have at it," he'd told them. "Let's see if your kings are up to the task."

"Three days," he repeated to me now. "If she's still silent, you can leave her there to rot."

Melek's eyes widened, his usual smirk dying behind a concerned mask. "*Typhos.*"

"Is there anything else, Azazel?" Typhos asked, ignoring his prince.

"No. I'll handle it from here," I promised him.

"I know you will," he agreed, confidence underlying those words. Or perhaps it was a bit of a threat.

Because Melek had established initial ties to Camillia, making this a very important task. One I couldn't fail.

It also meant I might not be able to hurt her the way I needed to in order to make her talk. *Because Melek can feel her,* I realized, meeting the male's hard gaze in question. *Well, shit.*

That was going to complicate things.

Of course, it wasn't my fault Melek had tied himself to her soul.

But it would be my fault if he was hurt through my actions, and Typhos certainly wouldn't appreciate that either.

Well, that complicates matters even more.

As does my still-silent Phoenix.

Fuck.

So how am I supposed to interrogate her when I can't force her to talk?

CHAPTER 3

MELEK

AZAZEL DISAPPEARED in a puff of ash, leaving behind a cold sort of darkness in the air that raised the hairs along my arms.

I tightened the sash around my robe and faced Typhos. "Leave her to rot?" I repeated, arching a brow at my lover. "Have you considered what that will do to me?"

"Perhaps it's a necessary lesson in mate-bonds," he drawled, his blue eyes narrowing. "You're the one who tied your soul to her."

"So now you want to punish me for it?" I asked, taken aback by his callousness. Typhos could be cruel, he could even be cruel to me, but this...

This wasn't like him at all.

I knew he had a lot on his mind right now, not to mention the strain the source was putting on him—a strain he either didn't notice or refused to acknowledge—but that didn't excuse his easy dismissal of my mate-bond choice.

"Camillia couldn't possibly be behind the portal," I told him. "And I highly doubt she's tainting your source, either. She's a Halfling Hell Fae."

"Of unknown origin," Typhos reminded me. "And Azazel couldn't locate her parents."

Okay, yes, that was concerning. As was her disappearing act for the last thirty days. *But...* "What would she have to gain by tainting the source?"

"Her escape, obviously," Typhos replied. "Which she succeeded in achieving, then disappeared for thirty days. And in those thirty days, we haven't had any other disturbances. Is that a coincidence or is it related?"

He folded his thick arms as he stared down at me, waiting for my reply.

"You know I don't believe in coincidences," I told him.

"Neither do I."

"But I don't think she's responsible," I continued. "I think she's resourceful and took advantage of the opportunity to flee."

Which made her formidable and intelligent, and maybe a little devious. All traits I found to be respectable, not distasteful.

Actually, her cunning behavior turned me on. It was part of what made her perfect for us.

I just had to convince Typhos of that.

Which was an impossible feat in his current mood.

"Just as I think some of our Nightmare Fae chose to take advantage of the opportunity to create a portal," I added. "Someone or something else is responsible for weakening the source. And their interference merely allowed a few other pieces to fall into place."

We knew from our discussions with Maliki that he hadn't expected the portal to work. But he'd attempted to create it with the help of a few hungry Ghouls from the Morpheus Kingdom. The Ghouls hadn't initially set out to find mates, just to feed on human nightmares. But playing was in their nature.

And they were horny little fae.

So they'd found a few mortal snacks to bring home.

Or that had been the plan, anyway.

But apparently this new reality had contained mortals who were suitable mates for some of Hell Fae kind. An intriguing development, considering the Hell Fae Source was notoriously selective, often rejecting mortals and fae who sought entry. However, something about these mortals was deemed acceptable.

Typhos didn't understand it.

But he was a good king, and he'd allowed them to remain with the requirement that every human be tested through the trials before officially mated.

Of course, he hadn't had much choice. He could either allow them to remain or kill them.

Because the portal had fizzled and burned once the last of our fae had returned home, closing the temporary door to the alternate universe and their infamous Monsters Night—which was apparently a holiday in that realm, not a term our fae had created. It was that world's version of the mortal holiday Halloween, which was very different from that of our own Human Realm.

Much more deadly.

With real monsters, not just mortals in masks.

And it was called Monsters Night instead of Halloween.

A fascinating concept that I would have loved to explore on a different day. Perhaps *after* we finished working through all the chaos inspired by the Nightmare Fae's little take-a-mate session with the alternate realm.

"I understand giving Azazel three days," I went on when Typhos continued to stare at me. "You need our Commander focused on regulating the Nightmare Fae, specifically on our various kings"—whom Typhos referred to as his *lieutenants*—"but leaving Cami to rot isn't a solution."

"What do you propose instead?" Typhos asked, his blue eyes narrowing. "That I let you keep her in a bedroom cage?"

A visual appeared in my mind of Cami naked in a cage with a collar around her neck. "Actually—"

"No. That would be a reward. And you don't deserve one."

My eyebrows rose at his cutting reply. "Oh? What do I deserve, then, Typhos? To be punished by feeling her starve?"

He flinched and shook his head, his expression immediately contrite. "No, I didn't mean that."

"Then what did you mean?" I knew he was under a lot of pressure to perform, but I wasn't going to stand here and take this nonsense from him. *I* hadn't tainted the source. *I* hadn't opened a portal. And *I* certainly hadn't helped Cami escape.

Well, perhaps I had in some unexpected way, if our shared link had anything to do with it.

But it hadn't been intentional. Why would I want her to leave? She had the potential to complete us. I wouldn't push her away for the world. In fact, I'd probably sacrifice the world just to bring her closer.

Typhos wrapped his palm around my nape and pulled me into his chest, his opposite arm branding my lower back. Then his head went to my neck where he sighed long and hard, his big shoulders heaving with the motion.

I blinked, surprised by his uncharacteristic display of need. He usually put me on my knees, his desire to dominate second nature to him.

But this... this was a side of him I rarely witnessed, even in all our millennia together.

"I won't let her hurt you," he whispered against my skin, his arm tightening around me. "I won't let anyone hurt you."

I embraced him in return, my lips going to his thick, dark hair. "Why are you worried about me, Ty?"

"Because I don't have the answers I need," he admitted. "And without answers, I feel as though I'm losing control."

His confession shocked me.

Typhos *never* admitted to losing control. He was the Hell Fae King. A fallen Virtuous Fae. One of the most powerful beings in existence. Fuck, he'd even created his own source of power.

"One dark strand doesn't mean you're losing control," I promised him. Although, I had noticed that his power had been growing wildly for centuries now with him as the only anchor, and I'd been worried about his ability to handle it all.

Not because he couldn't, but because he was the type to take it all on himself rather than lean on others for help.

Others like me.

Because he didn't want to burden me with the responsibility of grounding the Hell Fae Source.

Which was why I felt we needed someone like Camillia, someone who could potentially provide us with a new way to secure the expanding bundle of energy. I wasn't sure why I suspected she could assist, but I did. And I wasn't one to ignore my instincts.

There was something special about her. Something that had endeared her to me immediately. Not just because she could read Typhos's book, but because of the way she'd approached her new situation.

She was a fighter.

Confident.

Collected.

Suitable for being a queen.

A queen who refuses to be kept in a cage, I marveled, thinking about how she'd managed to escape the Hell Fae paradigm. *But she'll succumb to my ropes.* Because I'd ensure she enjoyed the feel of that silky texture against her skin.

And I'd give her a reason to crawl.

Only in the bedroom, though.

Never outside of it.

She would be ours. Our intended queen. I was almost certain of it. Even if Typhos doubted her. However, he needed a challenge, someone who wasn't afraid to stand her ground and demand that he bow under certain circumstances.

Such as the one he was currently in with the source.

Typhos needed help. He needed someone capable of balancing *him.* And I sincerely hoped Camillia De la Croix could be that someone.

Because I hadn't proved to be a sufficient enough strength for him. It was nothing either of us had done, just the way fate had played our cards.

I accepted that.

Someday, he would, too.

We needed a circle to maintain the source and ensure our Hell Fae King didn't truly fall.

I won't lose you again, I thought, careful not to let the message enter his mind. *You're mine to protect, too, my king. And I'll do anything to make sure you're safe.*

I kissed his hair and ran my palms up and down his strong back. "Would you like a distraction?" I asked him softly. "Something to take your mind off everything for a little while?"

He sighed again, his palm flexing against my nape. "I don't deserve you, Melek."

I smiled. "Then tell me what you do deserve, my king." I purposely twisted our earlier words, just to show him that I wasn't upset and that I understood he was hurting and needed an outlet.

I could be that outlet if he indulged in a game I wanted to play, but not if he wanted to use me as a verbal punching bag. However, a physical one where he punished me with his cock was more than acceptable.

"You've been in the mood to play with rope," he hedged. "Because you want to be tied up or because you want to tie up a certain female?"

Typhos was the only one I would ever allow to tie me up. But I typically preferred to be the one wielding the rope. "I keep picturing her decorated in red silk," I confided. "Under her breasts. Between her legs. Her arms bound behind her back." A renewed image populated my mind, making me painfully hard beneath my robe.

"Do you want to fantasize while I kneel for you?" Typhos asked, his voice soft against my neck.

"That doesn't sound like a distraction for you, my king," I murmured, my fingers trailing down his spine. "I offered you an outlet for a reason."

"Taking care of you is the distraction I crave." His lips moved up my throat to my chin. "I need to know that I can still control something." His mouth whispered along my jaw. "I need to know that I can still keep you safe and make you feel good."

"You always make me feel good, Ty. And I know I'm safe with you."

He hummed, his lips moving to softly brush mine. "Prove it to me, little prince. Let me pleasure you while you tell me about your rope fantasy. Maybe it'll convince me to spare her."

Now he was teasing me. Because I knew he would do

more than spare her. He'd wrap her up in a bow as a gift if I required it. Assuming Azazel could prove her innocence, anyway. Until then, Typhos was unlikely to let me near her, even though I could more than handle myself.

Still, he was giving me an apology in his own way. Letting me revel in my baser needs by thinking about Cami while sharing the intimate details of my desires with my king.

"Would you fuck her after I tied her up?" I wondered aloud. "If I wanted to watch?"

He grinned against my mouth. "Are you asking for my limits where she's concerned, little prince?"

"Yes."

"Consider me limitless, then. Because I would do anything you ask of me."

"Including not leaving her alone to rot?" I asked, my eyes finding his.

"Including ensuring she's healthy and fine, even if she's locked up in a cage far away," he replied, the words a breath against my lips. "Azazel won't hurt her. He knows it'll hurt you. And hurting you hurts me."

I nodded, my mouth brushing his with the movement. "I don't think she's our culprit, my king."

"Yes, you've made your opinion clear." His fingers drifted upward into my hair. "So share your fantasy with me, little prince. Tell me how you would tie her up. Give me every detail. And then tell me what you would want me to do to her while you watch."

My cock ached at his words, my groin pressing into him. "Yes, my king," I whispered, easily giving in to his request. "I would start by removing her clothes. Slowly. Ensuring she feels every fiber glide against her soft skin, preparing her senses for what's to come."

Ty's palms traced my arms, sliding up to the collar of

my robe and down to the sash. "Like this?" he asked, demonstrating my words by gently pushing open the material and drawing it down my shoulders and biceps, revealing my skin inch by inch.

I swallowed. "Yes, like that. And I would kiss her throat, lightly, and graze my teeth along her collarbone."

Ty followed my words with his mouth, making it hard for me to concentrate. Especially as he revealed my lower half, thus allowing my cock to kiss the air before feeling the texture of his own gown.

It all made me so sensitive.

Just like I would do to Cami.

"Her nipples would be hard little peaks, begging for our mouths. But we wouldn't give her what she needs. We'd tease her instead."

"Hmm," Ty hummed, his fingers tracing a path down my abdomen to the top of my groin. "I like teasing."

"I know." I grabbed his shoulders to hold on to him, my veins lighting up with exquisite need. "That's why I would ask you to pick the rope. Your choice would tell me how you want me to tie her up."

"You wouldn't decide?" He sounded surprised.

"I want her tied up in a thousand different ways," I admitted. "So for our first time, I would let you lead. Because making you want her would only turn me on more."

He drew back to stare into my eyes, his own giving nothing away. "You really want to share her."

"With you, yes."

"What about Azazel and Ajax?"

"I wouldn't say no to watching them fuck her, too," I replied. "Shall I bring them into the fantasy or leave it as just us?"

He considered me for a long moment. "Just us for now."

I smiled, then hissed as his palm skimmed my shaft.

"Keep going," he demanded. "And I choose the red silk. I agree it would complement her skin."

Fuck. I was ready to explode, and we hadn't even really begun yet. But he was indulging me, and I refused to waste this opportunity by coming too quickly.

Blowing out a breath, I returned to my fantasy and said, "I would ask you to stand behind her and pull her arms backward to clasp against her lower back."

He demonstrated with my arms, moving around me to press his chest to my shoulder blades, his lips at my ear. "And then?"

"And then I would introduce her to the silky texture with light strokes against her skin, preparing her for more..."

CHAPTER 4

AJAX

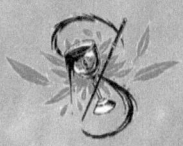

I HATE IT HERE.

Not the old Council dungeon, but this *realm*. I rarely returned to the Midnight Fae world, partly to avoid memories I'd rather not revisit. But the real reason I hated this place was the constant influx of power.

Power that reminded me of the very one that had taken everything from me.

I supposed that was why I'd chosen this location to take Camillia De la Croix—because I despised her almost as much as I despised the Midnight Fae Council.

She'd used me. *Distracted* me from doing my job. All the while playing on a piece of my history that I desperately tried not to think about. I'd mentioned Emelyn to her, perhaps not by name, but that wasn't needed. I'd given Camillia enough by admitting that she reminded me of someone from my past.

And she'd used that information against me, finding a moment of weakness where my guard was down and choosing that precise moment to escape *my* prison.

I was the Hell Fae Warden. Not Ajax, the Midnight

Fae who'd lost everything. But a being of power and respect. And this female had tainted that image, reducing my worth in the cruelest of ways.

Well, now she would pay.

Because she was in *my* Hell now.

"I've already told you. I don't know," she said, her gray eyes reminding me of a brewing storm. "You asking me the same question a hundred times isn't going to change my answer."

I narrowed my gaze at her. "We'll see." I was just biding my time until the real help appeared.

Honestly, I was surprised he hadn't arrived already. Shade typically foresaw situations such as this, a benefit of being part Fortune Fae, part Midnight Fae. Although, knowing my oldest friend, he was making me wait for a reason.

I twirled my wand between my fingertips as I circled Camillia for the thousandth time. She was covered in snake vines—nasty little creatures with a penchant for biting when they felt threatened.

Which explained the three marks on Camillia's nude form.

She'd quickly learned that moving beneath their writhing bodies was a bad idea. I could have warned her, but she didn't deserve my help. Not after what she'd done.

Still, I wove a little spell through the air to aid in her healing. It wasn't because I cared, but because I needed her mind focused on the interrogation, not a minor snake bite.

Alas, she proved to be quite stubborn.

"This would go easier on you if you simply told the truth," I said conversationally. "Of course, I won't believe a damn word you have to say anyway." Which defeated the entire purpose of this activity.

I angled my wand upward and muttered a spell to nudge Shade. Just a little puff of glitter that would express my impatience.

He'd likely have a few things to say about it when he eventually arrived. But if it made him move faster, then it would be worth his choice remarks.

"Then what are we doing here?" Camillia asked, her tone exasperated. "You won't believe anything I say, and I'm not changing my answer, because it's the truth—*I don't know.*"

"I'm waiting for permission to kill you," I lied.

"For what?" she demanded. "For not knowing how I ended up in my old dorm room?"

"For distracting me with your damn pussy and using that distraction as a chance to flee, thereby ruining my entire fucking reputation as Warden," I snapped at her.

Her eyebrows flew upward. "Oh, so your ego was wounded and that gives you cause to kill me. I see." She flinched as the snakes hissed around her in warning, not liking her tone.

Useful little pets, I decided. I used to hate their slithering vines around the Academy walls, but I definitely found them interesting now as they slithered and writhed around Cami's midsection. They were hiding her tits from my view, which was fine. I didn't need to be tempted into another *distraction.*

"You know, Azazel warned me that you would probably call our time together a mistake and run away in the process. But he failed to mention that you'd also revert to being an asshole again." Her voice was softer now, but her expression was just as hard as before.

"I'm not running away from anything, Camillia. And I never stopped being an asshole."

She grunted. "You stopped long enough to orgasm at least."

I spun around to face her, furious at the accusation underlying those pointed words. "Are you trying to say *I* used *you*?"

"Maybe you did." She shrugged and immediately regretted it when one of the snakes sank its fangs into her upper arm.

This time I didn't weave a spell to help numb her to the pain, too furious by what she was implying. "*You* used *me*, Camillia. You tricked me into bed and then escaped while I was in the shower trying to clear my head. Don't even think for a minute that you can turn this around on me."

She bit her lip, her eyes tearing up from the fresh wound in her arm.

Yeah, snake vines hurt.

But they only bit those with nefarious motives, and clearly, Camillia De la Croix had those in spades.

"I didn't use you," she gritted out, wincing as the snake finally withdrew from her skin. "*Fuck*, that burns."

I scoffed at her claim and rolled my eyes. "No, you just snuck out while I wasn't paying attention, then fucked off to some untraceable realm for fun. All the while not giving a fuck what would happen to me or Az when Lucifer found out."

"Why would I care?" she demanded in a low whisper that sounded similar to the snakes hissing around her. "It's pretty fucking clear that neither of you cares about me. So why should I care about either of you?"

Well, she had a fair point there.

Because I didn't care about her. At all. Not even a little bit.

"Hmm, I suddenly see why you called in a truth spell

request," Shade said as he appeared beside me. "But now I'm not sure who it's meant for."

I glared at him. "About fucking time."

"Actually, I think my timing was absolutely perfect," he drawled, his black cloak billowing around his legs like a perpetual dark shadow. Appropriate, given his name. His ice-blue eyes shifted toward Camillia, his gaze assessing her like prey.

She glowered right back at him. "Keep your fangs to yourself, vampire."

He laughed dryly. "Who knew you had such good taste, Ajax?"

I rolled my eyes. "Did you bring what I need or not?"

"Sort of," Shade said vaguely as he started circling Camillia. "You chose a fitting location for this, Ajax."

"Did I?" I asked, already bored by whatever riddle my best friend was about to weave.

"After all, Aflora and I had our first date here," he continued, acting as though I hadn't spoken. "And look how happy we turned out to be."

"This isn't a date."

He glanced up at me from behind her, his expression exuding a confusion I knew wasn't real. "She's naked and bound by snake vines, Ajax. Perhaps I've been hanging out with Kols and Zeph too long, but that certainly sounds like a date to me."

"I would never use snake vines on Aflora," a deep voice interjected as a door appeared in the wall, the outline glittering with emerald magic.

Warrior Blood enchantment, courtesy of Zeph, I thought, suppressing a groan.

"Now, regular tree vines? Yes," he said, stepping into the room.

He tsked at the sight before him, making my shoulders

tighten in annoyance. I'd never been a huge fan of the Warrior Blood, but he and Shade were mated to the same female, making him a necessary evil in my life.

"Proper domination grants the submissive true control." His green eyes narrowed at Cami's bound form, specifically at the bleeding snake bite on her arm. "I'm surprised she hasn't safeworded you yet."

"That would require my *prisoner* to have a safeword," I snapped at him. "This isn't a date or some kinky bedroom play. This is an interrogation."

"Interrogation makes for great foreplay," a third voice murmured.

Zakkai.

I was about to correct him when he appeared in the doorway holding a dark-haired little fae in his arms. Her big blue eyes immediately went to Shade as she spread out her arms and shrieked, "Daddy!"

I blinked, incapable of understanding the scene before me. While I knew Shade had indeed fathered a little hellspawn—I'd even met her before—it was difficult to comprehend what I was seeing.

To witness my oldest friend shadow directly to her side to sweep her up into a big hug was... mind-boggling.

My rebellious best friend who had bitten a pretty little Earth Fae against her will, thus forcing the mate-bond upon her without permission.

My crude best friend who'd commonly skipped classes when we were young just to piss off his Councilman father.

My cruel best friend who had wielded secrets like daggers, somehow saving the Midnight Fae world with his slippery thoughts and quick-witted ploys.

My loving best friend who is now nuzzling his nose against the four-year-old in his arms.

I blinked again and shook my head. "You brought

Florica to witness this interrogation?" I couldn't even fathom what Aflora would do about this when she found out. She'd probably wrap tree vines around all three of their dicks and hang them upside down near a burning thwomp.

"No, I'm picking her up from Zakkai and Zeph so they can help you with your truth pursuits while I give Florica a tour of this historic site." He gave her a devilish smile. "Are you ready to play with fire, baby girl?"

She held out her palm and showed him a glowing ball of cerulean magic. "Yes!"

"That's my little princess," Shade cooed, kissing her on the cheek.

She preened, her big eyes smiling until she spotted Camillia in the chair, dressed in snakes. I winced a little as Florica's happy face melted into a frown. "Who's that, Daddy?"

He followed her line of sight to Camillia and replied, "That's your uncle Ajax's intended mate."

My jaw clenched at his description, an argument lining up on my lips.

But he wasn't done talking.

"They're currently playing a game, somewhat similar to the ones Daddy Zeph likes to play with Mommy." He cast a cheeky glance at Zeph, but the Warrior Blood merely grunted in reply while Zakkai smirked.

"Ohhh." Florica's lips formed a big "O" with the sound. "Like hide-and-seek?"

"Yes, a lot like hide-and-seek."

Her little nose curled upward. "But with snakes?" She cupped her hand over her mouth to loudly whisper, "Snakes are grossss. They hissss."

"They do hiss, but not all snakes are gross. You like Raph," he pointed out, referring to Zeph's familiar—a three-headed snake. Because of course the Warrior Blood would have a deadly creature as his magical familiar.

Florica's eyes lit up. "Daddy Zeph's snake is my friend."

"He's Mommy's friend, too," Shade agreed, casting another wicked look at Zeph.

The Warrior Blood simply shook his head.

"And now Uncle Ajax is trying to convince the nice lady in the chair to play with his snake, too," Shade went on, making me want to deck him. "So why don't we let them play while you and I go cast some spells, hmm?"

Florica lit up like the sun, reminding me very much of her Earth Fae mother. "Yes!"

Shade kissed her again on the cheek before saying, "You all play nice now." He glanced around me. "And, Camillia, I apologize for Ajax's lack of manners. I'll make sure he introduces us properly at Lucifer's Ball in a few months."

I glared at my fortune-telling best friend. "Shade—"

"Let's go make a big fire in the former council chamber, hmm?" His eyes were on his daughter while he spoke. "We can start with your grandfather's old chair, then we'll find evil Constantine's old roots and burn them, too."

Her eyes lit up with excitement, a spell twisting from her lips that caused her arm to go up in flames.

Zeph winced while Zakkai took a step back, but Shade's gaze was filled with pride. "You're beautiful, little inferno."

The two of them winked out of the room, leaving me to pinch the bridge of my nose in frustration. "How long do we have before your little firestarter destroys the building?"

Zakkai and Zeph shared a look, one that had Zakkai sighing.

A hint of an ocean breeze tickled the air as he engaged his magic, the cerulean flames similar to Florica's. She'd clearly inherited the Quandary Blood traits from her mother—traits her mother had technically received when Zakkai had mated her.

Which made that little girl of theirs incredibly powerful because while Shade might be her biological father, she had Aflora's blood running through her veins, and Aflora's blood was tied to all four of her mates.

Midnight Fae lineages were complicated.

And given the wonder on Camillia's face right now, she was suddenly realizing that as well.

Or perhaps it was Zakkai's immense energy that inspired her current expression. He was the Source Architect and therefore one of the strongest fae in existence. Even Lucifer seemed uneasy around him.

Which meant I now had a very worthy fae to use to intimidate Camillia into speaking.

It's time for the truth, I thought, catching her gaze. *I can't wait to hear what you really have to say.*

CHAPTER 5

CAMI

Zakkai, Zeph, and Shade.

I recognized those names. Particularly, Zakkai. He was the Midnight Fae Source Architect. Which was a fancy way of saying he could rewrite fae magic. I'd heard rumors about his power, just as I'd heard rumors about Aflora and her four mates.

They were abominations, but different from Hell Fae.

Aflora was connected to the Earth Fae Source, her royal Elemental Fae lineage granting her exquisite abilities at a young age. But Shadow, or *Shade*, as Ajax had called him, had bitten her, which had been a huge breach in fae politics a little over a decade ago.

His bite had transitioned Aflora from being an Earth Fae into something else entirely.

And their story evolved from there to somehow include Zephyrus—*Zeph*, which I assumed was his preferred nickname since Shade had referred to him that way—Zakkai, and Kolstov.

They were all various types of Midnight Fae, thus providing Aflora with a well-rounded circle of power.

Together, they were thought to be formidable. But I suspected that even apart they could hold their own just fine in a battle.

Not that I wanted to fight any of them.

Actually, I really didn't want to be on any of their bad sides.

Yet I was the one strapped to a chair, held down by violent snakes, while Zakkai weaved some sort of hypnotic magic in the air. I couldn't see it, but I could smell it, the sweet, ocean-like perfume washing over me in warm welcome.

Some part of me sighed, pleased with the abundance of energy lurking in those electric currents.

"The building is fortified," Zakkai said, his silver-blue eyes flickering with embers as he stared at Zeph. "She'll be able to destroy things over and over again to her little heart's content."

Zeph arched a dark brow, the color matching his thick hair. "Are we talking about Shade's satisfaction or Florica's?"

"Both," Zakkai deadpanned before looking at Ajax. "What is it that you need me to do, Death Blood?"

"I believe he prefers to be called *Warden* now," Zeph offered.

"He isn't my Warden," Zakkai replied, folding his thick arms as he continued to focus on Ajax.

I leaned forward a little, intrigued by this whole dynamic, only to jolt as one of the bastard snakes bit my arm again.

All three males glanced at me with interest as I tried not to scream from the excruciating pain shooting through my veins.

When I figure out how to get out of this mess, I'm going to kill

Ajax, I decided, closing my eyes to hold my burning tears at bay.

"Impressive." Zeph's deep baritone made his voice easily decipherable. "I know Warrior Bloods who can't even handle that."

"Is there a reason you're punishing an innocent?" the other male asked, giving me pause.

I nearly opened my eyes to gape at him, but I didn't want to be tricked into revealing my tears.

"Innocent?" Ajax scoffed. "She managed to escape Lucifer's trials and disappeared for thirty days without a trace. She is *not* innocent."

"You mean a female fae ran away from the bridal trials she was forced into against her will?" Zakkai rephrased. "That's incredibly shocking." His deadpan tone coaxed me into peeking at him through my thick lashes. "And that also does not make her guilty of anything other than desiring free will."

All right. Zakkai might be intimidating, but I would absolutely buy him a beer at a bar if he wanted one.

"She used me to escape," Ajax said through his teeth.

"That sounds like a disgruntled lovers' spat, not a reason to strap an innocent to a chair and threaten her with snake vines," Zakkai returned, his wand appearing in his hand as he whispered a spell that surrounded me in a cloud of cerulean smoke.

I gasped in relief as my lungs expanded on a full breath —the first one I'd taken since the snakes had appeared.

"This isn't your interrogation, Zakkai," Ajax snapped.

"Wrong, Death Blood. It became mine the moment you reached out for help."

"I didn't ask *you* for help."

"No, but it's my help that you clearly need." Zakkai

sounded regal in his reply, his tone befitting a king. "Now get on with your questions before I get bored."

The cloud disappeared, causing my eyes to immediately shift downward. The snakes had been covering my nudity before, and without them, I expected to be completely exposed.

But no.

I somehow wore a tank top and jeans.

My fingers ran over the fabric, half expecting it to be a mirage. However, it was definitely real. And it was the most clothing I'd been given since this hell had started last week. *Nope. Scratch that—over a month ago.*

"I think I would have preferred Kolstov in this situation," Ajax muttered.

"Kolstov is busy seducing our mate." Zeph's voice seemed to deepen impossibly more with his words. "Which I would prefer to be watching over this interrogation. So I agree with Zakkai—get on with your questions before *we* get bored."

"Fine." Ajax looked at me, his dark irises going to my now free hands before narrowing upward at my face. "What happened thirty days ago?"

"Thirty days ago?" I repeated. "I have no idea. I was probably in class or doing homework."

His brow furrowed. "I thought you said she was ready to be questioned?"

"She is," Zakkai replied as he leaned back against the stone wall behind him.

Ajax shifted his glare to the Source Architect. "But she's still lying."

Zakkai held his gaze without flinching. "Or you're not asking the right questions. What has she said so far?"

"That she doesn't know anything," Ajax summarized.

"Which is true," I inserted. "He keeps asking me how I

escaped, and I don't know how I escaped. I wasn't actively trying to go anywhere. I mean, I wanted to, don't get me wrong, but I didn't actually attempt to leave."

Ajax pointed at me. "See? She's still lying."

"She's not," Zakkai said before I could speak. "I would feel it in the energy if she were, and she's not even trying to lie to you. She's telling the truth."

"That doesn't make any sense," Ajax argued.

Zakkai slid his hands into his pockets, his wand having disappeared without a trace. "I didn't come here to help you make sense of it, Death Blood. I came here to help you pull the truth from her, and that's what I'm doing."

"Detail your last twenty-four hours." Zeph's voice caused me to look at him, noting his billowing cloak laced with dark green leaves along the edges. The color matched his eyes, which I suspected was the point. It seemed like the kind of gift a woman might give her mate, making me wonder if Aflora had made it for him. Because the leaves seemed to move, almost as though caught up in a breeze.

I blinked away from the draw of magic surrounding him and focused on his words. *"Detail your last twenty-four hours."*

"It was a really long fucking day, but all right." I started with the trial, talking about the Centaurs.

"That wasn't—"

"Let her finish," Zeph interjected, cutting off Ajax.

Finishing up my account of the Centaur trial—where I mentioned being able to see through the veil into their true actions—I started into the Minotaur maze.

Zakkai and Zeph watched me with intrigued expressions, while Ajax appeared ready to kill me.

But I ignored him and focused on the other two men, hoping they might actually believe me and help me escape this situation.

Hell Fae Rule #9: Allies Exist in the Most Unexpected of Places.

When I wrapped up the maze, I talked about ending up in my cell, Melek's unwelcome visit, and waking up in Ajax's bed.

Which led me to provide a rather explicit description of what came next, something I hadn't meant to do, but I couldn't seem to stop talking.

Zakkai and Zeph both reappraised Ajax while I spoke, some fucked-up sense of admiration coming through. However, I didn't comment on it because I was too busy detailing how I woke up again and my quick conversation with Az.

Then I continued with what Ajax had said and how he'd gone off to shower, and ended with the book's appearance and the strange events that had followed.

"I went to get some water, and suddenly, Az and Ajax were there in all their pissed-off glory. Then they manhandled me here and tortured me with snakes," I summarized at the conclusion. "The end."

"Well, that's... that's quite the day you've had." Zeph sounded surprised and a tad bit mortified. "You must be starving."

"I am," I admitted. "And thirsty. And really fucking pissed off."

He nodded as though understanding my situation. "So you really don't remember thirty days slipping by?"

"I'm not even convinced thirty days have passed by. I woke up in bed, ready to play with Az and Ajax again, then things just... literally went to Hell."

"So you enjoyed playing with Az and Ajax?" he pressed.

"Very much so, yes." *Why am I admitting that out loud?*

"You like them? Or at least, you did before now?" That came from Zakkai.

"Before now, yes. Right now, no, I really don't." *Okay, stop talking, Cami.* "I thought we were becoming... something. But they've made their feelings for me very clear." *Seriously, no more talking.* "Instead of listening to me, or even attempting to believe me, they've treated me like a prisoner. Which hurts... And I really want to stop rambling now."

"Side effect of the truth spell, I'm afraid," Zakkai explained. "If I'm understanding the situation correctly, then from their point of view, you disappeared for thirty days without a trace. What's your point of view?"

"I woke up feeling gratified and ready for more, only to be thrown into another version of hell where I'm being rudely interrogated by the two assholes who were just giving me pleasure mere hours ago," I answered, wincing at how sad I sounded. "Well, two assholes, and now two much nicer fae."

Zeph smirked. "I don't think anyone has ever called me *nice* before."

"Well, nicer than Az and Ajax," I muttered.

"Meaning your point of view is mere hours compared to their thirty days," Zakkai translated for me.

"I guess, yes. I don't know how I lost thirty days. But apparently, if I'm to believe the two asshole fae, then I did."

Zakkai canted his head, causing his long, silvery white hair to fall across his handsome face. "So you didn't use Ajax to escape?"

I snorted. "No. I mean, I thought about asking him to help me, but I knew he wouldn't, so I never did. And I wanted to escape on my own. I've been trying to find a loophole in the book."

"The book that took you on a journey to the source?" Zakkai asked.

I nodded. "Yeah. It's full of Lucifer's deals and a lot of random Hell Fae knowledge. Melek says I shouldn't be able to read it, but…" I shrugged. "I can."

"Because you're powerful." Zakkai pushed away from the wall to come stand beside my chair. "Powerful *and* innocent."

Ajax hadn't spoken a word, his dark eyes swirling with emotions I couldn't decipher. He seemed to be trying to pull the shadows in the room around him, to hide from the scene before him.

"Her aura is clear. She's not lying." Zakkai's wand appeared again, the tip a little too close to my neck. "But she's also not what she seems."

My eyelashes fluttered as I turned to look up at him. "What?"

"Who are your parents?" Zakkai asked me, his wand flickering with power.

"Um, Mystika De la Croix and Pierre De la Croix."

"One is obviously a Hell Fae, yes?"

"My father. He's the one who made a deal with Lucifer."

Zakkai nodded. "And your mother?"

"She's human," I told him.

"You're certain?"

"What else could she be?" I countered.

He shrugged. "I'm not sure, but I would wager something powerful. Or your father has a relative he's not aware of somewhere."

"What do you sense, Kai?" Zeph asked, the nickname suggesting intimacy between them.

"An equal," he replied, his wand vanishing as a cloak settled around his shoulders. "Well, this was more insightful than I anticipated. But it seems Ajax certainly has his hands full." He looked at the Warden and added, "Do let Lucifer know that I'm available for when he needs help figuring this one out."

With that, he disappeared, leaving Zeph smirking in his wake. "He's an insightful dick, but he grows on you." He clapped Ajax on the back and walked out through the door. "I'm going to go see if Florica manages to set Shade on fire again. That's always enjoyable."

The door disappeared in a blink, leaving nothing but a wall behind.

Midnight Fae magic, I realized. Because that door hadn't been there before either; Zeph had somehow conjured it. Or perhaps it existed behind some sort of veil.

Regardless, it didn't matter.

What mattered was the silent Warden standing across from me. He said nothing, his gaze assessing, his lips pressed in a firm line.

"Let me guess—you still don't believe me." I folded my arms and winced as it pulled at the snake bites decorating my skin.

Feeling those reminded me of how much I wanted to kill Ajax for inflicting that torment upon me. But I suddenly felt too weak—too *dejected*—to move. And not because of some weird spell, but because I was just, well, *exhausted.*

When was the last time I ate something?

Did I even sleep in the last thirty days?

Maybe I truly was running the entire time, trying to escape the ball of fire...

I shivered, recalling how intense it had felt, how *real.* Apparently, it had been real. *But what even was it?* I had no one I could ask. No one I could talk to. No one I could trust.

Hell Fae Rule #4: Don't Trust Anyone.

I hadn't exactly forgotten that rule, but I had been a bit too relaxed as far as that one was concerned. Fortunately, Az and Ajax had quickly reminded me why that rule existed.

So now I wouldn't be forgetting it. Nor would I be forgiving them.

They're my captors, not my lovers.

Which inspired me to create a new rule.

Hell Fae Rule #47: It Doesn't Matter How Beautiful They Are; They'll Always Disappoint You in the End.

CHAPTER 6

AJAX

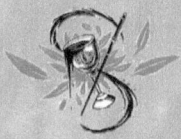

I STARED AT CAMILLIA, unable to answer what I assumed was a rhetorical question.

"Let me guess—you still don't believe me."

The problem was no longer that I couldn't believe her; it was that part of me *did* believe her.

Because I'd felt Zakkai's magic suffocating the room, demanding truth from everyone inside. There was no circumventing it. No way to hide.

Even my thoughts had become truthful.

Such as the one that expressed remorse over her snake bites, and the very real internal confession that I had been healing her because I cared. I just didn't want to care.

If it had been any other Midnight Fae who had wielded that magic, I'd question the strength of the spell. But Zakkai was the fucking Source Architect. The only one who could surpass him in power was Aflora, and she had to try very hard to do so.

There was no way Camillia had been able to circumvent his spell.

Although, his comments about her power left me

reeling. *What did that even mean? She's not what she seems in what way, exactly?*

And what was all that stuff about a book? Was it one she'd found in my room?

I considered the few texts I had in my quarters and frowned. None of them belonged to Lucifer, and they certainly didn't have information about his deals.

"Melek says I shouldn't be able to read it, but... I can."

So whatever book it was, he knew about it. And it had apparently shown her something about Lucifer's fall, which had led to her seeing a source of light.

Was it *the* source of light, as in the Hell Fae Source? Or something else entirely?

Does she really not know where she's been? I ran my fingers through my hair, my frustration mounting with each breath. *What the fuck am I supposed to do with that?*

I drew my palm down my face and sighed. I needed a break. Some fresh air. A way to clear my head.

And I really needed to talk to Az.

With a wave of my wand, I created a bed for Camillia. Then I added a tray with some spaghetti—one of my favorite human foods—and a glass of water. It wasn't an apology. Not even close. But I wasn't entirely sure I owed her one yet.

If I did, it was going to take a hell of a lot more than a bed and some food to earn her forgiveness.

"Don't try to escape. Zakkai might have released you from the snake vines in here, but there are more guarding the exterior. And there's also a grumpy old gargoyle who shrieks like a Banshee." I didn't offer her any more words, still unsure of what to say. I simply shadowed out of the room and into the corridor.

"Grumpy old gargoyle," Sir Callahan grated out. "I'll show you *old*."

He pulled out a wicked-looking sword, his beady red eyes challenging.

Rather than accept his duel, I shadowed outside to stand on the gravelly path. I'd accidentally kill the little gargoyle in my current mood, and I really didn't want to do that.

I wove a spell behind me, telling it to alert me if Camillia tried anything funny in the room—including touching the walls—and started walking.

It'd been a long time since I'd been anywhere near this ancient building and its deadly landscape. All the trees here were black, their tops burning with hiccups of fire that never died. It was eerie, and ancient, and so incredibly gothic.

The stone walls all added to the effect.

As did the black torches billowing with smoke.

I glanced up at the perpetual Midnight Fae moon and found it oddly comforting. I suddenly missed the constant sea of night here. The cool kiss of air on my skin. The buzz of familiar magic.

It's a trap, my mind whispered. *We hate it here.*

But for the moment, I accepted the familiarity of it all and tried to clear my head. However, Zakkai's assessment revolved through my thoughts instead.

"Her aura is clear. She's not lying."

Somehow, he and Zeph had taken charge of my interrogation, asking all the questions on my behalf—including a few I would have preferred not to hear the answer to.

"You like them? Or at least, you did before now?"

"I thought we were becoming… something. But they've made their feelings for me very clear. Instead of listening to me, or even attempting to believe me, they've treated me like a prisoner. Which hurts…"

Camillia's response had me rubbing my chest.

You are *our prisoner,* I'd wanted to argue. *How else am I supposed to treat you?*

But a softer part of me had thought, *Is this how Emelyn felt when everyone misunderstood her?*

Emelyn had been viewed as a bit of a bully in our youth, her haughty persona covering years of hurt and familial trauma. Her entire life had been decided for her, without her permission. So whenever there'd been an opportunity for her to dictate to others, she'd taken it. And she'd been villainized in response.

I'd picked apart her shell, learned more about the female beneath, and I'd fallen madly in love with her. We'd planned to run away together, perhaps to the Human Realm, where she could escape the requirements bestowed upon her at birth.

But I hadn't always liked her.

There'd been a time when I'd seen her through the same narrow window as everyone else—an entitled bitch with a power complex.

However, one night had changed that. A night when I'd found her at her most vulnerable and heard the way her father spoke to her.

It was like I'd fallen witness to a second beginning, my narrow window broadening into a full-blown sky as I suddenly viewed Emelyn through new eyes.

Would I have ever given her a second look had it not been for that night? Likely not.

But it left me wondering about Camillia now.

Was I being narrow-minded again? Looking at her through a pinpointed view rather than taking in the scenery around her?

She'd touched a part of me I couldn't define. A part of me I'd thought had died with Emelyn. Was that all a trick?

Or was it real?

"No. I mean, I thought about asking him to help me, but I knew he wouldn't, so I never did. And I wanted to escape on my own. I've been trying to find a loophole in the book."

How did she know I wouldn't help her? I supposed she wasn't wrong, but why did hearing that unnerve me?

I'd wanted to help her survive the next trial. Did that not count for anything?

Why did I want to help her? I wondered, wandering through the paths of the burning thwomp garden. *Do I still want to help her?*

I'd spent the last thirty days thinking she'd used me to escape. Thirty very long, angry days. But now... now I no longer knew what to think.

I paused near one of the larger tree stumps, watching the embers play over the burnt limbs, aware that a very large explosion was about to occur. The fire gnats danced in the air in expectation, looking forward to the fireworks that would inflame their wings.

What if she's telling the truth? What if she truly has no memory of the last thirty days?

Then my priorities would need to shift, wouldn't they? I'd need to find out what had actually happened to her. Because it might have been bad.

"Is there a reason you're punishing an innocent?"

Zakkai's question had irked me before. Now it just left me uneasy.

Was I punishing the wrong person? Should I have spent the last thirty days trying to save her instead of capturing her again? A powerful vibration rocked my spine, this uncertainty unnerving my very spirit.

I'd been so sure of my course, so steadfast on what I had to do to fix my reputation. Then Zakkai had lit everything on fire with a truth serum that had worked in entirely unexpected ways.

I kept thinking of that narrow-window view, the one Emelyn had been trapped behind, and wondering if Camillia had that in common with her, too.

They were so much alike. Strong. Defiant. Emotionally impenetrable.

"You mean a female fae ran away from the bridal trials she was forced into against her will?"

That sarcastic query repeated in my head, Zakkai's words wrapping around my heart and squeezing. Because he was right. It wasn't all that shocking that Camillia would try to run. Emelyn would have done the same thing.

Gods, she must think I'm just as bad as the Councilmen, I realized, thinking about how Emelyn would look at me if she could see me now. She'd be horrified.

Taming cursed Nightmare Fae creatures was one thing.

Rounding up unwilling brides for a series of deadly trials was entirely another.

And then I'd secured one of those brides to a chair with snake vines...

I blew out a breath just as the burning thwomp exploded, its fiery display reaching high into the sky above.

Who even am I? I marveled, staring directly into the flames. *Who do I want to be?*

My mind revealed nothing, the response impossible to fathom. So I observed the inferno instead, reveling in the heat waves pulsing through the previously chilly air. They reminded me of the Hell Fae Realm—my new home.

But is it my true home?

Being here was fucking with my head.

Seeing Shade hadn't helped matters.

And Camillia's replies, well, those certainly hadn't improved a damn thing.

My teeth clenched together as I suppressed the urge to shout into the night. But then a flicker of black flame caught my attention, drawing my eyes up to the top of the burning thwomp's blaze of glory. It was beginning to subside now, lowering back to its burnt limbs, and on top of it was a rare Black Phoenix.

Az.

His bird appeared agitated even while it roosted on the top of the flames, the wings an exotic mix of obsidian feathers and bright orange embers.

I arched a brow at him. "Out for a midnight flight?" I'd expected him to appear in a cloud of ash as he usually did, not as his Phoenix.

He didn't reply, incapable of human speech while in this form. His feathers ruffled, their majestic gleam glinting in the moonlight.

Az usually considered shifting to be an intimate affair. But he often shifted in front of me when he felt like showing off. However, flying in like this suggested he'd needed a break to stretch his wings—which he did now as the fire died completely, leaving him perched on the burning thwomp.

I had to admit, his wingspan was impressive. Intimidating, even. But he didn't appear to be trying to fight me, just reveling in his magnificence.

"Well, if you want to sit there and listen for a bit, that works for me," I admitted, my hands slipping into my pockets.

Az replied by pulling his wings back into his sides, his black irises studying me intently.

"I don't think she remembers anything," I told him. "Zakkai administered the truth spell, and she stuck by her story, saying that, to her, only a few hours have passed. And she mentioned something about a book."

I recounted everything she'd said while he sat there quietly, and then I started into my own thoughts on the matter, telling him that I wasn't sure how to feel about any of it.

"There's no way she's lying. I felt the pressure of that spell on my own mind. But then, there's also no way she escaped the ward." I palmed the back of my neck. "So maybe Zakkai's cryptic commentary about her being powerful is right. Maybe she's more than just a Halfling Hell Fae."

But I had no idea what she could be or what it might mean.

"I don't think she meant to escape, though. Not like that. Which means she wasn't using either of us. And we... we just interrogated her for no reason." I flinched as that last part left my mouth, that dreaded uncertainty circling again. "I don't know what to do now, Az. I don't even know what to think anymore."

She'd turned it all upside down on me with a few honest answers.

"And this place is fucking with my head," I added, my voice holding a touch of a growl to it.

Because all I could do was think about what Emelyn would say to me right now, how disappointed and pissed off she'd be at me for my life decisions.

Az's feathers fluttered, drawing my attention to his descension as he floated gracefully down to the gravel path I stood upon. Only, he didn't land on his talons; he landed on his feet, his shift appearing effortless as he returned to his human form.

He folded his arms over his bare chest, his irises still black rather than violet. That told me his Phoenix was still very much in charge.

"Perhaps I need to taste her power for clues," he said, making me frown.

"What do you mean?"

"If she's powerful enough to escape the ward and circumvent Zakkai's truth spell, then we need to determine what she is. I can do that." The black in his gaze seemed to flicker, like the violet was trying to peek out but failed. "Let me taste her. *Really* taste her."

"You already have to an extent," I reminded him. "The last time we played."

"I was more focused on your power than hers. I'll focus on hers this time."

"So your solution to us not knowing how to move forward is to fuck her?" I asked incredulously.

He lifted a shoulder. "We can do more than fuck. We can play, too."

I frowned at him. "This doesn't sound like you." In fact, it sounded more like his Phoenix than the man I knew. "What did Lucifer say?"

"Not to hurt her," he replied without blinking. "Hurting her hurts Melek. We are not allowed to hurt Melek."

We, *as in me and you? Or we, as in Azazel and his Phoenix?* I wondered. "I'm not sure she's going to want us to fuck her right now," I hedged, trying to figure out what was really going on here. "She's pretty angry."

He took a step forward. "Did you harm her?"

"No."

His eyes searched mine. "A lie." His palm wrapped around my throat as he lifted me into the air. "*You harmed what is ours.*"

I grabbed his wrist, squeezing. "What the fuck is wrong with you?" I demanded, my voice coming out in a rasp as he closed his grasp around my windpipe, cutting off my air supply.

I kicked out at him as he hissed, the sound very much like his Phoenix and not at all like the man beneath.

Fuck.

His animal was obviously very much in charge.

Not only that, but apparently he also thought I'd threatened Camillia in some way.

I knew enough about Phoenixes to know that this was a very bad situation to be in. They were extremely possessive and aggressive when it came to their fated mates, and if Az's Phoenix thought she was theirs, then...

This is going to fucking hurt.

CHAPTER 7

AZ

STOP THIS! I shouted at my Phoenix. *We like Ajax, you fucking bird!*

I watched helplessly as my beast threw Ajax across the charcoal-bladed field into the stump of a nearby burning thwomp.

Everything had been fine until it wasn't.

I'd been in complete control, ready to return to Ajax and Camillia to finish up the interrogation, when my Phoenix burst free from his confines and took flight. I'd been trapped in him ever since, along for the ride.

I'd apologized. I'd groveled. I'd even promised to let him out more often. But nothing had worked. He wasn't listening to me at all.

But then he'd spotted Ajax, and he'd headed straight for him.

The conversation had placated my animal while we'd listened. I'd thought he might give me back control when we'd shifted back.

But no.

He'd led the conversation, or rather, he'd instructed me on what to say—a feeling that had never happened before. And he'd been fine. Content, even. He wanted to play again.

This time with the focus on Camillia, but his vision included Ajax. He liked sharing her with him, which was telling in and of itself. Ajax had earned my Phoenix's respect.

Until Ajax had said Camillia was angry.

A switch had flipped, and all hell had broken loose inside. And now my animal wanted to kill.

You can't kill him, I said through my teeth. *He's our friend*.

"You hurt Cami," my Phoenix raged instead, forcing my mouth to voice the words my animal felt deep in his soul.

Ajax groaned as he rolled onto his side. The charcoal fields in the Midnight Fae Realm were lethal—the grass resembling sharp rocks, not the softness of leaves. Blood swept down his side, seeping into his cloak, from the small pinpricks they'd left behind.

"I seem to remember you were the one with a blade over her heart just a few hours ago," Ajax muttered as he forced himself back up to his feet.

Unfortunately, his comment only made my Phoenix rage harder.

He hadn't been the one to threaten the female.

He blamed me, and rightfully so.

"A mistake that will be paid for in blood," my Phoenix vowed.

I wasn't sure if he meant Ajax's blood, mine, which was technically *ours*, or both.

My peripheral vision picked up fresh black flames that billowed from behind my shoulders, nearly engulfing me as we flew forward.

My Phoenix was powerful, but I'd never felt him take control like this. He'd never overpowered me before.

Of course, he'd never been obsessed with a potential mate before, either.

While I understood why my animal was attracted to Camillia, she had threatened Typhos, and that could not be tolerated.

Perhaps Ajax's story was true. Perhaps not. Really, it didn't matter. She had escaped. We couldn't even find her family.

And if the Source Architect saw her as powerful, then she was dangerous.

Too dangerous to be allowed to live, perhaps.

My Phoenix sent a rumbling roar through my throat in response, having heard my thoughts.

Shit. He couldn't truly hurt me, but he could take out his rage on the male before us. A male he saw as on my side and not his, thanks to Ajax's lie.

Run! I shouted, willing my mouth to form the word, but my beast had his talons sunk deep into our shared spirit. He wasn't letting go until his bloodthirst was sated.

The dark flames turned into blades and shot like bullets at Ajax.

Stop this! I repeated for the thousandth time, but it was futile.

He was really trying to kill the Midnight Fae. Lucifer's chosen Warden, whom I had approved. Someone who had our allegiance. Who had *earned* it.

A fae who deserved our protection after all he had done for us. He was one of the few beings in the world who could contain my Phoenix's energy. He was an outlet for us.

But more than that, he was our friend.

Rare fear gripped me when two of my black blades embedded themselves in Ajax's chest. Blades I'd thrown.

No, not me. *My fucking bird.*

However, that didn't stem the deep-seated ache of betrayal inside me from blossoming with guilt. *We love Ajax, you fucking bird. Don't kill him!*

Fortunately, Ajax wasn't going down without a fight. He grabbed the hilt of one of the magic knives and drew it out, sending dark, tainted blood splattering onto the charcoal-bladed field.

He threw it back at me—at my Phoenix—which was a pointless move. These blades were conjured by my beast, causing this one to puff into smoke just before it would have impaled my face.

"You hurt Cami," my Phoenix hissed again. "*You will die.*"

It seemed my animal worked on very simple terms. He saw Camillia as his intended mate; therefore, anyone who harmed her would pay.

Including me, as evidenced by how my Phoenix had shoved me down into the pits of my own body, forcing me to watch him murder one of the few fae I actually cared about. Perhaps he felt this was justice for me binding him earlier. An equal betrayal to what I'd done to him.

But really all it would do to us was rip us further apart.

Alas, my damn bird wasn't thinking about the future. Only now.

Why aren't you running?! I shouted in my head as Ajax pulled out the second blade and gripped it. This time his words moved on a spell as he wielded his wand with his other hand.

While Ajax was formidable and had experienced almost a decade of sparring with me, he couldn't take on my beast.

Very few could.

The dagger sailed through the air, and a rush of energy swept around me as my Phoenix tried to disintegrate it like the first one, but it didn't work.

Pain exploded through the left side of my chest as the knife buried itself in my human form.

Directly into my heart.

A roar ripped from my throat as agony burned through my muscles, bone, and skin. I crashed to my knees and dug my fingers into the rocky field. Blood trickled down my palms as my entire body shook with the effort not to pass out.

Fortunately, a strike to the heart couldn't kill me, something Ajax knew. A Black Phoenix would just be reborn. While it wasn't a pleasant process, it was one I'd experienced countless times before.

Maybe it'll act as a reset, I hoped. *Give me control again and help me tame my beast.*

However, my body didn't disintegrate the way it should, making me realize that Ajax had done more to the dagger than reprogram my Phoenix magic.

"Now that I have your attention, I need you to listen to me," Ajax said as he limped toward me.

I hadn't noticed the third blade in his leg. More blood drizzled down his pants and left a stain on the ground as he walked.

He towered over me as I peered up at him, my Phoenix still very much in control. My hands moved without my permission as my beast wrapped my fingers around the dagger and started twisting it free from my chest. I tried to stop him, to give Ajax more time, but it was futile. I was trapped in the back of my soul, just as my beast had been mere hours ago.

Touché, I thought at him. *But you can't control me forever.*

85

Which was probably what my animal had thought at me earlier when I'd bound him, too.

"Camillia is okay," Ajax started. Up this close, his obsidian eyes danced with dark blue flames. There was something else there, too.

I often saw his torment reflected back at me, but this was different.

He'd said that this place was fucking with him, but it was more than that. His emotions were troubled, perhaps because he was seeing relics of his past. Or maybe because of his time with Camillia. Likely both.

Twist.

Ajax had maybe twenty-five seconds before that blade was fully dislodged, so he'd better start talking faster.

Only, he stared my beast down without fear. He should have been terrified. He should have been using these few moments to run for his life. Instead, he was trying to reason with my fucking bird.

"But you asked me if I hurt Camillia. And yes, I did. I watched as snake vines sank their fangs into her and spread their poison."

What are you doing? I demanded. *How do you think this is helpful?*

I'd been bitten by a snake vine before. It hadn't been pleasant. To be bitten more than once suggested Cami must have been in agony. And since I knew that, my bird also knew that.

Thus, his words only fueled my Phoenix's ire even more.

"But that's not why she's angry," he went on.

Which caused my Phoenix to pause only for a second.

"She's angry because we—*you* and I—chose to interrogate her rather than try to talk to her." His eyes squeezed shut before opening again, revealing more of those conflicted emotions swirling in his dark orbs. "She said she thought there was something between us. But we ruined it through our actions."

What was the idiot doing? He was digging his own grave. As evidenced by my Phoenix reigniting his efforts in pulling out the dagger.

"But I realized something," Ajax continued. He lowered with unsteady movements, landing on one knee so that we were at eye level.

Not many managed to be this close to a pissed-off Phoenix and survive.

If Ajax didn't start running in the next ten seconds, he probably wouldn't.

But I was starting to wonder if that was exactly what he wanted. If he'd finally given up.

If that damn female had finally pushed him over the edge.

"I realized why she reminds me so much of Emelyn." A shiver of pain ripped through him at the name.

I knew there was a female in his past that had broken him. But he rarely ever spoke about her.

Unfortunately, my Phoenix didn't really care about the revelation right now, though. It was only the dagger in my heart that kept my beast from shredding Ajax into pieces.

Ajax worked on a swallow. "I... I loved Emelyn, but she's gone. Nothing will change that." He glanced up, meeting my gaze unflinchingly once more. "Camillia is here. She was put on my path for a reason, and as her Warden, it was my job to secure her. When she escaped, I was angry."

As was I, I thought at him.

As were you, I reminded my bird, too. *You didn't like that we couldn't find her, that she'd evaded us. Remember?*

Although, I was beginning to understand that perhaps

it was losing his desired mate that had pissed off my beast, not the fact that she was magically thwarting our efforts to track her.

Ajax's jaw clenched. "I—*we*—wrongly took that frustration out on her. If she's telling the truth, which I think she is, then she did nothing to earn our anger. We should have been helping her figure out what happened rather than considering torturing the information out of her."

My beast snarled at the word *torture*, confirming that Ajax was definitely trying to die. There was absolutely nothing he could say now that would—

"Let her take out her revenge on me," he said, making my bird go still. "If you kill me, you will be hurting Camillia. Because she wants to hurt me, too. She's angry. So let her punish me."

My Phoenix tilted my head to the side, probably making me appear somewhat crazy and birdlike. But I supposed that was an accurate appearance.

"Punish?" my bird forced me to say, my fingers still against the hilt of my dagger despite the pain lingering in my veins. "Cami punish Ajax?"

My beast liked that idea.

He wanted to *watch*.

"Yes," Ajax confirmed, making me groan inside.

This isn't going to end well.

Especially since I could feel my animal's glee over the prospect of presenting Ajax to Camillia as a gift. He'd probably give her a dagger, too.

Agony burned through my chest as my Phoenix finally tore the blade out completely, whatever spell Ajax had used to keep it there disappearing. "Cami punish Ajax."

My bird used my hands to grab Ajax by the nape.

And started dragging him toward the old Midnight Fae Council building.

Fuck.

CHAPTER 8

CAMI

I STARED at the food on the bed, uncertain of whether or not to touch it.

My stomach seemed on board with the plan, the hungry rumble echoing in the small cell chamber.

But my mind wouldn't stop shouting what-ifs at me.

What if it's a trick?

What if it's spelled with something nefarious?

What if it's poisoned to kill me?

I glared at the plate, irritated by the questions it inspired. It felt like a taunt. Or maybe even a dare.

Ajax had conjured it before disappearing without a word, leaving me alone and confused and really fucking pissed off.

I'd given him the only truths I had. What more could he possibly want from me?

Did he not think I was equally concerned about missing thirty days of my life? That maybe I was a little terrified by the prospect of the source hallucination having been real?

No. He didn't care about any of that. He was too bent out of shape over his tainted reputation.

I crossed my arms with a huff while the food stared back at me with invisible *Eat Me* eyes.

"Are you not fond of spaghetti?" a silky voice asked behind me, making me literally jump out of my chair.

"Melek," I breathed, placing my hand over my heart. "You scared the crap out of me."

"I've never been fond of that human colloquialism, as it's never true. And besides, the image of someone shitting themselves in surprise isn't all that appealing."

He pushed off the wall he'd been leaning against and stepped toward me, his multicolored gaze sweeping over me in an instant.

"You're hurt," he said, frowning as he moved closer to me. "That's not acceptable."

My eyebrows rose, surprised by the vehemence in his voice. It had me taking a step back into the wall as he approached, which caused him to freeze.

"Camillia." There was a note of concern in his voice that seemed to radiate through his expression. "You're afraid of me?"

"I…" Was I? "No, not really." It'd just been a really long day, and I hadn't expected to see him here.

I didn't know what to expect at all.

Everything was so confusing. I'd apparently missed thirty days of my life, and rather than trying to figure out what that meant, I'd been too caught up in being interrogated.

I rubbed my hand over my face and winced at the dull pain shooting down my arm. *The snake bite.* I'd forgotten about it while focusing on the food. Technically, I had multiple wounds that were going to leave marks.

Twisting my arms, I started searching for the other ones before lifting my shirt to check my torso.

Melek's sharp intake of breath reminded me of his presence, but I didn't bother acknowledging him. It wasn't like he hadn't seen me in various stages of undress. After all, he'd provided some of my *bridal wardrobe*.

"Are there any snake bites on my back?" I asked him as I turned around. "Ajax failed to provide a mirror."

"Snake bites?" Melek repeated, his fingers brushing my skin and sending a subtle shiver through my being in response. "What kind of snake?"

"You'd have to ask Ajax about his hissing friends," I muttered, starting to pull my shirt down again.

But the fabric caught on Melek's hand as he quickly yanked it in the opposite direction.

"Hey!" I snapped as he removed it completely from my head with a deft tug. "This wasn't an invitation to—"

His soft murmur cut me off, the words gibberish to my ears.

"What?" I tried to rotate toward him, but he stopped me with a hand on my hip while his opposite palm branded my back.

I flinched at the heat pouring off of him, then sighed as it spread across my skin.

Oh. That... that feels nice.

I hadn't considered how cold I'd become until now, his warmth a blanket I hadn't realized I'd needed.

A hum of contentment filtered through me, my body relaxing into his touch as he continued speaking in soft tones. I didn't understand anything he was saying, but I couldn't bring myself to care. All that mattered was the warm sensations swimming through my veins.

His arm came around me, holding me back against his

chest as he whispered some of those foreign words in my ear.

I melted, his comfort drugging my senses.

I'm no longer alone. No longer cold. No longer hurting.

My eyes fell closed, my limbs suddenly heavy.

I'll just rest for a few minutes, I decided. *It's been so long since I last slept...*

I felt as though I was floating on a cloud, my body one with the air, my soul flying free.

It was disconcerting yet beautiful. So soft and placid. Reminding me of feathers drifting on the wind.

Maybe I have wings, I thought groggily.

A giggle escaped me at the notion, my mind clearly high on whatever Melek had just done to me.

I paused.

Wait...

I shouldn't be enjoying this. I... I should be fighting this. What rule had I just created?

Hell Fae Rule #47...

What did it say?

It Doesn't Matter How Beautiful They Are...

They'll Always Disappoint You in the End.

My eyes flew open to meet Melek's sparkling gaze, the colors vibrant and rampant as he stared down at me. His emotions were veiled behind a pleasant smile, one I found rather appealing until I realized I was being cradled in his lap. With my head against his shoulder.

Fuck.

I scrambled off of him and scurried across the bed until my back hit an icy wall. Fortunately, my shirt somewhat saved my skin. Which told me he'd put it back on me at some point.

"What just happened?" I demanded.

"I healed you." His blunt reply momentarily stunned

me. Melek usually spoke in riddles or avoided answers with cleverly worded statements. But he'd answered me without hesitation.

"Why?" I hedged, curious to see how far this forthcoming side of him would go.

"Because you were hurt and because I can." He shrugged. "You're not technically a Hell Fae Bride at the moment, so there are no rules at play. I can give you whatever I want, including a new meal, if you're hungry."

My stomach chose that moment to respond for me, causing his lips to twitch.

"Your spaghetti is cold, and your Warden is busy playing with a pissed-off Black Phoenix. So I see no reason why I can't provide you with the comforts you need, if you'd like them."

"Does one of those comforts include getting me out of this snake-infested hellhole?" I asked dryly.

He smiled. "Maybe. I suppose that depends on how your truth session with Ajax went."

"You mean he didn't tell you?" I couldn't hide the sarcasm in my voice. "He doesn't believe anything I've said. And he probably never will. All he cares about is his wounded reputation."

"Hmm." Melek's noncommittal hum seemed to reverberate around me. "What have you told him?"

Part of me wanted to say, *Why don't you go ask him?* But instead I replied, "Why do you want to know? I imagine you won't believe me either."

"On the contrary, Camillia. I think I might be the only one who would." His use of my full name and the seriousness of his tone had me wondering if that was true.

But Rule #47 repeated in my thoughts.

I couldn't trust any of these fae. They didn't care about

me. Not really. I was just a toy for them to play with, a doll to be married off at some future trial.

Except Melek had said I was no longer a Hell Fae Bride. *At the moment.* Had he meant that? "Why am I no longer a Hell Fae Bride?"

He arched a brow at me. "I thought you didn't want to be one?"

"I don't. So I want to know how I'm suddenly not one. And what you meant by *at the moment.*" I did a poor imitation of his voice, but he didn't seem to notice.

He shrugged. "The trials are on hold. You're also currently under observation as a potential threat to the Hell Fae Source, which disqualifies you from the bridal games."

I blinked at him. "A threat to the source?" I didn't want to be a bridal candidate at all, but that somehow sounded much worse. "Wh-what does that mean?"

"It means nothing until we determine what happened thirty days ago." His forthcoming answers were starting to unnerve me. I preferred the playful Melek and his cryptic replies. Not this blunt version that talked to me like...

Like I'm a true prisoner.

"Will you share with me what you told Ajax? I would ask him, but as I said, he's busy at the moment." He waved his hand through the air, allowing a translucent screen of sorts to populate the space.

My eyes widened as it showed Ajax being thrown through the air by an irate Az. I'd known they were both powerful, but this... this was *intense.*

"It's their version of foreplay, I suppose," Melek murmured before using his fingers to diffuse the image.

"How did you do that?" I wondered aloud.

He lifted a shoulder. "I can do a great many things, little angel. And perhaps I'll share them all with you someday. But I need to know what happened thirty days ago."

Right. The question everyone wants an answer to. "I'd like to know that as well," I muttered. "But rather than helping me figure it out, everyone keeps insisting that I already know."

"I imagine that's because you were the one who went missing, so everyone assumes you know where you've been." Melek shifted on the bed to place his back against the same wall as me but left the space between us. "But your response tells me you don't remember."

"It's not that I don't remember; it's that only a few hours have passed for me since I was in Ajax's room. I mean, prison."

"You mean *room*, which I know because I put you there," he replied. "But go on. Tell me what you do remember, and perhaps we can solve this puzzle together."

I stared at him, somewhat surprised by his offer. He was the first one to suggest we work *together* rather than treat me like a prisoner.

I still can't trust him, I thought, Rule #4 running through my head. *But maybe I can use him.*

"Okay." I cleared my throat, but before I could continue speaking, Melek produced a bottle of water and held it out toward me.

"Hydrate first, then continue. And my offer for food still stands."

I stared at the drink, my throat suddenly parched. It was possible he'd done something to it—perhaps added his own version of a truth spell—but I had nothing to hide. He knew all about the book and how it showed me things. Just as he likely assumed I'd wanted to escape the entire time I'd been in the Hell Fae Realm.

What more could he learn?

And he wouldn't want to kill me before learning those answers.

So the water was probably fine. Some food wouldn't hurt either.

"A pepperoni pizza would be amazing right now," I admitted as I took the water from him. "Thin crust, preferably. Extra crispy. And maybe some mozzarella sticks. Oh, and garlic bread. Extra garlic." That way, he wouldn't try to kiss me.

Because I definitely don't want that. At all. Ever. Nope.

His lips curled as though he knew exactly why I'd requested that last item. "As you wish, my angel."

An Italian smorgasbord appeared on the bed between us, along with a set of silky napkins and two more waters. That latter was good because once I started drinking the first one, I couldn't stop. I downed it all in a matter of seconds before snatching up the second, then the third.

More water appeared each time I set down an empty bottle, Melek's sinfully decadent scent filling the air with each swirl of magic.

He watched while I devoured the food, his gaze holding an amused glint to it that probably should have unsettled me. But I was too busy enjoying the meal to let it ruin the moment.

If he'd drugged me, so be it.

At least he was feeding me in the process.

However, as I finished, all I felt was replete. No dizzying sensations. No cloudlike dreams. Just a fulfilled appetite and a very full stomach. "Thank you."

He dipped his chin. "I'm just taking advantage of the rules and giving you as much as I can, while I can."

I wasn't exactly sure what he meant by that, but I didn't press it. Instead, I started telling him everything I'd already admitted to Ajax. Because maybe Melek had really meant what he'd said—that he wanted us to figure out what had happened together.

When I got to the part about the book appearing and showing me Lucifer falling through the sky, I paused and added, "You were there. You were smirking."

He nodded. "Yes, because I knew what Ty was about to do."

I blinked. "Wait. You mean this was real?"

"Of course. Everything in the book is real," he replied, canting his head to the side. "You grew up in the Human Realm. Surely this story reminds you of another famous one the mortals like to believe?"

"You mean, the religious one about a fallen angel sent by God to rule Hell?"

"The very one." His lips curled. "A lot of human folklore stems from some realistic experience. In this case, Ty's legacy has been morphed to scare human children into repenting for their sins. But he doesn't mind. Much, anyway."

"So you're saying what I saw really happened? Even the part about touching a light source?"

His shoulders stiffened. "What part now?"

Right, I hadn't gone into that detail yet. So I wrapped up everything I saw of Lucifer's fall and how the vision had changed into me being drawn toward the hot bulb of power and how I'd been compelled to touch it. "But then the strand changed colors, and the energy grew... *violent*."

I told him how I'd started to run, which had eventually led me to waking up in my old college room.

And how Ajax and Az had shown up a few minutes after that.

He stared at me for a very long moment before saying, "You told Ajax this?"

"Yes. As well as Zeph and Zakkai."

His eyebrows rose. "The Midnight Fae consorts to the queen?"

"Yeah, they were helping Ajax with his... *interrogation.* Although, they were much nicer about it than he was. Zakkai gave me these clothes." I glanced down at the plain tank top and jeans. "He also got rid of the snakes."

"I see." Melek sounded thoughtful. "Did they say anything else?"

"Not really. They just asked me how I felt about Ajax and Az, and then Zakkai asked about my parents."

"What did he want to know about your parents?"

"Their ancestry, I guess. I told him my dad is a Hell Fae and my mother is human. But he seemed to question that." I frowned. "He also kept saying I'm powerful. And he told Ajax to tell Lucifer to call him when he's ready to figure things out."

Melek hummed again. "Interesting."

"I take it Ajax hasn't passed that message along yet?"

"No, but he's otherwise occupied at the moment. And I'm not sure he understands the gravity of what you've revealed." He waved his hand over the dishes to make the empty plates, used napkins, and bottles disappear.

"That sounds ominous," I said, his words weaving dread through my thoughts. "Have I done something wrong?"

"No. But Ty may not realize that."

Another menacing statement. "Except you know I didn't do anything wrong, so that... that has to count for something, right?" I couldn't hide the unease in my tone.

Nor did he attempt to dispel it.

Instead, he studied me with unreadable eyes, his expression giving nothing away.

"Thirty days ago, you managed to escape without a trace. However, that's not the only thing that happened. A portal was opened in the Netherworld Kingdom that allowed several Nightmare Fae to go on a romp through an alternate reality."

"Okay… And this happened at the same time…?"

"Yes. It all happened concurrently when Ty noticed a darkened strand in the Hell Fae Source." He stared at me. "A darkened strand that appeared to have been *touched*."

"Oh." *Well, shit.* "So it's all related?"

"I used to think that. However, now, I don't think it's related at all. I think you somehow touched the source—which shouldn't be possible, but that's a discussion for later—and when you did, the source forced you out as a defensive measure."

"Which would explain all the running," I guessed.

"Indeed. As well as your loss of time and the fact that our best tracker, Azazel, couldn't find you."

"And you said Ty—" I swallowed, wincing at my use of what had to be an intimate nickname between Melek and Lucifer. "Sorry, I meant King Lucifer. You said the trials are on hold because of a threat to the Hell Fae Source. And that threat… it's… it's me?"

Because I touched the source, thereby potentially causing the portal to open to an alternate reality? I shivered, the intensity of my situation rolling through my mind. *Fuck. Lucifer is going to kill me.*

"No." Melek's single-word denial had me snapping my attention back to him. "If you were a true threat, the Hell Fae Source would have killed you to protect itself. Instead, it simply pushed you out. Almost as though you weren't ready to embrace it yet."

My eyebrows rose. "Ready to embrace it?" I recalled the vivid sensations the source had thrown at me. "I don't know about that. It seemed pretty fucking pissed at me."

His lips twitched. "Yes, I imagine it would. The source

is Ty, just as Ty is the source. He isn't one to embrace change with ease. And he doesn't trust those outside his circle either."

None of that made any sense to me. But I was still hung up on the *embrace it* part. "I wasn't trying to *embrace* the source. I was just reading the book."

"Yes, it seems the book wanted to test your compatibility. And given that you survived, I'd say you passed. But it's certainly come with some challenges." He ran his fingers through his blondish-brown hair, the edges teasing his ears. "Fortunately, challenges are my specialty."

Good for you, I nearly said. "I don't want to be a challenge."

"Unfortunately, fate has other plans for you, little angel," he murmured, his irises reminding me of glittering opals as they flashed various colors at once.

Why does he have to be so beautiful? It was distracting, his soft features giving him an almost innocent glow. Although, that glow disappeared every time he opened his mouth. Because there was absolutely nothing *innocent* about this fae.

"Fortunately, however, it seems the portal wasn't caused by someone tainting the source," he continued. "Knowing the two incidents are unrelated is a relief. But now we need to figure out who gave Maliki and the Ghouls the tools to create that portal."

He slid off the bed, his expression one of determination.

"You've helped me immensely, little angel. I'll be sure to repay the favor soon. But in the interim, feel free to make Ajax suffer. Az's Phoenix will approve." He disappeared before I could say a word in response, but left behind a water cooler in his wake.

A literal cooler.

With a giant jug on top, a stack of cups, and temperature controls.

On the floor beside it was a vial with a note that read, *Truth Serum for Ajax.*

I arched a brow at it. Ajax must have requested that from Melek, probably because he still didn't believe what I'd said while under the influence of Zakkai's spell.

Asshole, I thought, rolling my eyes. I supposed the term applied to both Ajax and Melek, but at least Melek had seemed to believe me. He'd also left me a water cooler, which was useful and appreciated.

But what's that on top? I wondered, noticing a subtle flicker of light.

I stood to get a better look. *A feather.* But it was no ordinary feather. It was glittering as though caught in some eternal light.

I glanced up at the dull bulb hanging from the ceiling, then at the smoke-laden torches.

Definitely not being lit up from any of those.

It was gloomy in here, making it a pretty standard dungeon cell.

Strange.

I picked up the soft item, allowing it to run between my fingers, and quivered as energy warmed my very soul. It reminded me of Melek's healing gift—the one that had made me feel as though I was flying through the clouds.

Feeling slightly disturbed, I went to set it back down. Only, it burst into a puff of glitter that coated my skin. I tried to scrub it off, but that only seemed to cause it to anchor into my limbs. It almost reminded me of lotion.

"What did you do to me?" I whispered, trembling as power thrummed through my veins. "What is this magic?"

But of course Melek didn't reply.

He was already gone.

At least he'd helped me figure out what had happened.

Unfortunately, that didn't make me all that confident in my future. If anything, it left me more uneasy than ever before.

I touched the Hell Fae Source.

Lucifer's *source.*

Yeah, I'm definitely a dead fae...

CHAPTER 9

MELEK

THE MOMENT I set foot in the palace, I knew something was wrong. *Ty?*

I'm in the council chamber, he answered shortly.

Frowning, I unfurled my wings and teleported toward his location. I didn't usually engage in my ethereal abilities around others, as I reserved that secret for those I felt intimately connected to, so I chose to land just outside the door.

Chaos greeted me as I entered, several screens fired up to display an array of Nightmare Fae Kings and their stern expressions.

Typhos was in the middle of speaking to King Neptune from the Underwater Kingdom, his voice carrying throughout the room. "Have you found the power source?"

"Not yet," King Neptune replied, his vibrant blue eyes a stark contrast against his long, dark hair. "But we've managed to put a temporary plug in it."

"How long will it hold?"

The godlike king shook his head, causing his mane to

wave around him like black water. "I'm not sure. Maybe an hour. Hopefully longer."

Typhos nodded. "That'll be enough time." He shifted his attention to King Pyre. "Gather as many Ruby Dragons as you can and head toward the Underwater Kingdom."

"Yes, my liege."

Ty addressed King Lazuli next, his boxy face resembling a boulder more than a human. "I need you to gather your Boggarts and compile as many stones as possible."

King Lazuli dipped his square chin. "Of course, my king." The words resembled gravel, which was appropriate given his species.

King Horus's gold eyes lit up the screen as Ty turned to him and said, "Send your Griffins to the Boggarts to collect rocks and meet King Pyre's dragons on the shores of the Underwater Kingdom."

"Consider it done, my liege," he replied, his silky tones sounding flirtatious, but that was just his usual voice.

"I'll be there within the hour to enchant the seal and replace the core," Typhos informed them. "As for the rest of you, scour your kingdoms for potential breaches and report back any inconsistencies you can find."

A chorus of "Yes, my liege" and "Yes, my king" followed.

Typhos nodded and ended all the calls at once. His shoulders sagged the moment they were disconnected, his head falling forward and causing his long hair to cascade over him like a dark waterfall.

I'd been so caught up in Cami that I hadn't felt the panic radiating from my mate, but I sensed it now, the cacophony resembling a beating drum against my heart.

"Ty…" I walked around to his front and palmed his cheeks, lifting his troubled gaze to mine. "The source?" I asked, not needing to voice a full question. He'd understand.

He shook his head. "No, I don't sense any dark strands or visible tampering." He pressed his forehead to mine, seeming to need my comfort more than ever. "But another portal has been opened. This time in the Underwater Kingdom, specifically in the middle of a Sapphire Dragon nest."

"To an alternate reality again?"

"No, it's opening to an ocean in our Human Realm. But it's acting like a vortex. At least twelve dragons were caught up in the creation and swept out of our world. King Neptune has already unleashed a search party." He shuddered out a long breath. "Two of them were found dead, perhaps from the impact of being sucked into the portal."

"So it's forcibly pulling Nightmare Fae out of our realm?" I translated.

"It seems that way, yes." He swallowed, then drew back to stare down into my eyes. "Where have you been?"

"I went to see Cami," I admitted, not wanting to lie to him. Normally, I would have tried to disguise my activities with something playful or cryptic, but that wasn't what Typhos needed right now. "I've been with her for the last ninety minutes or so. She needed some healing and some food."

Typhos expression hardened. "Where were Ajax and Az?"

"Battling in a Midnight Fae courtyard nearby." I slid my hands down to his neck, holding him to me. "It seems our Commander lost control of his Phoenix." Something that hadn't surprised me. I'd noticed he was throttling his animal when he'd visited Ty earlier, and I'd guessed that it was Cami-related.

Typhos growled under his breath and tried to pull free from my grip.

"This is good, my king," I told him. "It means Cami had nothing to do with the portal. Otherwise, I would know."

"Perhaps not *this* portal, but what about the other? What about the source?"

"Two portals in our world in such a brief time suggests a pattern, yes?" My fingers locked behind his neck. "I doubt she would be responsible for one and not the other. Additionally, she has nothing to gain from a portal. The source, however, may be a different matter."

He stopped trying to yank free from me, his dark blue eyes locking on mine. "She told you something interesting."

"She told me something interesting," I echoed, confirming his statement. "Something you're not going to like."

Something I'd intended to keep to myself for a while, but with Ajax already being aware of her truth, it wouldn't be wise to hold this information back.

Moreover, these details would be better coming from me rather than someone else.

"Your book showed her the source of your power." There was no mincing the truth or wrapping it up in riddles. We didn't have time for that, and I needed Typhos to focus and listen to me, not play a game.

"*What*? My book?"

"Vita," I confirmed, causing his eyebrows to hit his hairline. "That's why it keeps running off. It's been visiting Cami."

"And you're just now telling me this?"

I lifted a shoulder. "It wasn't relevant before."

"Not relevant that *Vita* is *talking* to a candidate?" He looked ready to kill me. "*Melek.*"

"I've been monitoring the situation, my liege. Cami originally picked it up in the library to look for a way to break your deal. But she's since been using it to learn certain things. As you know, the book has a mind of its own. It shows Cami what it wants her to learn, not what she's actually asking to see."

He gaped at me, his expression telling me he needed a minute to process this. "Fuck," he breathed. "That's why you chose her," he realized aloud. "Because she can read the book."

I smiled. "One of many reasons, yes."

"She shouldn't be able to read it."

"I know." Only Ty, Az, and I technically could. "But she can. I've seen her do it several times."

"And each time you witnessed this miraculous act, you failed to mention it to me?" he demanded.

"As I said, it wasn't relevant before." Not exactly true, I just hadn't felt it was pressing information to share yet. Now... now it unfortunately was. And Ty was taking the news about as well as I'd expected him to.

"An outsider being able to read *my* book is always fucking relevant, Melek."

"I wanted to see where it would go before I said anything."

"It led to her learning information about me—about *us* —that she isn't meant to know," he fired back at me. "That makes her a threat, Melek. Don't you see that? Or are you too busy playing one of your games?"

I was always playing a game. He knew that better than anyone. However, this game had an ending I hoped would one day please him.

Just not today.

Because if he thought the part about her being able to read the book was a threat, then he really wasn't going to like what else I had to tell him. "There's more, my king. Vita has been very... well, similar to me, I suppose. Meddling? Conniving? Beautifully intelligent?"

Ty narrowed his gaze, his lips flattening into a disapproving line. He clearly wasn't amused by my humor.

"Vita didn't just show her the source. It, well, it led Cami to the heart of it. And she touched one of the strands, which is why it turned black."

"That's impossible. Vita would never do that."

"Nor would it usually present itself to an outsider, as you called Cami. But Cami's explanation is the truth. The book showed her the story of your fall, then led her to the source, where she was drawn to the light. One of the strands darkened beneath her fingers, and she ran away. And, Ty, the source *allowed* her escape."

He stared at me, unspeaking.

So I elaborated with "If the source truly saw her as a threat, it would have killed her, just as I know you're considering doing now. But the source of your power tested her for thirty days and decided to let her live. That has to mean something."

"It means she's far more powerful than we realized and needs to be exterminated."

I tightened my grip on him before he could attempt to teleport to the Midnight Fae Realm and handle her. "It means we need to figure out what she is and determine whether or not she's useful to us."

It wasn't exactly what I wanted to do with Cami—I saw her as much more important than a general resource —but I knew how to talk to Ty. How to convince him to see something as a benefit more than a threat.

"She's scared, Ty. She doesn't understand what

happened. She woke up in Ajax's bed a few hours ago, fell into a historical story within the pages of your book, faced one of the mightiest sources in all the fae realms, and returned only to be interrogated by two very pissed-off fae males."

I paused to let all that sink in.

Then I concluded by saying, "That's not someone who is a threat, my king. That's someone who is naive about her own power and has the potential to be very useful if trained appropriately."

Or has the potential to be a perfect mate for us all, I thought, careful not to telegraph that to Ty. He wasn't ready to hear that part yet. But someday, he would be, and I couldn't wait to present her to him as the ultimate gift.

Because she was the ideal candidate and her visit to the source proved it. She could help anchor Ty, ground the source, be the outlet he truly needed.

But only if he allowed it.

Only if he was able to see beyond his own fears, his own bias, his own history, and potentially trust again.

Cami might be the key, but only if he accepts her.

"The source tampering and the portals are unrelated," I continued when Ty didn't speak. "Which means we need Azazel and Ajax to come home. We need them to track the culprit. And in the interim, you and I can work with Cami to determine her true origins." Because whatever she was, she was more than a mere Halfling Hell Fae.

"If she's as powerful as you're claiming her to be, then I don't want you anywhere near her," Ty said through his teeth.

I chuckled. "You know better than to label something as forbidden to me, my king. That'll only make me rebel more." I'd already proved that by venturing into the

Midnight Fae Realm to see her when I knew he wouldn't approve at all.

It was dangerous for one as high-ranking as I was to venture into another fae world without permission. However, that hadn't stopped me from seeing my darling angel.

Of course, had I been caught, I would have just argued that her being there with Az and Ajax made it acceptable for me to visit. I was mated to her, after all. Just at the first level, but it still qualified me for entry.

"I mean it, Melek. She's dangerous."

"She's not," I promised him. "If she were, the source would have killed her." It didn't hurt to repeat that out loud because it was a worthy argument. And the way his pupils dilated told me he knew it, too.

"She could have tricked the source," he hedged.

"Possibly," I agreed. "And if that's true, you'll discover that trickery for yourself when you talk with her."

His gaze narrowed. "I haven't agreed to that."

"But you will, my king. It's the practical recourse and you know it. Bring Azazel and Ajax home to help with our portal problem while you handle the former Hell Fae Bride."

"I also haven't agreed to remove her from the trials."

"I think we both know that's a guarantee because you're going to either keep her here for observation or kill her, both of which will disqualify her from your bridal games." I ran my thumb along his pulse as I added, "And I know you won't kill her because it'll hurt me, something you vowed never to do."

Pain flickered across his expression, his mind processing what I'd just said. I'd saved that playing card for last, knowing it would hit home.

Because I was right. Her soul was tied to mine. If he

ended her, I would feel it. More than that, I'd have to carry it around as a burden for the rest of my very long existence.

He wouldn't want to do that unless it proved necessary. Which I hoped it wouldn't, but it was the risk I'd taken on when I'd decided to bestow my initial vow upon her.

"I need to get to the Underwater Kingdom," he said, his forehead touching mine again. "We'll continue this conversation when I return."

That was better than his initial response to kill her; it meant he was going to think about what I'd said and come to his own terms for how to proceed. There would likely be a negotiation in our future. There always was when it came to us.

"I'll come with you." I trailed my fingers down his arm to his palm. "Our Nightmare Fae need a united front right now. Remaining here would make it appear as though you're trying to protect me. But I'll never be afraid with you by my side, and they need to see that."

He squeezed my hand, gratitude showing brightly in his gaze. He'd needed to hear that I still had faith in him, as I suspected he was losing faith in himself. Two portal breaches in a month was more than we'd ever had in our entire history, and he was clearly concerned about it.

"I'll be your extra eyes and ears while you focus on fixing the portal. Perhaps there's a clue we're missing. And we'll go from there." I pressed my lips to his chin. "We're going to figure this out, Ty. Then vengeance will be yours."

His grip tightened with my words, his excitement palpable as he considered what kind of retribution he would deliver to those who'd wronged him. He'd probably create another Nightmare Fae species, like he'd done with the Sirens, just to revel in the torment and punishment of the offenders. I couldn't wait to see what he did.

"Thank you," he murmured, his mouth brushing mine. "I would be lost without you, little prince."

"You wouldn't," I promised him. "But you would probably be quite bored."

He grunted at that. "Very," he agreed. "Let's go."

CHAPTER 10

AJAX

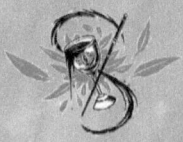

I HADN'T REALIZED how far I'd ventured away from the Council building until we began our trek back. Normally, I would have shadowed. But Az's Phoenix forced me to walk.

Or hobble, anyway.

He'd really done a number on me with those blades. *Dick.*

I'd never seen Az like this. He was usually in control of his animal—even if barely—but never the other way around.

Apparently, Camillia was a sensitive topic. Considering how broken up I felt about her and everything that had happened between us, I wasn't surprised.

At least I'd found a way to keep Az's beast from killing me. His glee had been palpable when I'd proposed that he let Camillia punish me.

Just as his excitement radiated around him now as he dragged me along beside him. I'd convinced him to put on a pair of black jeans and a dark shirt, telling him that Camillia would probably be a little unnerved by my bloody appearance and his naked one.

His bird had narrowed his gaze in suspicion, but then he'd held out his hand and had accepted the clothing I'd conjured.

The moment he'd finished dressing, he'd grabbed me by the nape again and restarted our journey, completely heedless of my injuries.

Camillia was probably going to kill me. Which would suck. But I'd always been familiar with death. Hell, there'd been a time when I'd courted it not so long ago. It was why I'd befriended Az. He was dangerous. Lethal. Maybe one of the few beings throughout the realms who could end me.

Only, he'd befriended me instead.

Ironic that he might be leading me to my death now, doing the very thing he'd forced me to fight against—the impulse to die.

He hadn't used words to distract me, but his fists. And it'd worked. Every beating had reminded me that I was still alive, that I could still feel, very unlike Emelyn and my parents.

They would be disappointed to know how much I'd craved my early grave all those years ago. They'd have told me to live when they couldn't.

But would they approve of who I am now? I wondered. *Would they approve of who I've become?*

Because I didn't feel all that respectable right now.

If they could see me right now, they would probably be disgusted.

I'd originally brought Camillia back here because it was a place I loathed, but somehow fate had twisted on me, making me realize that I'd also taken her close to the graves of fallen loved ones. My behavior acted as a desecration of their existence.

I tortured an innocent woman with snake vines.

I wanted to kill her.

All for what? To save my reputation?

No, that wasn't true. It was so much deeper than that. I'd felt betrayed. Disappointed that I'd let someone under my skin when I'd vowed never to do that again after Emelyn.

And I'd felt *used*.

But that wasn't an excuse for how I'd behaved. I should have believed Camillia when she'd first spoken, should have realized that she was scared and confused and incapable of such betrayal.

I barely know her, I thought, trying to defend myself. *We've played one time. Spent a few hours in a cell. That's it. How was I supposed to know she was truthful?*

I shook my head, exhausted by this argument, pained by Az thoroughly kicking my ass, and just flat-out done with being in this realm.

Az practically dragged me up the obsidian stone stairs to the main doors, hauling me inside as snake vines hissed along the walls. They didn't lunge at him, something I found surprising, given the amount of hostility radiating off his large frame.

Perhaps they sensed that his retribution was due.

And maybe they were right.

My leg ached as he tugged me down the hall toward the back stairwell. It was still enchanted with old spells, ones I had to whisper to let us through, then down we went toward the dungeon beneath.

Gargoyles lounged lazily near knobless doors, their jobs long since expired since Queen Aflora had decommissioned the use of this building.

I wondered if Shade had used any of the cells as fire practice for Florica before going up to the main council chamber.

There hadn't been any residual damage that I could smell, likely as a result of Zakkai's cleanup spell.

Az suddenly jerked to a halt, his nose twitching and making me wonder if I'd missed the stench of burning wood somewhere.

But then I saw what had Az's focus—Sir Callahan. He was strung up in glittering strands near the top of the ceiling with a gleaming red apple stuffed in his mouth. His beady, ruby-colored eyes glared with rage.

"Shit," I breathed. Then I caught a familiar scent of ambrosia, causing my eyes to narrow. "Hold on…"

I pulled out my wand to open the bespelled door outside of Camillia's cell and pushed it open to see her sitting on the bed beside a water cooler that hadn't been there when I'd left.

"Melek," I said, more to Az's Phoenix than to Camillia. "Of course he couldn't stay away." The prince always seemed to be meddling with Camillia.

What is it about this female that has all of us so tangled up?

She had Melek's full attention, Az's Phoenix caught up in some sort of mating high, and me lost in the clouds of my past.

I shook my head, then winced as Az shoved me into the room with a force meant to make me stumble. My bad leg gave out, taking me to my knees in front of a very startled Camillia.

The gargoyle made an unintelligible sound behind me, the apple preventing him from speaking. I supposed we'd help him later.

Because the door shut and disappeared as Az stepped through the threshold.

Camillia's gaze left me to stare up at Az, her eyes widening in surprise. She had part of a chair leg in her hand, the rest of it lying in pieces before me. Apparently, she'd decided that would make a good weapon.

How very human, I wanted to muse aloud. *But Midnight Fae can't be killed with a stake through the heart.*

Alas, it was best that I didn't speak. Otherwise, Az's Phoenix might try to rip my throat out and present it to her as a consolation gift.

"Cami is okay," Az's Phoenix said, relief evident in his tone. "I protect Cami from Az and Ajax."

Camillia gaped at him. "What?"

"His Phoenix has taken control," I told her softly. "He has Az locked up somewhere inside him." It was the best I could offer in terms of an explanation, as I didn't actually know how it all worked since I wasn't a shifter.

"Yesss," Az's Phoenix hissed, the *s* more pronounced than before. "And I brought you a presssent." I wondered if his new lisp was a sign that Az might be trying to break free.

Or perhaps the bird was overcome at seeing Camillia and struggling to form proper words.

"I'm the present," I translated.

"Yesss," the Phoenix agreed. "Cami punishes Ajax."

One of her blondish-brown eyebrows arched upward, his lips flattening as she looked from me to Az. Her incredulous expression asked, *What game are they playing with me now?*

She didn't trust this, and I didn't blame her. Mere hours ago, we'd been interrogating her with violent snakes. Now Az's Phoenix had dragged me in here like a beaten animal and had thrown me at her feet.

Her eyes went to the wound in my leg, which was barely healing, thanks to Az's spelled daggers. They sucked the energy from their victims, which was partly why I felt so weak right now.

I could technically use my wand to heal, but I suspected that would just set Az's Phoenix off again.

Meanwhile, the hole in his chest was gone, leaving only a smattering of blood soaking through Az's shirt.

"What exactly am I punishing Ajax for?" Camillia asked carefully.

"For hurting my you," Az replied, his broken words making it very clear that it was the beast speaking, not the man. "My Cami. You."

"I… I see." She tilted her head, which caused Az to do the same. "Is this some sort of trick?" She blinked, then huffed a laugh. "Never mind. If it was, you wouldn't tell me."

Az stepped forward, producing a dagger in his hand, and knelt beside the bed. "Another gift for my Cami."

Both her eyebrows hit her hairline. "Now I know you have to be fucking with me."

"He's not." I pitched my voice low, focusing on keeping it soft and trying not to anger the Phoenix. "I suggested he let you punish me. It was that or death."

"And you're not worried I might kill you?" she asked.

I lifted a shoulder. "You probably will. But I would rather it be you than Az."

"Why?"

"Because you would be exacting revenge and I can accept that. Hell, I deserve it. But if Az's Phoenix did it… Az, the man, may never forgive his beast." It had seemed right to give her the truth, considering everything we'd shared in this room today. So I did. Whether she believed me or not was up to her.

"Cami punishes Ajax," Az's Phoenix repeated, again holding out the blade. "My Cami accepts my gifts?"

She stared at him, her lips seeming to work soundlessly as she considered what he was offering. She had to know what all this meant—Az's Phoenix was courting her.

Camillia would be a fool to turn down his gifts, especially after all we'd done to her. All *I* had done to her, anyway.

She'd wanted to escape the bride trials since the very beginning. But I had been the one to finally subdue her and take her to the paradigm for imprisonment. Just as I had been the one assigned to her cell when Typhos had decided to relocate her to the prison. And today, I'd been the one to lead the majority of her interrogation.

I more than deserved her wrath.

She was an innocent woman caught up in a debt that truly had nothing to do with her. Her father had been the one to give her away. He was why she'd been ensnared in a contest and forced to play against her will. Not because she'd done anything wrong, but because her father had chosen that fate for her.

But I'd been the one to ensure she stayed.

I'd been the one to track her down with the threat of taking her back after she'd magically managed to free herself.

Only, she hadn't actually freed herself at all. She'd been provided help by some magic book. For all I knew, Melek had orchestrated all of this. It would be just like him to give a candidate a bespelled text that would allow her to flee, just so he could watch us all track her down and torment her for information.

Is that why he visited? I wondered. *To check in on his little pet project?*

"Please?" Az's Phoenix said, his tone very unlike the Az I knew. "Accept my gifts?"

Camillia studied him for another long moment, then

looked at me before staring down at the dagger. Her eyes narrowed, then she reached for the blade.

Az's Phoenix positively preened in response, pleased that she had accepted his weapon. She tensed like she expected some sort of repercussion for her actions, but when none came, she finally started to relax.

It seemed to be dawning on her that this was real.

That she not only had me at her mercy but also had a violent, birdlike male ready to burn down the world for her if she asked him to.

"So you're Az's Phoenix," she murmured, studying him again.

"Yes," the beast replied, lowering his head once more. "And you are my Cami."

"Am I? Because your other half doesn't seem to think so."

"My other half isss not in charge," Az's animal replied.

"I can see that." She twirled the blade between her fingers. "Thank you for this."

Az bowed again, then stood and backed away. "Cami punishes Ajax."

The bird really seemed to like that phrase.

"Yes, I would very much like to punish Ajax," she agreed, her gray eyes finding mine. A wild sort of grin spread across her face, painting an expression of bloodthirsty glee that I'd only seen from Az's Phoenix.

Compatible indeed, I thought.

And regardless of Camillia's true heritage, she was definitely half Hell Fae. That much was confirmed, given that Lucifer knew her father.

Meaning she had a ruthless side to her just like all Hell Fae did.

"I was shoved into this room completely naked and tied up with ropes that turned into snakes," she said as she stood, her words making Az's Phoenix hiss in response. "I think Ajax should experience what that feels like."

Az cocked his head like he was considering it. "Yesss."

"Will you undress him for me?" Cami asked, her words seeming to be a test for how far she could push Az to do her bidding.

The Phoenix made a clicking sound, one I recognized as eagerness. Which meant he was all too happy to comply with her request, something that didn't shock me at all. His bird had always been a sensual creature. Violent, yes, but he absolutely loved sensual torment most of all.

He moved toward me and ripped my cape off first, then lit up his fingers with black fire to burn off my shirt. I flinched, the heat singeing my skin. It didn't quite burn, telling me he hadn't wanted to hurt me. He'd just wanted me to *feel* his power.

My pants were next. Az yanked at them, uncaring of my wound and the blood that oozed toward the ground. Then he used his fire to remove my boxers, the heat along my groin a carnal torment that had me growling in response.

Az knew all about my preference for pain during sex.

It was why I usually let him pierce me for fun.

But the way he was staring at the barbell in my cock right now told me he was thinking about ripping it out, just to watch me bleed.

Instead, his eyes met mine as he hissed out, "Snake rope. Now."

I sighed. As the Midnight Fae, I would have to conjure them. With a wave of my hand, I called my wand to me and created a new chair for me to sit in, then muttered another spell for the snake vines to appear, effectively wrapping myself up in my own magic.

"I know you said rope, but this way you don't have to touch them," I told Camillia, meeting her gaze.

"If you conjured them, I assume they won't bite you?" she guessed.

"Oh, they'll bite me," I promised her. "They don't care who created them. They exist to defend and bite when they feel threatened." I lifted a shoulder to demonstrate and winced as one of the snakes sank its fangs into my skin. "Like that."

She stared at the wound, her lips twisting to the side in a way that suggested she didn't like it. Perhaps because she hadn't been the one to inflict it.

"They won't attack me again unless I move in a way they don't like or think malicious thoughts." The former I could easily do, but the latter... that would be more difficult.

Because right now I just felt defeated.

Disappointed in myself.

Confused.

I'd spent thirty days enraged and hurt by betrayal. But when all of that had been ripped out from under me, a void had been left behind.

A void from my past that only seemed to widen with each passing second in this place.

Camillia said nothing for a long moment, her focus seeming to shift to the slowly healing wounds on my naked body.

She examined the dark mark on my shoulder, near where the snake had bitten me, likely noting the difference in coloration. The bite wound was fresh, the blood red and normal there. While the other was black, my essence tainted by Az's magic that continued to feed on my energy.

She found a similar one near my rib cage, then glanced at the one on my thigh again before her gaze trailed upward to my groin. I was half-hard, thanks to Az's fiery touch.

And maybe I was a little turned on by the fact that I was tied up, naked, and under threat of pain while a beautiful woman observed.

I'd never been into typical sex. I preferred danger. Agony chased by bliss. Dark themes. *Blades*.

She arched a brow at my growing arousal. "You like this?"

I shrugged. "I don't hate it." Nor did I hate her. On the contrary, I quite liked her. Even in that fitted tank top and jeans, I found her undeniably sexy. Which was saying something, given that I'd seen her in a variety of revealing outfits during her time as a bridal candidate.

I probably should be trying to fight my arousal for her, especially considering she was likely going to slowly torture me and kill me. But I didn't see the point in hiding my attraction. We'd come here for honesty, after all, hadn't we?

Still, hunger wound through me when she softly bit her lower lip as her gaze fell again. It was likely an unintended gesture, but it did things to me that only made my cock harden.

She frowned. "I need to do more." She glanced around, her gaze going to the water cooler and then to the ground. "Melek's present he left you."

"Melek left me a present?" I asked, confused.

She picked up a vial and showed it to me. "Truth Serum for Ajax," she read.

My lips curled downward. "I didn't ask him for a truth serum."

She blinked, then looked at the item again. "Oh. It's for me." She met my gaze again. "To use on you."

Of course it was. Either Melek had overheard my offer

to Az, or he was suddenly a fortune teller. "Clever fucking fae," I muttered. Then I opened my mouth while holding Camillia's gaze, making it clear that I would drink it without force.

If she wanted my truths, I'd give them to her. Although, I had no idea what she could possibly want to know. But it seemed she was hell-bent on re-creating the interrogation I'd put her through, so I'd play along.

She walked over to me and dumped the contents into my mouth, then pushed upward on my chin as though she was afraid I might spit it out.

I swallowed instead, all the while staring her down.

Her stormy gray irises swirled with a dozen emotions, chiefly among them being anger. But she didn't say anything, her eyes searching mine for something.

I waited, letting her lead while Az stood just behind her, his reverent gaze on her. It was a look I'd never seen from Az before, one I hadn't even known he could make.

He had to be pacing angrily inside his mind right now, demanding that his Phoenix release him. And I feared what might happen when he did.

Hopefully, he didn't punish Camillia for his bird's insanity. But if Az felt she was a threat to him and his beast, he just might try to kill her.

What will I do if that happens? I wondered. *Will I even be alive to find out?*

"What are you thinking about?" Camillia asked me, her question catching me off guard.

"I... I was thinking about whether or not I'll be alive when Az takes control of his Phoenix again," I admitted, wincing when I realized the truth serum was definitely already working. The words had practically rolled off my tongue.

"You think I'm going to kill you?"

"I'm not sure," I answered honestly. "You absolutely could. I guess it depends on how mad you are."

"How mad I am," she repeated as though considering the words. "Well, you did interrogate me with snake vines and force the truth out of me, which wasn't all that different from what I had already admitted. And you still don't seem to believe me even now."

I gazed up at her, aware that she hadn't asked me anything, yet feeling it necessary to clarify regardless of her lack of inquiry. "I believe you now. And I feel like an ass for not believing you before."

"You... you what?"

I repeated what I'd just said, the truth serum forcing me to speak. Only this time, I added, "I thought you betrayed me. It clouded my judgment."

Her brow furrowed. "You mean I harmed your precious reputation and you felt the need to get retribution. That's your definition of betrayal?"

"No, my definition is confiding in someone only to have those confessions used against me for the other person's gain," I stated flatly.

She blinked. "And you think I did that?"

"I thought you did, yes. But after hearing your truth... I'm no longer sure." Because she could have been planning to exploit my weaknesses at some later time.

Or maybe she hadn't planned to take advantage of me at all. Camillia had said herself that she'd considered asking for my help but had decided against it. So it stood to reason that she hadn't planned to manipulate me or use my past in some nefarious way.

Some of the fire died in her gaze, her expression turning thoughtful. "Why would you think that?"

"You disappeared while I was in the shower. I thought you seduced Az and me in order to lower our guards, just to escape. And…" I swallowed. "And I thought you used my past as a way to infiltrate my defenses."

"Used your past?" She shook her head. "I don't know enough about your past to do that."

"But you do. You know more than most. About… about Emelyn." It hurt to say her name aloud, but that was the truth serum working its magic. I couldn't fight it, and I wasn't even sure I wanted to. I just felt so tired. Mostly due to Az's dark weaponry and the energy-zapping wounds he'd inflicted upon me with them, but also because of this place. The last thirty days. Everything I'd endured.

"Who's Emelyn?" Camillia asked, her question sending a dagger through my heart. "No, wait. Is that who you said I reminded you of?"

I nodded. "Yes. She was a fighter. Strong. Stood up for what she believed in, even when all the odds were stacked against her. She never gave up. Just like you."

"Where is she now?" Camillia sounded more curious than angry now, but her inquiry cut right through me, the truth tugging sharply at my soul.

"She's dead."

"Oh." She cleared her throat. "Do I want to know how?"

I huffed a laugh, then flinched as two of the snakes bit me at once. *Fuuuck.* I fucking hated snake vines. Yet I'd inflicted them on Camillia earlier, because I'd thought I'd hated her, too.

I'd wanted to, anyway.

Grinding my teeth, I tried to ignore the pain as the potion yanked the truth from my mouth. "You probably don't want to know. No one really does. But it's a well-known death. She stood up for the abominations, just like my family. Just like me. And Constantine turned them all to marble while forcing several of us, myself included, to watch."

Camillia winced.

And I looked away. "I vowed never to care about anyone like that again. But you... you're too much like her. Yet you're not like her at all. You're even stronger. Resilient, too. I never thought you could escape, but you did."

"You just thought I used you in the process," she replied.

"Yes. No." I shook my head. "I did feel betrayed, yes. But mostly, I... I didn't want to admit how I felt about us, how I felt about *you*. And to think you might have used me... used *us*..." I glanced at a silent Az before looking back at Camillia. "It infuriated me."

"But you told me you were upset about your Warden reputation and how I'd tainted it by breaking free from your prison. That's true, too, right?"

"My reputation as Warden is all I am now. So yes, that's also true. However, I used that excuse to mask my real hurt. It was easier to be upset about a slight against my record than to admit my feelings were hurt by a woman I'd started to care about."

Fuck. If I survive this, I'm going to kill Melek. His spell was reverting me to the fae I used to be, the one who wasn't afraid to feel things.

And I really did not want to feel anything right now.

Nor did I want to be telling Camillia all of this.

She'd stopped twirling Az's blade, her expression no longer exuding the murderous rage I'd seen on it before. Instead, she appeared... complacent. And I had no idea how to interpret that.

"How do we get rid of the snakes?" she asked, her gaze going from me to Az.

"Ajax can whisper a simple command to remove them," Az replied, causing me to glance at him. His irises glittered a vibrant violet shade, making my heart squeeze in my chest.

You're back, I nearly said, more relieved than ever to see my friend. I wondered how long he'd been standing there silently, listening to Camillia's interrogation without intervening.

Hell, he'd probably heard everything.

But I was surprised he hadn't tried to take over or subdue her. Perhaps he'd come to some sort of compromise with his Phoenix. Whatever it was, I was just thankful to have him back in control.

Camillia didn't seem to notice, her focus on me. "Despell the snakes."

I wasn't going to wait for her to say it twice and obeyed by uttering a few words. The vines vanished in an instant, leaving me naked and fully exposed on the chair.

"Can you heal yourself?" Camillia asked.

"Yes."

"Then why haven't you?"

I shrugged. "Because that would defeat the purpose unless you want me fully healthy before you kill me." She wouldn't be able to now that Az was back—something his narrowing eyes told me—but I wasn't going to fight her if she tried.

"I don't want to kill you, Ajax." She slid the blade into her jeans pocket rather than handing it back to Az. "I mean, I wanted to a few hours ago, but now..." She trailed off, her shoulder lifting and falling. "I think all of us have misunderstood each other at some point."

"Yes, I'm beginning to agree with that sentiment," Az murmured as he stepped closer to Camillia.

"Az," I warned him, my instincts starting to fire. "Don't."

"Don't what?" he asked in a silky tone, his vibrant eyes locking on Camillia like prey.

She suddenly seemed to understand that the Phoenix at her back was no longer in charge, her shoulders stiffening as she slowly turned to face a very pissed-off Commander.

"I'll be taking that blade back now," he told her, his hand appearing palm up. "Please."

CHAPTER 11

CAMI

Az's PUPILS PULSATED, his violet irises thin and enlarging around them as though he and his Phoenix were still at war for control.

But clearly the man inside him had taken over once more.

Leaving me staring at a very pissed-off fae instead of a besotted Black Phoenix. I wasn't sure why his inner beast had decided to claim me; however, it'd been nice while it'd lasted.

"Blade," Az repeated. "*Now.*"

I looked up at him, my gaze narrowing. "You know what? No. I don't think so."

Both his dark brows rose. "Excuse me?"

"I'm certain you heard me, but I'll repeat it just in case —*No.*" I folded my arms across my chest, unfazed by the simmering male before me. "*My* Phoenix gave it to me as a gift, and I don't feel like returning it."

Az's nostrils flared as obsidian flames overtook his eyes, only to be squashed by a wave of vibrant purple. "It's not a request, Camillia. That blade is mine."

"No, it belonged to your Black Phoenix. But he gave it to me. And I'm keeping it." I was probably playing with literal fire here, but I was done being pushed around for today.

Unfortunately, Az had other ideas, something he proved when he grabbed me by the throat and shoved me up against the wall.

"*Az.*" Ajax appeared right behind him, his expression wary. "Don't do this."

"I want my blade back." Fury underlined Az's tone, sending a chill down my spine. His Black Phoenix might like me, but the man he cohabited with very clearly did not.

And both were equally lethal.

Yet, I found myself holding his gaze without flinching. If he wanted that knife back, he'd have to take it off of me himself. At least then I wouldn't be offending his animal side by giving up so easily.

Az's grip tightened, cutting off my air supply as his opposite hand went to my hip. "You have no idea who you're challenging, little warrior."

I wasn't trying to challenge anyone. I was simply doing what felt right—which included raising a brow back at him in response. Wasting my air seemed impractical when I could convey my reply nonverbally.

His eyes slanted into a glare that rivaled my own, his body coming closer to crowd me against the wall. I didn't try to fight him. Didn't wrap my hand around his wrist in an effort to negotiate my release. I simply stared at him, waiting for him to do whatever the fuck he planned to do.

Electricity charged between us, causing all the hairs along my arms to stand on end in warning.

This being is dangerous. Old. Capable of killing me without blinking.

My instincts fired on all ends, my lungs burning with the need for air.

Yet I couldn't seem to back down. It felt wrong, like I would be losing something incredibly important if I gave in to his demand.

"Az," Ajax tried again, his palm landing on Az's shoulder. "Let her go."

The stubborn male before me didn't budge, his grip cemented around my throat and threatening to crush my windpipe. His violet rims began to appear ominous, darkening with lethal promise. But I caught the hint of his Phoenix in his pupils, the flicker of fire acting as a beacon of his approval.

Or perhaps I was just reading into the situation and morphing it into a fantasy.

Maybe I even had a death wish.

After everything that had happened today, I wouldn't be surprised. I hadn't even been able to properly torture Ajax. Because the moment he'd started revealing his truths, I'd been paralyzed by my own emotions.

He'd lived through hell.

That didn't make up for what he'd done to me today, and I wasn't sure I truly forgave him. However, at least I understood *why* he'd done it.

It had helped us come to a tenuous agreement, one we hadn't actually spoken about, but he believed me now. And I believed him.

That might allow us to move forward.

Assuming Az didn't kill me.

"Azazel," Ajax snapped. "This is between you and your Phoenix. Camillia—"

Az cut him off with a growl that reverberated against my chest, the sound so feral and cruel that I couldn't help the silent gasp my lips attempted to form. But there was no air left for me to breathe.

"*Fuck.*" The word vibrated my tongue as Az captured my mouth with his in a punishing kiss, his oxygen becoming mine as he loosened his grip on my throat. I inhaled sharply, my lungs demanding the very essence it needed to survive.

But all I could take in was Az.

His air.

His taste.

His addictive cologne.

I moaned, the sensation of being revived making my limbs tingle with rejuvenated energy. I'd been drowning, *dying*, punished by his dangerous palm, and now he was rewarding me for surviving.

This is so messed up, I thought. Yet I couldn't stop myself from kissing him back, my tongue dueling with his in a renewed crusade led by our souls.

His palms went to my hips, holding me against him, forcing me to feel his arousal through our clothes. I wrapped my arms around his neck, my nails biting into his shoulders in response, my need to draw his blood an overwhelming craving inside my mind.

He didn't stop. If anything, he pushed me to do it, to mark him, to *claw* him.

Fuck, this is insane. I could barely think, my senses lost to this monstrous male holding me against the wall, devouring me to my very spirit.

I gasped again, my throat raw from his roughness, my lungs still demanding *more*.

More Az.

More scent.

More *everything*.

But my world spun before I had a chance to indulge in the oxygen I craved, his palm once again at my throat as he branded my lower belly with his arm.

A strangled sound left my mouth as he yanked me backward into his muscular body, his chest to my back, his lips at my ear. "Ajax needs to heal," he said, his voice silky and dark and barely edged with violence. "You're going to help him heal."

My chest heaved with exertion, my mind spinning as I tried to decipher what was happening and how we'd ended up here.

I'm supposed to be mad.

I am mad.

Except I'm also...

Oh, fuck, I'm also hot.

Ajax was still naked, his body still covered in blood from his fight with Az, the snakes that had bitten him, and whatever else he'd been doing.

But he was also hard. *So... fucking... hard.*

"Az," he warned, sounding pained.

"Shut up and take what you need, Ajax," Az demanded, walking me forward into the other male. "Take *her.*"

"This is wrong," the other male growled, even while his hand found my hip. "We can't."

"We can," Az corrected him, his arm tightening around my abdomen. "Challenge him, Camillia. Show him we can."

I swallowed, uncertain of what he meant and aroused by it at the same time. *Challenge him to do what?* I wondered, my gaze roaming over Ajax's chiseled features. His face had been unmarred, while his body...

My eyes slanted into a glare. *Hold on...* "I told you to

heal yourself." My gaze flew back up to his. "Why haven't you healed yourself?"

"Because he feels he deserves the pain," Az murmured, his lips brushing my pulse with his words. "And he *likes* pain." Az's hips pressed into mine, forcing me to feel both his erection and the one before me. A tremor worked through my being as Ajax's pierced tip touched my lower belly, that metal bar momentarily distracting me.

I want to lick him again, I thought.

But more than that, I wanted to feel him inside me.

I wanted to feel them both.

Fuck, this is bad.

I should be trying to kill them… not… not indulging in them.

However, a cloud of pine, mint, and overpowering masculinity consumed me in the next breath, my senses drugged by the two intoxicating males surrounding me.

It was familiar, yet new. Safe, yet underlined with dangerous currents. Sensual, yet violent.

"Help him heal, Cami," Az whispered again. "Kiss him. Show him that he's not nearly as horrible as he believes himself to be."

"Fuck you, Az," Ajax said, his voice low and menacing. "I don't need this."

"You do," the male behind me countered. "You've been living in a world of grief for so fucking long, refusing to talk about what happened, and failing to accept that there was nothing you could do."

Ajax's grasp tightened against my hip, his body seeming to vibrate in response to Az's words.

However, the man at my back wasn't done.

"Everyone makes mistakes. Fate's a fucking cunt. But that doesn't mean you can't have a future." Az's lips skimmed my ear as he added, "Give him a glimpse of what our future could taste like, little warrior. Show him what we could be."

That sounded like a terrible plan. But also a great one.

Ajax had shown me his bleeding heart, his secrets no longer trapped beneath his angry veil. And he'd sort of done so willingly, at least to an extent. Because he hadn't fought me on the truth serum. He'd simply swallowed it.

He'd also volunteered himself for my retribution, stripping himself bare and trapping himself beneath a sea of deadly snakes.

Snakes he could have bespelled with just a few words, I reminded myself, thinking about how easily he'd freed himself when given permission. *Yet he'd subjected himself to the pain for me.*

Well, partly for Az's Phoenix, too.

Or maybe primarily as a result of Az's beast.

I wasn't really sure. Except Ajax had seemed contrite. He'd also admitted that it hadn't really been about his reputation, but about how he'd been starting to feel things for me.

"It was easier to be upset about a slight against my record than to admit my feelings were hurt by a woman I'd started to care about."

I lifted my hand to his cheek, his words playing through my head. I felt something for him, too. Something I couldn't define. Something I absolutely shouldn't be feeling at all.

But we were connected in a way. Or maybe we were just living in the moment.

Still, I found myself wanting to help him heal. Perhaps not physically, but at least a little mentally.

And I could do that by showing him a little bit of forgiveness.

Because he wasn't as horrible as he claimed himself to be. Yes, he'd interrogated me rather cruelly, but he'd thought I'd betrayed him. That I'd used him. That'd I'd fled without a trace.

No one could really blame me for wanting to escape. But that was a discussion for later.

Right now, I wanted to make him feel better, to remove that sadness from his dark gaze, making that ring of blue fire appear around the edges of his irises again, and convince him to let himself heal.

"You don't have to do this," he whispered as he stared down at me.

"I do," I told him. "But not because Az is telling me to." I went up on my toes to brush a kiss against his plump lips. "I'm doing this for me. For you. For *us*." My palm slid to the back of his head, trapping him in case he chose to flee. "You need this. You need *me*."

I wasn't sure how I knew that, but I sensed it in the stiffness of his form, could see it in his sad gaze.

He needed a distraction. Or maybe this was more of a reminder.

A reminder that he was alive.

"Kiss me," I requested, the words a breath against his mouth. "Apologize to me with your tongue, and I'll consider apologizing, too."

He groaned, his other hand grabbing my opposite hip to pull me closer. "I fucking hate both of you."

"A lie," Az said, sounding amused. "Good thing my Phoenix isn't still in charge, hmm?"

Ajax made a rough noise in the back of his throat before finally claiming my mouth.

He wasn't nearly as rough as Az, his kiss almost gentle in comparison, like he didn't find himself worthy of this moment and wanted to ensure I felt cherished as a result. Or perhaps he truly was trying to apologize, to make me feel adored, respected, *admired*.

His velvet tongue seemed to be whispering more truths against mine, truths he didn't want to admit even to himself but was willing to share with me here, so long as we agreed to keep this secret between us.

I allowed it, receiving his unspoken words and exchanging a few of my own.

I don't really hate you.

I want you.

But I don't want to want you either.

This is wrong, isn't it?

Except it feels right. Why does it feel right?

He couldn't actually hear my thoughts, nor could I hear his, but something told me we were thinking on a similar wavelength.

Because his tentative strokes grew bolder, as did my thoughts.

Why am I overthinking this?

I should just enjoy it.

Embrace it.

Fucking own *it.*

Az rumbled in approval behind me, and I suspected the noise came from his Phoenix. It almost resembled a purr. He kissed the back of my neck, his hands roaming up my sides beneath my shirt and around to cup my breasts.

I arched back into him, my hips meeting Ajax's as pleasure engulfed my being.

Their touch was hypnotic, their mouths a hazardous addiction. I hardly even noticed Az removing my tank top, Ajax's lips only leaving mine for a second.

But I felt Ajax's hard chest against mine, his wounds providing a texture I found more arousing than revolting.

So strange, I marveled. Apparently, I liked his pain. His blood. His harsh intake of air when the worst of his injuries brushed my unmarred skin.

It was probably because a part of me still wanted him to hurt.

Or, more likely, I found his sacrifice enticing. Those cuts had to be excruciating, but he was choosing to play with me over focusing on his own healing.

Because he thought he deserved it.

Maybe he did.

However, I told him with my tongue that he didn't. Told him with each kiss that I wanted him to be whole, to be alive, to be... to be Ajax again.

Either he didn't understand me, or he didn't want to comply, because he continued to bleed as his fingers went to the top of my jeans.

Az's hand met him there, his own fingers tugging at my zipper while Ajax popped the button. Then they worked together to pull off my pants, leaving me naked between them.

Ajax's pierced cock hit my belly, the bulbous head weeping in expectation.

I wanted to taste him again. But I also needed something different.

What would all that power feel like inside me? Would it make him bleed more? Would he give me everything, despite the pain?

Az's hands went to my hips, his lips once again by my ear. "I want him to fuck you against me, sweet warrior. Use me as a wall, let me support you while he takes you."

I shuddered, that proposal painting a vivid picture in my mind, one I refused to deny.

Then he increased my need by removing his own shirt, placing his hot skin to my back, and branding me with his heat.

"Yes..." The word was in response to the sensation, but also to what he'd offered. Because yes, I wanted that. All of it. To feel them. To experience *this*.

Ajax pulled back to study my expression, his eyes searching mine for something I didn't understand.

Whatever it was, it could wait, because I was ready for him, my thighs slick with obvious desire. I wrapped my palm around his base, pulling him toward me and angling him downward as I went up onto my toes again.

He hissed as his head met my wetness, his entire body seeming to jolt as though in agony.

Then Az lifted me, giving us a better position and allowing me to wrap my legs around Ajax's hips.

"Fuuuck," Ajax groaned as I rubbed his cock against me, proving that I wanted him, that I was more than ready to take him.

Or so I hoped, anyway.

I felt primed and ready from our last play session because it didn't feel like that long ago to me.

Although, Ajax was thick. And he was *pierced*.

I had no idea how that would feel, but I knew I could take him. I had to. I *wanted* to.

His forehead went to mine, his eyes closing on a wince as he grabbed Az's shoulder for support.

"Take her," Az encouraged him. "I want to feel you fuck her against me."

"It's going to make me bite her," Ajax warned, his throat working on a swallow. "I won't... *can't*... mate her... against... her will."

"Then I'll bleed her for you," Az offered, the stubble on his chin tickling my neck. "Assuming I have your permission, little warrior?" The words were hot against my skin, his teeth skimming my pulse.

"Shifter bonds," Ajax gritted out. "Your Phoenix—"

"Isn't in charge right now," Az murmured. "I am." His tongue teased my thrumming vein. "May I bite you for Ajax, Cami?"

I shivered, the offer oddly euphoric even while it should be terrifying.

But my life had never been calm or normal. I'd always been surrounded by danger and intrigue, and this moment was no different.

So I said the only thing I could say. "*Yes.*"

CHAPTER 12

AJAX

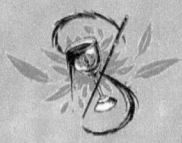

Fucking Phoenix.

Fucking Az.

Fucking… fuck…

I couldn't fight Az's damn charisma. He was incredibly alluring when he wanted to be, fucking addicting, and Camillia…

Camillia was fucking *perfect*.

Her firm grip around my shaft held me captive before her, lost to the sensation of her damp pussy rubbing against my pulsating cock.

I wanted her more than I wanted to breathe.

But what if Az's Phoenix is doing this? He was magnetic. Sensual. *Hypnotic.* It came so naturally to him that half the time he didn't even realize he was doing it.

Has Cami fallen under his spell? Or is this her? Does she actually want this?

Her body said she did. Fuck, even her eyes confirmed her arousal. As did her words.

And her moan…

The scent of her blood hit me with a force that stole the air from my lungs, her grip around me tightening as Az sank his teeth into her neck, right where I desired to mark her.

It was madness.

I couldn't mate this female. She wasn't mine to take. Wasn't mine to even taste.

Yet, I couldn't deny her, not when my body responded so profoundly to her own. She was a craving I hadn't known I desired. A meal I hadn't even realized I needed.

"She's ready," Az murmured, his lips bloody as he pulled away from her throat.

I leaned toward him on impulse, needing to lick the essence from his mouth. It caused my arousal to rub even more against Camillia as I sandwiched her between us, my hunger for her blood and Az driving my actions.

She released me, only to grab my nape, her fingers teasing my hair as she brought me closer to Az.

His lips curled against mine, his smile victorious. It told me his Phoenix was riding him hard, dictating his movements even while allowing Az to lead.

But I was too far gone to comment.

I merely accepted a preview of Camillia's addictive flavor directly from his tongue and groaned as her essence slid down my throat.

More, my instincts raged. *Take* more.

I pulled away from Az with a gasp, my focus going to Camillia's slender throat and the blood waiting for me there.

It was too tempting to deny.

She was too tempting to deny.

"Are you sure?" I somehow managed to ask her.

Camillia responded by pressing herself against my

groin, her wet kiss a clear invitation. But I wanted to hear her say it.

"Tell me what you want, Camillia. Tell me in explicit terms, and I'll give it to you." I wanted her consent. I wanted to know this was real. I needed to believe this wasn't just Az's Phoenix seducing us both. "Please, Camillia. Tell me what you *need*."

"You," she said, her nails biting into my nape. "I want you inside me. To feel that piercing. To feel *you*. And you need me to bleed." She arched her neck. "So drink from me and fuck me."

Az purred in approval, the vibration one he rarely made and very much coming from his Phoenix. I caught flickers of black fire in his gaze, confirming his animal was exceptionally close to the surface. But the violet remained, grounding my friend as he continued to hold Camillia up like a damn offering for me to fuck.

Her thighs tightened around me, her pussy pushing against my cock. "*Please*, Ajax. I want to feel your power."

I caught her hip, my hand brushing Az's as he slid his touch up to her waist. "You sure about that, Camillia?" I asked her, sliding between her slick folds. "I might hurt you."

"Then we'll bleed together." Her fingers trailed away from my nape to my shoulder, her thumb brushing one of my snake bites before applying enough pressure to make me groan. "Give me everything, Ajax."

This was not at all how I'd expected our time together to go. But I was done second-guessing it. Done worrying about Az's interference. Done *overthinking*.

I just wanted Camillia.

Her heat.

Her moans.

Her *pleasure*.

I moved back enough to reposition myself against her, only for Az to reach down and grab my base, his grip firm and cruel as he forced me to meet his burning gaze. "You're going to tell me how every inch of her feels, and you're going to make her come at least twice before you empty yourself inside her."

Fucking Az. Of course he would dictate this, just like he controlled every other encounter together.

But I wasn't about to argue with him.

If he wanted me to make Camillia come, then I'd make her fucking explode.

He must have read the agreement in my gaze because he angled my head downward toward her wet opening, guiding me right toward the heart of her.

I didn't think; I acted, thrusting forward the moment he released me.

Camillia cried out at the impact, her thumb digging harshly into my wound as Az returned his lips to her neck to bite her again.

A curse slipped from her mouth, her body tensing between ours and giving me pause. "Are you okay?" I asked, needing to know we hadn't truly hurt her.

"Yes," she breathed. "More than okay. Now fuck me, Ajax. *Hard.*"

Fuck. This female was going to dismantle every part of me, destroy all my preconceived notions, and force me to do more than feel.

She was going to make me fall hard.

She might just make me love again.

I refused to allow the thought to infiltrate the moment, my mind shutting down as I focused on how she felt. "So fucking tight," I breathed, doing my part in telling Az the details he'd demanded. "I feel like I barely fit."

"Then loosen her up," he suggested, a sinful note in his voice. "Make her take you."

Camillia responded to his words by squeezing the shit out of my shaft, her inner muscles stronger than I would have anticipated. "She definitely likes hearing your commands," I told him as I slid out to the tip. "Her cunt contracted around me the moment you spoke."

I slammed back inside, earning a scream from Camillia and a groan from Az. He'd felt the power of that thrust through her, likely making him envision himself sliding into her from behind. But rather than take part, his hands went to her waist again, holding her in place while I gripped her hips and drove into her again.

And again.

And again.

She moved against me, eagerly accepting my pace and meeting me with gyrations of her own.

It was seamless perfection, our bodies dancing as one while Az added his own filthy commentary.

"You're taking him so well, little warrior."

"Fuck, look at that beautiful pussy swallowing Ajax's big cock."

"I can't wait to feel you."

"Thrust harder. Make her scream."

"Hmm, that's it. Pant for him, sweet girl. Beg him to let you come."

Camillia moaned, her sheath pulsating around me as her climax started to climb. "Keep talking to her," I told Az. "It's going to make her explode."

"Or I could touch her," he murmured, his arm banding around her stomach. "Maybe her tits need some attention."

"Yes." The word left Camillia on a moan, her arousal grounding against mine. "*Please.*"

Az palmed her breast, his thumb circling her nipple. "Like that?" he asked. "Or like this?" He pinched the bud, twisting it sharply and drawing a scream from Camilia. "Hmm, yes, definitely that."

The tightening around my shaft confirmed his words. "She definitely preferred that." I used my grip on her hips to angle her slightly differently, then slid into her again, this time rubbing her clit with the movement.

"Ohhh, *more...*" Her words sounded raspy, her voice strained from all her moaning and screaming.

I repeated my action while Az played with her tits, both of us spurring her onward and drawing a decadent flush across her skin.

Then I leaned down to lap at the blood on her neck, my tongue prodding the holes Az had left behind.

And Camillia detonated.

I grinned against her throat, relishing the throbbing sensations she inspired below. "She's even tighter now, Az. Pulsing around me. Trying to force me to come with her."

"But you won't."

"Not yet," I agreed, sliding in and out of her while she rode out her orgasm. "She definitely needs to come again. She's too wet not to. Too *needy*." I suckled on her neck, groaning at her exquisite taste. *Like renewed life,* I marveled. *A new day.*

I hadn't even realized that had a flavor, but it absolutely did. Like pollen on a spring day in the Human Realm.

I groaned again, my teeth aching to sink into her flesh, to truly indulge in her.

But I held myself back, choosing to suck on her open wound instead, taking more of her blood into my mouth and swallowing.

So fucking good...

"Slip your hand down your stomach and stroke your clit," Az murmured into Camillia's ear. "Ajax needs to feel you fall apart again."

"I… I don't know if… I can." Camillia's chest heaved with the words, her breaths uneven, her gratified state palpable.

"You can," Az promised. "You *will*."

She gasped as he toyed with her nipple again, her body jolting against mine and driving me even deeper into her. I'd slowed my pace during her orgasm, choosing to drink from her and savor the sensations blossoming between us.

However, I shoved myself inside her again, harder, just to drive home Az's point. Because Camillia would absolutely come again. I'd make her.

I moved my hand to her lower abdomen, my thumb slipping downward toward her clit when she didn't obey Az. She groaned in protest, her hand going to my wrist, but I didn't stop, my need to make her burst apart again too strong to be denied.

She whimpered, her exhale sharp.

"Shh, let him please you," Az murmured. "You deserve to feel good, little warrior. Especially after everything we've done. Let us make it up to you."

I hummed in agreement, my mouth still against her neck.

But then I realized she needed more than this.

More than me drinking from her vein.

More than my thumb against her sensitive nub.

More than my cock.

She needed to be *worshipped*. To feel like a goddess. To be the center of our existence.

I drew my lips up her neck to her chin, then captured her mouth in a kiss meant to devastate her. A kiss that would seal an unspoken vow to cherish her. Respect her. *Pleasure* her.

Her hands went to my shoulders, making me wonder if she was going to push me away. But instead she tried to bring me impossibly closer, her shudder one born of emotion more than physical need.

And she positively melted between us.

My motions slowed once more, drawing out her desire, coaxing the fire within her to burn higher. Her breath hitched, her inner muscles clamping down again. *So close*, I thought. *Come for me, little rebel. Let me hear you scream.*

She couldn't hear me.

But she could feel my intentions. She could *taste* them in my mouth. Sense them on my tongue and in the way my thumb continued to massage her below.

She was incapable of stopping the inferno from engulfing her. It was building inside her—*around my throbbing dick*—and threatening to destroy us all.

Az must have noticed it, too, his palm cupping her breast as he banded his opposite arm around her once more, holding her and keeping her safe as she neared the edge of oblivion.

She was going to take me with her this time.

I could feel it in my balls, the way they were tightening in preparation for release. And I didn't try to hold myself back. I wanted to go over that cliff with her.

"Come on, Camillia." Az's words were a demand laced with sensual need. "Come for Ajax. Make him spill inside you. Milk him with your sweet pussy."

She clamped down around me, her orgasm seeming to teeter on the brink for what felt like an eternity.

And then she screamed into my mouth, her body convulsing, her inner walls creating a vise around my shaft that refused to let me go until I followed her into rapturous bliss.

I didn't fight her, instead choosing to dive headfirst after her with a groan that vibrated my being all the way to my toes.

My thumb pressed down on her clit, forcing her ecstasy to last, coaxing her into a wave of delicious aftershocks that rocked us both while I continued to pulsate inside her.

It'd been too long.

So long.

Since I'd felt the warmth of a woman's touch.

And my body seemed hell-bent on coating every inch of her with my seed.

Claiming her in the most basic of ways.

Owning her.

Possessing her.

Marking her as mine.

My incisors ached with the desire to *bite*. To mark. *To mate.*

The tendons in my neck hurt as I clenched my jaw, refusing to force Camillia into such a binding. She wasn't mine. Not in that way.

Not yet, a dark voice whispered in my head, making me shudder.

I buried my face in her neck, my chest heaving from the exertion of my climax and the emotion it had unleashed.

This time was so much more powerful than before, so much more *meaningful.*

A heavy weight seemed to settle in my chest, the anchor belonging to Camillia.

Fucking Camillia.

But I couldn't stop it from forming, my soul somehow

already marked by hers. *We're not mates,* I told myself. *We can't be mates.*

Yet my spirit seemed to feel otherwise.

Impossible. I pulled back to look at her, noting the pleasure-drunk glaze in her pretty gray eyes. If she felt a similar pull, she didn't show it. She just appeared drowsy and well fucked, her cheeks pink with the effort of our time together.

But Az's gaze held a different glint, one that said he suspected what I did.

Fortunately, he didn't comment on it. Instead, he kissed Camillia's throat and said, "Heal her."

I whispered an enchantment to do just that, prioritizing her over myself. She didn't seem to notice, too lost to the residual sensations to focus.

She clenched around me again, her aftershocks coming and going in subtle waves that massaged my still-hard shaft. I wasn't exactly ready for another round yet, but I could definitely go again in a few minutes. Fae were insatiable.

But Camillia was supposedly part human. *Unless Zakkai's cryptic statement is to be believed…*

However, just because Zakkai saw something else in her didn't mean she was as unbreakable as a full-blooded fae.

With that in mind, I slowly pulled out of her, aware that she would need a bit of time to recover, even with my healing spell weaving magic through her veins.

Az caught her up in his arms before her legs could fall to the floor, his Phoenix making a brief appearance in his features before the violet took over again.

"She's not ready for you yet," I told him, afraid that he might try to fuck her now. I could barely contain his energy on a good day; I couldn't imagine Camillia receiving it now.

"I know," he said, laying her down on the mattress before gently spreading her thighs. "I'm just going to help clean her up."

Camillia yelped when Az's lips descended upon her abused sex, her hands going to his hair to try to pull him away. He simply caught her wrists in one of his palms and pressed them to her stomach.

"Shh, just relax and enjoy, little warrior." He spoke the words right against her clit, making her cry out in response.

I walked over to kneel beside the bed, my palm finding her cheek as I tilted her head toward me. "Tell me if you want him to stop, and I'll distract him."

Az grunted in response, then he did something with his tongue that had Camillia bowing off the bed with a surprised moan.

Unintelligible words spilled from her mouth, causing my lips to curl. "Yeah, he's talented." I knew because I'd experienced his mouth a few times before. Not often, though. Because Az considered kneeling to be a display of submission.

Thus making his choice now exceptionally interesting.

He's apologizing, I realized with a start.

All of this had been his way of trying to apologize to me and Camillia.

He wasn't one for placative words, but he strongly believed in actions.

That was why he'd held her up for me as an offering— he'd wanted to please me. And now he was ensuring that she was thoroughly taken care of, too.

I decided to help him out by kissing Camillia,

apologizing in my own way with my tongue. Or maybe I was thanking her. Likely a bit of both.

Because she'd blown my mind with her perfection.

The way she'd encouraged me to bleed, taking my cock without hesitation, coming twice with me inside her.

Fuck.

I really could do it all again right now.

Pound her into the bed.

Force her to scream for hours on end.

But I wanted to ensure she was okay, that she was fully healed, that she didn't hate us for everything that had happened today.

It was all so fucked up.

We should have talked more. We still had no idea what had truly happened to her.

Oh, I believed what she'd said. But that just confused the situation more.

Where did she go for thirty days? What happened to her? Did it hurt her in some way? Will she be okay?

The questions pelted my mind while I kissed her, my heart aching in my chest, that anchor tugging on my insides with dark intentions.

All the while, Az was driving Camillia toward another climax, one that was probably going to knock her out.

Perhaps that was his plan. If she passed out, we could finally talk.

But I wanted her to be part of the conversation. I didn't want to make decisions for her anymore. That hadn't worked in the past. We needed to collaborate. Talk. Figure this out.

Who even am I? I marveled, this line of thought contradicting everything I'd built within myself for the last ten years.

I sounded like the old Ajax.

The one who had been determined to help Emelyn.

The one who had lost everything as a result.

But have I really been living these last few years? I asked myself. I'd been breathing, yes. But was I truly happy?

I blinked, pulling away from Camillia as the words percolated through my mind.

Her eyes opened to capture mine.

Then they widened as she focused on something over my shoulder, and a scream escaped her.

I glanced over to find Melek sitting in the chair, one leg crossed over the other and a bowl of ice cream in his hands. He had the spoon poised right against his lips as Az came shooting to his feet.

"What?" Melek asked conversationally as Camillia started scrambling across the bed to cover herself. "Is Azazel the only one allowed to indulge in a snack?"

"What the fuck are you doing in here?" Az demanded, stepping in front of Camillia to shield her.

"Well, I came to deliver a message from Typhos, but I didn't want to interrupt. Thus..." He gestured to his ice cream with the spoon and shrugged. "I figured you were going to be another five minutes or so, and the show was making me... hungry."

Az ran a hand over his face, a curse slipping from his lips. "This isn't what it looks like."

Melek's eyebrows shot upward. "Oh? You weren't trying to make dear Cami come a third time?" He cocked his head. "Then what were you doing?"

I swallowed, Melek's words confirming he'd seen a hell of a lot more than Az being on his knees for Camillia.

He'd seen me fuck her, too.

The Warden.

The fae whom Lucifer blamed for losing Camillia.

The one the Hell Fae King had put in charge of interrogating the runaway bridal candidate.

And what a bang-up job I was doing with that.

The minute Melek delivered his report to Lucifer, I was a dead man. Or a fired one, anyway.

Because there was no way Lucifer would trust me again after this.

And if he couldn't trust me, then I wouldn't be welcome in the Hell Fae Realm.

Which meant I no longer had a home.

I no longer had anything at all.

CHAPTER 13

CAMI

Az PLUCKED his shirt off the floor and handed it to me while staring down Melek. He hadn't yet answered Melek's question, which didn't surprise me since Melek's summary was pretty accurate.

I slipped into Az's black T-shirt, the fabric practically fitting me like a dress. I supposed that was easier than pulling my jeans and tank top back on. Besides, the ash-like scent smelled nice. Like the dying embers of a beautiful bonfire.

That must be Az's Phoenix, I thought, shivering.

"What's Typhos's message?" Az demanded, his back blocking my view of Melek.

But I could still see Ajax —who hadn't bothered to put on clothes. I admired his firm ass, then frowned when I realized he had yet to heal his leg.

Actually, he hadn't healed himself at all.

Why?

"He needs you back at the palace," Melek replied. "All three of you."

Ajax stiffened.

Az merely folded his arms. "We have three days."

"Not anymore." The sound of a chair moving echoed through the room, then Melek appeared as he approached Az. "Another portal opened in the Underwater Kingdom. And this time, there were casualties."

This time, Az tensed. "How? Was the source disturbed again?"

"The source is fine. That incident appears to be unrelated to the rogue portals." Melek glanced at me with his words. "But Ty needs your help in tracking down whoever is opening these illegal gateways."

"What about the source problem?" Az asked.

"Ty knows what caused that issue and will be handling it himself." Melek again looked at me, his warning clear.

The Hell Fae King knows I touched the source.

And now he plans to deal with me directly.

Shit.

Az nodded, accepting that plan without realizing what it truly meant. Not that it would really impact him anyway. His Phoenix might like me, but I doubted that was a powerful enough motivator to stand up to Typhos Lucifer on my behalf.

"Has the portal been closed?" Az's businesslike tone almost made him sound bored.

"Yes. Several of Ty's lieutenants pooled resources to help him seal the breach. But we still don't know how or why it happened. The other one led to the Monsters Night celebration. This one just opened to a Human Realm location."

"In our reality?" Az asked, his question making my brow furrow.

As opposed to what? I wondered. *And what's a Monsters Night celebration?* It sounded creepy as fuck and not the kind of party I'd want to attend.

"Yes," Melek replied. "We were able to pull most of the Nightmare Fae back, but our death count is up to six now. We think it's because the portal functioned like a black hole, sucking unsuspecting fae into the other realm and its foreign waters."

"So unlike the one in the Netherworld where the fae voluntarily left," Az translated.

"Correct."

"Do you have any leads? Any magic for me to track?"

Melek hesitated. "I think that's why you should meet with Ty. He'll provide you with the details you need." His focus shifted to Ajax. "And he wants to see you, too. I think it's regarding a different matter."

Ajax dipped his chin in a show of reverence. "Of course, my prince."

The formal reply struck me as odd. But neither Az nor Melek reacted to it.

"I suggest you both report directly to Ty." Melek took in Ajax's nude state. "Well, maybe put on some clothes first. And heal yourself, too. You'll need to be at full strength when you face him."

Ajax simply bowed his head again. Then his wand appeared in a blink, and the scent of pine tickled the air.

My eyebrows rose as Ajax's magic whirled around him, clothing him in jeans and a shirt in less than a second.

"Heal yourself entirely, Warden," Melek told him, his tone stern.

"I'll make sure he does," Az inserted. "What about Cami?"

"Oh, I'll handle our little angel," Melek murmured, his grin revealing a pair of dimples. "I've been given permission to show her around the palace and introduce her to the guest quarters."

I stared at him, my thoughts trapped somewhere

LEXI C. FOSS & J.R. THORN

between sarcastic glee—because of course Melek would be my tour guide—and horror at the thought of what those *guest quarters* might look like.

Az glanced over his shoulder at me, his violet gaze unreadable. Ajax, however, kept his focus on Melek.

Does he regret what we've done? I wondered. *Is he going to revert back to being an aloof asshole, like he tried to last time?*

"Ajax will shadow us to the east wing. Then you can take Cami on your tour," Az said. "We'll meet you there, Melek."

The Hell Fae Prince considered me for a long moment, his multicolored irises giving nothing away. "She needs to change first. Your shirt isn't suitable for her tour."

"And I imagine you have something else in mind?" Az drawled.

Melek positively beamed. "Yes. Yes, I do." He leaned into Ajax and whispered in his ear, causing the Midnight Fae to shake his head as he pulled out his wand. Melek continued murmuring, ignoring Ajax's reaction, and waggled his brows. "Go on, Warden."

Ajax sighed and waved his hand through the air while muttering a spell.

A black leather skirt appeared on the bed beside me with a red corset top lined with black sequins.

Wait, no.

Not sequins.

Diamonds.

I gaped at it. "I am not wearing that when I have a perfectly nice pair of jeans and a tank top over there." I pointed to the clothes in question.

Which caused Melek to glance from me to the other outfit—an outfit that promptly disappeared into a pile of glitter. "Oh, that won't do."

I glared at him. "Then I'll keep wearing Az's shirt."

"I can make that turn into glitter, too," Melek warned. "Shall I?"

"Just put on the clothes, Camillia," Ajax said, sounding tired. "We won't win this game."

We? I thought. *Where is the* we *in this situation? I'm the one being forced into a corset.*

"I'm not a doll to be dressed up," I told Melek more than Ajax. "If you're going to make me change, at least let me pick what I want to wear."

The Hell Fae Prince looked me up and down and hummed, "Hmm, all right. What would you like to wear, little angel? I can tell you if it's court appropriate or not."

"Black jeans and a tank top. Preferably with undergarments."

He studied me for a long moment before whispering into Ajax's ear again.

The Midnight Fae aimed his wand at me, his expression one of utter exhaustion as he wove his pine-scented magic through the air. I yelped as it crawled over my skin, forcing me into an outfit of their choosing.

My mouth opened to protest—or curse—only for me to realize that Melek had mostly allowed my choice.

Black pants—not jeans, but a soft material—complete with knee-high leather boots with killer heels.

A deep red strapless top that tied up the back like a corset, but more comfortable. I couldn't see the strands, but I felt them. The sweetheart neckline cut beautifully across my cleavage, making me look biker-bar-ready.

And a pair of dark, lacy gloves adorned my hands all the way up to my elbows, the fabric shimmering as it moved.

"Okay." I could accept this outfit, even if it clung to me like a second skin.

"Just one more thing," Melek murmured, his hand in his pocket.

My eyes widened as he pulled a familiar necklace into view. "Oh, no. No, no, no. That necklace is trouble."

"It's protection," he countered. "And you're going to need that in the palace, little angel."

"The last time—"

"If he has the talisman back, then Typhos gave it to him," Az interjected. "Which means you have permission to wear it."

I blinked. "But…" *But Lucifer knows I touched the source. Why would he allow this?*

"Trust me," Melek murmured, stepping around Az's large frame to reach my neck.

"Trust you," I repeated incredulously. "I can't trust any of you."

"A very wise statement," Az agreed. "But I would accept Melek's gift. It might be the only one you'll ever get."

I narrowed my gaze, realizing what he meant. *My blade.* The bastard had distracted me with that kiss—and everything else—just to take it back.

"We'll see," I told him, accepting the challenge in his vibrant gaze.

His lips twitched. "Yes, I suppose we will." He held his hand out toward Ajax. "Go ahead and take us to the palace. Melek can handle Camillia."

I nearly snorted. *So much for us all traveling together.*

Ajax's eyes met mine, his wariness hitting me right in the chest. It was a brief glimpse of emotion that he probably didn't mean to show me, but he was worried.

Which made me worry.

He clearly knew something bad was coming.

Because he knows I touched the source, too, I realized. *I admitted that during my interrogation.*

And now we were all going to see Lucifer. Well, Ajax would visit with him first, and he would have to confirm whatever Melek had already shared with the Hell Fae King.

Sex couldn't change the truth.

Nor would it change my fate.

A hint of an apology seemed to lurk in his expression, there and gone in a blink.

Then he grabbed Az's hand and disappeared.

CHAPTER 14

AZ

CAMI'S TASTE lingered in my mouth, pleasing my inner Phoenix. It was a distraction I didn't need right now, not with Typhos requiring my attention.

A portal in the Underwater Kingdom. Fuck.

At least my half brother couldn't be blamed for this one. He was still being held captive over the first illegal breach.

My feet touched down in an east-wing palace corridor with Ajax beside me. He immediately dropped my hand as he looked around, his expression timid.

I frowned. "What's wrong?"

"Nothing," he lied.

My inner Phoenix bristled, not liking that one bit.

Frankly, neither did I.

I grabbed him by the neck and pushed him up against the wall—similarly to what I'd done to Cami, only much rougher now—and forced him to meet my gaze. "Speak."

He rolled his eyes. "Fuck you, Az."

"Oh, you have no idea how much I'd like to fuck right now." My playtime with Cami had been unduly interrupted. Of course, I hadn't planned to seek out my own pleasure from her.

Not today, anyway.

No, all of that had been for her and Ajax. My way of trying to make amends for my wrongs.

My errant bird had tried to kill Ajax, something I could never truly apologize enough for. And Cami, well, I wasn't quite sure why I felt the need to please her. I wanted to believe it was because my Phoenix had demanded it, but I would be lying to myself.

I'd wanted to please her. To make her feel good. To reward her for her strength, for standing up to me even when she shouldn't, to revel in her magnificence.

It'd all been entirely selfless on my part. I'd simply wanted them to feel pleasure, and it had only seemed appropriate to offer Cami as a gift to Ajax after everything I'd done to him.

Not to mention the heartbreak of his confession.

He never talked about his past. While I was familiar with what had happened, it hadn't prepared me to hear the anguish in his voice as the truth serum forced him to speak.

I swallowed, the memory of it clouding my mind and making me loosen my grip on his throat. But I didn't release him.

Instead, I pressed my mouth to his and told him without words that I cared about him. That I was here. That while we might not be the sort to emotionally share with one another, we were still bonded by brotherhood. By life. By *experience*.

Perhaps mine was different from his, but that didn't belittle the friendship between us or the affection I felt for him.

He tried to shove me away, but I didn't let him, my

mouth demanding that he accept my possession. *You're my friend. My lover. My something more. I'm sorry I couldn't control my Phoenix. I'm sorry about the truth serum…*

"Stop," Ajax growled against my mouth. "Just stop."

"No." I grabbed his hip, grinding him into the wall, and forced him to take my tongue. *Mine.*

His jaw started to clench, but he stopped at the last second, aware of what would happen if he fully clamped down. *A mate-bond.* Midnight Fae couldn't help it. One bite was all it took to ignite the spiritual link between two fae.

Oh, a human was fine. He could bite them all he wanted, and did since he required their blood to fuel his magic.

But he couldn't bite me.

Not without marrying our souls.

It was why he hadn't wanted to bite Cami either.

My Phoenix would one day share a similar act, and I, too, would only need a single bite. But Shifter Fae had to be in their animal form for an imprint to take place, and as a Black Phoenix, I was technically part Shifter Fae. Which meant I could do all the biting I wanted while in my human form, something I intended to take full advantage of where Cami was concerned.

Because her blood tasted euphoric, making it something I would absolutely be doing again. Especially if it was for Ajax's benefit.

His tongue traced mine as though he were thinking about it. Or, more likely, he was tasting our sweet little warrior's pleasure in my mouth.

It was combined with his unique flavor as well, their fucking having created a decadent dessert I'd enjoyed just moments ago.

Until Melek interrupted, I thought, remembering why we were back in the palace.

I didn't like to keep Typhos waiting, but Ajax seemed to need me. And I felt compelled to make sure he was all right before we went searching for the Hell Fae King.

"Tell me what's bothering you," I whispered against Ajax's mouth. "Is it what just happened with Cami? Because trust me, Ajax, she enjoyed that even more than you did."

"We were supposed to be interrogating her, not fucking her," he growled.

I huffed a laugh and shook my head. "Sex is a fantastic interrogation tool. You know that better than anyone." I pressed my groin against his, purposely reminding him of our first few times in bed where I'd sensually tormented him for hours. My Phoenix had wanted to make sure he was trustworthy—not just for me, but for Typhos.

And he'd proved to be quite admirable indeed.

Ajax narrowed his gaze. "That's not what I meant."

"Are you feeling guilty for fucking her?"

"I should be, yes."

"Ah, but that's not what I asked. Do you feel guilty?"

He ground his teeth together, his annoyance palpable. "No."

"And that's bothering you because you think you should feel bad about fucking the prisoner when we were supposed to be working," I translated, understanding his mind after years of friendship. "That's ridiculous."

"It's not ridiculous. I fucked up when she escaped, and it was my job to capture—"

"*Our* job," I interjected.

"—her again," he finished. "And I was tasked with gathering answers, which I did, but they're not going to appease Lucifer."

"Why not?" I asked, genuinely curious. "Zakkai

administered a truth spell, and she told you everything, didn't she?"

"Yes, she did. Which, in summary, is that she has no idea what happened to her because some magical book took her on a journey to a bright light before she woke up in her old university room," he snapped.

"Vita," a deep voice interrupted, causing the hairs along my nape to stand on end.

I hate *when you do that,* I said, glancing sideways at the Hell Fae King. *You could at least shimmer the air to announce your presence.* Fuck, Melek could do the same. Alas, the Hell Fae Prince liked sneaking around and surprising people, so I was used to his antics.

Typhos, however, usually provided a warning to my senses before blatantly appearing.

You were taking too long, Typhos replied, his voice bored inside my mind. "The book Camillia De la Croix mentioned is named Vita," he added aloud, his focus on Ajax.

My brow furrowed. "Cami had Vita?"

"Apparently." The barest hint of annoyance touched that one word. "It seems Vita has been visiting her and showing her things it shouldn't."

That didn't make any sense. "Even if that's true, she shouldn't be able to read it."

"According to Melek, she can and has." Typhos lifted a shoulder. "I intend to investigate the matter personally, which is why I requested that she be brought here. So where is she?"

"With Melek," I told him, finally releasing Ajax's throat. "We were just on our way to see you."

"Were you?" Typhos sounded amused. "Because it seemed I caught you both at an interesting time."

"Like that hasn't happened before," I deadpanned,

referring to the many occasions where I'd caught Typhos in a similar situation—typically while dressed in far less clothing—with Melek.

His lips twitched. "Indeed it has." He refocused on Ajax. "You've disappointed me as Warden, but I'm not going to banish you. I have another task in mind for you to redeem yourself. So stop fretting over your mistakes and focus on redemption."

My forehead creased as I considered Typhos and then Ajax. "That's what has you so bothered? Typhos punishing you for fucking Cami?" I nearly laughed, but the expression on Ajax's face had me sobering almost instantly. "He'd have to punish me, too. And he won't."

I won't? Typhos asked in that silky tone of his, the words for my mind alone. *What makes you so sure?*

Because you need me, I answered without looking at him. *So stop fucking with Ajax and tell us about this new portal.*

I'm not fucking *with Ajax,* he replied, that velvety quality still gliding through his tone even while he blatantly lied.

Yes, you are, my liege. I infused those last two words with as much sarcasm as I could, knowing it would infuriate him to hear the formal title coming from me. *You told him you're disappointed in him when you're not. He's been a fantastic Warden and you know it.*

Perhaps. But he's clearly distracted by Camillia De la Croix's pussy.

Yeah, well, it's a pretty fantastic cunt. Maybe you should give it a taste? I suggested, boldly meeting his gaze. *We both know your little prince wants to.*

Hmm. It wasn't a denial, more of a dismissive noise. "I didn't ask to see you both to talk about the former candidate," he finally said aloud. "Well, Ajax's new assignment involves her. But we'll get to that. We need to discuss the new portal and what I sensed around it."

I arched a brow. "What did you sense?"

"Not here," he said. "My office."

With that, he vanished with the same stealth magic he'd used to mask his arrival.

I shook my head. *Show-off.*

Stop wasting time and get your ass in here, he demanded.

Yes, my liege.

His mental growl was the only reply.

I smirked and looked at Ajax—who didn't appear as concerned as before but still had a broken quality in his gaze. "He's not going to banish you," I told him, reiterating what Typhos had just said.

"The problem isn't about the potential for banishment. It's how I feel about it."

I frowned. "What do you mean?"

He looked like he was about to reply but thought better of it. "Never mind. We shouldn't keep him waiting. My issues can wait. This portal is more important."

I wanted to argue, to force him to open up. However, he was right. These rogue portals were a more pertinent issue.

As was Cami's ability to read Vita. Very few could understand the language in that text—only me, Melek, and Typhos. And that was because the book belonged to Typhos. It was part of his magic. Which was why his mates could read from the pages.

But Cami wasn't one of Typhos's mates.

So why can she read it? I wondered as Ajax and I started walking down the corridor toward Typhos's main office. *And how does Typhos intend to handle the situation?*

I would have to ponder those questions more thoroughly later.

After we discussed the breach to the Underwater Kingdom.

It was my job as Commander to manage the Nightmare Fae throughout all of the Hell Fae Realm. If one of them was causing this problem, I'd find him and end him.

And if it was someone else outside of our world, I'd track that culprit, too.

It was my job.

My life.

My pledge.

CHAPTER 15

CAMI

A Few Minutes Earlier

"Is it really necessary to carry me?" I protested as Melek held me aloft with my legs hanging over one arm as his opposite arm supported my upper back.

He didn't reply.

Instead, little pinpricks of energy danced across my skin as a whooshing sound startled my ears. I yelped and clung to him, the sudden change in atmosphere leaving me reeling.

And then all I could see was him.

His perfect face.

That chiseled jaw.

Sparkling eyes.

Kissable lips.

Something told me he'd chosen this method of transportation on purpose. Because nothing Melek ever did was innocent, and holding me in his arms while blocking my view of everything except his handsome features certainly qualified as devious.

"How do you feel?" he asked, ignoring my question entirely and further proving my suspicions.

The word *fine* rolled over my tongue, only to be swallowed back as an unwelcome wave of nausea hit me before I could respond. I narrowed my gaze, even while lolling my head against his shoulder.

It was as though his words had unleashed a maelstrom of sensation.

I groaned, incapable of forming words. *Including cursing*, I thought, irritated by whatever he'd just done to me.

And I was doubly annoyed when my groan made him chuckle.

"I thought that might be the case, little angel," he murmured. "Flying between realms is a learned skill, one your body will become accustomed to with time."

Ajax shadowing me to the Midnight Fae Realm hadn't made me feel this way, I wanted to tell him.

Instead, I just closed my eyes in an effort to fight the dizzying spell threatening my vision. One stunning Melek face was enough. I didn't need to see double or triple versions of it.

"Here." His voice was soft, his breath a kiss against my temple. "I'll help."

A soothing wave of power caressed my skin, sending a tingle down my spine. The decadent scent that was all Melek washed over me, drowning me in a sea of blissful solace.

I suddenly felt tired.

Just like before… when I became a cloud…

Part of me knew better than to embrace it, but *ohhh… just a few seconds… won't hurt… right?*

Melek had told me mere minutes ago that he would need to touch me for his teleportation magic to work. I'd expected him to grab my hand.

But no.

He'd swooped me up into a bridal carry, eliciting my protest. However, now I couldn't remember why I'd cared.

This felt nice. Safe. *Warm.*

The fabric of my black pants swished together as my high-heeled leather boots dangled in the air. My position also plumped up my breasts in the tight corset-like top, mostly because my arms were wrapped around Melek's neck.

Why did I care about the outfit? I wondered, frowning. *Why am I upset at all?*

I peeked at Melek, searching for some hint as to why I'd bothered protesting. *There's something,* I thought. *Some reason I don't want to be held like this...*

Melek's dimples appeared as he smiled at me, his amusement palpable.

Does he have to be this beautiful? I wondered.

"To answer your earlier question, little angel, no, I didn't need to carry you. But I wasn't sure how you would react to my ethereal abilities." He brushed his lips against my temple, the brief kiss shooting sparks to all my nerve endings. "Plus, I couldn't let you touch the floor of this wing until you were wearing the necklace."

When I opened both eyes again, I saw him staring expectantly down at me with those multicolored irises of his.

He was... hypnotic. Different from Az's Phoenix, but just as alluring.

When I realized he was expecting me to do something, I blinked at him.

"I'm holding the necklace with my left hand, if you care to retrieve it," he said, then his dimples returned. "Unless you'd like me to carry you for the duration of your tour. I would not be opposed."

"And what happens if I touch the floor without your necklace?" I countered as I squirmed to pull away from him. I needed space. Air. *Distance.* "Is the palace made of lava or some—"

My words cut off when I adjusted enough to see beyond Melek's mesmerizing face.

"Oh…" *Holy… shit…*

My guess hadn't been that far off. The walls were made of fire, burning with black and red swirls of smoke and flames that billowed in vertical sheets, leaving the blood-red floor unmarked.

Although, I didn't feel any heat from them. Maybe because Melek was protecting me.

The ground was made up of some sort of glimmering stone that reflected the energy radiating from the walls. That could also be why I wasn't feeling the warmth of the fire.

I studied the texture before glancing around some more.

We're not alone, I realized.

Chained every few feet was a Hellhound on a large lead. I was used to seeing them in their human forms, but they were terrifying in their shifted ones. Their sharp ears had perked up, and all of them were staring at us with intense fiery eyes.

There were several other Hell Fae roaming the hallway, too.

Okay, so Melek wasn't joking about the attire, I thought, noting their formal outfits. *It's like he teleported us into the middle of a hellish art gallery.*

All the fae around us wore suits and diamond-studded cuff links. Some had ties with black silk, and others donned vibrant red colors. I didn't spot any weapons—none that were visible, anyway—but most Hell Fae didn't need a weapon to be a threat.

And even if there was a concern, I suspected all they'd have to do would be to unleash the Hellhounds in the event of an intruder.

I'd dispatched plenty of Hellhounds when Lucifer had been trying to bring me down for the bride trials, but that had always been one-on-one.

Playing with all of these beasts at once? No, thanks.

Although, their chained-up states suggested that the Hellhounds weren't allowed to shift in the palace. I wondered what they had done to earn that treatment, or if Lucifer just preferred them in their animal form.

With a quick scan, I even noticed that the Hellhounds wore spiked collars studded with diamonds and black onyx.

Well, obviously no expense was spared for the palace and the members within it.

"No," Melek said, drawing my attention back to him. "The floor isn't made of lava."

I blinked, not understanding his change in topic.

Then I remembered that I'd just asked about the floors and the reason for the necklace. "Oh." I seemed to be a woman of many words this evening. *Er, uh, morning? Afternoon? Whatever time it is.*

"No part of the palace does, actually," he went on. "The walls are made of Hellfire. At least in this wing. But the east wing is flameless, mostly because it's reserved for business meetings and out-of-realm visitors."

He tucked me closer to his chest, blocking my view again. My breath caught at the proximity.

"But we're not in the east wing. Which means you need protection." He flicked his gaze somewhere behind my shoulder. "You'll have to reach for the necklace."

It took me a minute to comprehend what he'd said. *Right. He was holding the necklace in his left hand.*

He hadn't answered my question about what would happen if I set foot on the floor of Lucifer's palace without it, but based on what I'd seen so far, I'd probably be burned alive or set off some sort of Hellhound alarm.

Stretching to twist around and grab the necklace, I brought it to my chest.

"Just hold it up for me and I'll help you put it on," he told me, gently setting me down without warning.

Heat instantly shot up my legs as energy zapped through my heels. A wave of immediate exhaustion cascaded over me. *Fuck.* I clutched the necklace, feeling it tugging at something inside of me. Something I didn't understand.

Melek had told me once that the talisman was a conduit of sorts. I wasn't sure if that meant it was a conduit for his power, or mine, or maybe both.

"Is this why Ty—I mean, Lucifer—said you could give me back the necklace?" I asked as Melek took hold of the chain and strung it around my neck.

He clasped it at my nape as he replied, "Ty will want to talk to you first."

That didn't answer my question.

And it also suggested that burning me alive or feeding me to the Hellhounds wasn't off the table, either. Lucifer was just too busy for me right now.

Because he's meeting with Ajax and Az while Melek distracts me with a tour.

My death was likely inconsequential to Lucifer, too. He'd see to it, but when it suited his timetable.

My eyes snapped up when one of the Hellhounds began snarling at me.

My hand fell to my hip on instinct, searching for a weapon. Except I didn't have one.

Because Az took back the dagger and Ajax hadn't bespelled a new one for me with this outfit.

Fuck.

Az had had no right to take that dagger back. His Phoenix—*my* Phoenix—had given it to me as a gift. I wasn't quite sure what that meant, but I liked that his beast seemed fond of me. It would hopefully afford me some protection.

Maybe.

But also unlikely, I thought. Because Az seemed like the type to keep his Phoenix on a tight leash. Which meant I had to win over the man before that protection would be a guarantee. And, well, I didn't see that happening anytime soon, even with all the sexy playtime we'd just shared.

However, I'd enjoyed the complete and utter devotion his beast had demonstrated. No one else had tried to protect me like that. No one else had been willing to *kill* for me. Not just in the Hell Fae Realm, but in general.

"Camillia," Melek called from several feet ahead, his expression expectant. "This way."

Right. Palace tour. Distraction. Got it.

It wasn't my first choice of activities, but it beat being eaten by one of the snarling Hellhounds.

Moving as fast as my annoyingly tall heels would allow without breaking an ankle, I followed Melek into a corridor that burned with more flames. Fortunately, the heat didn't seem to be impacting me at all now.

Because of the necklace? I wondered.

My fingers went to the talisman, and I found the metal cool against my touch. When I concentrated on its stone, a refreshing wave swept through my body.

"So, uh, this is Lucifer's palace?" I already knew the

answer. I just wanted Melek to start talking. *Preferably about Lucifer and what the hell he's going to do to me.*

Not just because he probably thought I'd seduced his Warden and his Commander, but because I'd touched his precious source.

Which shouldn't have been possible.

None of this makes any sense.

"Part of it, yes," Melek said noncommittally as he turned a corner and walked past two sentry-like guards into what appeared to be a private space.

Or I assumed it was private because we were the only ones in the hall, leaving all the Hellhounds and other fae behind.

He continued in silence for a few minutes, leaving me to admire the Hellfire walls and stone floors.

No windows.

No doors.

Just an endless corridor of blood and flames.

It felt ominous. Deadly. *Like I'm walking to my own execution.*

However, the hallway ended in a large open space framed by a huge balcony. But it was the object at the center of the room that captivated me.

Because it was *massive.*

My eyes widened as I took in the statue of Lucifer, his body adorned in red marble and threaded with gold.

If someone had asked me to artistically depict the Hell Fae King, I would have set him on a throne and shown him ruling over his subjects. But this wasn't like that at all.

Instead, the colossal piece of art showed a broken Lucifer stretched out on the ground with his head bent. The statue appeared almost lifelike with the individual strands of his hair visible as they layered over him and fell to the ground.

My heels clicked against the floor as I began the journey of making a slow circle around it.

Every muscle was taut in the depiction, demonstrating pure agony without even showing the emotion on Lucifer's face.

Then when I reached the back, two bloody scars ripped down the sides of his spine. They looked painful. Agonizing, even. *Realistic.* It provoked the strangest urge within me to reach out and offer him comfort.

But I refrained, only slightly aware that this was an inanimate object.

"Ty asked for this to be placed at the entry to his personal wing so that all those who are close to him remember what brings us together," Melek informed me softly, his presence by my side both welcome and startling. I'd almost forgotten he was here.

"And what brings you together?" I asked. *Pain? Sacrifice?*

"Rejection," he replied, the word one I hadn't considered yet but found made perfect sense with what I'd recently learned.

Lucifer had fallen.

That was what the book had shown me. However, it was so much more than that. His fall had been significant, but I suspected it was whatever had happened *before* his fall that truly defined him.

He had been cast out of his home and, I could only assume, *rejected* by those who were supposed to be his family.

Just like all the abominations he had taken under his broken wings.

Unable to resist, I returned to the front of the statue. I stepped forward and ran my fingers over the perfect stone. It was so large that I could only brush its fingers—but to my surprise, it was warm.

I felt like I was understanding Lucifer better now. The creation of a new source hadn't been a show of grand power or control.

He'd just been trying to survive.

And in doing so, he'd brought other fallen races under his protection.

Some might even call that admirable.

Minus the whole kidnapping-forced-brides issue.

Melek went to the balcony and tucked his arms behind his back. His soft blondish-brown hair swayed with the heated wind, reminding me of feathers.

I joined him and sucked in my breath as I finally took in the outside view.

It was impressive, to say the least. Buildings of red and gold and black decorated a marble street in the distance, with courtyards of flames and charcoal rock separating the palace grounds from what I assumed was the town.

"Is this the heart of the Hell Fae Realm?" I asked, unfamiliar with all the various kingdoms within Lucifer's gates.

"This is the Hell Fae Kingdom," Melek murmured. "It's where Lucifer and I live, as well as his Hell Fae and the outcasts—or *abominations*, as the other realms like to call them—under his command."

I nodded slowly, my gaze attempting to see beyond the glittering town buildings. "So the Barren Lands..." I trailed off, not seeing anything nearby that resembled the dry landscape I'd recently become acquainted with during the trials.

"The Barren Lands is another kingdom," he replied. "It's one of the many areas where Nightmare Fae reside."

I frowned. "And what's the difference?"

He was quiet for a moment, his gaze on the outside

world rather than on me. "The book showed you Lucifer's fall, but did it explain how or where he landed?"

I recalled the pain I'd witnessed in Lucifer's features, how I'd seen a glimpse of Melek's smirk, and the visceral fury that had followed, how it'd shaken me to my very core... and then... "Everything derailed after he burst into light," I whispered, my throat suddenly dry. "He was so angry..."

"Rightly so," Melek murmured, his expression darkening for half a beat before he refocused on me. "When Lucifer fell, he landed in the pits of Hell. That was where, we'll call them *outcasts* for this discussion, were sent. You would know those *outcasts* as today's Nightmare Fae."

I studied Melek's profile, surprised that he was speaking in terms I understood rather than in riddles. But I refrained from commenting on it, as I didn't want to risk ruining the moment.

"There weren't many at first," he continued. "But there were enough. They didn't have any order or a home, no kings or leaders to guide them, just dejected souls scurrying about in a plight to survive."

Melek glanced back at the statue, a note of admiration in his features.

"Lucifer took on the burden of becoming their light. Over the vast millennia, he's provided structure and protection. Kingdoms were created, the lands perfectly suited to the Nightmare Fae who reside there. But the harsh environments are not suitable for all, which is why this was created." He gestured to the palace and the city beyond it.

"The Hell Fae Kingdom," I said, reiterating his term from earlier.

"Yes. A place where fae with mixed backgrounds, such as yourself, can safely reside without judgment or the threat of violence from the other fae realms. We don't use the term *abomination* here. We simply embrace fae kind, taking in those the others fear, and give them a home."

"But they're considered different from Nightmare Fae," I hedged, trying to ensure I understood.

"Yes. Nightmare Fae are more specific; their origins typically align with a single species rather than several." He leaned against the balcony rail and met my gaze.

"Okay, meaning they're not Hell Fae because they don't have a mixture of fae types inside them," I said, starting to understand.

"Yes. Thus a Naga, for example, is a Nightmare Fae because he is solely of Naga origin. Whereas Azazel is a Hell Fae because he has mixed ancestry. His father was a Hell Fae—part Paradox Fae, Corpse Fae, and Ghoul— while his mother was a purebred Black Phoenix Fae."

I hadn't known that about Azazel. Well, I'd known the Phoenix part. But the other half was just as intense.

However, I still didn't comprehend one thing. "Why not just refer to the Naga as, well, a Naga?"

"Because Nagas are a type of Nightmare Fae. Just like Ruby Dragons and Centaurs and Minotaurs. They're all types of Nightmare Fae."

"Because they're, uh, sort of like monsters? Therefore, they're Nightmare Fae?" I guessed. I wasn't trying to stereotype; it was just that I'd never known these mythical beings actually existed until I'd become a Hell Fae Bride. Lucifer had obviously hidden them all well.

So what does it mean that I'm learning about all this now? Because Melek just felt like sharing and trusted me not to say anything? Or because he knew I won't be alive long enough to use the information?

Melek lifted a shoulder. "That's one way to define it. I choose to see them as misunderstood creatures rather than monsters, but many of the fae realms would reject them for the latter, calling them *nightmarish* and *monstrous*."

Hearing his definition had me reconsidering my own terms. "Misunderstood creatures sounds better."

"It does, doesn't it?" he mused, smiling at me. "It also happens to be true, something I think you recently learned in your trials, yes?"

The mirages, I thought, translating his words. *He's talking about the mirages.*

I'd noticed the auras around certain Nightmare Fae while running through the Barren Lands. Certain Centaurs were violent, while others... others seemed to be almost kind. Loving, even.

But something Melek had said made me frown. "You said this kingdom was built for Hell Fae that can't survive in the Nightmare Fae environments." It wasn't exactly what he'd said word for word, but it'd been implied.

His hypnotic gaze sparkled from the incoming light, giving him an otherworldly glow that almost distracted me from my train of thought.

Except I was rather hung up on a certain detail now, one that had me narrowing my eyes.

"So how are the Hell Fae Brides supposed to survive in the Barren Lands? Unless that kingdom is considered habitable?" I couldn't help the note of sarcasm in my voice. Because no way in Hell's realms was that environment considered hospitable.

He smiled. "The Nightmare Fae mate-bonds will ensure the Hell Fae Brides survive."

I didn't return his smile. "Meaning the choice will be for the brides to either mate their captors or die?"

"Those who find themselves to be suitable mates won't deny the bond. That's the whole point of the trials." He canted his head. "Did they look terrified to you, or pleased?"

A trick, I thought. Because they had looked absolutely horrified until I'd seen through the mirage. "Their screams suggested they weren't thrilled by the prospect," I hedged.

Melek studied me with a knowing look while amusement flirted with his lips. "Well, I suppose we'll see how you feel after the next trial."

I blanched at the thought. "And when will that be?" *Does that also mean I'll still be alive for it?* I added mentally.

"That's a question for Ty," he murmured. "Which reminds me, we should continue our tour."

He didn't give me a chance to ask anything else, instead turning away from the balcony and leaving the room through a different exit—this one also guarded by silent sentries.

I nearly tripped over my heeled boots in an effort to keep up. "I'm going to break my neck in these things," I muttered.

Melek's soft dimples returned. "Proper Hell Fae attire will grow on you. After all, you're likely going to be staying here for a while."

"At the palace?" *And does that also mean I'll still be alive?* I wondered again.

He guided me into another creepy corridor shrouded in flames and directly to a pair of obsidian double doors. He whispered a few words that I didn't catch, causing the rock to melt before us. *Literally* melt. Like a black waterfall.

My eyes widened at the display, my attention immediately going to the ground. But the liquid rock—or whatever material it was made of—simply disappeared.

And then Melek led me through the threshold.

A sharp snap echoed behind me the moment I stepped into the new area, causing me to whip around with a gasp.

The doors were back in their place.

And we were very much alone in yet another hallway.

"What happened to all the other Hell Fae?" I asked, suddenly uneasy.

"They're still in the public areas." He paused as though considering them. "Most of them hold various positions here in the palace. But a few were just visiting. My guess is they wanted to catch a glimpse of Lucifer for reassurance purposes."

I wasn't sure what he meant by that last part, nor was I all that focused on those details. It was the first part that had me more preoccupied. "So, we're no longer in the public area?" I hedged, swallowing.

Then his words about the statue came tumbling through my mind.

"Ty asked for this to be placed at the entry to his personal wing…"

"We're…" I trailed off, swallowing. "We're in Lucifer's personal quarters?"

Melek grinned. "That we are, little angel. Now come along. There's much to see here."

CHAPTER 16

CAMI

I'M in Typhos Lucifer's private wing.

Home of the Hell Fae King.

The very one who may or may not want to kill me.

My throat suddenly felt very tight, my legs moving beneath me like lead blocks. *So this is what it feels like to knowingly walk to one's execution. Fuck.*

Melek had already started walking again, his strides long and confident.

I glanced back at the door behind me. *Definitely no way out.*

But at least there weren't more Hellhounds here.

Cursing under my breath, I started after Melek, my heels clacking loudly over the stone floor below. There would be no running in these boots. Not that I knew where to go anyway.

"We'll primarily focus on Lucifer's private wing for today," Melek said as I caught up to him. "There's just too much to show you in one tour, and I thought it might be best for you to see where you'll be staying first."

The tour is in the wing where I'm staying…

I repeated those words in my head, trying to wrap my mind around them.

"But this is Lucifer's wing," I said dumbly.

A mischievous glimmer entered Melek's fractal eyes. "It is."

"And this... this is where I'm staying?"

He nodded. "Yes."

My stomach dropped, and I felt like I'd been teleported by Melek's magic all over again.

I supposed it was better than being put in a dungeon. *But is it?* I wondered. *Do I want to be this close to the Hell Fae King?*

A shiver traversed my spine, rendering my limbs stiff as I forced myself to follow Melek. I didn't know what to say or what questions to ask anymore. I was too lost in my own confusion to focus.

Melek said something about a certain hallway that I didn't quite catch. The word *playroom* was all I caught. And I didn't bother to ask for clarification. I wasn't sure I wanted to know what type of "playroom" the Hell Fae King would entertain.

We kept moving for what felt like hours but was really only minutes.

Just to come to a new hallway with more Hellhounds. But these weren't chained up to the fiery walls; they were sitting on leather platforms. And many of them were in their human forms.

I blinked at them, then startled as a tuxedo-clad Hell Fae wandered by with a Hellhound on a long lead.

"Um..." I watched the Hell Fae head down the corridor we'd just exited. "Is he going to be punished like the others or something?"

Melek glanced back at me, his eyebrows flying upward. "Punished?"

"Yeah." I cleared my throat. "Like the Hellhounds in the other room that were chained up to the fiery walls?"

He stopped walking and faced me. "They're not being punished. Hellhounds like fire. And they take commands better in their canine form."

One of the Hellhounds nearby snorted, his beady black eyes meeting and holding mine as a ball of fire formed in his palm. I half expected him to throw that burning inferno my way, but instead he tossed it to the shifted Hellhound across the room.

Who proceeded to catch the fiery sphere in its muzzle and crunch down while wagging his tail in excitement.

Then he sprinted on four legs toward the other one and tackled him to the ground, the two engaging in a wrestling match of man versus flaming dog.

"See?" Melek sounded amused. "They're very playful creatures. This is one of the rooms Lucifer has gifted them on this side of the palace to relax in while on break. Their security wing is a good mile away, and while that's nothing for a Hellhound, many of them prefer to chill here instead."

"Security," I echoed. "Hellhounds are the primary security for the palace." That made sense. "But they need leashes?"

"As I said, they obey commands better in their canine form. But they can be messy creatures, their penchant for fire frequently causing destruction. It's easier if a Hell Fae helps them swap posts." He shrugged and started walking again.

Melek was being uncharacteristically forthcoming, which told me he was likely preparing me for something. I'd learned a little bit about his tells after the last however many days or weeks we'd spent time together. Everything he did and said had a purpose. This was no different.

And he had yet to say anything about Lucifer's intentions for me. That couldn't be a mistake—he didn't want to comment on it for a reason.

I just wished I knew *why*.

My fingers itched for a knife, something to help protect me from whatever was coming, but the sharpest items on me right now were my heels.

Heels that continued to click loudly across the blood-red floor.

The next part of our "tour" included a walk through a trophy room—which had way too many skulls in it. Then Melek showed me the kitchens, both staffed and self-serve, and a few reading nooks, as well as various libraries stacked with books.

It didn't surprise me that Lucifer appreciated literature.

Probably because I'd become familiar with one of his books.

I started to notice a pattern as Melek showed me around—every room had some sort of incredible art piece or statue in it. Sometimes Melek commented on them; sometimes he didn't. But when he did remark on a piece, it was always related to Lucifer in some way.

"Ty commissioned this about two thousand years ago to commemorate the creation of the Underwater Kingdom."

"This was created to honor Ty's negotiation with the Mythos Fae. The collection of hands represents their monumental agreement, but if you look at it this way, you can see that it forms a cage. A very telling piece of art, some would say."

"The Hellhounds made that for Ty. It's… well, it's unique. But Ty cherishes it, which is why it's in his favorite library."

"My king feels very strongly about his deals and those

who have wronged him. That's what this Siren statue represents—an ultimate form of punishment."

"Whatever you do, don't ever touch this golden feather. I know it's alluring, but it's a bespelled relic from a very old fae realm. Ty would keep it in glass if he could. However, the magic refuses to be contained."

That last item was floating in the middle of one of the reading nooks, the soft tendrils glittering with a light that reminded me of the Hell Fae Source. I gave the item a wide berth as I continued down the path Melek had set.

"And this is the contract room," he said, gesturing to a set of massive double doors made entirely of metal. A crisscross of chains kept it secure, and a skull-shaped fastener with flames sputtering from it assured me that I would not be picking that lock. Not that I wanted to.

Okay, maybe I did a little.

I would *love* to see if there were more details on the deal my father had made with Lucifer. Because the contract I'd read couldn't be everything.

Or maybe it really was that simple. It wasn't like my parents had ever really cared about me.

"But most fae only see a regular flame wall here," Melek added, a note of curiosity in his tone.

It took me a moment to realize what he was saying. He'd been testing me. *Did he interpret my scrutiny as trying to see through the mirage, or as me evaluating the doors?*

Likely the latter.

It wasn't like my ability to see things I shouldn't be able to see was a secret. So rather than comment on it, I simply arched a brow and waited for his next move.

His lips curled in that devilish way of his, telling me that he knew exactly what I'd seen. But he didn't outright say it. He simply said, "The residence area is next."

That sounded like a promise and a threat, and reminded me of my unknown fate.

I trailed after him in silence, my mind spinning with a mixture of curiosity and dread. The former won as we moved through another melting door into a wide hallway glowing with more flames.

There were several Hellhounds in the corridor here, all of them sitting sentry by the walls again.

I swallowed. *Definitely walking to my execution.*

That thought only darkened as Melek stopped by a shimmering red barrier in the middle of the hallway. "After you," he said.

I arched a brow at him. "You want me to walk through that?"

"Yes." Those damn dimples flashed. "Unless you would rather sleep with the Hellhounds?"

I glowered at him. "What's waiting on the other side?"

Melek gave me a playful look. "You'll see."

When I didn't immediately move, he shrugged and stepped through the barrier, leaving me alone.

The urge to run locked onto my lungs and held me captive for a moment, my mind reeling with the maze in our wake. *There's no escape. The doors fucking melt here. There are Hellhounds everywhere. I'm literally in the heart of the Hell Fae Realm.*

Or the Hell Fae Kingdom.

Whatever it is.

It's Lucifer's palace.

Fuck.

Even if I knew how to escape, I'd just be tracked down again. And then I'd definitely be killed.

Or taken in by Az and Ajax to be interrogated again.

Followed by more sex. Maybe. Hopefully.

Heat rushed over my already warm skin as memories

flickered behind my eyes. I gripped the talisman and focused on its cool energy, needing to ground myself and focus.

Yes, it was amazing. The best sex of my life. But that's not important right now.

It was wishful thinking that it would happen again, especially if I escaped. Which I didn't even know how to do. So there was no point in even thinking about it.

Or reveling in the memories.

Or craving more.

Particularly when I might be walking into my death.

Focus, Cami, I chastised myself, my gaze on the barrier. *You can do this. Shoulders back. Head up. Face it straight on. You've done nothing wrong. You just need to convince Lucifer of that.*

Besides, I'd faced plenty of devils throughout my life. Assholes at frat parties. Freaking Hellhounds. Not to mention my own father.

Of course, this was the literal devil, and he scared the shit out of me—an accurate phrase even if Melek didn't care for it.

What's Lucifer going to do to me? I wondered. *Only one way to find out.*

Stealing a deep breath, I pushed through the barrier and flinched as my necklace hummed to life. White light flittered over my vision, making me temporarily dizzy before Melek's handsome form came into view.

"There's my little angel," Melek murmured, holding out his hand. "Come along, then. The best has yet to appear."

I had no idea what he meant, nor did I know why I took his offered hand, but my mind felt cloudy like before, making me oddly susceptible to his charm.

He was probably drugging me.

Because it definitely had nothing to do with the fact

that Melek had just led me into what were clearly his intimate quarters. And it absolutely wasn't related to his angelic looks or that devastating smile he kept throwing at me.

Nope. Not attracted to him at all. Definitely not.

His hand squeezed mine as though he could hear my thoughts. *Liar,* that action said.

Or maybe that was my conscience tattling on me.

Melek hadn't truly tried to hurt me despite his propensity for courting trouble on my behalf. He'd actually been the first one to really believe my story about my missing time. And he also seemed to be somewhat concerned with my protection. That was how I translated the talisman gift, anyway.

What about the feather? I wondered. *What had that done to me?*

It was on the tip of my tongue to ask, but as we moved by a door with horned rims, Melek distracted me by saying, "My hell."

I blinked at him. "What?"

He merely winked and led me to another door just a few paces away. "And this will be your home sweet hell."

"Do you mean *room*? I mean, *home*?" The saying was *home sweet home,* right?

Rather than reply to my rambling—which I knew I was doing due to nerves—he pushed through the threshold to reveal a gorgeous suite beyond it.

My eyes widened. *This is certainly an improvement from my previous cell.*

Which I supposed made sense since we were in Lucifer's personal quarters.

Suddenly, I much preferred my old accommodations with the metal bars and bespelled bed. Because this room was far too close to the Hell Fae King.

He's going to kill me while I sleep, I realized. *Or worse.*

A hint of warmth fluttered over my skin, one that felt mysteriously like the feather again. Only there were no feathers and Melek wasn't even looking at me when I glanced at him.

Odd.

Swallowing my nerves, I stepped into the room and allowed myself to take in the space.

A marbled foyer gave way to an oversized living area with black leather couches, blood-red rugs, and a massive black screen—one I assumed functioned like a television in the Human Realm. Beside it was a kitchen with a bar area that appeared to be fully stocked.

And there were also some odd-looking metal beams that resembled...

Hold on.

"Are those stripper poles?" I asked, incredulous.

"Only if you want to use them as such," Melek murmured. "There's also a master bedroom and luxury bathroom down the hall to the right. Both of which are built to handle group play—I mean, multiple guests."

I glanced sideways at him, fully aware that he didn't mean that last correction at all. "Uh-huh." I was about to correct him—by saying what, I wasn't sure, because he had just caught me with Az between my legs and Ajax at my mouth—when he started whispering to himself.

My brow furrowed as the area distorted around me. *Wait. Was all this a trick? A way to pass time? Am I being taken to...?* My thoughts slowed as the room reappeared, but with several new additions.

A pizza oven had joined the kitchen area, equipped with real flames. An espresso machine now rested on the breakfast bar. And a wine cooler had been set up near the black screen in the living space.

"Oh." Well, that… that was nice. "Thank you."

Melek's dimples returned, seemingly pleased with my approval. "I added a few of my favorites to the fridge as well," he said. "Human foods, I mean. Like cheese."

I started toward the kitchen, curious to see what else he'd added, when the door to the room slammed open, making me jump.

Oh, no. He's—

"Ajax?" Relief caused my shoulders to fall on a puff of air, my heart rate instantly slowing. *Thank God.*

Except he didn't look all that pleased to see me. In fact, he seemed quite pissed off about it.

He dropped a duffel bag on the floor just inside the room and headed straight for the kitchen. "There had better be liquor in here."

My eyebrows flew upward while Melek chuckled. "There is now," he replied with a twinkle in his gaze. Then he looked at me and said, "It appears my shift is over. But if you need anything at all, don't hesitate to call for me."

Uh… I wasn't sure I wanted him to leave just yet, especially with Ajax revealing his broody mood. "You don't want to stay?" I hedged, hating the needy note in my voice. It wasn't like me at all, but I felt so unprotected here—so at the mercy of the literal King of Hell.

And so unprepared for whatever was about to happen next.

"You're in good hands, little angel," Melek told me. But then he wandered over to whisper something to Ajax that made the Midnight Fae frown.

I frowned, too, wondering what he'd just said. But before I could ask, he disappeared, leaving me alone with the Warden.

Whatever it was, it made Ajax grunt a second later as

he opened one of the cupboards and pulled out a bottle of amber liquid.

He unscrewed the top and took a healthy gulp, not bothering for a glass.

I stared at him, waiting for an explanation as to his current mood. But he didn't provide one.

Az's warning played through my mind, the one he'd given me after I'd woken up in Ajax's bed.

"This is going to make him feel. He'll do his best to push you away as a result."

"He'll think he regrets it. But it'll be a lie."

Is that what this is? I wondered. *Is Ajax regressing into asshole mode again?*

Because I refused to accept that. Not after everything that had happened between us. He'd interrogated me. Used snakes to torment me. Then he'd come in all contrite —albeit led by an angry Phoenix in the process, but I'd felt his remorse—and had allowed me to do the same right back to him.

He'd shared his secrets, his hurts, his *past*.

And then he'd fucked me more thoroughly than anyone ever had before. He'd practically *owned* me.

So no. We would not be going backward, especially when I might not be alive much longer.

"Tell me what's bothering you," I told him. "Speak so we can work through it."

His dark eyes gleamed in the firelight provided by the walls, the blue edge around his irises taking on a purplish shade that reminded me a bit of Az. "I'm not a Hellhound, Camillia. I don't adhere to commands."

I folded my arms. "Well, I don't accept brooding assholes darkening my personal space without good reason. So. Start talking."

He snorted and took another drink before setting the

bottle on the obsidian countertop. "This isn't your personal space; it's Az's." He glanced around, his eyebrows drawing together. "Or it was until Melek's little embellishments."

When he narrowed his gaze at the stripper poles, I assumed he was also including those in his list of *embellishments*. That didn't surprise me. Those metal beams had Melek's name imprinted all over them.

"And I'm not being an asshole. I'm just thinking," he added. "But I can be an asshole, if that's what you fancy."

He pulled his wand from his pocket and waved it through the air, causing a pair of handcuffs to appear with one edge secured to my wrist. A gust of wind followed, sending me right toward one of those beams.

And the opposite cuff snapped around the pole.

I narrowed my gaze. "Undo it. Now."

"No." He picked up his bottle to take another drink, then set it on the counter. "I'll release you after I take a shower. Until then, *stay*."

"*Ajax*." I could handle handcuffs in a kinky situation, but this wasn't that. "You are not handcuffing me to a fucking stripper pole."

"I already have," he replied, waltzing past me to pick up his bag. "Now try to behave and I'll reward you with the key."

My eyebrows flew upward. "You've got to be fucking kidding me. Az warned me you would try to push me away, but I had no idea you'd be so damn skilled at it."

He paused on the threshold to the bedroom—or what I assumed was the bedroom since Melek had said it was down that hallway—and glanced back at me. "I'm not trying to do anything other than keep you here, which is my new assignment. And the last time I went into the bathroom, you fucking disappeared. That won't be happening again."

New assignment? "What do you mean? You've always been my Warden. How is that a new assignment?"

"I've always been *the* Warden." He faced me fully. "But now I am *your* Warden only. My position has been temporarily filled while Lucifer decides what to do with you and what to do with me. So do me a favor and fucking behave. Because I have no interest in dying for you."

With that, he left me gaping in his wake.

Shit.

So we would be sharing this room? I supposed that explained his duffel bag. It also explained his dark mood.

"My position has been temporarily filled…"

Meaning Lucifer had removed him from his post.

Because of me.

Except I hadn't done anything wrong. I hadn't meant to escape. I hadn't meant to touch the source, either.

So what does this mean for both of us? What will Lucifer decide to do?

I sat on the floor, my eyes glued to the hallway Ajax had just disappeared down. All the frustration I'd felt for him melted away as I realized he was probably just as much in the dark as I was.

Because Lucifer blamed him for what had happened with me.

I'd been in Ajax's bed when I'd not only magically fled Hell but also ended up near this realm's heart of power.

It stood to reason that Lucifer would suspect Ajax of being involved somehow, or having indirectly helped me in some way.

Which made Ajax both my ally and my enemy.

An ally because we were now in this together.

An enemy because he hadn't chosen to be involved in any of this at all.

I curled my knees into my chest, wrapping my arms

around my shins as best I could with the cuff latched onto one wrist.

The words *I'm sorry* lingered on my tongue, although I wasn't sure what I was apologizing for exactly. Still, they floated around in my mouth until Ajax finally reemerged. He wore a pair of gray sweats and a white T-shirt that hinted at the muscular frame beneath. His dark hair was damp from his shower, his expression one of pure exhaustion.

He flinched when he saw me curled up on the floor and muttered a spell under his breath that wove magic around my wrist.

I massaged my skin as the cuffs disappeared, my ire having died entirely in the last however many minutes. I was just as tired as he was, maybe even more so, considering everything. Or maybe less. It was hard to say.

"I'll sleep on the couch," he told me softly. "The bedroom is yours."

"Well, technically it's Az's," I replied, attempting to lighten the mood with a little humor.

But Ajax didn't smile. "It's technically a guest room meant for those Lucifer considers family, but Az is the only one who qualifies. So that's why I said it's his room."

"Then it's a bit strange he's keeping us both here when we're obviously not his family," I said.

"Not strange, it's strategic. He could put us in a dungeon, but I'm the former Warden. I know those cells better than the inmates inside them. And you've proved to be a magical problem that requires extreme levels of babysitting. So he's keeping us close by where he can watch us himself."

Yeah, that's not ominous at all, I thought, gulping. "Right." Although, it was admittedly kind of nice to have an *us* in this situation.

A realization that only made me feel guilty because there shouldn't be an *us* at all.

I ran my hand over my face and yawned. A warm shower and a bed sounded amazing right about now. But I'd probably fall asleep beneath the water. So maybe I'd take a nap first.

Ajax conjured himself a pillow and a blanket, then disappeared into the kitchen to grab a water. He grabbed one for me as well, handing it to me without a word, then went to the couch to lie down. "Try to get some sleep. I think we're both going to need it."

Swallowing again, I nodded and started toward the bedroom. "Good night, Ajax."

When he didn't reply, I sighed and left him to rest.

But just as I was closing the door, I heard him whisper, "Good night, little rebel."

CHAPTER 17

TYPHOS

My BED FELT cold without Melek's presence beside me, his warmth one I typically craved when I first awoke. I instantly searched for him in my mind, needing to know he was safe and comfortable.

I miss you, too, he whispered to me, obviously sensing my need. *We're still in the Netherworld Kingdom with Maliki.*

Has he given you anything useful? I asked.

He's engaged in some sort of battle of wills with Az at present, so no. Melek sounded tired. *Maliki isn't apologetic. He said the Ghouls were hungry and someone had to feed them.*

Yes, that was the same excuse he'd given me when I'd paid him a visit. Maliki had a Corpse Fae for a mother and shared a mixed-fae father with Az. Which meant they both had Paradox Fae, Corpse Fae, and Ghoul inside them.

But that had never made Az give Ghouls any special treatment. Very unlike Maliki, who felt the Ghouls were his kin, sometimes more so than the Corpse Fae. He was a complicated male that I should probably have killed for his defiance.

However, he was related to Az.

And his motives were unfortunately admirable.

Because he was right—the Ghouls were starving. Which was why their trial had been moved forward. They were going to have their chance in the mating ring right after the Corpse Fae.

Until their little Monsters Night initiative had ruined everything.

I ran my palm over my face, exhausted from the last thirty-plus days of mayhem.

My Nightmare Fae were growing restless, their need to taste the bridal offerings a palpable presence in the back of my mind.

But on top of all that was a deep-seated sense of uncertainty, one caused by the formation of *two* illegal portals in my realm.

No one had directly questioned my powers or strength yet, but it was coming. Because these acts were undermining my authority and threatening my position.

They needed to cease immediately.

We'll figure this out, Ty, Melek whispered into my mind. *Az wanted to try talking to Maliki first, and to reinvestigate the site of the portal here to see if we can find a trace similar to the one in the Underwater Kingdom.*

I nodded even though he couldn't see me. *We were so distracted by Monsters Night that we likely failed to sense it.*

That's what I told Az, although he already had a similar thought.

Of course he did. That's why he's our Commander.

Yes. So trust him and your favorite prince to figure this out.

I snorted. *You're my* only *prince.*

Just as you're my only king, he returned. *So please go easy on Cami today. For me.*

I already let her rest for fifteen hours, I reminded him. *That was our only deal.*

Melek had agreed to help Azazel track the source of magic so long as I vowed to let Camillia and Ajax rest for a minimum of fifteen hours before I began my interrogation. I could have forced him to go with a few coaxing words—such as pointing out that this issue was far more important than a Halfling's comfort—but it was much more fun to engage in Melek's games than to thwart his efforts.

Would you like to make another one? he offered now.

I always want to make deals with you, little prince. But I think I've made far too many where this female is concerned. She's mine now. I'll report back when I'm finished.

As you wish, my king, he replied, his flirty tone a kiss against my senses. *I'm here if you need me.*

I know. And I would forever be grateful for that. *Stay safe.*

I'm in your world, Ty. Here, I'm always safe.

I wished I believed that as much as he did. Because right now, nothing felt safe to me. Someone had infiltrated my domain, and worse, I had a Halfling that could not only read my book but had also touched *my* source.

Things felt chaotic.

Like I'd somehow lost control.

I'd spent a thousand years preparing for the Hell Fae Bride Trials. There were thousands of plans, all with caveats and twists meant to anticipate even the smallest of deviances. But nowhere had I factored in these rogue portals and Vita showing a female the source.

Well, at least I could do something about the latter now.

I slid out of my bed and frowned as a mug full of freshly brewed coffee appeared. Melek's ambrosia-like scent circled through the air, telling me he'd bespelled that to happen the moment my feet hit the ground.

Thank you, little prince.

Just ensuring you're cared for, he replied. *Now I have to focus on Maliki. He seems to be caving to his brother's will. Finally.*

I didn't respond, letting him focus, and took a sip of the heavenly brew that only Melek seemed to know how to make. He did something with his magical essence to freshen the flavor; I was certain of it.

With the majestic hot drink reviving my senses, I went into the bathroom to prepare for the day.

Technically, I was giving Camillia even more time to rest than I'd originally promised, but Melek had put me in a good mood. Which had probably been his goal, the sly little prince.

After a long shower—where I thought about Melek's fantasy involving red silk and a certain female—I put on an all-black suit. I didn't really like other colors, but I occasionally indulged Melek's requests when he had specific outfits in mind.

I warmed the bristles of a comb and ran it through my long hair, the strands instantly drying from my heated magic. Then I pulled it all back at my nape and gave myself a once-over in the mirror.

Why do I care what I look like? I wondered. *I'm the fucking king.*

This girl meant nothing to me.

Well, that was a bit of a lie. She'd somehow managed to tangle herself up with two of my mates, and she'd seduced my Warden—someone I had begun to trust.

Az had been right yesterday about me not truly being disappointed in Ajax. He'd proved himself to be most admirable. I wasn't going to dismiss him over a fling with a female, especially when my prince and Commander desired her, too.

Still, I needed to make it appear as though he were being punished for his mistakes. A bridal candidate had escaped on his watch, and several of my Hell Fae knew it. I would be seen as weak, or possibly showing favoritism, if I didn't address that problem.

Of course, I could do whatever I wanted as king, including allowing him to be with the girl despite his non–Hell Fae status.

But I would have to play the pieces on the board correctly for it to work. Because now was not the time for me to make moves that could be construed as fallible or uncharacteristically soft.

I needed to appear strong and capable and in control. It was the only way to ensure that my constituents would feel safe. I needed them to fear me in order to respect my rule.

Because a cruel king would handle the threat against his realm and end it without flinching, while a tenderhearted king would be inclined to negotiate, which could risk innocent Hell Fae lives. I would always be the former and never the latter.

With that thought in mind, I left my quarters and headed down the hall to the room Melek had given Cami. It was deep within my personal wing and typically reserved for Az, but Az rarely stayed the night. Lately, he much preferred his cottage just outside of the bridal arena, or occasionally, Ajax's place in the woods.

I briefly considered knocking on the door but decided better of it. This was *my* domain. A king didn't have a need to knock.

So I teleported into the living area instead.

Melek's scent assaulted me the moment I materialized,

making all the hairs along my arms dance as I half expected to find him lingering somewhere inside the room.

But no.

It wasn't my little prince; it was his *magic.* Everywhere.

Because he'd completely redecorated the formerly modern space.

Oh, the reds and blacks had remained—as was the usual theme throughout my home—and the walls were still burning beautifully.

But everything else was different.

"Is that a pizza oven?" I asked, making my presence known.

Ajax bolted upright from his position on the couch, his face riddled with sleep lines.

Apparently, fifteen hours hadn't been enough.

Camillia walked in with a towel on her head, her body clad in a silky red robe that reminded me of the ribbon Melek had weaved through his fantasy.

The moment she saw me standing in the living area, her jaw dropped and she instantly started looking around the room as though hunting for someone or something.

I frowned. "Are you searching for a weapon? Because I promise you it won't save you."

"N-no, Your Highness. I... I'm not sure... Am I supposed to bow? Or curtsy? Or...?" She ended up executing an awkward move where she bent her knees while leaning forward at the hips and nearly face-planted on the floor. Instead, only her towel touched the ground as it slipped off her head, leaving her damp strands hanging around her like a wet mop.

I blinked at her. This *is the female that has all my men tied up in knots?*

Sure, that robe was sexy and short and probably revealing her tight ass right now as she attempted to remain in her strange position, but the lack of elegance and grace left a lot to be desired here.

"What the fuck are you doing?" I demanded.

"I think she's trying to formally greet you," Ajax said, sounding amused. "Instead, she looks like a demented flamingo."

Camillia snapped right back up and glared at him. "How am I supposed to know how to greet the Hell Fae King? It's not like you or Melek have taught me much."

"No, but I hear my book has taught you plenty," I drawled before Ajax could reply. "And he should be addressed as *Prince* Melek, especially when speaking to his kingly *mate*."

She swallowed, the fire she'd just displayed in front of Ajax disappearing in a second. "My apologies, my... uh... sir."

Ajax snorted at her failed address.

I merely stared at her. "Your father obviously didn't introduce you to this world." It wasn't a question but a statement.

However, it made her scoff. "My *father* didn't do a lot of things he probably should have, including warning me that he'd sold my soul to the literal devil."

"Cami," Ajax whispered.

But she ignored him, her gray eyes flaring with renewed flames as she boldly met my gaze.

"I know you're here to talk about the source, or maybe to just outright kill me. However, I only started reading that book to learn about loopholes in the agreement you made with my bastard father. Then the book started showing me things. And..." She trailed off with a shrug. "I'm not sure what else to say."

Hmm. Maybe I could see a bit of the draw now. She sort of resembled a drowned cat with her wet hair and narrowed eyes, but she definitely had courage.

And she was also covered in Melek's angel dust, something I hadn't noticed until just now as the light glittered across her skin.

You sneaky prince, I said to him. *She's covered in your feathers.*

Only one feather, he corrected. *But I'd hoped that would be enough to persuade you not to hurt her.*

I nearly rolled my eyes. *I can easily override your protection, Melek.*

You could, he agreed. *However, I hope you won't.*

I didn't reply. Because he knew I wouldn't dare touch his protective cloak. That feather was just as much a part of him as it was her now.

Which meant it would hurt him to dismantle the charm.

That absolutely qualifies as a tangible gift, little prince, I told him, my gaze going to her neck. *Just like the charm you managed to steal back from me.*

She's no longer a candidate, my king. Therefore, the terms of our previous deal no longer apply. But if you want to renegotiate, I'm yours to play with.

I sighed, both outwardly and inwardly. *You win this round, little prince.*

His pleasure warmed my heart, considerably lightening my mood again. "Let's start this again," I said, locking gazes with Camillia. She didn't even flinch, her spine set in a confident line that had me respecting her more by the second.

This was much better than her—what had Ajax called it? A demented penguin pose? Or was it some other awkward animal? Regardless, it was much better than *that.*

"I don't believe we've officially met, but I'm Typhos Lucifer. Most refer to me as 'my king' or 'my liege.'

However, you've developed certain relationships that bend the rules of normalcy."

I wasn't just referring to my men, but to something else.

Something that had been created by my very spirit.

"*Vita. Ven ad me,*" I said, calling the book to me.

Camillia's gaze widened slightly as the leather-bound item appeared beneath my arm.

"So you may call me Lucifer," I concluded. "For now."

CHAPTER 18

AJAX

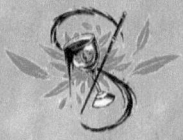

CAMILLIA HAD no idea how big a deal it was that Typhos Lucifer had just given her permission to address him by his surname.

I'd worked for him for nearly eight years before he'd told me to drop the formal address and call him *Lucifer*. And that was leagues before many, many others.

Hell, even his lieutenants typically referred to him as *my liege* and *my king*.

The only reason I'd been brought into the inner circle was because I had a relationship with Az.

So I supposed it made sense that Lucifer would grant Camillia similar leeway, what with her having a very clear connection to Az, me, and Melek.

But after the disrespectful way she'd behaved, it was even more astonishing that he would allow this familiarity to grow between them. She'd called him the *devil*, which was a nickname he despised. Az had warned me long ago never to even whisper the term in the Hell Fae Kingdom, or Lucifer would hear it.

Yet she'd basically referred to him by that name, and

he'd responded by saying, "You can call me Lucifer. For now."

Well, he'd said a few things before that. However, it was surprising nonetheless.

Camillia held out her hand. "I'm Camillia De la Croix. My friends call me Cami. Your people call me Candidate Sixty-Six."

Typhos smirked and took her hand. "I'll be calling you Camillia." He turned toward the sofas, his gaze flicking around the room again as he grimaced.

I understood because I'd slept in this room before with Az. Melek had definitely redecorated with Camillia's tastes in mind.

Minus the stripper poles.

Those were absolutely for Melek. Although, I wouldn't complain if Camillia wanted to shed her clothes and swing around a few times.

In fact, she could easily do so right now—just drop the robe and climb up the pole.

But instead she sat beside me on the couch while Lucifer took over the adjacent sofa. His long legs parted, his muscular form appearing regal against the black leather, as though he'd just created a new throne for his intimidating presence. Because only Lucifer could maintain a domineering stature while sitting down with a book resting against one thick thigh.

Cami pulled her legs beneath her, completely unfazed by lounging in a robe. She actually seemed more concerned with her damp hair, her fingers running through the dark blonde strands as though she longed to tame them.

I had the sudden urge to find her a brush and offer to comb her hair for her. Thankfully, my mouth was smart enough to refuse the urge when it tickled my tongue.

Because no.

I was not going to offer to brush her hair.

What the fuck is wrong with me?

"This is the book you've been reading, yes?" Lucifer asked, breaking the silence, his gaze on Camillia.

"Yes. It appears to me at random, then hides. And sometimes Melek has it," she replied, causing Lucifer's eyebrow to twitch upward. "I mean, *Prince* Melek."

"Has my Melek been using you to help the candidate?" Lucifer seemed to be talking to his book and not to Camillia because he stroked his hand over the leather binding while he spoke. "What exactly has he told you to show her, hmm?"

The pages fluttered, the book opening on its own to display a blank canvas. I frowned at it, wondering what that meant. But when I glanced at Lucifer, he seemed to be reading.

"*Quomodo tame a bestia,*" Lucifer read aloud with a smirk. "Beast-taming spells." He glanced up at Camillia. "You didn't use any of these."

"No, I didn't."

"Because you forgot them?" he pressed.

"Because I don't trust Prince Melek," she returned. "He read a whole passage to me about talismans and gave me this." She pointed to the charm hanging from her slender neck. "And that didn't end well."

Lucifer considered that for a long moment before saying, "Are you sure about that? Because from my standpoint, it landed you in the Warden's cell, which eventually led you to his and Az's bed. And now you're in a guest suite reserved for those I consider family rather than stuck in the bridal barracks with the other candidates."

Both of Camillia's eyebrows lifted. "Are you suggesting I strived for all this to happen? That I asked Melek to"—

she held up her hand—"sorry, *Prince* Melek, to show up in my room unannounced countless times with strange gifts, just so I could end up here, with *you*?"

She scoffed loudly, clearly not seeing the thunderous blue waves rolling in Lucifer's gaze. I almost reached for her leg to give it a warning squeeze, but she wasn't done.

"I'll admit, a meeting with you in the beginning might have appealed to me a little, if anything so I could renegotiate whatever deal you struck with my asshole sperm donor, but this?" She waved her hand around the room. "The burning walls. Stripper poles. Okay, the pizza oven is nice, and I don't mind the bar, but trust me when I say *none of this* has in any way been a goal for me. I just wanted to go home."

"Which you managed to do," Lucifer pointed out. "By way of *my* source."

That made her pause, her chest heaving from the exertion of her outburst. "Well, that wasn't planned either. The book led me there. I didn't understand any of it."

"I think you understood plenty," he replied. "My fall. The creation of the Hell Fae Source. It might have seemed unbelievable, but you know it's all true, just like everything else Vita has shown you." He looked down at the item in question. "Tell me about that day, Vita. Show me what you showed her."

The pages whirled with magic once more, only to reveal yet another blank slate.

However, obviously there were words I couldn't see. Words Lucifer was reading without issue, and—I looked at Camillia—she seemed to be reading them, too.

I was beginning to feel like I shouldn't be in this room, like I was being shown things that might lead to my death.

Because these were Lucifer's private dealings, a book he clearly considered important.

Perhaps not being able to see any of it would save me. But something told me I was in far too deep now for Lucifer to just let me walk away without a scratch. And not just because of today. I'd been clawing my way up the ranks into his inner circle for years without even trying.

All because of Az, really.

We'd started as friends who enjoyed fighting and fucking.

However, things had evolved. And Camillia... she seemed to have pushed us a full step further, making it feel even more impossible to back out now.

"That's not what the book showed me," Camillia said after a minute. "That's... something different."

Lucifer glanced up at her, then set the book on the obsidian coffee table. "Vita, stop fucking around and show me what happened when you took Camillia De la Croix to the source."

The leather binding appeared to vibrate in reply, almost as though it was saying, *This, you idiot.*

Camillia seemed absorbed by whatever the book was displaying, her eyes scanning over the text as she shook her head. "I don't understand. The book showed me your fall, like you said. But I felt like I was there and experiencing it with you. This... this is a bunch of circles. And..." She tilted her head. "What looks like a family tree."

Lucifer turned the page without a word.

"Well, it *definitely* didn't show me that." Her eyes widened as she looked up at him. "I have no idea why it's displaying me in a crown while holding a ball of fire. Or maybe it's someone who looks like me? But that's not what happened. At all."

Rather than reply, Lucifer flipped to the next section, his attention on what again appeared to be a vacant page to me.

But it clearly had something bad on it because Camillia's features went white. "And that also didn't happen. If Prince Melek says otherwise, he's lying. I did not do that to him."

That had my eyebrows lifting, my curiosity piqued.

However, Lucifer just kept skimming pages, almost as though he was reviewing a picture book instead of text. Which, given what Camillia had said, might be accurate.

"Oh God…" Her eyes were as round as saucers.

"Wrong deity," Lucifer murmured. "But that reminds me, I owe a certain Mythos Fae an update on the trials." He pulled the book back into his lap as he continued to scan whatever it was showing him, his expression giving nothing away.

Meanwhile, Camillia looked deathly pale. "I don't have any interest in your source. The book took me to it, I touched a strand because it… it called to me… and then it vibrated with anger, and I ran for what felt like minutes but was apparently thirty days."

"I'm aware of your version of events, Camillia." Lucifer didn't look up while he spoke. "I'm now learning Vita's point of view."

"But the book is lying. All of those things… none of them happened."

"Yet," Lucifer replied. "They haven't happened _yet_."

Camillia blinked. "What?"

"I believe Vita is trying to explain itself by showing me why it's decided to appear to you." He finally looked at Camillia again. "Vita sees some sort of potential in you, which again has me wondering about your origins. It's too bad your father eluded Azazel's hunt."

Camillia's jaw clenched. "My father is a Hell Fae."

"Yes, I'm aware. An abomination. Some sort of hybrid fae, which is the definition of a Hell Fae. Or perhaps he has Nightmare Fae roots. The question is, *what* made him a Hell Fae?"

"I… I don't know," she admitted. "I've honestly never asked. But I don't think he's a Nightmare Fae. I didn't know those existed until… your trials."

Lucifer nodded. "Yes, I've done my best to hide them within the Hell Fae world's various kingdoms, guarding them with the Hell Fae Source. They would be hunted and killed in most other realms, just like all the others I protect within my gates."

The abominations, I translated, very familiar with those after everything that had happened in the Midnight Fae Realm a decade ago.

Hell Fae were, as Lucifer had said, mixed-fae breeds. Which many other realms referred to as *abominations*. However, Lucifer took it a step further by also protecting all the species beneath the Nightmare Fae umbrella because he considered the Nightmare Fae to be a type of Hell Fae.

The Nightmare Fae were all created from various magical anomalies and chaotic power fluxes. So their existence essentially defined the meaning of *abomination*. And then Hell Fae were true hybrid mixes of various fae types.

It was all tied together, but the heart of the matter for Lucifer was in protecting those he felt were wrongly discriminated against.

Many other fae didn't realize that. However, the moment I'd learned of his true purpose, I'd committed my fealty. Because I'd wanted a chance to help safeguard those who needed it since I'd spectacularly failed to do so in my youth.

"Well, it seems clear to me that my Vita has high expectations where you're concerned," Lucifer said as he closed the book. "Whether or not those expectations are good remains to be seen. But you obviously can no longer participate in the bride trials. You're hereby disqualified."

Camillia sat up straight. "I am?" A hint of excitement entered her voice, only her expression took on a suspicious gleam in the next second, her mind catching up with what that might mean. "Does that mean you're going to kill me?"

Lucifer grunted. "As much as I would like to, I can't right now. So it means I need a new role for you." His lips curled into a sly grin that reminded me a bit of Melek. "I do own your soul, after all. But maybe if Az can find your father, we'll have a chance to renegotiate."

"If that's your way of trying to get me to reveal his location, it won't work, because I don't know where he is. Trust me, if I did, you'd be the first one I'd tell. I'd love to see you kill him."

Amusement teased at Lucifer's features. "You're bloodthirsty, hmm? No wonder Azazel likes you." He glanced at me. "Ajax, too."

I swallowed, uncertain if that was a positive recognition or a negative one. With Lucifer, it was impossible to tell.

"Well, I think I'm done for now." He set the closed book on the table as he stood. "But as you'll likely be staying for a while, I think it would be wise for Ajax to properly school you on what it means to be a Hell Fae. He's been studying for a decade. I'm sure he can provide excellent insight." His intense gaze met mine. "Yes?"

"Of course, my liege," I told him. "As you wish."

He heaved a sigh. "I might have temporarily relinquished you from your Warden responsibilities, but that doesn't mean I've removed you from my circle. And you know how much the formal bullshit bores me. Don't piss me off with it."

"Sorry, this is all… very confusing," I admitted.

"On that, Ajax, we very much agree." He gave me an unreadable look and started toward the door. "Oh, and, Camillia, if I find you near my source again without permission, I will kill you. So don't let the book tempt you into sin. It won't end well for you."

With that, he disappeared from the room, not bothering to use the door.

And left Camillia gaping at the now empty foyer.

CHAPTER 19

CAMI

I RETREATED into the bedroom muttering something about getting dressed while I processed the shitshow of my first actual meeting with Lucifer.

The Hell Fae King.

Likely the most powerful fae in all the realms.

And I'd just presented myself as... what had Ajax called me again?

Right—a demented flamingo.

"Great job, Cami," I grumbled to myself as I towel-dried my hair.

Then there was the other issue of what the book had shown Lucifer.

Very, very disturbing images, I thought.

The back of my mind echoed a different choice of words.

Very, very delicious, *too.*

"Focus," I hissed at myself as I slung my used towel into a black hamper. It vanished in a puff of smoke.

It would probably be better if I just erased the book's

images from my head because none of that was happening.

Instead, I'd concentrate on the task at hand. Which, right now, was to wear more than a robe. Fortunately, I had a whole closet to choose from.

That's a nice change from having all my outfits chosen for me, I thought, entering the walk-in closet. I took my time running my fingers over the various choices.

They were all tight-fitting, and apparently I was only allowed to choose something black, red, or a mixture of the two—but for the most part, there were enough options to suit my tastes.

Picking a red top, I pulled the strapless, midriff baring over my head.

Black leather pants came on next. I'd prefer jeans, but there didn't appear to be any. Besides, the leather felt nice against my bare skin.

Rather than put on shoes, I went barefoot, tied my hair into a ponytail, made sure my necklace was still on, and headed back out to the living room.

Fortunately, Lucifer hadn't spontaneously returned in my absence. Not that I'd expected him to, but with the way he'd surprised me earlier, I couldn't be sure.

I just met the Hell Fae King, I marveled again. *And he didn't try to kill me.*

Instead, he'd told Ajax to "properly school" me on the Hell Fae. I wasn't sure what that order really meant, but being trained as a Hell Fae didn't sound much better than being trained as a Hell Fae Bride.

Rather than ask about it, I looked at Ajax and said, "Um, so, that went… well?"

He grunted in reply. "He didn't kill you, so yes."

I winced. "Nor you."

"Nor me," he agreed. "Instead, he wants me to teach you. But I want to finish eating and take a shower first."

We'd both spent most of the last fifteen hours asleep, so that didn't surprise me. It'd been the first thing I'd done upon waking up.

Then I'd walked out to find Lucifer in the living room.

And... my brain had immediately died, taking my sanity and pride with it.

Ajax stood, leaving his half-eaten breakfast on the table. I wasn't sure how or when he'd made that, but I assumed magic was involved.

He returned with a tray and handed it to me. "It's nothing special, just some eggs and bacon. If you want something else, let me know and I'll conjure it."

"Um, thanks." I gave him a half smile and joined him on the couch. There was cutlery and a glass of orange juice along with the food he'd mentioned. However, he appeared to be drinking a Bloody Mary, which I assumed was actually just blood.

Because he's a Midnight Fae. Right.

My neck tingled from where he'd drunk from me before, my mind immediately producing memories of how it had felt to experience his lips against my skin.

I cleared my throat, forcing the memory away. Because now wasn't a good time. Especially after Lucifer's visit... and the warning he'd left behind.

That isn't all he left for me, I thought, glancing at the book. *Vita.*

I wasn't sure why he'd left it here when he'd warned me not to be tempted by it.

Maybe it's a test?

I nearly snorted. *Well, if that's the case, then that's an easy test to pass.*

Because I wasn't going to touch that damn thing ever again. Not just because of Lucifer's warning, but because of everything else it had done to me. Lost time. Showing me the source. *Depicting a potential future I don't even want to contemplate…*

I shoved some eggs into my mouth, forcing myself to focus on food instead of the images that threatened to follow. *Nope. Not thinking about it. Ever.*

The book and I were done. Finito. Finished. *Goodbye.*

My hands slightly shook when I took a sip of my orange juice, something Ajax seemed to notice because he murmured, "Lucifer can be intimidating."

No shit, I thought, clearing my throat. I eyed the espresso machine and set my tray to the side. "I need something stronger than juice."

Before I could stand, a glass of coffee appeared with whipped cream on top. My eyebrow arched. "What the hell is that?"

"A very strong coffee," Ajax replied, his gaze twinkling. "Irish style."

I canted my head and picked it up, curious. "Irish style, huh?" That implied he'd added some whiskey to the mix. "Okay." I took a sip and groaned at the decadent flavor. "Ohhh, yes. More of this, please."

Ajax chuckled and two more populated my tray. "Consider it an apology for how I acted last night."

I glanced at him sideways. "Just last night?"

"To apologize for everything else, I'd need to conjure up a lot more Irish coffees," he confirmed.

"That's true," I agreed, smiling a little at him. This was kind of nice, us having a somewhat normal conversation. So I didn't bring up the *schooling* part or what it meant, as I didn't want to disturb the moment.

We ate in silence for a bit, though I mostly focused on

the delicious Irish coffee drink. It was probably going to make me drunk, but my supernatural metabolism would fix that quickly enough.

"It's a good sign that Lucifer let you refer to him informally," Ajax suddenly said into the quiet. "That's not common."

"Yet he told you he hates the formal titles," I pointed out.

"In certain situations, yes. But as I told him, things feel confusing at the moment. It makes me unsure of how to proceed." He finished his drink and set it down. "However, I at least know how to bow properly when required."

I scowled while he chuckled.

"We can make that lesson number one when I'm done with my shower," Ajax added, causing me to roll my eyes as he cast a spell that made his tray vanish. "Are you finished with that?"

I grumbled something unflattering and took a final bite before nodding. "Thank you," I told him when the dishes disappeared, but one Irish coffee remained.

"You're welcome." He tilted his head with a soft grin. It sent his messy black hair sprawling over his forehead, somehow making him look even more attractive and edgy. "But seriously, we'll need to work on your curtsy."

I frowned. "Is that part of being a Hell Fae?"

He shrugged. "It is now, as I'd prefer you don't almost fall on your face when you see Lucifer again."

I couldn't tell if he was being sarcastic or not. There was a devious twinkle in his gaze that left me uncertain.

"As long as you're training me to be a Hell Fae citizen and not a *bride*, I might cooperate," I told him.

He leaned in, the sudden proximity cutting off my air. "Oh, I'm going to make sure you cooperate. I can't afford to fail. *Again*."

I swallowed as a new lump formed in my throat, Ajax's boyish charm having been replaced by the powerful fae simmering inside.

Ajax could certainly be convincing when he wanted to be. And my mind tumbled on all the ways he might solicit my cooperation.

Like kissing me right now. That would make me pretty compliant.

Only a few inches separated us on the couch. Ajax wasn't wearing a shirt. He must have taken that off to sleep on the sofa after finally healing himself. I hadn't really noticed his state of undress while Lucifer had been here, but I did now.

Just like I noticed those delicious gray sweatpants again.

Yeah, he could definitely ensure that I cooperated… It wouldn't be hard.

I really need to stop thinking about this.

About him.

About sex.

I cleared my throat, my mind spinning to find a distraction. *What were we talking about?*

Oh, right. My potential preference for being a Hell Fae citizen rather than a bride.

"They are two different things, right?" I asked, my voice raspier than intended. "Being a citizen versus being a bride, I mean."

His gaze went to my mouth. "I suppose that depends on if you choose to take a Hell Fae mate. Training to become a bridal candidate is both preparation for the source's tests and for keeping up with a Hell Fae male."

The unsaid words lingered in the air. I hadn't exactly been accepted by the source, but it hadn't killed me, either.

And if "keeping up" with a Hell Fae male was

anything like being between him and Az, then I most certainly wished to qualify.

What rang out to me, though, was the specific phrasing he'd used.

"If you choose *to take a Hell Fae mate."*

That was a pretty stark difference. Bridal candidates weren't given a choice.

Then I registered the nuance of his statement.

"I would only be allowed to choose a Hell Fae?" I asked as I tilted my head.

Ajax wasn't a Hell Fae. He was a Midnight Fae.

He gave me a sad sort of smile. "You would have to work that out with Lucifer. I'm not even sure if you can stay unmated. The Hell Fae Source doesn't really accept females. Which is essentially why these trials were created."

"To test the worthiness of the brides?" I guessed.

"Yes, to find worthy candidates for mating. While male-male mating absolutely happens, there are those who prefer females. Females are also needed for procreation." He shrugged. "So Lucifer is trying to find a safe way to please his constituents."

"By forcing female fae to participate in the bride trials," I deadpanned.

"Not all of them are forced, Camillia. Many of them want to be here."

"I don't," I said quickly. "I didn't agree to any of this."

His gaze went to my mouth again before slowly returning to my eyes. "I suppose that's true. But Lucifer isn't the one who forced this upon you; your father did. And perhaps, with time, you'll understand why Lucifer has had to make certain choices."

With that, he stood and stretched his arms over his head, the conversation apparently done for now.

I admired his flexing muscles while he moved, my

mouth going a little dry at that delicious V cut into his hips.

But Ajax isn't a Hell Fae.

So I can't pick him as a mate.

I frowned at my thoughts. *Why am I thinking about him as a mate?* I could just fuck him, right? And I might not even want a Hell Fae mate.

Shit, I wasn't even sure I wanted to be a Hell Fae at all. While that might be part of my genetic makeup, it didn't define who I was.

"I need to shower," Ajax said, drawing me out of my thoughts. "But when I'm done, we're going to talk about the Hell Fae Kingdoms. That'll be a good place to start your training."

That was the abrupt conversation change I needed. A fresh bucket of proverbial ice to extinguish the bizarre flames growing inside. "Kingdoms?" I echoed. "Um, yeah. Sounds good."

Melek had mentioned we were in the Hell Fae Kingdom, and I knew the Barren Lands was another one. Ajax had also mentioned a Netherworld Kingdom before, too. Learning more about all those places, and any of the others, could be beneficial.

"Don't go anywhere," Ajax said before walking away.

I almost asked, *What? No cuffs?* But I refrained.

Instead, I admired his back and the way it tapered down to his ass. *Such a beautiful man.*

Stop that, I chastised myself. *Yes, he gives good dick. But there are more important things in this world than sex.*

Maybe it was this room that kept messing with my head. Knowing Melek, he'd left behind some sort of aphrodisiac meant to spike my libido.

But as I watched Ajax's shoulder droop just before he

reached the door, my heart cracked a little. Loneliness seemed to drape around him like an invisible cloak.

Perhaps I was just imagining it, making up perceptions based on everything he'd admitted while under the truth serum. However, he seemed… sad. Misplaced. Uncertain.

Because he's no longer the Warden, I realized. While he'd said that hadn't been his primary driver for wanting to interrogate me, he had admitted that it'd been a factor.

Knowing what I did about him now, I could somewhat understand why. He'd lost everything in the Midnight Fae Realm. But he'd found happiness—or a version of it, anyway—and purpose here in the Hell Fae Realm as the Warden.

But that'd been stripped away from him.

Because of his affiliation with me.

My lips twisted, frustration inching a path across my brain. I wasn't to blame for what had happened, and yet, something sharp pricked at my heart, something that felt a lot like guilt.

I blew out a breath and grabbed my Irish coffee, needing a distraction. The black screen before me seemed to wave a warm welcome, except there didn't appear to be a remote for it anywhere in sight.

"Okay, how do I turn you on?" I asked, my eyes scanning the room once more. "Hmm."

I started to stand, intending to see if there was a switch on the wall or on the screen itself, when something hit me hard on the thighs, causing me to fall back onto the couch with an "Oomph."

Gaping downward, I found the book vibrating in my lap.

I scoffed. "Yeah, no," I told it as I grabbed the binding and shoved it back onto the table. "The last time I listened to you, I lost thirty days. Forgive me for not being interested."

The book blinked out of view, then landed in my lap again.

"I said *no*," I told it, lifting it once more, only for it to vanish from my hands and plop right back down on my thighs.

Damn stubborn piece of parchment.

I glared at it. "No."

It responded by flinging itself open.

I screeched and slapped my hands over my eyes. "Will you stop it!" I shouted. "Lucifer said he'd kill me if I went near the source again, you fucking book!"

Vita pulsated, like it was nudging my legs.

I growled in annoyance and folded my arms. "I refuse to read you."

Part of me recognized that this was the most ridiculous thing that had ever happened to me in my existence—I was arguing with an inanimate object.

An inanimate object that was beginning to pulse even more fiercely. So fiercely, in fact, that my jaw was starting to rattle from the vibrations ricocheting up my spine.

"*Fuck,*" I cursed, finally looking down. "If you pull me into the source again, I swear I will burn all your pages."

The book shuffled, the pages in question making a fluttering sound that almost resembled a giggle.

I'm losing my fucking mind.

Lucifer had just told me not to mess with his source again, and here I was, staring down at the very item who'd taken me to it to begin with.

Of course, he hadn't said I couldn't read the book. Hell, he'd even left it here.

Probably as a test, I reminded myself. *A test I'm now failing because I'm looking at an open page.*

I shook my head and sighed. "Fine. Show me something worthwhile, then. I should at least enjoy myself before I die." Maybe it would display that circle again— the one with a naked female between four men.

Four men who had looked suspiciously like Ajax, Az, Melek, and Lucifer.

I wonder which of them fucks the best, I thought. *Maybe the book can tell me that as a dying wish.*

Alas, to my great disappointment, there weren't any unsolicited dick pics on the page. Nor were there any sexual profiles.

"That's fine," I murmured. "I can use my imagination."

Ajax was the thicker one, his piercing allowing for interesting tingles below.

Az was the longer, more dominant one, his thrusts... they would be bruising in the best way.

Melek would be attentive, maybe even kind and gentle, and exceptionally thorough.

And Lucifer... well, Lucifer would be punishing. He probably enjoyed doling out pain. A lot of it.

I shivered, all four of them running through my mind, thanks to the book's depiction of explicit images while Lucifer was here.

The page now was blank, making me wary as to what the book was about to display. But when it sensed it finally had my full attention, it flipped to a new canvas that illustrated a picture of my father.

Definitely a mood killer, I thought, glaring. "Are you showing me my sperm donor because you know where he is?" I asked the book.

Because that would actually be worth risking Lucifer's wrath for.

From what Az had said, Lucifer wanted my father

found. So if the book wanted to reveal his location, I'd happily pass along the information. If nothing more than to see the bastard killed for getting me into this mess.

"All right, I'm listening," I said while I held up a finger. "But if I even see a glimpse of a blinding light, I'm shutting my eyes and throwing you across the room."

The book didn't shuffle its pages this time, instead replacing my father with an image of a glittering star.

I raised a brow.

"Uh, okay?" I waited for more, only for the book to jump up at my chest and fall back into my lap. "Ow!" I snapped at it. "What the fuck?"

Vita shook in response, not in fear, but in what appeared to be a motion of insistence.

"I don't remember you being this violent before," I muttered at it, rubbing my chest. The damn pages had nearly embedded my talisman into my...

Hold on.

I glanced down at the talisman hanging down toward my breasts. *A glittering star.* I looked back at the book. *Just like that.*

"Are you saying I can use this to find my father?" I asked the book.

I'd been so wary of using Melek's gifts that I hadn't considered what the talisman could actually do for me. However, he'd called it a conduit. And he'd provided a few spells, too.

What if this amplifies my blood connection with my father? I thought. *Would that help me track him down?*

My fingers slipped around the necklace as an icy shiver ran up my spine.

This was dangerous.

Risky.

Would probably end in blood.

But that's my life now, isn't it?

Drawing in a shaky breath, I clung to the necklace when the page revealed something new.

This time it was a transcript of a spell.

Was the book trying to trick me again? I wasn't sure what it gained by taking me to the source in the first place, or if it wanted to do it again. But this might let me find some answers and get a little payback against my father for everything he'd done.

That reward alone was far too good to pass up.

My heart sent blood roaring in my ears as I mouthed the words, *"Invenire. Inveniunt. Aperi ianuam."*

My hair flung back as a massive portal opened, dousing the flames along the walls to produce smoke.

No, not smoke. *Shadows.*

A flickering oval revealed another world behind it, one littered with gravestones dimly lit by the moonlight above. It almost reminded me of the Midnight Fae world—or what I'd expect it to look like outside the dungeon, anyway. But this world had dark shadows moving in the distance, ones that didn't look very Midnight Fae-like at all.

Uh, this can't be good…

"My father is here?" I whispered at the book, afraid to speak too loudly and be heard by anything lurking on the other side. "In a graveyard?"

The book didn't reply, the same page laid out before me as though it expected me to read it again.

Or walk through the portal, I realized, a shiver skating down my spine. *Yeah, no,* that *was not going to happen.* Even if it didn't resemble a freaky haunted cemetery, I'd learned my lesson the last time. *No. Leaving.*

Not until I had a real escape route in place, anyway.

And a plan for *after* I escaped.

Which was likely never going—

A familiar voice drifted across the sea of black headstones, the words nearly too quiet to be heard, until they carried into the room on a subtle gust of icy wind. "Do you feel that?"

I frowned. "Az?"

The portal whirled, suddenly showing me Az and Melek as they stood in the middle of a gravesite.

My eyes widened. "Oh. Uh, hi?"

Neither of them replied, their focus on the ground.

My brow furrowed. *Can they not see me?*

And what does this have to do with my dad?

I glanced down at Vita, but the page still hadn't changed.

"I do." Melek's wary tones wavered on the wind, giving his voice an eerie quality. "It's the same as what I sensed in the Underwater Kingdom—Virtuous magic."

Az nodded, his fingers running through his thick, dark hair. "But why would they appear after all this time?"

"Time is subjective," Melek replied, the shaky breeze flowing through the portal distorting his voice once more. "Especially for ones as old as us. But they're clearly behind the portal. The question is, what were they really trying to achieve? Because releasing Nightmare Fae into the Human Realm wasn't their end goal."

"No, that's just a distraction." Az's violet eyes narrowed. "We need to talk to King Onyx, maybe even Hades. See what other clues they might have missed while distracted by Monsters Night."

Melek hummed. "Agreed."

I leaned forward, curious to learn more, but the portal abruptly went dark, the smoke sputtering as though out of fuel. I grabbed my necklace, ready to utter the spell again, when Ajax shadowed into the room wearing nothing but a towel.

Oh.

Oh, shit, I thought, realizing what this looked like.

The last time he'd gone to take a shower, I'd disappeared for thirty days. And he'd probably just sensed the portal in the living room, therefore jumping to conclusions.

"Ajax," I started. "It's not—"

"What the *fuck*, Camillia?" he roared, tackling me to the ground before I could finish speaking.

I glanced around, dazed, searching for the book, to explain what I'd been doing.

But it was nowhere to be seen.

Of fucking course.

CHAPTER 20

AJAX

"I CAN'T *BELIEVE* YOU," I snarled.

Fuck, I couldn't believe that I'd trusted her, that I'd bought her lies, that I'd thought she was innocent.

But now I knew the truth.

A portal. That *was how she escaped.*

And she'd almost managed to do it again. But I'd caught a hint of the magic in the air and stopped her before she could flee.

Her tight leather pants clung to my skin as I braced one arm at her throat, pinning her to the ground. I'd lost my towel in the process, but fuck that.

And *fuck her.*

I'd basically bled myself at her feet, thanks to that fucking truth serum, and this was her response?

To try to run? *Again?*

"If you'd… just…" She squirmed and pushed at my weight, but I wasn't going to let her up until I was certain the portal had completely dissipated. It was flickering behind me, sputtering with dying power.

Because I broke her concentration.

Just in time, too.

Lucifer might not kill me for failing—*again*—but he would absolutely shove me out of his inner circle.

Losing my Warden title would no longer be temporary; it would be permanent. And he might even go as far as severing my loose connection to the Hell Fae Realm, thus casting me out entirely.

On top of all that, he'd also kill Camillia. And while I might want to do that right now, I didn't actually want to see her die. I wanted her to *survive*. To *live*. To…*to be free.*

I frowned. She couldn't be free here. Not truly. But she could be alive. And maybe she would learn to love it.

That must be why Lucifer wants me to teach her—to help her understand this realm and give her reasons to stay.

She had no idea how important that opportunity truly was, particularly for a *female* Hell Fae. They were so rare here, the source rejecting ninety-nine percent of them.

But Lucifer seemed to think Camillia might be able to stay. And he wanted my help in guaranteeing she survived.

Alas, I couldn't do that if she kept trying to fucking run away.

"While I appreciate your fight, little rebel, I really wish you would take a moment to consider the opportunities you're being offered here. Because I can assure you they're better than whatever you have waiting for you in the Human Realm."

She rolled her eyes and tried to shove me off her again. "Ajax," she managed to get out before I pressed my arm into her throat again.

The portal's energy was nearly dead behind me, but I refused to move until I was absolutely certain she couldn't use it.

"You're not going anywhere," I informed her, pressing my weight on her chest.

I eased off her throat enough to let her breathe again while I waited for the chill in the air to dissipate.

She'd opened up a portal.

To the Netherworld Kingdom.

What the fuck?

Not a place I'd use to escape, but maybe that was the real way she'd evaded Az and me for so long? Had she been hopping around the various Hell Fae Kingdoms while we'd been off searching the various fae realms?

That seemed... impossible. And also ridiculous. She would have been eaten alive in most of the kingdoms, and we would have felt her.

So maybe it'd been a temporary jump?

Did she travel to the Netherworld last time and escape through the Monsters Night portal? Was she hiding in an alternate reality for thirty days? Why come back?

"*Ajax.*" She twisted her hips. "Get. Off!"

She shoved her knee between us, making pain bloom in my groin.

Low blow, little rebel.

Momentarily distracted, she managed to roll out from beneath me and scampered behind the couch.

As if that would save her.

"Reveal yourself, Vita. Help me out." She glanced frantically around the room. "*Come on.*"

A whirl of pages appeared on the couch, making Camillia sigh with relief.

"Thank you," she said before looking at me. "Now hear me out for a second." She reached over the couch for the book. "I was just reading this—"

Cursing, I dove to snatch the book away from her. Because maybe that part of her story was true—that the book had helped her escape. She'd just failed to mention the part about *how*, instead lying and sharing that the book had pulled her toward the source.

Maybe the alternate story had been close enough to the truth to trick Zakkai's spell.

Well, I'm onto you now, little rebel.

"You are *not* summoning another portal," I growled as I gripped the book. It vibrated in protest, but I ignored it. "You're staying right here. With me. Your *Warden*."

I'd worked hard to build up my new identity. While there was some room for growth, I was still Lucifer's Warden. Just in a different capacity right now.

Camillia crossed her arms and glowered at me like I was an idiot. "I don't think Vita likes to be manhandled like that."

As if to confirm Camillia's statement, the book heated until it burned, making me bite off another curse as I dropped it to the floor.

"And I wasn't trying to escape," she added.

"Really?" I drawled, stalking around the couch. "Because that's what it damn well looked like."

I called my wand and summoned the cuffs I should have put on her in the first place. Just like I'd done last night. It'd been a mistake to ever take them off.

She loosened her arms and took a step back. "You're not putting those on me."

I whirled my wand, sending the cuffs on a path to snag around her wrists.

But she deflected it, a bright light appearing from her necklace as the cuffs clattered uselessly to the floor.

It seemed that she'd learned more tricks than just summoning portals.

I raised an eyebrow. "So everything has been a lie?" I asked her. "All your stories? The seductive games? Your pretend feelings?"

She appeared startled, like she hadn't expected me to call her out on her bullshit. "*What?*"

"You heard me." I took a step toward her. "Your lies have all been revealed now, Camillia. I *see* you." For a few unbelievable moments, I'd actually fallen for her tales of innocence.

And who could blame me? She was clever. Beautiful. Alluringly determined.

Fuck, I was getting hard right now just staring at her. All that crafty energy and cunning intelligence made her so incredibly strong, so fucking *gorgeous*.

I shadowed directly in front of her and backed her up against the flaming wall, pressing her into it. She jolted at first, clearly afraid of being burned, but her inner power burst out to protect her, confirming everything I needed to know.

"You are so much more than you say you are, little rebel," I murmured, my hands against her hips, my knuckles brushing the walls. "But so am I."

As I proved now by holding on to her even while the flames surged.

I might not be a true Hell Fae, but my power had been realigned by Zakkai. It'd been at the request of Lucifer, his way of ensuring my safety while working in his realm.

The realignment made me a true abomination, to be connected to both the Midnight Fae Source and the Hell Fae Source. Not many even knew about the link, the tenuous bond more of a test than a permanent connection. But it protected me now as the Hellfire burned hot behind Camillia.

However, Camillia's magic felt different. It seemed to glow across her skin, making my brow furrow. Because it was distinctly unlike a Hell Fae's.

Actually, it… it reminded me of Melek.

Because of her necklace? I wondered, noting the shining star. That had also been what she'd used to deflect my cuffs.

My frown deepened. *Is she using spells he taught her? Or is this something else entirely?*

I met her gray gaze, noting the sheer panic dilating her pupils. She appeared frozen despite being pressed up against a hot wall, her jaw clenched tight.

"Am I hurting you?" I asked, the words rough against my tongue. Because part of me wanted to hurt her, to throttle her, to berate her for trying to trick me—*again*. But a deeper part of me, one I'd ignored for a very long time, worried that I'd just made a terrible mistake.

She didn't reply, her expression almost ghostlike and reminding me of the very kingdom she'd nearly escaped to.

Except... she hadn't been anywhere near the portal. She'd been on the couch instead, simply leaning forward as though watching a riveting movie or television program.

I tried to recall the full scene in my head, to picture what I'd truly seen. I'd been so consumed with stopping Camillia and closing the portal that I'd mostly focused on her. But there'd been glimpses of the Netherworld.

And there'd been voices, too.

Az's voice.

I'd sensed him, too. Just like I'd sensed the enchantment.

That doesn't make sense. Why would she open a portal near the Hell Fae Commander?

Was it an accident? Had she been trying to find the right place to run to, but she'd stumbled upon Az instead?

Another pulse of power burst from her necklace, coating her in a shimmering dust that made her shiver, her lips beginning to tremble.

A hint of decadence followed, reminding me very much of Melek again. *Because it's his talisman*, I thought once more. *But something isn't right here.*

I took a step back, leaving her up against the wall.

She didn't move, seemingly frozen.

With a sigh, I grabbed her hip with one hand and her nape with the other, tugging her away from the flames.

She felt brittle in my arms, like she'd morphed into an ice cube. However, her skin wasn't cold, just chilled.

I led her to the couch and lowered her to a cushion. The book bristled, the pages fluttering as it relocated itself from the floor to the table, the sound reminding me of a female "hmphing" at me.

Strange fucking book, I decided as I called for my wand. I needed some fucking clothes, mostly to hide my physical reaction to Camillia. Not that she'd seemed to notice. Her eyes appeared a little lost, which had me cursing at myself for my reactions.

Maybe she'd been trying to escape again. Maybe she hadn't.

At this point, I didn't have a damn clue. But one thing was certain—I was tired of games. Whether they be in the form of interrogations or just Melek's infuriating meddling, I just wanted a real conversation with some real fucking answers.

Summoning royal attire, I fitted myself with an open-vested suit that showed off my chest, complete with court-favored diamond cuff links and blood-red trim. I wanted to be ready in case I had to venture out to find Lucifer.

I also magicked a new pair of cuffs, ones that came without a key, and affixed them to my belt before sitting beside a still-shivering Camillia.

"I d-don't understand th-this mag-gic," she chattered, flinching at the end. "Th-the p-portal… sh-showed Azzz and Mel..." She closed her eyes, her expression one of frustration. A low growl built in her chest, one that had me instantly hard in my pants again.

She obviously didn't appreciate feeling weak.

I could understand that.

Taking a seat beside her, I conjured up some apple tea —one of my favorite remedies to chase away a chill—and held it out for her. "Here. Drink this. Then we'll talk."

She peeked at it, her face instantly wary.

"It's similar to hot apple cider, just a little thinner. And it's not drugged." I added that last part because I knew she suspected otherwise.

"Even i-if you did, i-it wouldn't r-really matter, hmm?" She trembled over the words but lifted one shaky hand to accept the drink.

"Why wouldn't it matter?" I asked, my focus on the rattling cup in her hand. I fully intended to catch that if she accidentally dropped it. The last thing I wanted was for her to burn herself.

Rather than respond, she brought the drink to her lips and closed her eyes. Then she began to sip it, her posture defeated.

It reminded me of how I'd felt yesterday—exhausted and just done.

Does she feel that way now because I caught her mid-escape? Or is it from the way I reacted?

Silence fell over us for a long moment, her throat working slowly as she swallowed small sips of the drink I'd crafted for her. By the time she finished, her quivering had subsided. A slight flush stole across her cheeks, providing her skin with much-needed color as she set the cup on the table.

Several more minutes passed while I waited for her next move, curious as to what she would try to do. But all she did was turn to look at me, her gray eyes cautious. "What happens now?" she asked. "Or is your spell tormenting me with waiting in suspense?"

"What spell?" I asked her.

She gestured toward the cup with her chin. "*That* one."

"It's already taken effect," I told her. "You're no longer shivering." But it wasn't actually a spell, just a warm drink.

She arched a brow. "You mean you were actually trying to help?"

"Yes."

"Why?" she asked incredulously.

"Because you needed it," I admitted. "You seemed frozen."

"I *felt* frozen," she replied, shuddering. Her attention shifted downward as she grabbed the talisman hanging from her neck. "It's this thing. I don't really understand it. Like how it deflected your cuffs or the cooling power it sends across my skin."

Another tremor visibly shook her shoulders, causing her to bite her lower lip and wince.

I leaned back into the couch, my arm stretching behind her.

"It's hard to know what's real and what's not with you, Camillia." I angled my body toward her as I brought my ankle up to rest across my opposite thigh. "And I'm really tired of guessing. Can we try for honesty? Please?"

She made a noise in the back of her throat and shook her head. "I haven't lied to you, Ajax. Actually, I've been pretty upfront from the very beginning."

"Then let's begin again," I suggested. "Tell me what you were doing with the portal, and I'll attempt to believe you."

CHAPTER 21

AJAX

Camillia glanced at me sideways. "Attempt to believe me. Right."

"I'm trying, Camillia. But none of this has been very easy. You—"

"You're right," she interjected. "None of this has been easy at all. From the very first moment that you dragged me to the Hell Fae Realm, it's all been pretty fucking difficult. And as much as I want to blame you for it, I can't. Because it wasn't *your* deal. It was between Lucifer and my father."

"Well, I'm partially to blame for capturing you and putting you in the paradigm," I pointed out. It only seemed right to own up to my part in it.

"You were just doing your job. Just like you were doing it again when you tracked me down and interrogated me." She shook her head once more and collapsed against the couch, her hair touching my arm. "My father is the real culprit."

"On that, we agree." Because she was right. She

wouldn't be here if it weren't for her father's bargain. "But I'm surprised you're not blaming Lucifer, too."

"Oh, he's certainly part of it," she said with a dry laugh. "But I don't know. He... There's something about him that makes me question his true motives."

I nodded, understanding what she meant. "He's an enigma."

"He is," she agreed.

Another beat passed between us before she turned a little to look at me, her gaze searching.

"I wasn't trying to escape," she told me. "The book was being insistent and kept landing in my lap, so I finally looked down at it, and it showed me a picture of my father."

Her nose crinkled with the words, making her appear adorably infuriated.

But rather than comment on that, I asked, "And then what happened?"

"Well, it showed me a star." Her fingers went to the talisman, her thumb stroking the glittering gems. "And then it revealed a spell."

So this is Melek's meddling again, I thought but didn't voice it aloud.

"I thought it was going to help me locate my father. Instead, it opened a portal. Except it wasn't really a portal. Or I don't think it was, anyway. Because it only showed Az and Melek. I tried to talk to them, but they couldn't hear me."

Her expression turned pensive again, her fingers still running over the talisman. I half expected her to try something nefarious, maybe utter another spell that would render me immobile while she escaped, but all she did was sigh again and release the star.

"Melek once said this was a conduit, so I thought that

maybe it was a conduit for some sort of blood-tie and that the book was trying to tell me how to use it, you know, to help me find my father. Then I let my need for vengeance take over." Her fingers clenched, her expression turning fierce.

Which, of course, had my cock reacting all over again.

This female is going to be the death of me.

"Anyway, the book tricked me, like it does, and showed me Az and Melek in a graveyard."

"The Netherworld Kingdom," I corrected. "It's a land full of Corpse Fae and Death Fae." It was supposed to be the site of the next trial a month ago, but that hadn't happened after the Monsters Night chaos. "I was supposed to help you learn more about them for the bride trial."

She slowly nodded. "I remember." Her gray eyes flashed. "Because that was just a few days ago for me. Or a day ago. I don't know. Time is really fucking with my head."

"Well, everything is fucking with mine," I replied, not bothering to hide my irritation. I wanted to believe Camillia, but it was a risk. Not because she might succeed in escaping, but because I didn't want her to be able to hurt me.

I'd lived through more than enough pain in my life. I didn't need any more.

But something about this woman had the cages around my heart threatening to shatter.

It wasn't just that she reminded me of Emelyn, although that was a large part of it. Or, at least, that'd been the instigator of my interest. However, every passing moment with Camillia drew me to her even more.

Like now, when I should want to wring her neck for the stunt she'd pulled, all I actually wanted to do was kiss her. Worship her. *Fuck* her.

It was counterintuitive to reason. And it was making me feel insane.

"What was the spell?" I asked, curious as to what the book had supposedly shown her.

"Oh, um…" She frowned. "*Invenire. Inveniunt. Aperi ianuam.*" Her eyes flew to the wall as though she expected the portal to reappear, and when it didn't, she released a relieved exhale. "Right. I have to be touching the talisman," she said, seemingly speaking to herself. "Or…" She glanced at me. "Did you want to see it?"

I shook my head. "No, the words are enough." And knowing that she needed the talisman to make it work told me what I needed to know, too. "That's not Hell Fae magic." I looked at her necklace. "And neither is that."

Which meant this was all Melek's meddling. *Fucking prince.*

"I don't think the book is really Hell Fae magic either," Camillia said, her gaze on the ancient text on the table. "There's something very… *otherworldly*… about it." She glanced back at me. "Can you read it?"

I shook my head. "No. The pages looked blank to me earlier."

"So at least Melek told the truth about that, I guess. He found me in the library reading it on my first day here. I'd been trying to look for a legal way to break my father's deal with Lucifer, and the figments brought me that book. But it didn't help in the way I'd anticipated." Her gaze narrowed at the item in question. "It never does anything that I expect."

"Sounds like Melek," I mused. "Except I can always expect him to do something devious."

She snorted in response to that. "Every. Time." Her expression turned thoughtful. "Although, he's been a lot more forthcoming lately. Serious, even. Like when he was talking to Az through the portal window thing, he didn't sound playful at all."

"What was he saying?"

"Something about Virtuous magic." She frowned. "Do you know what that means?"

I slowly shook my head, my lips curling downward to match hers. "No, I haven't heard of that." Which was troubling. Because if Az and Melek were discussing a type of magic I'd never heard of before, then it meant no one was supposed to know about it.

Lucifer hadn't even taught me about Nightmare Fae until I'd passed a series of tests and earned a higher level of trust. They were well hidden from the fae population for their own protection. Lucifer didn't tell just anyone his secrets. I'd learned about them because I'd earned the knowledge.

Most of that had been because of Az.

"Yet you're supposed to be my Hell Fae tutor?" Camillia asked, a hint of teasing in her voice. When I didn't laugh, she cleared her throat. "Sorry, I just... I thought you might... Never mind."

"If it's something I don't know, it's something none of us are meant to know," I told her. "Lucifer has a great many secrets. One of the first lessons I learned in this realm is to never pry. Everything here happens for a predetermined reason, even things I might not like."

She stared at me. "Things like the bride trials?"

"I might not agree with some of the methods used, but I understand the overall purpose of the trials, thus allowing me to respect them."

"And what is the overall purpose?" she asked, genuine curiosity in her tone. "Other than forcing fae to mate against their will?"

"No, that's just it—it isn't against anyone's will. The

Hell Fae mate-bonds can only snap into place when both spirits are willing, and the trials are meant to help sort those who are worthy from those who are not."

"And what happens to those who are considered unworthy?" she pressed. "They die?"

"It honestly depends on why the source considers them unworthy. Most females are just sent back to where they've come from. But if the candidate possesses ill will, or a darkness inside, the source will exterminate the intruder, if nothing more than to protect those beneath its umbrella of power."

"Okay, so if that's true, then why am I here?" she asked, her blondish-brown eyebrow arched upward in a haughty display of annoyance. "The source *literally* sent me home. Yet you and Az dragged me back."

"True," I agreed. "But I'm talking about the candidates who are determined unworthy of all the fae within this realm at the end of the trials. Your situation is unique in that you touched the source, and it wasn't during the trials at all."

She twisted her lips to the side, seeming to want to argue, but there was no disputing the truth.

"Do you want to know the true purpose of the trials?" I asked her. "The whole reason they were created?"

"To find mates for Nightmare Fae and Hell Fae?" she guessed.

"To an extent, yes. But it's so much deeper than that, Camillia."

"Enlighten me, then, Professor Ajax. Teach me."

I could tell she was being facetious, but I ignored her sarcasm. Because she really did need to understand this. It was the heart of her contention—being forced into these trials. And while I understood her anger, I needed her to understand why it'd been necessary.

"Several of the Nightmare Fae species are bordering on extinction because there are no females, and no females means no procreation. However, the source is incredibly selective about who it allows within the realm gates. The whole point of this realm is to protect the monsters every other realm refuses. And all it takes is one or two bad fae to ruin everything Lucifer has built."

"And for some reason, the source rejects females rather than males?" she asked, her tone shrouded in doubt.

"Yes. I don't know why, but it seems females are less likely to be compassionate toward monsters. Perhaps out of fear, or repulsion. However, it doesn't seem to be a problem among male fae nearly as often."

"So even Hell Fae females tend to be rejected," she said.

I nodded. "Yes. Although, Hell Fae females are rare in general. Most Hell Fae are born male. But Lucifer has spent the last one thousand years hunting for the right candidates—Hell Fae and other fae alike—to participate in the trials. He only made deals for those he knew the source would allow through the gates. The trials are set up to determine if all his research and work prove fruitful."

She considered that for a moment. "So he found bloodlines of females who should survive in his world, but only if they are truly compassionate or worthy of his misunderstood creatures."

"Yes," I confirmed. "And if they prove themselves as true candidates, their souls will align with a fae and a mate-bond will be formed. But it has to be accepted by both of them."

"Hmm." She didn't sound completely convinced, but I could see the pieces slowly falling into place. "So now I'm no longer eligible because the source sent me home."

"You're no longer eligible because you're proving to be

a handful," I corrected her. "The source has neither accepted nor rejected you yet. And Lucifer is trying to determine what to do next."

"Kill me or keep me," she mused. "Excellent choices."

"Or a good reason to try to run," I hedged.

She looked at me, her gaze sharp. "You still don't believe me?"

I held her angry stare for a long moment before saying, "Honestly, I think I do believe you. About all of it." I reached forward to touch her talisman, noting the icy texture of it. "Melek is playing a game that involves us both. I just have to figure out if I want to remain a player on his wicked little chessboard."

"What about Az?" Her voice lowered an octave with her words, causing my focus to lift away from her necklace to her lips and farther up to her stunning irises. They were flickering with power as her pupils dilated, making me wonder what the talisman was doing to her right now.

Or is that hint of magic just her?

"What about Az?" I repeated back to her. "Are you asking if he's a pawn, too?"

"Yes. No. I don't know. I just… You two seem close. And he obviously knows Melek well. Can you talk to him about all this?'

"I likely will, yes."

"And will he tell you about the Virtuous magic?" she pressed. "About what he and Melek were talking about, I mean?"

That… I wasn't so sure. "It depends on if I need to know."

"Why wouldn't you need to know?"

I shrugged. "Sometimes secrets, even between friends, are a necessary evil."

I'd learned that lesson from Shade years ago. There

were things he'd done to save the Midnight Fae Realm that I would never know anything about, and I was okay with that. Mostly. I had to believe that if he'd known what had been about to happen to my parents and Emelyn, he would have done something. Warned me. *Anything.* Because to believe otherwise…

I swallowed.

To believe otherwise would ruin a lifelong friendship.

Pushing the thought from my mind, I focused on Camillia and distracted myself by asking, "Did you hear them say anything else?" I probably shouldn't be inquiring, as she'd essentially eavesdropped on a private conversation. But I couldn't help the curiosity brewing inside me.

She shook her head. "They said something about talking to King Onyx and, uh, Hades, about other clues, but I didn't really hear the rest because you slammed into me like a maniac."

I smirked, amused by her descriptive term. "I suppose I did. Sorry for tackling you *like a maniac,* Camillia."

Her lips parted. "What?" She blinked. "Did you… just apologize?"

I lifted a shoulder. "I'm capable of owning up to my mistakes. Don't act so surprised. But while we're on the subject, I'm also sorry for shoving you up against the wall. I didn't expect you to *freeze.*"

She flinched. "Neither did I." Her fingers went to her talisman again. "I don't trust this thing, but I also can't afford to take it off. It's clearly trying to protect me."

"So it seems," I agreed. "So how about we do something to take your mind off it for a little while? Take your mind off of all this?"

She studied me with open skepticism. "What did you have in mind?"

I canted my head toward the pizza oven. "A tutorial on how the hell we use that."

Her gaze followed the angle of my head, a sweet little smile gracing her features. "It's pretty simple—you put a pizza together and set it on the fire."

"Then how about you help me make a pizza and I'll man the fire?" Because I needed a distraction from the hunger growing in my groin, as well as the chaos brewing in my mind. And I suspected she needed the same— particularly in regard to the latter.

"I would suggest you just magic-wand us some pizza, but cooking actually does sound like fun," she admitted. "It almost sounds normal." She flicked her eyes at the walls. "You know, apart from being in a hellish castle and staying in a room down the hall from the Hell Fae King himself."

"Let's do our best to forget that part. At least until we finish eating," I offered. "Deal?" I couldn't help the phrasing, aware that it was a direct play on her situation.

Fortunately, her smile only strengthened in response. "Deal," she echoed, holding out her hand for a proper shake.

I accepted and helped her up off the couch.

Then I followed her into the kitchen and pretended like we were just two normal fae about to share dinner.

Afterward, I'd become her Warden again.

But for now, we'd live in the present as simply Ajax and Cami.

CHAPTER 22

CAMI

A Few Days Later

Ajax and I had developed a bit of a routine over the last few days.

We ate breakfast together, discussed different types of Nightmare Fae, had lunch, visited one of Lucifer's many libraries in the afternoon to read, ate dinner, and spent our evenings just being us.

Last night we'd even watched a movie from the Human Realm, one I'd been hoping to see last month.

When I'd mentioned it to Ajax, he'd conjured a device that contained the film. Then we'd lounged on the couch with some popcorn and transformed the living area into our own little theater.

It turned out that the black screen wasn't operated by a remote but by specific commands, something Ajax had taught me so I could use it as desired.

Alas, it was mostly filled with Hell Fae surveillance videos rather than entertaining shows.

So I'd mostly been intrigued by the various books

within Lucifer's library. Hence the one I'd set out on my bed to read once I finished getting ready.

Only, I couldn't decide what to wear today because my routine with Ajax had been disrupted.

He'd been called away this morning by Az, derailing our usual breakfast plan. Rather than invite me along—which I'd stupidly hoped he'd do—Ajax had told me to stay in the guest suite and read for a bit. Then he'd conjured some sort of magical net all around me, ensuring I couldn't leave.

"I see you still don't trust me," I'd muttered at him, bothered by being excluded and his babysitting spell. A practical part of me had recognized that his actions made sense, but that hadn't stopped a part of me from feeling disappointed in being reverted back to captive status.

"I'm not sure about that," he'd replied, giving me a cryptic look. "But I don't trust *that*." He'd pointed at Vita on the coffee table—the place it'd been since the other day. "Please don't create any portals while I'm gone. If Lucifer comes in here and sees it, he won't be pleased."

With that unnecessary warning, Ajax had disappeared, leaving me to make my own breakfast. I'd decided on coffee, then taken a shower, and proceeded to stare at my closet now as I tried to determine what to wear.

I wanted something comfortable, but most of the pajamas were lingerie sets. Which was why I'd spent the last few nights wearing a tank top and lacy panties to bed. They were the most practical. But also cute. *Just in case a certain Midnight Fae decided to join me,* I thought with a sigh.

However, he hadn't. He'd simply slept on the couch the last five nights instead.

My eyes narrowed. Ajax hadn't so much as touched me, either. Well, aside from our tumble the other day after the portal incident, anyway.

But even last night, he'd kept a foot between us on the couch while we'd watched the movie. Like he'd actively been trying not to be near me despite our close proximity.

He'd actually seemed quite relieved to hear from Az this morning, his eagerness to run away a palpable presence in the air when he'd announced his intentions. Maybe I was just reading too much into the situation. It wouldn't be surprising, given everything that had happened since being forced to the Hell Fae Realm.

Blowing out a breath, I focused on my clothes again.

Maybe I should go for comfortable yet sexy, I pondered. *Who knows how long Ajax will be gone? I can at least feel good about myself while alone, right?*

And perhaps a devious part of me hoped he wouldn't be gone all that long and would just happen to walk in on me dressed in something provocative.

We'll see how good your resolve is then, I thought, my lips curling.

Because I knew he was attracted to me. I'd seen the evidence of that in all its glory the other day when he'd pinned me to the floor and again to the wall.

It wasn't like he didn't know if it was mutual or not; we'd had sex less than a week ago. Obviously, I was drawn to him. *And his thick, pierced cock.*

I could admit that was part of my disappointment over not being invited to tag along today. I'd wanted to see Az, too.

Because I'm broken.

Or I'd simply been destroyed by the two male fae. They'd awoken a libido inside me that now demanded attention—with or without logical reasoning intact.

Rolling my eyes at my hormones, I selected a sexy little number that was more like a revealing babydoll dress than a proper dress. The vibrant reds shimmered as if the material was made from fire rather than silk. It was surprisingly warm, too, suggesting there was some enchantment behind the fiery color.

That's a nice touch that would be useful if I were actually going out in this dress, I thought.

But I wasn't.

So I paired the dress with a matching robe and reveled in the sensual fabric. A few glittery, diamond-like studs decorated the sleeves, giving it an opulent flair that made me smile.

I wasn't one to play dress-up, but this felt nice.

With a nod at my reflection, I returned to my room to find Vita lying on top of my chosen book.

"Ha. No." I pushed it aside and settled myself into the pillows for a reading session with a *safe* book.

Vita vibrated at me, but I ignored it, choosing instead to grab my lukewarm coffee mug.

I briefly considered wandering into the kitchen to brew a new pot but decided to push the ceramic cup up against the flaming wall instead, leaving it resting on the nightstand.

The walls framed the bed's headboard, giving the room a fiery glow. And now it was going to be useful in reheating my coffee, too.

"Right. Let's get started, shall we?" I opened up the book titled *Marsh Lands: A Historical Documentation of Degradation.*

Vita pulsed again in response.

"I'm not talking to you," I told it and turned back to my chosen text.

A depiction of a lush forest waited for me on the introduction page, causing my eyebrow to arch. *Definitely wasn't expecting that,* I thought.

However, the next page explained that the visual was a relic from the past...

Once a forest filled with Centaurs and Griffins, there was plenty of space for life in this vast stretch of fertile land. However, these species had managed to hoard a significant area between what is now the Underwater Kingdom and the Barren Lands. Unfortunately, with no ruler to guide these creatures, their efforts quickly became unstable and formed a bridge between the two regions, resulting in what is now the Marsh Lands.

I turned the page, curious. It seemed that Lucifer had done more than establish the various kingdoms; he'd also stopped the existing "outcasts" from making things worse.

Typhos Lucifer appointed kings of two compatible species to rule the Marsh Lands. The Naga and the Unseelie were tasked to work together to cultivate their domain and help it prosper.

A sipping sound made me drop the book and jump up to my knees.

Glancing sideways, I found Melek drinking my coffee. "Hey!" I chided, startled and annoyed by his unexpected presence. "Get your own coffee."

He didn't respond.

Instead, he stared down at me with the cup poised against his lips, his gaze roaming over my chosen attire.

My robe had apparently fallen off my shoulders when I'd jumped, revealing my babydoll dress.

He lowered the beverage slowly as a pleased grin stretched across his handsome face, securing his iconic dimples. "Well, I certainly didn't expect you to accept that particular gift so soon."

My face heated, and it had nothing to do with the surrounding walls.

Clearing my throat, I slid off the bed—because it suddenly felt like an invitation in my current state—and fixed my robe before cinching it around my waist with a messy knot. "What are you doing here?" I asked him.

His grin disappeared as he frowned at the center of my robe's tie. "Is that how you tie a knot?"

I looked down, my brow furrowing. "What?"

"Sweet angel, no," he continued, acting as though I hadn't responded. "This is simply unacceptable."

He set down the coffee cup and stepped toward me, his hand going to the strip of silk binding my midsection. I squeaked as he deftly unbound it, his movements quick and purposeful.

"What are you...?" I trailed off.

He draped the silky ribbon over the curve of my hip and resecured the robe neatly over my breasts before ensuring the fabric was fully aligned down to my belly button. Then he grabbed the tie again and created a decadent knot against my stomach, one that formed the shape of a rose. "Much better."

I gaped down at it. I suddenly felt like a gift-wrapped present. The question was, whom had he just wrapped me up for?

With a quick shake of my head to stir me from any unwanted thoughts, I asked, "Why are you here, Melek?" *Wait, no.* "Sorry, *Prince* Melek."

Or did I only need to refer to him that way around Lucifer?

I hadn't bothered to use the formal title when talking about Melek with Ajax since we'd always called him by his name alone. But now that I'd met the Hell Fae King, I wasn't sure of Melek's appropriate address.

He raised a blondish-brown brow. "Prince?"

"I, uh, yeah. Lucifer said I should be referring to you as *Prince* Melek."

His lips twitched. "And yet you're calling Lucifer without a title?"

"That's what he told me to call him." I went to run my fingers through my hair, then remembered I'd pulled it back into a ponytail.

Ugh. Why do I feel so jittery?

I released a long breath and shook my head. Melek typically made me uneasy because of his perpetual riddles. But this was different. I felt... *nervous.* Like I wasn't sure how to act around him. Or what to say.

A frustrated noise escaped my mouth. *This isn't me. I'm not inept or insecure. I'm Cami. I live by a set of rules. I kick ass and take names. And I do not bow.*

Except to Lucifer, apparently.

Like a demented flamingo.

Another groan threatened to leave my lips, but I swallowed it on a wince.

"Do you want to call me 'prince,' little angel? Or maybe 'sir'?" Melek offered, his silky voice pulling my attention back to him. He stood closer now, his all-black suit a scant inch from my robe. "Or do you want to hear my preference?"

"I don't want to play any games today," I admitted. "Not even one related to titles and names."

He considered me for a moment, his gaze softening. "Then I'll tell you to call me Melek. Because with you, I don't have a title. I'm simply yours."

"Mine?" I nearly snorted, though the part of me that was melting from his words kept the incredulity from coloring my tone. "You're Lucifer's mate."

"I am," he agreed. "But I'm also yours."

My brow furrowed. "You're not my mate." It didn't come out as defensive so much as confused. Because what he was saying didn't make any sense.

He merely smiled. "Then we'll say I *intend* to be yours, if you choose to one day have me." He brushed his knuckles across my cheek, sending a shiver of warm energy over my being. "But that's not what I've come to discuss with you today."

I... I didn't know how to reply to him.

"I intend to be yours," he'd said.

As... as a mate...

CHAPTER 23

CAMI

Melek intends to mate me?

That wasn't at all what I'd expected him to say.

Is it a trick? Some sort of lie? A new game?

Do I want to mate him?

I couldn't answer that. I could barely even think.

His knuckles continued a path down my neck, more of his warmth bleeding into my skin. That decadent scent of his followed, wrapping me up in a sensual blanket that left me shivering beneath his touch.

I kept repeating his words over and over in my head, trying to decipher the hidden meaning. He never spoke the truth to me. Not directly, anyway.

Except, recently, he actually had.

On the tour, he'd been forthcoming when telling me about Lucifer and his history. He'd also helped me understand my lost time by deciphering what the book had done to me.

And now he's claiming that his intentions are to mate me.

"Why?" I blurted out. "Because I can read the book?"

"Ironically what I wanted to discuss," he murmured. "But what do you mean?"

"Why do you want to mate me?" I reiterated.

He smiled. "Because you're special, little angel. Why else?"

I gaped at him. "But we hardly know each other. And Lucifer…" *Is your mate? Already might want to kill me, and this will make him want to kill me more?* I wasn't sure which of those continuations was best.

But Melek had another in mind as he said, "Lucifer will take some time to appreciate this development, yes. Which is good because that means we have time to learn more about each other, too." He pulled his hand away and sat on the bed. "Now, about Vita, why are you neglecting him?"

"Him?" I repeated, surprised by his choice of pronoun and still stunned by everything else he'd said.

He lifted a shoulder. "*It*, if you prefer. Why are you avoiding Vita's information?"

"Uh, well, because Vita keeps getting me into trouble," I offered as one very good reason to avoid the magic book. "It took me to the source, and Lucifer made it very clear that if it happens again, he'll kill me. And just the other day, it had me make a—"

"Ty said what?" Melek interjected.

"He said if I went near his source again, he'd kill me," I repeated.

Melek's hair fluttered around him on an invisible wind as golden glitter shimmered just above his skin. "I see." His tone deepened with those two words, the sound oddly menacing. Or perhaps it was his glittering eyes that gave me that impression.

Is he… angry? I wondered.

"I'll talk to Ty." That sounded more like a threat than a

promise. "But have you considered that it wasn't Vita that took you to Lucifer's source?"

I blinked at him. "Well, I definitely didn't do it." *How would I even know how to?*

Melek didn't seem convinced. "Are you certain?" he pressed. "Perhaps the book was simply trying to prepare you for your destiny by showing you the past. And maybe you took yourself to the source to see the present."

"I wouldn't even begin to know how to do that," I promised him. "It had to be the book."

"Hmm, but you're in the Hell Fae Realm now, little angel. Anything is possible here. And there's something very unique about you. I mean, why else could you read Ty's book? How else did you touch the source and survive?"

He canted his head, causing a strand of his blondish-brown hair to roll across his forehead and into his eyes.

"No, little angel. I don't think it was the book at all," he went on. "You're something very powerful. A mystery for us to solve. But not today."

Something powerful, I repeated to myself, those words reminding of the ones Zakkai, the Midnight Fae Source Architect, had said the other day.

I'm just a Halfling Hell Fae, I wanted to argue.

But if Melek's suggestion that I'd reached Lucifer's source on my own was true, then my life was definitely in danger.

Because I didn't see the Hell Fae King tolerating that sort of threat.

"If all of this is true, then I'm already dead," I whispered. "Lucifer is going to kill me."

Melek didn't seem fazed. "No, little angel. He's not. And you're going to help protect yourself by getting to know him better—by reading his book."

I stared at him. "How will that help me get to know the Hell Fae King?"

"Because the book *is* Typhos Lucifer," Melek replied. "It's part of his soul. Which is why I found you so intriguing the first day I met you and why you continue to fascinate me. You're strong. Courageous. Extremely intelligent. Resourceful." He glanced over me with those hypnotic irises. "Beautiful, too."

My cheeks heated beneath his perusal, only for my pulse to start racing as he stood and advanced toward me.

"Understanding how to communicate with Ty will only secure your safety, Cami," he said softly. "The book is the key to learning how to do that. Because, as I said, the book is Typhos Lucifer. Part of him, anyway. And that part of him wants to know you. Otherwise, you wouldn't be able to read it."

His palm met my cheek as his opposite hand went to my hip.

"I think that's why you were able to reach the source, too. It's a piece of his soul, just like Vita. And those pieces have chosen you. Embrace them and Ty will embrace you, too."

"Why would I want that?" I asked him, my gaze holding his. "Why would I want any of this?" I frowned. "And how do I know this isn't your doing?" He'd been there the day I'd found the book. "Maybe you're the reason I can read Vita."

Humor touched his gaze as he moved closer, his body pressing into mine. "I may be Ty's mate, but I don't have the power to let anyone touch his soul. Only his eternal magic can do that."

I pondered that for a moment.

Eternal magic? What did that mean? It almost reminded me of what I'd overheard through the portal.

A portal the book had encouraged me to create.

To learn more about Lucifer? I wondered. *More about the realm? More about Melek and Az?*

They were both important to Lucifer. So maybe it'd been about them.

Or maybe my first instinct was correct—that the book had been trying to teach me about Lucifer.

"Virtuous magic," I said slowly, recalling the term I'd overheard that day.

Melek's eyes widened, giving me a full view of the array of colors sparkling around his pupils. "Little angel. It's not often that I'm surprised." He tilted his head. "So you have been reading a little, then."

"Not enough to know what it means," I hedged.

"Then I suggest you open up the right book and continue your education," he replied, his words warm against my mouth. "Now, before I go…"

His hand slid from my hip to my lower back as his other palm went to my nape.

I trembled beneath his touch, shocked that he was holding me so close, so intimately, so *perfectly.* I'd been craving a male's touch all week, my hormones begging for a repeat performance with Ajax or Az.

But this… this I hadn't expected. This I hadn't realized I'd even wanted until now.

Which was a lie.

A complete and utter *lie.*

Because I'd been attracted to Melek from the first time I'd seen him. His games were a deterrent, yet also insightful, and I found his candor most recently to be quite charming.

So why isn't he kissing me yet? I wondered. *Why is he holding me so closely without closing the distance between our mouths?*

"To heighten the moment," he whispered, sending a

shock down my spine. *Can he hear me?* "And to remind you of our vows," he went on, his thumb brushing my pulse. "You are my intended, Camillia De la Croix. But it will be your choice in the end. A temporary courtship or a lifelong eternity?"

There are his riddles again, I thought dizzily.

But as his mouth finally touched mine, I couldn't focus enough to decipher his meaning. I was too lost to the energy spilling across my skin from his nearness, his potent magic drowning me in his sinful aroma.

I parted my lips, longing to taste that luscious purity from his very mouth, and he eagerly fed it to me with his tongue. I moaned, relishing the intensity, losing myself to his touch, his power, his *kiss*.

It was slow and purposeful. A thorough introduction to what he had to offer me—*erotic ecstasy.* Melek wouldn't be gentle, but he wouldn't be cruel either. He'd be masterful. Knowing. *Deliciously meticulous.* I could feel it in each stroke of his tongue against mine, his unspoken promise of what he would do to my body, how he would unravel my pleasure with delicate twists and meaningful binds.

His fingers danced along the sash of my robe, making me wonder if he planned to take this further.

But when he paused near the knot, I realized he was trying to convey another message entirely. Something only he seemed to understand. Something I *wanted* him to explain.

Because it felt very much like a licentious pledge, a way of telling me the future without actually speaking any words.

Soon, that touch said. *When you're ready.*

He pulled away, his eyes having darkened to a deep golden hue. "Powerful indeed," he murmured. "Read the book, Camillia. Trust me."

I shuddered, incapable of a response.

Then his eyes went over my shoulder, causing me to freeze.

Oh God. Is Lucifer behind me? Please… please don't be Lucifer.

"Ah, Warden," Melek said, his greeting causing my shoulders to droop with relief.

Until I realized that the *Warden* had just witnessed me kissing Melek.

Fuck.

"I have a training suggestion for you," Melek went on, his hands leaving me as he produced a folded paper within his palm. "Based on what I've seen so far, Cami is in dire need of training on this topic." He walked around me, presumably to hand Ajax the letter.

I turned slowly, afraid of what I would see on the Warden's face, but he was merely looking at the paper with interest.

"Also, Vita has the knowledge Cami is going to need to pass Ty's tests," Melek went on. "Not those dusty old books. So don't waste precious time on something that won't help her in the end."

Tests? I thought. *What tests?*

"She might not be a part of the bride trials anymore," Melek continued, his knowing eyes meeting mine, the color still burning with gold flames. "But I suspect she is undergoing Ty's version of a trial, as are you."

With those cryptic words, he vanished in proper Melek fashion.

Ajax frowned at the space he'd just occupied, then focused on me, his gaze instantly widening. "Did Melek spell that for you?" he asked, his attention shifting down to my attire.

I blinked, the abrupt change in topic leaving me a little bewildered.

And maybe Melek's kiss had something to do with that, too. "I, uh, no." I cleared my throat as I attempted to find my misplaced sanity. "He... I mean, *I* chose this. I assumed I should just make myself comfortable for a while. And it's not like my closet is packed with sweats to wear."

It sounded much lamer than I'd desired. After all, I'd hoped to use this to seduce Ajax, or to garner some sort of a reaction. But now my brain was too fried to focus.

"I like it," Ajax said, surprising me. But then he seemed to pull himself out of his trance and looked down at the paper in his hand. He unfolded it, which made his eyes widen more than before. "Right." He balled up the paper and lined it up with a nearby container, ready to throw it.

A container that would burn it into ash if it passed the rim, just like the laundry hampers did around here.

Acting on instinct, I dove and caught it, needing to know what Melek had suggested for training.

"Don't," Ajax growled. "It's just Melek being Melek."

Ajax's insistence that I not look at the page only made me more inclined to *definitely* look at it.

Working the paper open, I held it up just as Ajax tackled me to the floor. I spun, using my legs to lock around his neck in a practiced martial arts move I'd learned long ago.

Hell Fae survival training with good old Dad.

At least he'd taught me a few useful tricks.

I drew in a breath when I saw that it wasn't a list of instructions but an illustration.

If Melek had drawn this, then he was talented. But it was more than that; it was the complexity of the sketch that held my attention and showed his true abilities.

Because it was me.

Bound in ropes.

In a very erotic pose.

And covered in knots. *Intricate ones.*

"*Camillia*," Ajax growled with a deep husky tone, one that sounded almost pained.

I looked down to see him still trapped between my legs, his cheek pressed against my silky red underwear.

Oh.

CHAPTER 24

AJAX

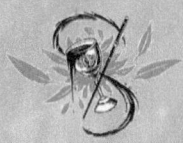

CAMILLIA'S FUCKING scent held me captive between her thighs.

It was like I'd lost the will to fight, my entire being freezing the moment her red panties had come in contact with my face.

All I wanted to do was devour her.

And that fiery outfit of hers wasn't helping matters.

It was warm. Sensual. *Fucking stunning.* I'd hardly seen any of it, her robe having covered the majority of the fabric.

But I'd caught enough of a glimpse to know it fit Camillia perfectly.

"Um," she hummed, squirming a little.

Which only brushed more of her lace-covered heat against my cheek.

Fuck. Her arousal smelled so sweet, so damn *alluring*. I wanted to rip her panties off and lick her. *Bite* her. Saturate myself in her addictive need.

Az had offered me a much-needed outlet just an hour ago with a rough sparring match. I'd been dying from spending the last several days locked up with this delectable female.

It'd taken physical restraint not to touch her. But I knew this was some sort of test from Lucifer. A way to measure my ability to not give in to temptation.

Camillia De la Croix was not meant to be mine. Hell, Melek had just demonstrated that with his kiss. I'd shadowed in just as his lips had taken hers.

I'd been too surprised to leave, my worked-out aggression returning with full force and making my knees shake with the need to react. To push Melek away. Or maybe to join him.

I hadn't known what I'd desired more. I still didn't, even now.

She's not available to me. Not because Lucifer had explicitly said so, but because I knew there would be repercussions if I took her.

That was how Lucifer worked. He might not banish me or kill me, but there would be some sort of punishment involved if I touched Camillia again.

He wanted me to take this task of guarding her seriously, not use it as an excuse to fuck her.

I gritted my teeth as she shifted again, more of her sensual aroma infiltrating my senses.

This was the ultimate trial in self-restraint. That image of her tied up in ropes flashed through my head, followed by her kissing Melek.

He did this to torture me, I decided. *He wants me to lose whatever game this is. But why?*

Melek had to know what Lucifer was up to, that this was all some elaborate way to determine my worthiness. Lucifer strove for control in everything he did. There were no coincidences or frivolous tasks. He did everything with purpose.

Including reassigning me to Camillia as her personal Warden.

I'd said as much to Az earlier after he'd asked why I wasn't playing with Camillia.

"Why the fuck would you sleep on the couch?" he'd asked after I'd mentioned my sore back. "That bed is more than big enough for the two of you, something I know you're aware of since we've shared it together before."

"I gave her the bedroom so she can have her privacy."

That had made his eyebrow arch upward. "Privacy? After everything we've done? Surely she's fine being naked with you now."

"I would really rather not know," I'd gritted out, wincing as Az had taken me down to the mat again. "She's tempting enough while clothed. I don't need her naked, too." My words had come out a little winded, thanks to the impact of Az's tackle.

He'd frozen above me. "Wait… you're not fucking her?"

"No." I'd taken advantage of his startled state and shoved him off me with a blast of magic.

Rather than counter or try to hit me back, he'd gaped at me. "Why the fuck not?"

"Because Lucifer is testing me and I refuse to fail."

Az had snorted. "That's a bullshit reason. Typhos wouldn't put you in a room with one bed if he didn't expect you to fuck her. Yeah, he might pretend to be mad. But he's a sadist. He just enjoys having a reason to punish those who are under his wing."

"But am I really 'under his wing'?" I'd countered. "I'm not a Hell Fae. Not really, anyway."

My power affiliation might have been realigned by Zakkai to secure my Midnight Fae abilities to the Hell Fae Source, but I was still considered an outsider here.

Az had responded with another tackle, this time pinning me to the ground as he straddled my hips.

"Stop second-guessing your place in this world. Stop ignoring your instincts. And stop using Typhos as a reason not to fuck Camillia. Your true fear is in your urge to bite her. Admit that, overcome it, and give her what you both need."

I'd growled in response, denying his accusation by throwing a fist at his face.

And then he'd handed me my ass in typical Az fashion.

But the beating had been a welcome distraction from the ache in my groin.

An ache that had reignited with a fury the moment I'd found Melek holding Camillia.

Now that ache was threatening my sanity as I inhaled deeply, taking in Camillia's flavor through my mouth.

She was wet. I could feel it against my cheek.

Needy.

Wanting.

Practically begging for my touch.

She still hadn't made an effort to move, almost as though she was paralyzed around me.

"Camillia," I repeated, trying again to make her move. "If you don't release me, I'm going to rip these panties off and fuck you with my tongue."

She jolted in response, pressing more of that damp fabric against my face. "Okay," she breathed.

Her thighs remained tight around me, her warmth seeping into my body. It was a sensual invitation, one I needed to refuse.

But a soft moan left her lips as she jerked again, her desire wrapping around my neck like a noose, tightening and threatening to suffocate me if I didn't react.

Az's words kept playing through my head, his

agreement that Lucifer had done this all for a reason, but for a very different reason from what I wanted to believe.

"But he's a sadist. He just enjoys having a reason to punish those who are under his wing."

Is that what this is? I wondered. *Some sort of twisted game? A way to give Lucifer a reason to take control and punish me… because he'll enjoy it?*

That didn't seem too far-fetched to me. Actually, it sounded a lot like Lucifer.

And it would be just like Melek to ensure his Hell Fae King mate was given exactly what he wanted.

I groaned, torn between fighting against their wicked intentions and giving in to the yearning blossoming on my tongue.

Camillia still hadn't moved. She'd even said, "Okay," as though accepting my threat as an offer.

This is fucking insane.

How am I supposed to deny her?

I'd tasted her pussy before, felt her pulse around my cock, and it hadn't been enough. It might *never* be enough.

I nuzzled her damp center as a growl built in my throat. "Melek turned you on." My voice sounded rough, like I wasn't getting enough air. "And now you want my tongue."

"*You* turned me on," she corrected, her body shifting to her back while her legs stayed locked around my neck.

I rolled with her automatically, hypnotized by her seductive form, and ended up on my stomach with my face poised perfectly to please her. I just needed to remove her panties first.

Her thighs squeezed my neck, her bare heels digging into my back.

"I've wanted you all week, Ajax. But you've refused to

touch me." Her tone held a hint of accusation in it as her fingers threaded through my hair.

"Because you're not mine to touch."

"What does that even mean?" she demanded. "I'm not a candidate, right? I can't be claimed. Unless…"

I met her stormy gaze from between her thighs. "Unless what?"

"Is it because of what Melek said? About how he plans to mate me?" The accusatory bite had left her voice, softening her words to a more thoughtful undertone.

"Is that what he told you?" I asked, a pang going through my chest. *Melek wants to mate Camillia?*

She looked a little perplexed. "Yeah, he said we're intended. But it's Melek. He always talks in riddles."

"Hmm." The reverberation from my hum made her jolt, her fingers tightening in my hair. I'd assumed Melek was playing some sort of game, perhaps even using Camillia in a grand scheme.

However, maybe he actually wanted her.

What does that mean for me? For Az?

And why am I even thinking about that? Camillia can't be mine. I can play with her, enjoy her in the moment, but I can't keep her.

Another pang shot through my chest, the sensation familiar yet foreign. Familiar, as I'd felt it countless times after losing my loved ones. And foreign because I didn't expect to experience that feeling with Camillia.

What did it mean?

Why did I care about Melek's intentions for Camillia?

Does Lucifer know? Is that all part of this elaborate test?

Wouldn't Az know about this, too? He was mate-bonded to Lucifer. He'd have to know if Camillia was potentially going to join Melek and Lucifer's dynamic.

Camillia tugged on my hair again, her gray eyes capturing mine once more. "Warden."

"Rebel," I returned.

"*Touch me.*"

I grinned against her wet lace. "I am."

She released an impatient sound, her legs releasing my neck. "If you're going to be difficult, then I'll just go handle myself."

I grabbed her hips as she tried to shimmy her way out from beneath me. Then I crawled up her sexy form and caged her with my arms. "Tell me what you want, little rebel, and I'll consider giving it to you."

Oh, it was a dangerous game I'd just started. But I couldn't help it.

She was temptation incarnate. A prize I wasn't meant to win. A female entirely out of my league.

But I had her pinned to the ground with her weeping heat right against my aching groin.

Because she wants me. She'd admitted it aloud, bringing all my dirty fantasies to life.

Melek might intend to claim her. But I was the one who had her now.

Maybe that was exactly what he wanted. Why else would he leave me with that enchanting drawing of Camillia wrapped up in rope?

I glanced at it now, the paper having been discarded to the side when Camillia had rolled.

It really was a work of art, her bound, naked body primed by silky strands. It made me want to nibble on her exposed nipples while tugging against the carefully placed knot between her thighs.

"Is that what you want?" I pressed, nodding at the drawing. "To be tied up?"

She swallowed. "I... I want your kinks. Your preferences. *You.*"

I blinked down at her in surprise. "You'd prefer that

over being dressed up in silky ribbons?"

"I'd prefer to experience you, Ajax. Your desires. Not Melek's." She lifted her palm to my face, her eyes taking on an intense gleam. "Az isn't here to direct. Melek's image served its purpose. As did my outfit, I think. Now I just want you."

My gaze slid down to her neck and to the robe falling off her shoulders. "You wore this for me?" I asked, amused.

"I wore it for me," she corrected. "But also to see how you reacted to it." Her fingers slid into my hair again, her touch drawing my focus back up to her eyes. "I want you, Ajax."

"I want you, too, Camillia," I admitted.

Part of me had wondered if Az's Phoenix had influenced our last two encounters, his seductive animal a natural beacon of sensuality and grace. While I'd known that I'd craved her—and still very much did—I hadn't been sure of her true inclinations.

Az's Phoenix was a powerful influencer, capable of hypnotizing its prey without even trying. Knowing that Camillia desired me now, here, *alone*, had my body tightening in unadulterated expectation.

She wants me. Just Ajax. Right here. Right now.

And it wasn't because of Melek's influence either; it was because of *me*.

How can I deny this? I marveled. Why *am I even trying?*

Lucifer wanted a reason to punish me? Fine. I could accept that if it meant indulging in this passion. A memory with Camillia was worth a thousand punishments.

She might not be mine for eternity, but she would be mine for today. This week, even.

Just mine, I thought, my gaze going to her mouth. *And I'm going to make every second of it count.*

CHAPTER 25

CAMI

Shadows swirled around me as Ajax engaged his power, making my breath catch in my throat.

I opened my mouth to protest, worried that he'd decided to disappear on me. But then my back hit the mattress of the bed, and Ajax's delicious weight settled upon me again.

I'd been forward with my needs, ensuring he understood exactly where I stood and what I wanted. *Him*.

Maybe Melek had helped stoke the fires burning within me, but it was Ajax who had ignited that flame initially. And I wanted to experience him. Only him. No outside influences. No expectations. Just a joining of our bodies in a sensual dance inspired by mutual gratification.

He'd been the one to bring me to Hell.

Now he would take me to Heaven, if such a plane truly existed.

It was dangerous to want him, but I was done worrying about right and wrong. So what if he was my Warden? Yeah, I might have a sort of fucked-up kidnapping kink going on here. However, my life had always been fucked up.

And I wasn't about to strive for normalcy now.

Ajax's dark gaze burned into mine, the blue rims seeming to disappear beneath a black inferno of lust-driven need. He hadn't told me what his preferences were, but I hoped he was about to show me.

His nose skimmed my cheek, his breath warm against my skin. "Your blood sings to me, sweet rebel," he whispered, his body shuddering on top of mine. "But I can't bite you."

"You can cut me," I offered, shivering at the suggestion. Az had nicked my breast the first time we'd played, giving Ajax the essence he'd craved. It'd stung at first, but then Ajax's mouth had stolen the pain away and replaced it with exquisite pleasure.

I wanted to feel that again.

To give him what he needed while he indulged in my expectations, too.

A low rumble left his chest as he started kissing my neck, his palms skimming up my sides. We were both still fully clothed—me in my robe and babydoll dress, him in gray sweatpants and a T-shirt. I could tell he'd showered again recently, maybe even with Az.

Did they fuck? I wondered. *Or did they fight?*

Maybe both.

My mind painted an erotic picture of them fighting while fucking, which only had my legs tensing even more around Ajax's waist. The two males were lethal creatures, their hungers darkly intense. I shared in that carnal desire, craving their roughness. Their masculine touch. Their fierce *need*.

Ajax's hands reached my shoulders, his mouth going to my ear. "As much as I like this silky material on you, I need it to disappear." His words were followed by a blast of magic that singed my skin, causing me to gasp.

Warmth flooded my veins, enhanced by the scent of pine and mint.

I shuddered, goose bumps pebbling across my heated flesh as the fabric seemed to melt away from my body, leaving me naked beneath Ajax. "That's a handy trick," I breathed.

He hummed in agreement, another wave of power removing his own clothes. "It is. But don't mistake it for me rushing the moment. I'm going to make you so ready for me that you'll be begging me to fuck you."

I was already halfway there, my boldness having forced words from my mouth before that I hadn't anticipated saying.

But somehow I'd known he'd needed to hear my desires voiced aloud.

And it'd worked.

Oh, yes, how it worked, I marveled as his pierced cock met my sensitive center. I arched into him in response, earning a chuckle from the male above me.

He nibbled on my ear, then resumed his path of kissing my neck down to my collarbone. I ran my fingers over his back, reveling in the cords of muscle and the way they bunched as he moved.

So powerful.

I could feel his potent energy humming beneath his skin, the magnetic pulse calling to my inner spirit. He was all strength and man, his Midnight Fae essence marking him as unbreakable and that much more intense.

His lips closed around my nipple, making me jolt beneath him, his teeth skimming my sensitive nub in a promise for more.

I scratched my nails up his spine, reminding him of my

offer. I wasn't afraid of feeling a little pain, nor was I afraid to give it. He groaned in response, his abdomen tensing as he shifted his hips downward, away from the apex between my thighs.

"I threatened to lick you, didn't I?" His words reverberated against my nipple as he followed them with a subtle tracing of his tongue. "Although, I suppose you did eventually move." He nipped my stiff peak, his wicked gaze flashing up to mine. "So what should I do, little rebel?"

"Definitely follow through on your threat." My reply came out husky, my core throbbing with need. "I want to feel your mouth on me."

"It is on you," he murmured, switching to my other breast. "I intend to taste every inch of you by the time I'm done."

Yes, please, I thought, gasping as the hint of cold metal touched my side. It was so sudden and unexpected that I froze, only for Ajax to trace the sharp item up my rib cage to my breast. A tinge of pine-scented magic followed, telling me he'd conjured the blade.

My heart skipped several beats as he brought it up to my chest, his dark gaze capturing and holding mine as though seeking my consent. Or maybe he just wanted to watch my reaction.

I licked my lips, my focus darting to the dagger before returning to his face. Then I dared him with my stare to continue, wanting him to use me. Claim me. Make me his. Even if just for this moment in time.

He drew the sharp tip along the fleshy part of my breast, not hard enough to bleed, just to tease, then pressed down right above my nipple to create a pinprick. A shiver traversed my spine, the subtle pinch exciting my nerve endings.

Ajax made a second cut, the two holes reminding me of a vampiric bite.

And then his mouth descended, his tongue gently soothing the sting.

I swallowed, my toes curling at the sensual touch. It wasn't overwhelming so much as a slow-burn sensation that crept along my skin, making my heart flutter in my chest.

Ajax created another set of cuts on my opposite breast, repeating the motion and sending more of that blissful warmth through my veins.

It was unlike anything I'd ever experienced, his touch not nearly as rough as I would have expected after our last two sessions. But this was Ajax. His preferences. His desires. It seemed he enjoyed drawing out pleasure, teasing my nerves, and stirring butterflies in my abdomen.

I trembled as he ventured downward, his knife following his mouth and pausing at my hip bone, where he made two more slices. They stung a bit more, the skin thinner there, but it added to the overall effect of his sensuality.

Every part of me felt primed, ready to explode, overheated by his arousing methods.

How is this even possible? I marveled. *It's like he's barely touched me, yet I feel entirely owned from those few marks alone.*

He added a fourth set along my inner thigh, his mouth sealing around the cuts to lap at my essence. My veins pulsed in the best way, my heart singing in time with his hypnotic tongue.

His dagger dug a little harsher into my opposite leg, causing me to flinch as he yanked me back from my foggy state, only to send me that much deeper into it as his lips closed around the new wound.

Now I could feel him drinking. Truly swallowing my

essence. Pulling my life into his own, drawing me further into this strange cocoon of blistering sensation.

I felt dizzy.

Overwhelmed.

So fucking hot.

It seemed knife play was one of Ajax's kinks. Or perhaps he'd reserved this just for me. Regardless, he was skilled, and I was utterly lost to his ministrations.

My fingers locked in his hair as I held him against my thigh, demanding more, wanting him to take his fill and continue to drug me with his Midnight Fae kiss.

But he moved away a few moments later, his mouth traveling upward to my weeping center.

"You smell fucking amazing," he murmured, his nose running up my damp slit to the sensitive beacon that begged for his touch. "I'm going to devour you, Camillia."

God, I already felt devoured by him, my entire body burning beneath his touch. Who knew knife play could be so damn stimulating?

"Please," I whispered, my fingers knotting even more with his hair. "I... I need more."

"I know, little rebel." His words vibrated my delicate flesh. "But I promised to make you really beg. And you will."

His mouth captured my clit before I could reply, his tongue eliciting a scream from my throat. My hips bucked against him, but his hand on my belly held me down, his blade lying dangerously beneath it.

If I moved again, the tip would dig into my skin.

And fuck if that didn't make me even wetter.

I liked the threat of a punishment should I misbehave, which probably made me insane. But it was Ajax. It was us. Nothing about any of this was sane.

Violent quakes threatened to overwhelm me as Ajax

swirled his tongue against me, his skill sending tingles through every ounce of my being.

I moaned his name, my grip in his hair tightening.

So close, I thought, shocked by how quickly he'd taken me to the edge. *So very close.*

Everything burned, my heart racing in my chest as time seemed to still.

And then it all stopped.

"*Ajax.*"

His stubble prickled against my stimulated flesh, his mouth forming a taunting grin that rivaled his evil look.

I growled, frustrated and turned on and fucking overwhelmed. "You're killing me."

"Am I?" His finger slid through my slick folds, finding my entrance and slipping inside. "Mmm, so wet."

He laved my sex again, eliciting a deep moan from my throat.

"So ready to come," he continued. "But I want to feel that sweet pussy strangle my cock again."

His finger and mouth disappeared, leaving me panting beneath him as he crawled up my prone form.

"Are you ready to beg, Camillia?" he asked softly. "Or would you rather take what you need?"

He settled onto his elbows on either side of my head, his cock a brand against my lower body. I was practically panting beneath him, ready to say whatever he wanted me to say, but his last question caught me off guard.

"Or would you rather take what you need?"

I liked the sound of that.

Grabbing his shoulders, I gave him a little nudge to see what he would do.

He grinned and said, "Option two, I see. All right, Camillia." He rolled off me and onto his back. "I have no limits. Take whatever you want."

Oh, I was very much going to take him up on that.

His smile grew as I straddled him, his cock hot and ready against my core. But I wanted to tease him like he'd teased me. More than that, I wanted to *taste* him. Feel that piercing in my mouth. Drive him to the point of madness. Make *him* beg *me* to come.

I leaned down to kiss him, reveling in my flavor on his tongue, and gently bit down. He groaned in response, clearly liking the subtle pain. I'd use that reaction to my advantage, see what other sounds I could coax from him.

Dragging my teeth away from him, I looked for the knife he'd used but didn't see it anywhere. He must have magically dispelled it at some point during our position shifts because now his hands were tucked behind his head.

"Don't move," I told him.

"As you wish," he returned, his shaft pulsing between my thighs.

So he enjoyed me taking charge a little, I mused. *Good.*

I licked a path down his torso, admiring the muscular dips and planes along the way. His eyes resembled two black pools as he watched me, his need a palpable presence that throbbed between us. I reciprocated that need but wanted to make this last.

To torture us both.

To *enjoy* the eventual gratification.

My insides clenched with the desire to take him to the hilt, to ride him, but my mouth required attention first. I wanted to swallow that pierced head, feel him pulsate in my throat, and take him to the edge of an orgasm, just like he'd done to me not moments ago.

Quid pro quo, I thought, reaching his groin.

Precum glistened on the tip of his arousal, the faint hint of my own pleasure touching his skin. I licked him from base to head before taking that sensual offering from him and allowing his flavor to blossom on my tongue.

He hissed in reply, his muscles bulging as he fought not to move and take control. I suspected this was a gift of sorts—him allowing me to lead—and I vowed not to belittle it by wasting time.

Instead, I opened my mouth and took him as far as I could without choking, which I found a little more difficult with his piercing.

"*Fuck.*" The word left him on a snarl of sound, causing my thighs to clench.

God, I want him inside me.

But not yet.

I need him just as lost to my touch as...

I moaned as more of his precum coated my tongue, his excitement an erotic flavor that ratcheted up my own yearning. I was captivated by his essence, his body a work of art that I wanted to conquer. To mark. To claim for the rest of time.

It was such a visceral reaction, so unexpected and new.

This craving for him is unnatural.

And yet, I couldn't stop sucking him, my mouth working up and down his shaft, his piercing nudging my throat each time. It was just as amazing as I'd anticipated, his girth a welcome presence in my mouth.

"*Camillia.*" He grabbed my hair, yanking me off his cock and dragging me up his body. "Put me inside you. *Now.*"

His control had clearly snapped, but I didn't care. His command was one I longed to obey. Every part of me was on fire, my veins exploding with an inferno only Ajax could contain.

I straddled his hips and positioned him, then screamed as he thrust upward into my waiting heat.

Reality spun into a dark web of euphoric hunger, both of us having lost our souls to the physical demand growing between us.

He sat up, his arms coming around me, his hand at my nape, and his mouth devouring mine.

I was barely aware of how he'd moved that quickly, of where my body started and ended, because every part of me was glued to Ajax. My legs curled around his waist, securing me to his lap as he thrust harshly into me.

That piercing, I marveled, my mind blanking as rapture threatened to consume me. *God, that piercing…*

He was so deep. So thick. So fucking unreal.

I matched his pace, my hips enchanted by his sexual dance. His prowess. His *vigor.*

"Oh God," I panted, my insides twisting sharply as pleasure churned through my lower belly. "Close…"

I couldn't properly form sentences, but Ajax had to know, had to *feel*, that I was about to come. That all of this pent-up need and energy between us was about to pour out of me in an—

Explosion.

Ajax swallowed my scream, his palm on my nape forcing me to continue kissing him as I unraveled on one of the most intense climaxes of my existence.

Then his opposite hand disappeared between us, his thumb circling my clit to draw violent tremors from my being. I squirmed, the sensations too much, but he wouldn't release me, his strength surpassing my own as his piercing massaged me from the inside.

Touching me.
So deep.
Right there.
Ohhh…

More quakes were building, another eruption already

on the horizon, every part of me too primed, overly stimulated, and weak in his arms.

"Ajax," I spoke into his mouth. "*Ajax.*"

"You can take it," he promised, his thumb and cock destroying me below. "Now *scream.*"

This time he didn't swallow the sound. He allowed me to fully erupt, his name loud and ringing through the room as my body raged in time with the fiery walls.

Ajax flipped me onto my back, his hips punishing mine as wave after wave of orgasmic bliss stole my consciousness.

I swore he made me come a third time. Maybe he did. I was too far gone in my oblivion to know. I just kept shaking, my limbs going numb with the force of my passion. *Too much*, I thought, delirious. *But oh, not enough...*

Ajax seemed to agree, his arousal throbbing inside me as he kept pushing, thrusting, *owning*.

My breaths came in sharp pants, my heart beating too fast, my being replete and half-paralyzed from our fucking.

Yet I could feel his cock enlarging inside me, his peak cresting and threatening to destroy us both.

Because he was going to make me explode again. I could feel it, my body reacting to his, learning his preferences, becoming his to master.

I grabbed his shoulder, my nail digging into his skin, needing to anchor myself to something.

Only to unravel in the next breath as we both fell headfirst over a cliff into a profound darkness where our entire existence solely revolved around each other.

I was barely aware of his tongue coaxing mine, his mouth claiming a kiss meant to cement our souls.

Not as mates. Not really. But as something far greater than mere lovers.

I didn't understand it. I doubted he did either. And

rather than question it, I reveled in it. Reveled in him. Relaxing. Existing. *Enjoying*.

His arms were around me, his body holding mine as he acted as a protective cage above me. Lazy kisses. Murmured platitudes. So much tenderness that I barely recognized the Midnight Fae inside me.

But it was perfect.

Beautiful.

Hot.

"We're doing that again as soon as you're ready," he whispered, his vow making my thighs squeeze around his legs.

He would get no complaint from me.

Because this was so much better than studying Hell Fae life. So much better than having to think about the future or what everything meant. So much better than worrying about Vita and the source.

This was simply living in the moment.

And I could certainly get used to that.

CHAPTER 26

MELEK

CAMI'S PLEASURE warmed my soul, improving my mood slightly.

But I couldn't shake the frustration darkening my mind, the very real anger I felt toward the one I loved most in this life.

I stood in our bedchamber, waiting for that love to return.

My Ty.

My reason for being.

My *mate*.

He knew I was angry, could clearly sense it in our link, but he hadn't tried to reach out yet. However, I could feel his presence nearing my own. Ty was on his way here, his mind no doubt prepared for battle.

I sipped my wine and paced, my silky robes swishing in my wake. I'd changed out of my royal attire the moment I'd felt Camillia's intrigue, knowing she and Ajax were about to play. And the last thing I wanted was to be hard beneath my uncomfortable trousers.

Silk was a much nicer fabric caress to my

uncomfortable erection. Maybe I'd let Ty truly relieve me of it.

But only if he begged.

"Lucifer made it very clear that if it happens again, he'll kill me."

"He said if I went near his source again, he'd kill me."

Cami's words played through my mind, making me nearly crush the crystal stem in my hand. It was very rare for me to feel upset. Very rare for me to experience true fury. But those few sentences from her had accomplished it.

Knowing Ty, he'd just been trying to scare her. However, I needed to be sure.

The source would have slaughtered her if it suspected she was a true threat. He knew that. I knew that. Everyone in this fucking kingdom would comprehend that if they were told the story.

While I understood that he felt a need to protect himself, us, the source, all of it, he couldn't threaten a soul so closely connected to mine.

She can touch that source for a reason, I thought. *Just like she can read Vita for a reason.*

And that reason was very clear to me—*she's meant to be ours.*

Not just mine and Ty's, but Az and Ajax's, too. The five of us would make a formidable circle. It would only make Ty stronger, allowing us all to even better protect his realm and those within it, and it would chase away this most recent threat.

Virtuous Fae.

Az and I had confirmed that their magic was somehow involved in these illegal portals. Which meant someone from the past had decided to restart old games.

Games they wouldn't dare play if Ty had a stronger circle.

Camillia was the key. I'd known it from the moment I'd found her reading his book. She could assume I'd done something to enable that ability all she wanted, but that would never make it true.

The truth was that Ty's soul had seen a potential match in her and had granted her access to his deepest secrets. *Vita*.

That couldn't be ignored. It couldn't be overlooked.

And it most certainly could not be *killed*.

"Hmm," Ty hummed as he appeared in the room, using his teleportation abilities rather than the door. "I see the Warden has finally given in to temptation. Are you angry because you weren't invited?"

I slowly turned to face him, my gaze narrowing up at him. "I wouldn't need to be invited. We both know if I wanted to fuck them, they wouldn't say no."

"But you do want to fuck them, Melek. So why not try?"

"Because it's not my time yet," I told him.

And it wouldn't be the right time until Camillia chose me.

Ajax, too.

Until then, I would court them in my own way. Well, maybe not Ajax. Although, I wouldn't mind some group play with Camillia between us. He was more to Az's tastes than mine, but I respected his potential for our circle and liked that he was taking care of my intended.

Thoroughly, it seemed.

Because they were already playing again.

The heat of Camillia's passion singed my veins, making my dick throb with need.

But staring up at Ty grounded me in the moment, my anger flourishing once more.

His eyebrow arched. "You're furious with me." Not a

question, but a statement. Because he could no doubt see the hues of anger swirling in my gaze.

"I am."

Some of his amusement seemed to melt into an expression of concern. He could easily look into my mind to find answers, but that wasn't how we played. We valued communication, and sometimes riddles disguised as games. He wouldn't intrude on my privacy unless he felt it absolutely necessary.

"Hmm," he hummed again, walking over to the bar to pour himself a drink—something I would normally do for him but hadn't bothered to now. "Would you like a refill, my prince?"

My prince instead of *little prince*.

A concession on his part.

Or perhaps a show of ownership.

Maybe a bit of both.

"No." I set my glass down and slid my hands into the pockets of my robe as Camillia's pleasure sang through my blood.

Yes, Ajax is certainly taking care of our intended, I thought, shivering as my groin tightened in expectation.

Ty turned and leaned back against the bar while he sipped his scotch, his intense sapphire eyes on me as he waited for me to speak.

Normally, I would dance around my words and play with him a little. But I was too angry to even try.

"You threatened Camillia." The words tasted sour in my mouth. "Told her you would kill her if she went near the source again."

"Yes. I did." No apology lurked in his tone, just resolve. "I don't tolerate threats to our realm, Melek. More so, I won't tolerate a threat that could hurt you or me. Nothing about that should surprise you."

Oh, it didn't surprise me. It just infuriated me that he couldn't see beyond his own need to *protect* to consider alternatives to the situation. "Can you for one minute think about what this could mean, Ty? Try to ponder the potential of why this female can not only read Vita but also touch the source?"

He stared at me. "I can see no positive reason for any of this, no."

"Because you're too blinded by your instincts," I argued.

"And you're too blinded by yours as well," he countered, slamming his drink down. "All you see is a pretty girl with a pussy you want to fuck. So go do it. Get her out of your system. Meanwhile, I'll be protecting you and the kingdom we created."

I bristled at the insinuation that I cared more about getting laid than supporting our realm. "You truly think I'm allowing my hormones to rule my mind? That all I feel for her is lust?"

Because that would make me a shallow angel indeed.

I stepped toward him, his words having added fuel to my already burning fire. "Everything I do in this life is for you, Ty. It's always been *for you*. Every deal. Every game. Every *decision*. Why would Camillia De la Croix be any different? Because you think I'm so desperately in need that I can't see beyond her beauty?"

His jaw clenched. "I think she has a magic snatch that has enchanted all my best men."

I scoffed at that. "It's not about her pussy, Ty. It's about *her*. She's special. And you're the only one who refuses to see it."

"Oh, I see it," he snapped. "I see exactly what she's done to you, to Az, to Ajax right fucking now. I just don't see *why*."

323

"Exactly." I stopped right in front of him. "Because you refuse to see beyond your own bias. She's a female and therefore can't be trusted. But not all women are Vivaxia, Ty."

He flinched at the forbidden name, the traitorous bitch one we rarely discussed. However, he needed to hear this.

"You've spent thousands of years hating female fae because of the one who wronged you, and I've stood by and allowed it because I understand. Fuck, I was there. But at some point, we have to heal. We have to believe again. We have to *trust*."

The source was a part of him. It rarely accepted females for a reason. It was time he realized that.

I pressed my hand to his heart, only for him to step away from me, his expression thunderous. "And you want me to do that with *her*? The female who curtsies like a demented pelican?"

I blinked at him. "What?"

He waved a hand. "It doesn't matter. None of this matters, Melek. She's a passing fancy, one I'm allowing you to have while the enjoyment lasts, but there will be no *us* involved here. She's your toy for you to fuck and throw away. I want no part of it."

"Then why is she in the guest wing?"

"Because *you* put her there," he returned. "I would have kept her in a dungeon, except she's proved she can escape them rather easily. So I allowed it and used it as an opportunity to test Ajax. A test he is currently failing, I might add, because he's just as hung up on this female as you are."

I shook my head. "Ajax doesn't deserve to be tested. He's faithful to us. He always has been. Az guaranteed that."

"Then why is he playing with the female when he's supposed to be guarding her?"

"Because Az's Phoenix has imprinted on her, and Az and Ajax are more mate-bonded than they realize. So both of them are drawn to her," I answered bluntly.

Shock was a rare emotion for the Hell Fae King, but his eyes widened with it now.

I merely looked at him. "You would have noticed this if you weren't so busy trying to vilify the female. If I didn't know better, I'd say you were a little jealous. Telling her to call me *Prince Melek*?" I snorted. "You know I hate that, *King Lucifer*."

Ty took a few steps away, his hand running over his face. "I've been distracted by the portal issue and managing the various Hell Fae Kings."

I allowed him the excuse, as it was a good one.

But that didn't detract from the point I needed to make.

"If you kill her, Ty, you'll be hurting everyone in your inner circle. Not just me. Hell, Az's Phoenix may not even let you. It tried to kill Ajax the other day for simply interrogating her."

Ty winced and sat on our bed, a variety of emotions spilling through his usually stern features. It was moments like this that allowed me to see the heart of my mate, the true vulnerabilities he hid beneath an iron shield of confidence.

But he didn't look all that confident now.

He looked concerned. A little broken. Forlorn.

"She's a threat," he whispered.

"If the source saw her as such, it would have annihilated her. Instead, it allowed her to live."

"By shoving her back to the Human Realm," he pointed out.

"I think she put herself there because she didn't know how to return to our realm," I told him. "So she went to the last place she'd felt safe. That wasn't the source's doing; it was her own."

I brought him his drink, but he didn't try to sip from it, just held it in his lap as he met my gaze. "Then why did a strand darken from her touch?"

"Perhaps it was meant as a sign, a way to tell you she was there." I shrugged. "There are a lot of reasons I could come up with, but they would all be guesses."

Which made it a senseless game of trying to say why the source had reacted the way it had. The important point was that it hadn't tried to kill her. That had to mean something, right?

However, rather than voice that part aloud, I said, "All I know is, the source is part of you. Vita is part of you. And those two parts have opened their gates to Camillia. Maybe she's a threat. Or maybe she's something else entirely. But you'll never know if you won't even try to get to know her."

"What makes you think she even wants to get to know me?" he asked, some of his hardness returning. "Or maybe that's the point of all this—a way to lure me into a trap. It's exactly what *she* would do."

"Camillia isn't Vivaxia," I told him, unafraid to use the evil bitch's name. "But a good way to confirm that would be to get to know Cami better, hmm? And you're correct— she probably doesn't want to know you right now since you *threatened her life.*"

A subtle wind blew around his shoulders, causing his long hair to ruffle like his old wings. "Your anger is unnerving me, Melek."

"Why? Because you want to counter it with some of your own eternal fire?" I taunted him, aware that my king possessed enough anger to burn the entire universe down a thousand times over. "You threatened my intended. I'm allowed to be angry."

"I'm trying to protect you," he grated out. "And you're being fucking ungrateful."

I took a step back, my heart squeezing in my chest. "I am not ungrateful, Typhos. But I'm starting to think you might be."

The fury fled from his features, replaced by a remorseful expression that made him appear so much younger than his ancient aura. "Melek——"

"I know you're under a lot of pressure to restart the bride trials. And I know this portal mess is stressing you out. However, I won't allow you to speak to me like this, Typhos. Nor will I allow you to hurt Camillia De la Croix without proper cause. Sometimes those we see as threats can become our greatest allies. But only if we let them."

There wasn't much else for me to say, so I disappeared into our closet to change. Cami's pleasure still swam through my veins, but my mood had plummeted to the depths of Lucifer's fall.

I was in the middle of pulling on my pants when Ty appeared behind me, his arms encircling my bare torso as he tugged me back into his chest.

"Don't leave like this, little prince," he whispered. "Please." He buried his face in my neck, his hair falling across my shoulders. "I'll always protect you, even when you don't want me to."

"I don't need you to protect me from Camillia."

"You can't be sure of that." His voice was soft, but his words were sure. "But you're right. I can't be certain she's a threat until I properly evaluate her. However, I haven't had time."

"I know." I turned toward him, my palms going to his

face. "And I'm not asking you to do it immediately. But I am asking that you not do anything rash—like kill her if she accidentally touches the source again."

His jaw clenched beneath my hands. "I don't want her near the source."

"I don't think she wants to be near the source either," I told him. "But she's struggling to control her power. Which tells me she has no idea what she is or where she actually came from."

"I'd have Az renew his search for her father, but we need him focused on the Virtuous Fae."

"Yes," I agreed. "So keeping Camillia here with Ajax for the time being makes sense. You can keep a closer eye on her and Ajax will guard her, all while Az and I continue our hunt."

Which had unfortunately not gone all that well so far, but we were still tracking a few leads. We'd only come back here to share our findings with Ty and gather some supplies. I'd handled the former before going to see Camillia while Az had put in a few sparring hours with Ajax and was now hunting for the items we needed.

Ty's forehead touched mine. "How can I trust Ajax to guard her when he's busy fucking her?"

"I would argue that him fucking her is going to make him that much more inclined to protect her, Ty."

"I don't want her *protected*. I want her *watched*."

My lips twitched. "Those two desires often go hand in hand, and our dear Warden is well suited for the position."

Ty grunted. "That remains to be seen."

"You just want an excuse to play with him," I told him. "You forget that I know you, my king. Punishment is your foundation, and Ajax has just earned one in your mind. You're not upset. You're excited. Tell me I'm wrong."

His blue eyes glittered as he met my gaze. "He's given

me a reason to remove her from the trials. One that I can actually explain to our fae."

"But he's not a Hell Fae," I hedged. "He can't claim her."

"No, but he can be punished for trying," he said, that hint of excitement I'd anticipated coming through in his words. He didn't sound excited, nor did he look it, but as I'd told him, I knew him.

"And she can be removed for being tainted by his Midnight Fae touch," I added. "Yes?"

He nodded. "She's no longer suitable for the trials. So I'll let the Warden have her, but not before I make an example of them."

"How merciful of you," I joked.

He lifted a shoulder. "It's better than explaining the truth. For now, anyway."

"You could say I claimed her. I wouldn't mind."

"But our Hell Fae might. I can't afford to play favorites. Not now. Not after everything that's happened."

"And that includes our Warden," I replied, following his logic. "You can't just give her to him as a gift; he has to earn it."

"Or be punished for trying to take it without permission," he countered.

"Locking them in a room together was all the permission he needed, Ty."

"He should know better than to accept something that easily. Nothing is what it seems in my realm."

My lips twitched. "Fair. And you'll make sure he understands that soon."

"I will."

"And you'll enjoy it, too," I said, my palm finding his hard cock and giving it a stroke through his black pants. "You're already enjoying the prospect of it."

"Maybe I'm just intending to enjoy you," he murmured, his palm going to my nape as his hot breath parted my lips. "Shall I kneel for you, my prince? Prove how grateful I am that you're in my life?"

I hummed, considering the offer. "It would be a decent start to the apology I desire, yes." Not that he would ever really voice it. Ty's version of remorse was usually more physical than verbal. Though, he could occasionally say the words when he felt they were truly needed.

His lips brushed mine. "Then allow me to start making amends," he said, his palm easily sliding into my pants, as I hadn't finished buttoning or zipping them yet.

Another explosion from Cami rolled through me at the precise moment Ty found my shaft, causing me to groan both at his touch and her overwhelming passion.

I swallowed, my mind fracturing beneath a wave of hot need. "Promise me you won't hurt her without talking it through with me first," I managed to get out. "Vow it."

"I promise not to hurt her unless she proves to be a viable threat or puts you in danger in some way," he replied instead.

It wasn't perfect.

But it was better than before.

I can work with this, I decided, nodding in acceptance of his vow. *We'll improve upon it in time.*

"You can start demonstrating your gratitude now," I told him.

He smiled against my mouth. "It would be my pleasure, little prince."

CHAPTER 27

AJAX

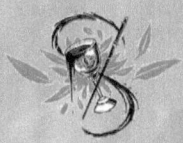

So BEAUTIFUL, I thought, my gaze on Camillia's resting form. She wasn't exactly asleep, just dozing in my arms as we both recovered from our third round of fucking.

Her stamina rivaled mine, proving my precious theories wrong regarding her human side making her more fragile. Whatever genetics she'd inherited from her father had clearly overshadowed her mother's mortal influence.

I supposed that made sense; most Halflings favored their fae heritage.

"What has you so thoughtful?" Camillia murmured groggily, her gray eyes half-open and staring up at me from my shoulder. She'd curled her naked body into mine, her arm resting on my abdomen while our legs tangled together below.

"Your heritage," I admitted. "Or rather, your durability as a Halfling and how your Hell Fae origin clearly overpowers your human side."

She considered that for a long moment, her brow furrowing. "Actually, that reminds me of what Melek said earlier."

I ran my fingers through her dark blonde hair as I asked, "What did he say?"

"That he doesn't think the book took me to the source. He thinks I did it myself." Her stormy eyes held a note of worry in them. "If I did, it wasn't intentional. And I have no idea how I did it."

I wasn't sure if she was confiding this to me because she assumed I already knew or because she wanted someone to talk to about it. Maybe both.

"He told me I need to read Vita more, that I need to trust it to guide me," she continued. "He also said the book is part of Lucifer's soul."

My eyebrows rose. "He said all that?"

She nodded. "I'm not sure what to think about it. Everything... it's a lot. Even the Midnight Fae Source Architect insinuated that there was something unique about me. But what could it be? My dad was just a normal Hell Fae."

"Maybe he wasn't that normal," I suggested. "I mean, he was able to evade Az's Phoenix. Just like you."

"So maybe he's been hiding near the source...?" she asked, her brow furrowing. "Wouldn't Lucifer feel him there?"

"One would think, but he didn't sense you, did he?"

"I don't know," she admitted. "But if he does again, I'm a dead fae."

"Maybe, maybe not," I hedged. "I know he said that, but if what Melek told you is true about wanting to mate you, then I don't think it's going to be that simple."

She chewed her lower lip, her brow crinkling again. "I don't know what to think about that either. I'm not sure if I want a mate. I'm... I'm not sure what I want in general."

"Probably not what most men want to hear after

spending several hours in bed with a woman," I joked. "But I understand."

And I meant it, too. I had no idea what I wanted either. All I knew was that I wanted Camillia. However, I couldn't keep her long-term. So I'd enjoy her while I could and go from there.

An uncomfortable sensation brewed in my chest, one that reminded me again of my past and of the lives I'd lost.

Camillia had gotten under my skin, maybe even clawed her way into my frozen heart. But I was a realist. I knew this couldn't go beyond the present. Lucifer would never allow it.

Unless Az is right and all he wants to do is punish me for fun.

So what would that mean? What would it look like for me? For Camillia? For Az? Was Lucifer playing a long game, using me as a pawn for some grander purpose?

Is Melek? I wondered in the next beat. *Is he trying to maneuver me into a certain place?*

Lucifer and Melek had always been enigmas to me. While I understood much of Lucifer's intentions with the Nightmare Fae and the Hell Fae Realm, I'd never truly understood him—the man behind the Hell Fae King mask.

But Az does, I mused. *And Az thinks Lucifer is playing with me.*

"You're thoughtful again," Camillia said softly, her hand reaching up to brush my face. "About what I said or something else?"

I pondered that for a few seconds, debating how to answer.

She'd been truthful with me, so I wanted to return the favor.

Mostly because we seemed to have reached a more

comfortable balance with each other, one that I didn't want to disrupt.

"I'm thinking about something Az told me earlier." I cleared my throat, trying to figure out a way to word it but decided to be blunt. "He didn't understand why I was refraining from touching you, so I told him I suspect Lucifer is testing me. Az laughed and essentially said any test designed by Lucifer is meant to be failed because the Hell Fae King likes to dole out punishment."

Her eyes widened. "That's why you weren't touching me? Because you think it's a test?"

"I know it is," I told her. "He reassigned me to guard you for a reason. He wanted to see if I could refrain from the temptation, or, if Az is to be believed, how long it would take me to refrain."

Her nose scrunched. "Oh. That can't be good."

I lifted a shoulder. "I accepted that a memory with you is worth whatever punishment Lucifer assigns to me."

Camillia startled at my words. "You... you decided that?"

I dipped my chin in confirmation, then shrugged again. "I don't regret it, Camillia. I think I would have regretted not fucking you again, though." I brushed my lips against her forehead. "I *know* I would have regretted it."

She stared at me for a long moment, emotion touching her gaze. "I actually think that might be the nicest thing you've ever said to me."

My lips curled, humor touching my chest. "I'm pretty sure I complimented your pussy about a dozen times this last round. That wasn't considered nice?"

She rolled her eyes. "Men in the throes of passion are willing to admit a lot of things they don't actually mean."

"True, but I meant every word."

"Well, I still think saying a memory with me is worthy

of punishment is nicer," she replied, her voice softening at the end. "It's almost as though you actually like me now, Warden."

"I think I do, rebel," I returned.

"Then maybe you can start calling me *Cami* instead of *Camillia*. You did a few times before… the incident."

"The incident?" I echoed. "You mean the one where you ran away?"

Her gaze narrowed. "I didn't run away. Not on purpose, anyway. But if you're going to—"

I grabbed her sides and tickled her, drawing a shocked gasp from her as she started to squirm.

"Hey!"

I continued my assault, dragging her beneath me as she giggled and fought, trying to thwart my hands and wiggle her way out of my hold.

When I had her right where I wanted her, I pinned her with my hips against hers and captured her wrists above her head. She was panting from the effort, soft laughs still escaping her as the residual sensations reached her nerves.

I grinned at her gorgeous smile, her angry eyes resembling furious storm clouds. It was an intoxicating combination, one that had me kissing her nose and then her cheek. "I know you didn't try to run away," I whispered softly. "I believe you, *Cami*."

She shuddered beneath me, those storm clouds immediately turning into something more intense, her body preparing for a fourth round.

I was just as ready as her, as evidenced by my hardness against her belly.

But right when I was about to kiss her, a deep voice said, "Attention, Hell Fae Kingdom."

I froze on top of Cami, then immediately looked at the black screen in the corner of the bedroom. Lucifer's face filled the area, his upper body clad in his usual black-on-black suit. Cami followed my gaze, her escalating heartbeat singing in my ears.

"I know you all have been eagerly awaiting an update regarding the Hell Fae Bride Trials," Lucifer went on. "After much deliberation, we have decided to resume the trials in two days' time. As with the last trials, I will be hosting a viewing party at Purgatory. All Hell Fae are welcome."

Yes, but not Midnight Fae, I thought. Which wasn't entirely true. If I wanted to go to Purgatory, Lucifer would allow it. But I'd never felt very welcome in the club, given my roots, so I hadn't spent much time there.

"If you have a candidate you're sponsoring," Lucifer continued, "I recommend gifts that may aid in surviving the Marsh Lands. Like last time, I won't elaborate on the trials beyond providing the location. There will be no favoritism when it comes to surpassing these challenges."

"Marsh Lands?" Cami whispered. "That's what I was starting to read about earlier."

I nodded, aware of the book she'd chosen.

"In closing, I will reiterate that the trials will not be extended to the Netherworld Kingdom or Morpheus Kingdom. The kings of those kingdoms are hosting their own trials with the Monsters Night brides. Those brides will not be eligible for Hell Fae mating."

He paused, his expression informing the kingdom that there would be no arguing that point.

"If there are any questions, I will be in Purgatory in two days' time to meet with you all," he concluded. "Thank you and good night."

The screen went black.

I swallowed. *The bride trials are resuming.* I wasn't exactly surprised, but I thought Lucifer would want to wait until after the portal issue was fully addressed. Apparently not.

"So…" Cami trailed off, her voice reminding me that I was still on top of her. I rolled to the side and she rotated with me, both of us sharing the same pillow. "Do we, uh, have to go to Purgatory to, um, watch?"

"Not likely. It would be too risky for you as the only female in the room, and I'm not exactly welcome there as an outsider."

She frowned. "You're an outsider?"

"I'm… distinctly other. A Midnight Fae with ties to the Hell Fae Source. It was the only way for me to become the Warden." I explained to her how Zakkai had reassigned my power to be a mixture of both. "He essentially turned me into an abomination."

"Melek said they don't like that term here. He suggested 'misunderstood creature.'"

I smiled. "Then I'm a misunderstood creature."

"That you are," she agreed, making my smile grow. "But I don't think you're an outsider. I think they're probably jealous that Lucifer has shown you favor. You have a title, and you're clearly closer to him than most."

"Because of Az."

"Why because of Az?"

"Because Az is mated to Lucifer, just like Melek," I explained.

Her eyes went round again. "*They're mated?*"

I chuckled. "Yeah, I reacted like that when he first told me. But it's a different sort of mating. They're more like best friends than lovers. While Melek…"

"Is his prince," she finished for me.

"Yes. But Az is just as important to him, and Az's friendship with me has given me a unique relationship with Lucifer. But we're not close. Not really, anyway."

"But closer than most," she pressed. "So I'm guessing you're not an outsider, just… envied."

"Maybe," I agreed. "However, to bring us back to your question, I have no interest in going to Purgatory. And I really doubt Lucifer will allow you in there. So we can watch the trials here if you want. It'll aid in your lessons on Hell Fae life."

"It'll be kind of weird to watch them after I've lived through them," she said slowly. "Especially with me knowing some of the candidates now."

"True. Or it might provide a unique perspective," I offered. "And you'll know if they're safe."

"Or if they die," she whispered, shuddering.

"Only the ones who truly deserve death will perish."

"Because the source will find them to have nefarious intentions," she added. "Yes. I remember you saying that."

"Watching the trials would show you it's true," I hedged. "It really will give you some insight into what's happening."

"Because I'll be able to see clearly through the mirages?" she asked.

I frowned. "Mirages?"

"The… visual… whatever…" Her lips puckered to the side. "Maybe they didn't exist on the screen and only on the field."

"I'm not sure what you're talking about, so maybe."

"Then watching the trials might actually be kind of interesting." Her gaze turned thoughtful. "Is there a way to check up on the candidates I know before then?"

"There are probably open feeds available on the screen, yeah."

Her head moved against the pillow as she nodded. "I may be interested in that. But first I want to know more about the Marsh Lands."

"I can help with that. Probably better than the book. We can pull some footage of the Nagas and the Unseelie, too. That'll help you understand them a little more."

Her expression told me she wasn't sure if she wanted to understand them or not, but she moved her head in the affirmative anyway. "Okay. But can we start tomorrow? I think I'd like to just be us for a little longer first. If that's okay."

My lips curled. "I would like that, too."

"Then we'll reconvene Hell Fae tutoring tomorrow," she murmured.

"Tomorrow," I agreed, leaning toward her.

Then I kissed her because I could.

Because I wanted to.

Because it felt right.

And I lost myself to the present, as the future could wait until tomorrow.

CHAPTER 28

CAMI

Two Days Later

"Hmm," I hummed to myself, dreamily wandering into the kitchen in a pleasant haze of satisfaction while Ajax finished dressing for the day.

He'd spent the morning trying to distract me from today's pending events, something I'd fully appreciated more than once. But now that I was standing in front of the espresso machine, reality started settling around me again.

The bride trials resume today. In the Marsh Lands.

From what I understood from Ajax, the Nagas and Unseelie primarily dominated the Marsh Lands. They were two very different types of Nightmare Fae, which meant there would likely be at least two sets of challenges, similar to the first round of trials with the Centaurs and the Minotaurs.

I nibbled my lip as I programmed the machine to pour me a normal cup of coffee.

"So if the source has already removed those with bad

intentions, no one should die this time, right?" I'd asked Ajax yesterday.

He'd shaken his head. "Just because it wasn't caught in the first trial doesn't mean it won't be caught now. There were over six hundred brides. That's a lot of auras for the source to test."

Which meant we might see some gruesome deaths on the live feed today.

I glanced at the big black screen, thinking about the various channels I'd discovered and the current feeds it was probably displaying.

How are the brides preparing? I wondered. *How much do they know?*

Ajax had said the sponsors could technically provide some warnings, maybe even say which kingdom and Nightmare Fae type to expect today. Because the whole purpose of a sponsor was to ensure the bride survived long enough to be chosen by a Hell Fae.

"It seems counterproductive for a sponsor to help their bride do well in the Nightmare Fae trial since that means he might lose her to another kingdom," I'd said to Ajax. "Wouldn't they be more inclined to try to help their candidate, I don't know, cheat in some way?"

"That's not how the Hell Fae and Nightmare Fae function," he'd replied. "They support each other, even when technically competing. Besides, the whole purpose is to prove that this can work so that maybe Lucifer will host another bridal event in a millennium or so."

"He plans to do this again?"

"Only if it proves worthwhile."

I had translated that to mean that it depended on how many brides made the cut. While in the arena last month, it'd felt like at least half of the brides had perished. But apparently the casualties were under twenty as a whole with about sixty brides being taken to the Barren Lands for the Centaurs and Minotaurs.

Which left just under six hundred candidates on the playing board for today's trial since Lucifer had started with six hundred and sixty-six total.

The machine beeped, telling me my coffee was ready. I picked it up and considered whether or not I wanted it black today. It seemed kind of appropriate, given what was about to happen.

So how are the brides feeling? I wondered, thinking again about the ones I knew.

They were probably all together now, waiting for the inevitable. I'd missed that gathering last time due to being stuck in a prison cell, thanks to Melek's antics.

I took a sip of my coffee and glanced at the screen again. Part of me didn't want to see the brides again. Not all of them had been kind. And those who had... I felt guilty on their behalf. However, a stronger part of me wanted to stand with them in solidarity and support them.

That stronger part was what had me walking over to the screen and turning it on with the command Ajax had taught me.

I didn't have to search for the channel I needed, because it appeared as though waiting for me, the excited chatter of feminine voices filling the otherwise quiet room.

My eyebrow inched upward in surprise. I hadn't expected to see so much enthusiasm.

Unless the cameras are purposely focused on this crew rather than the others.

I could see a few frightened candidates in the background, but not many. Most were smiling, some of them were stretching, and several were showing off their gifts.

As I settled myself on the couch and coddled my

coffee, I recognized some of the familiar faces. One with a punk look, whom I'd seen at the Centaur trial, as well as another, named Sarah, that I'd seen on my way to the library.

One group stood out with more "gifts" than the rest. It was their attitude that gave them away, though.

"The Elites," I said to myself, recalling the group of brides I'd encountered during one of the trials.

They'd been prepared, arrogant, and *rude*. But knowing what I did now, I understood them better. They'd been training for this all their lives.

They'd been... looking forward to it.

And their rolled-back shoulders and lifted chins implied that nothing about them had changed.

They were Hell Fae Brides in every form of the word. Beautiful. Powerful. Confident.

And they'd obviously earned plenty of gifts from Hell Fae suitors. Magic practically oozed off the screen as I examined them.

Their tight leathers showed plenty of skin, but there was a magical sheen to them that told me they had special protections, as did many who wore talismans not unlike the one Melek had given me.

The talismans they had on certainly weren't the same, but they were magical in nature. I noted one had a necklace made of pure fire that didn't burn her. Instead, it seemed to coat her in warmth.

"I'm hoping we head to Unseelie territory first," she informed the others. "I'll definitely turn some heads with my new magic." She demonstrated red flames licking across her fingers. "My sponsor taught me to summon Hellfire."

Another girl clad in blades scrunched up her nose. "But Unseelie don't like fire."

Based on what I'd read about the Unseelie, that was true. Which suggested the Elites had done their homework.

Are their sponsors giving them these details? Or did their parents prepare them?

Having a Hell Fae father would certainly give a candidate an edge, assuming he'd bothered to explain the Nightmare Fae.

Mine certainly hadn't.

Although, I supposed my parents had tried to prepare me in a bizarre sort of way, if the grenade birthday cake was any indicator. My trust levels were low and my ability to survive was high as a result of their awkward training.

But no expectations had ever been placed on me as far as mating was concerned.

My parents had taken very little interest in my love life other than to often remind me that fae males possessed a natural birth control—they could only procreate if they intended to, and typically only with a mate—which at least gave me a carefree experience with a fae like Ajax.

So there were no faeling accidents.

That wasn't the case with human males.

Meaning that I knew my existence had at least been planned. Unfortunately, now I knew why.

I was just an asset for my father to trade to Lucifer.

Fucking Father of the Year Award goes to good ol' Dad.

"I know," the first bride responded as she closed her fist. "I'm not looking to impress the Nightmare Fae. I like my Hell Fae sponsor. So I'll win this trial by proving I'm more trouble than I'm worth."

Right, because failing a trial still meant death. Leaving two remaining options for candidates—become a Nightmare Fae Bride and live with the monsters in their inhospitable land or make it to the end of the trials unscathed and become a member of Lucifer's Court.

Another candidate snorted and crossed her arms. "You actually want to be a Hell Fae Bride and live in the Hell Fae Kingdom? Not me. My sponsor is *so* annoying. I'd gladly live in the swamp to avoid him."

I winced when I realized this woman probably didn't know she was being broadcast right now.

"I'm hoping to be picked by a Naga," she added with a wink. "I hear they have special *tails*."

She seemed pleased with herself until a flash burst through her necklace, breaking it.

Another girl, one I'd dubbed "Queen Bitch" during the first trial, barked a laugh. "You're an idiot. We're probably live right now and your sponsor just heard you. There goes your gift. Good luck passing the trial now."

The girl's face fell as the screen moved to another side of the room, scanning the less excited candidates who didn't seem to have as many gifts as the Elite crew.

"What's an Unseelie?" one female whispered to another.

"No clue. What's a Naga…?"

"I heard there was a secret section of the library that has insight into the trials and the monsters we're facing. The Elites seem to know where it is, but they won't tell us."

Ah, that explains their knowledge, then. Although, maybe a parent or a sponsor had told one of them about that section. Regardless, they definitely had a leg up on the others.

However, all this confirmed was that the brides were just as inadequately prepared as before.

So what were they doing for the last month?

Ajax entered from the bedroom with his damp hair hanging attractively around his eyes. He glanced at the screen and hummed as he sat beside me on the couch, a cup of coffee magically appearing in his hand.

"I see the brides are having their last meal," he murmured, his gaze scanning the screen. "That means the trials will be starting in two or three hours."

I swallowed. "Right." Lucifer hadn't actually given everyone a time, but Ajax had projected it would be around midday like the last trial.

"The real purpose of the meal isn't to feed them, though. It's this." He gestured with his chin at the live feed. "It's all a test, a way to ensure their hearts are in the right place."

"I suppose that explains why one of the girls just lost her gift—she said some unpleasant things about her sponsor."

Ajax grunted. "Yeah, that would do it."

I frowned. "Okay, but the only way a bride can win a gift is by flirting with a sponsor, which is... wrong. Right? And to punish them for doing exactly what they're supposed to do...?"

I probably wasn't making any sense, my mind struggling to comprehend the whole *sponsorship* process. I also didn't really like the Elites, but I still felt bad for the girl who had lost her token. She'd just been playing the game the way it was designed to be played.

"No one is being punished," Ajax said, his focus on the screen. "It's just a consequence. If a Hell Fae gives a gift, it's because he wants that bride to survive to become his. If she doesn't want him, then she shouldn't have his gift. She'll be better off looking for a different suitor."

"Okay, except I thought the whole point was to ensure the brides survived. If not for the Hell Fae himself, then for the potential Nightmare Fae mating."

"True," he agreed. "But if she's going to try to manipulate the game in her favor, then she might not be worthy of either. Or she might be an ideal candidate for another Nightmare Fae entirely. Of course, the Unseelie are pretty fond of tricksters. So this trial might be her fate after all."

"Are they watching this, too?"

"I'm not sure," he admitted. "I've only seen the broadcast on this side of the realm, not on the Nightmare Fae side."

"So they might not know what she's done or said."

"Perhaps not, but they're intuitive creatures. Actually…" He waved his hand toward the screen and uttered a command for a different channel. "Yeah, I figured this would be playing. A similar one was on before the last trials for the Centaurs and Minotaurs. Watch."

The feed morphed from the bridal candidates to a marshy landscape, but not everything was mushy foliage.

There appeared to be an object in the distance. An object sparkling with color. Ajax maneuvered his hand in a gesture that caused the screen zoom, making me feel like I was on a flying ride over a swampy kingdom. But then a beautiful castle came into view, the towers covered in vines that glittered with power.

Fluttering creatures flitted in and out of existence, making me think something was glitching on the screen. But then a masculine voice boomed from the speakers with, "We honor the bridal garden."

I blinked a few times as the screen moved through the castle, past various halls filled with living floral arrangements and wet footsteps appearing on the mirrorlike stones.

The image on the screen followed some sort of invisible entity. I couldn't make much out except for a shimmer of magic that seemed to seep through the screen.

Then I gasped when it reached what could only be called a fairylike graveyard. It didn't reek of death like the

Netherworld Kingdom. This one was more of a remembrance of those lost and filled with life.

Statues of lifelike, beautiful female beings with sheer, silky wings raised their hands to the skies. They wore flowers that grew on vines, wrapping the figures in a living embrace. Their stones were the same mirrored material that reminded me of moving water.

What struck me with a strange sort of melancholy was that mirror tears seeped from their eyes.

"What is that?" I asked.

Ajax stretched his arm out behind me on the couch as he said, "It's all that's left of the Unseelie females, minus a small hidden handful that are still alive. A civil war once broke out among the Unseelie as males in the upper court tried to hoard females for themselves."

I raised a brow. "I don't remember seeing a chapter on that in the Marsh Lands book."

"There wouldn't be one, as it's not allowed to be documented. Lucifer knows that history tends to repeat itself, so he prefers history to be remembered in certain ways." Ajax nodded to the screen. "Such as the cost of infighting. Many females died during the war, leaving the Unseelie particularly starved for brides."

"I thought it was the source that keeps removing females and that was the reason Lucifer needs brides?"

"It's a combination of a lot of events. But it's rumored that the source might have played a role in the Unseelie female extermination— it removed the point of contention to halt the war."

"Oh." I supposed that made sense. And given what I'd learned about Lucifer, it seemed like something his soul would do.

More fluttering appeared on the screen, drawing my attention back to the Unseelie. Now that I'd seen some of the statues, it made it easier to identify the creatures flying about.

The tall, incredibly gorgeous creatures moved almost too fast for me to see. They all had sheer wings that flitted behind them, reminding me of a hummingbird's wings. Glitter shimmered over their skin with a metallic, mirrored quality, breaking the light as they moved. It probably had something to do with why it was so hard to focus on them.

While masculine bodies and impressive muscles assured me these were males, they still had soft features and a wild beauty about them that had me doing a double take.

"Wow," I breathed. "They're... very pretty." I didn't normally use that word to describe a male, but for the Unseelie, it definitely fit.

I could see why some brides might be interested in the Unseelie if they were all like that.

Ajax chuckled. "Yeah, I hear the Unseelie are pretty stunning. Although, I've never seen one. But don't let their beauty fool you. They're dangerous as fuck. Ruthless, too."

"You can't see them?" I asked, more confused by that than the other things he'd said. I pointed at the screen. "They're on the screen."

He shrugged. "That must be your Hell Fae talents coming out to play, because I don't see anything except shimmering light. Az says they move too fast to be seen."

"So he can't see them either?"

"Oh, no, he can see them. But he's exceptionally powerful. He's also picky when it comes to appearances, so I trust his description when he says they're pretty creatures." Ajax leaned in to brush his lips against my cheek. "I mean, Az thinks you're as beautiful as I do. So I'd say he's a good judge."

"Oh, I'm beautiful, am I?" I asked, allowing his flirtatious distraction.

"Very," he said, now nibbling on my earlobe.

Leaning into Ajax's embrace, I relished the butterflies taking flight in my lower abdomen. *Maybe another round would help me relax more*, I thought, turning and straddling him. *We have time, right?*

Ajax arched a brow as my short robe ran up my legs, revealing my lacy underwear beneath. "Eager for more, are we?" he asked.

"Shut up and distract me," I told him as I grabbed the tie on his waistband.

I was just about to rip it undone when a sudden influx of heat and power made me freeze on top of him.

Turning, I found Lucifer glowering down at us. "I didn't expect the bridal banquet to be your type of foreplay, Camillia."

Damn it all to Hell, I growled in my head as I worked to scramble off of Ajax's lap.

Except we were already in Hell.

And I was most certainly damned, because I'd just been caught straddling the Warden while trying to take off his clothes.

Despite endless practice of curtsying to ready myself for this moment, I snagged my foot on Ajax's pants pocket and landed face-first on the ground.

"I preferred the demented penguin," Lucifer said as I righted myself.

"Flamingo," I corrected, only to swallow down my wounded pride when I locked gazes with the powerful King of Hell.

His hard-set jaw and chiseled features were intimidating this close up. His eyes also practically burned with the Hellfire he commanded, assuring me that this wasn't the time for jokes.

"King Lucifer, Majesty, sir," I rambled like a moron.

He narrowed his midnight-blue eyes as his dark hair danced around his face. A heated wind unfurled from the bedroom, then settled a moment later.

"As I've said, just Lucifer is fine," he reminded me, then waved toward the bedroom. "I've placed what you'll be wearing on the bed."

"What I'll be wearing?" I dumbly repeated as I cinched my morning robe closed.

"You'll need to get dressed as well," Lucifer said, ignoring me as he turned his attention to Ajax, who was now standing at attention and adjusting his obvious hard-on. "You'll be joining Camillia and me at Purgatory to watch the bride trial."

"Purgatory?" I squeaked with alarm, familiar with the club name since Lucifer had announced he would be there with his Hell Fae later today. "Wait, why? With all the fae?"

Lucifer ignored me again, his intense gaze on Ajax. "I've called a car for you. It's waiting at the front of this wing, so once she's dressed, escort her to Purgatory. Your job today is to ensure there are no disruptions where Camillia's concerned, and to stay and guard."

The Hell Fae King looked at me, his fierce expression making me want to run and hide.

"And you," he said, his voice brooking no argument. "Don't forget to wear the coat."

He vanished, leaving me stunned and gaping at the space he'd just occupied.

Because apparently I was about to be shoved into a car and sent to a club.

A Hell Fae club.

And why would I need a coat in literal Hell?

"We aren't going to watch the trials here?" I numbly asked Ajax even though I knew that clearly we weren't.

I just wasn't sure what all of this meant.

Ajax was obviously as worried as I was, because a new vein had appeared in his neck. "Apparently not. Just... go get dressed, Cami. We'll talk about it in the car." He conjured himself a new outfit, one I hadn't seen in a while.

His original Warden clothes.

An open cloak gave him access to his wand on the inside pockets while heavy boots promised a painful, swift kick if any of his creatures rebelled. Except each item had been upgraded a bit for today's events.

Rubies and diamonds glinted in the fiery light from the walls, and a leathery whip trimmed with red rested on his waist next to a set of cuffs.

This is bad, I thought. *Very bad.*

And Ajax's expression confirmed it.

Rather than try to negotiate my way out of this—because there was nothing Ajax could do, and I already knew that—I headed toward the bedroom.

And stopped short when I saw the "outfit" waiting for me on the bed.

"I'm not fucking wearing *that.*"

CHAPTER 29

CAMI

I PACED BACK and forth in the bedroom, a variety of curses spewing through my mouth.

Because no. *Hell* no. Fuck this. Absolutely fucking not. *No.*

Ajax must have heard me swearing, because he entered the room behind me. "What's going on?"

"*That* is not an outfit," I snapped.

He took one look at the chains on the bed and winced. "Well, it could be in Hell. Which is where we are."

I whirled around to face him, furious. "This is not a joke, Ajax."

"No, it's definitely not," he agreed. "But you're going to have to wear it, Cami."

"Wear it?" I repeated, picking up the chains threaded with red lace. "This is not something I can *wear*. It's… it's… *metallic lingerie*." Which actually did sound like a joke, except I wasn't laughing.

And neither was Ajax.

The only acceptable item on the bed was the coat. It was beautifully embroidered with golden feathers intertwined with red flames. But it subtly matched the decorative chains, proving that Lucifer did, in fact, expect me to put all of this shit on.

He would allow me to cover up.

But when was I going to be forced to take the jacket off?

And who was going to see me in this monstrosity?

Was it for his personal benefit? Melek's? Or would I be presented like some sort of damn trophy to be won during the trials?

Maybe Melek had tried to talk to Lucifer about his intention to mate me and this was a kind of sensual test. *Does that mean Lucifer intends to mate me, too?* Because he certainly had a fucked-up way of showing it.

Aside from that, I didn't really want to mate Lucifer, either. Sure, he was beautiful, but he was also the Hell Fae King. The male terrified me.

Shit, he would probably kill me just as fast as he would fuck me.

But this wasn't about sex. This was about obedience. He was testing me, trying to see if I could adhere to his order like a good little female Hell Fae.

My arms wrapped around my chest, my mind giving a resounding *"Fuck that"* in response.

"Cami, Lucifer isn't someone you say no to," Ajax said softly. "If you don't, he'll just force me to conjure it on you."

Anger flared in my chest. "And if he told you to jump off a cliff, would you do that, too?"

Ajax didn't flinch. He wasn't even moving, suggesting he was holding his breath. Finally, his muscles flexed as he exhaled. "We don't know what game he's playing. For now, it's best to just play along."

That wasn't an answer to my question.

And usually it was Melek playing games. Right now, I preferred the Hell Fae Prince's antics to this.

Whatever *this* was.

Stretching out the chains, I tried to figure out what was supposed to go where. Red strappy loops suggested it could be tied. Some of the chains were smaller to the point of forming dainty loops. Others were thicker with the center openings covered in vibrant woven fabric. It *might* be enough to hide some of my more sensitive bits.

Maybe it's an erotic sort of puzzle? I wondered.

Or maybe I was just being wrapped like a present.

Perhaps Lucifer had also been intrigued by the images he'd seen in Vita and wanted to play them out in some capacity.

This is not going to end well.

"Do you need me to help you?" Ajax offered, making me shiver.

"No," I immediately replied. I was already humiliated enough. I wasn't going to have Ajax drape these chains over me and pity me when he saw how little they covered.

"Okay," he said as he eased back through the doorway. "Then I'll wait for you. We'll go down when you're ready." His obsidian irises glimmered with fire, suggesting he was almost as unhappy as I was about this. But I somehow doubted this was impacting him as much as it was impacting me.

He left without another word, confirming that he wasn't going to do a damn thing to stop this. Not that he could. But it still stung to know I was on my own here.

Just like always, I thought, growling to myself. *This is such bullshit.*

I tossed the chains onto the sheets, then unraveled my robe and removed my nightgown.

Standing naked by the side of the bed, I arranged the chains in the way I thought they should go.

Might as well see how bad this is, I decided. It would help me calculate just how pissed off I should be by this situation.

Based on what I was seeing so far, pretty damn pissed.

The thicker chains wound up on top, which might be enough to cover my breasts, but then that left little to nothing for my lower half.

Frowning, I turned it upside down and glowered at the offensive configuration.

This was definitely how it was meant to be worn, which meant my breasts would be completely visible, minus a few barely-there drapes of small chains. But it was the only way to cover my groin and ass.

Fuck.

Grinding my teeth so hard that my jaw ached, I slowly stepped into the loops and wound them up my thighs.

"If this shows anything private, I am not keeping it on," I vowed.

Some part of me hoped a magical gown would appear to replace the chains after I passed this "test" of obedience.

Except, when I put the first layer on, I realized that wasn't going to be the case at all.

Because once it was on, it wouldn't budge.

And the ends magically fused together, sealing the piece in place around me with a finality that made my lips part.

Shit.

"Surely it's just…" I mumbled to myself as I yanked at the metal, trying to adjust the tight grip it now had on my upper thigh.

It didn't move.

"*Fuck.*"

Once everything was in place, this so-called outfit would not be coming off, not without some magical assistance.

But it wasn't like I could stop now.

Damn it.

With no other recourse, I continued dressing.

Grim acceptance wound icy snakes around my heart as I continued pulling the lacy chain in place. One thick metal strip ran from my belly button to my mound, covering my intimate parts entirely.

Well, there's that.

Except the knobs of the chain rubbed right up against a certain bundle of nerves, making me curse every time I moved.

My fists wrapped around the chains looped over my hips as I tried to tug and adjust it, but the magic sealed it in place, just like the part around my thigh.

Meaning I was now stuck with a metal configuration that stimulated my clit every time I moved.

Fantastic.

"If this was Melek's idea, I'm going to kill him," I vowed.

But I doubted this kind of mindfuckery was Melek's doing.

This seemed to be about humiliation, which was most definitely Lucifer's forte.

And I would be thoroughly humiliated even if I didn't have to take off my coat. Because every step shot friction through my core and it would force me to remain very, very still throughout the rest of the day.

Which would be an extremely long time, given that it was still morning and the trials would likely run through the night. Perhaps even until tomorrow.

I hate this.

Once I was finished "dressing," I ran my fingers through my hair under the pretense of being presentable, then snatched up my jacket and put it on.

Ajax was nervously pacing behind the couch by the time I exited the bedroom.

He glanced up and frowned. "You're not ready yet?"

I gave him a raised brow. "I'm wearing the damn chains. You just can't tell because there's not much to them. And I am *not* removing this coat."

He shook his head. "No, I meant your hair. And you need shoes."

I looked down and realized I was still barefoot. "Okay, fine. Maybe I need shoes. But what's wrong with my hair?"

Instead of answering me, Ajax pulled out his wand and pointed it toward me.

Impatient much?

I glowered at him as his pine-scented energy circled around me. "Eager to see him take off my coat?" I snapped.

Magic tugged at my hair, adding something to my long strands, while a pair of strappy red heels wound up my calves. "No," he said.

But he didn't elaborate.

When the spell dissipated, I ran my fingers through my hair and found that he had added red lace braids to the mix.

"Why are you so on board with this?" I asked.

I'd intended for my question to come out angry, but instead I just sounded hurt.

Why aren't you standing up for me?

Ajax's anger was still there, but simmering underneath another emotion. One I had seen on the Warden far too many times to not recognize it.

Acceptance. It created a cold shield around him, one that seemed to justify the blurred lines when it came to his king.

"I don't have a choice, Camillia. And neither do you."

Oh, it's Camillia now? Not Cami anymore? I wanted to ask.

Instead, I countered with "You could at least conjure me a weapon if you're going to be altering things."

Ajax simply gave me an exasperated look as if he just wanted this day to be over with already. "Let's go."

He didn't wait for me to reply, simply led the way. I narrowed my gaze at his back. Well, even if he'd accepted this fate, it didn't mean I had to.

I'd find a weapon. I'd use my teeth, my feet, my hands, my *magic*—if I could figure out how to conjure it.

But if I was so "powerful," then I didn't have to put up with this shit. If I was asked to take off this feathery coat, I'd make sure there was hell to pay.

Or that was my plan, anyway.

Until the throbbing between my thighs took over my mind.

It grew with each step as we headed toward the palace's ground level, the metal knobs rubbing against my sex and making it hard to breathe.

We paused after passing a group of Hellhounds, giving me an opportunity to rest. I leaned on one of the red marble stones for support and sucked in gulps of warm air while I clutched my talisman for a refreshing wave of cool magic.

"Are you okay?" Ajax asked with a note of concern. "Is there some kind of draining magic on the chains?"

He reached out to touch me, but I stopped him with a raised hand and a strangled sound.

Feeling Ajax's energy right now might just tip me over the edge, and I *really* didn't want to explain why I was about to have an orgasm in the middle of the palace. He'd given me enough of those to realize what was happening.

No, not magic. Just friction...

"I'm fine," I said instead once I was able to stop trembling.

Ajax matched my slower pace and didn't ask me if I was okay again, but the tension was palpable.

He knew something was wrong. Which was apparent because he kept sneaking glances at me.

Sweat dripped down my hairline when we reached the palace gates, and I regretted not opting for a ponytail.

Ajax nodded to the Hell Fae guarding the doors and patiently waited while they opened them for us.

A magical snap rushed over my skin when we left the compound, but I almost didn't feel it when the city came into view.

I'd managed a glimpse of the dark buildings from the upper balcony with Melek, but being on the street provided a new experience. The city reminded me a bit of Chicago with its laid-back vibe and subtle winds, only the surroundings were cleaner and the breeze was hot rather than chilly.

It was exactly the kind of environment that suited me.

Powerful.

Dark.

Exciting.

I felt like I was in the middle of a controlled storm, one with various currents and channels that worked in unison to create the thunder that boomed all around us.

I hadn't realized I was smiling until Ajax's shoulders sagged in clear relief. He was probably glad to see that nothing too serious was going on with me. "I've been wanting to bring you down here," he admitted. "But I wasn't sure if you'd like it. Nor was I sure if it was allowed."

His words reminded me why I was here, causing my smile to slip a little.

"It's okay," I lied, shrugging and then wincing when the motion tugged at my sensitive area. "Let's just get this over with." I looked at the busy street. "I thought a car was supposed to be waiting for us?"

Ajax pointed toward the front of the building beside us, indicating that we were at valet parking.

The royal "parking spot," if one could call it that, took up three car lengths. It was completely unnecessary, given that Lucifer could teleport.

"That's... excessive," I said as I stared at the limo-like automobile.

Although, I supposed it was the kind of car one would imagine for the King of Hell.

It gleamed as if made from black steel, and embellishments of skulls and feathers decorated the sides. The design was stylish and made it clear who owned this car. The darkened windows wouldn't allow any peek inside, either.

Hell Fae wearing black suits waited for us, reminding me of the Secret Service. *If the Secret Service had blazing red eyes and sharp teeth, that is.*

One opened the door to the back when we approached.

Clutching my coat to ensure it didn't open, I hurried into the back seat.

Ajax entered from the other side, and I glanced at the dark glass that blocked my view of the driver.

"Why didn't we just"—I waved my hands and made a *poof* sound—"to the club, you know?"

Ajax chuckled. "Maybe Lucifer wanted you to see

where you'll be living." He kept his mouth open as if he was going to add to that, then shut it.

Tension seeped back into the air as he glanced out the window.

I didn't have to read his mind to finish that sentence —*Assuming you survive...*

Or maybe he just wants to make a show of something special traveling to the club, I thought.

A sinking feeling settled into my gut as the city rolled by. The buildings were beautiful in architecture. Somewhat modern, but also stylish with a European-like flair. *So, definitely not Chicago, then,* I decided. *A mix of, well, everything.*

Several Hell Fae stopped to observe the car along the way, but I knew when we were about to reach the club because the attire quickly changed from casual to *expensive*.

It occurred to me that not all Hell Fae would be able to sponsor a bride. Even with an original six hundred and sixty-six candidates, there wasn't enough for everyone.

Which meant those who would be at the club were the upper echelon of Hell Fae. Those going past roped areas wore suits and diamond-studded boots. Some had multiple piercings along their brows, and others boasted Hellish tattoos that were more a mark of power than artistic preference.

I was grateful for the tinted windows as the leering looks became more prevalent.

That sinking feeling turned my stomach sour, because these Hell Fae looked *hungry*.

"What's Lucifer going to do?" I asked.

I couldn't stand the various possibilities rolling around in my head. I was starting to think he'd had us go in the car to torment me with the what-ifs just because he knew it would drive me nuts.

"I don't know," Ajax said softly. His hand rested on my

thigh, forcing me to turn to him. "Whatever happens, Cami, I'm going to be with you every step of the way. Okay?"

He was trying to be comforting, but it wasn't a promise that he would stand up for me if things went too far.

What if Lucifer planned to unwrap me for himself? Would Ajax allow it? He didn't strike me as possessive, especially since he'd shared me with Az, but would he let me go so easily?

What if Lucifer plans to do something worse than that? I wondered, swallowing. *What if he plans to kill me? Will Ajax help me then?*

Or would he watch with cold acceptance?

There's one way to find out, I guess... "Will you please give me a weapon?" I asked Ajax. "So I can defend myself?"

His promise to be with me wasn't enough.

I needed something tangible.

Something *sharp*.

His Warden mask slipped over his features again, turning my stomach as our ride came to a stop. "No, Cami. I can't give you a weapon."

Of course you can't, I wanted to say, tears taunting the back of my eyes. *Because I'm alone in this. Just like I've always been.*

Forcing the betrayal away, I embraced the hot surge of anger that followed, and opened the door before the suited men could.

I'll do this on my own.

Lucifer might be trying to teach me a lesson, but he was about to learn a thing or two about me first.

Because no one humiliates me.

Not even the King of Hell.

CHAPTER 30

TYPHOS

A DISTURBANCE BROKE out at the entrance to the club, assuring me that my package had arrived.

Excellent, I thought, pleased with the unfolding events.

Perhaps it made me cruel, but Camillia needed to be tested. And Ajax had more than earned this punishment. He would be her official escort for the afternoon, forced to guard her while my Hell Fae enjoyed the show.

It was my way of seeing how badly he truly wanted her. *Is this just sex? Or is it more?*

He wouldn't be the only one I intended to evaluate. Az and Melek would be observed, too. I needed to determine how much this female truly meant to all of them, to decide how important it was that I allowed her to live.

After my conversation with Melek the other day, I suspected it was going to be extremely important, something I could never have anticipated at the beginning of the trials.

Alas, here we are, I mused. *So let's find out what all the commotion is about, hmm?*

Camillia was a gorgeous woman. But was she enough

to tempt even me?

I suppose we're about to find out.

"Mmm, I think I like that look," Melek murmured as he leaned back in our private booth, his multicolored irises sparking with interest. "You have something planned."

"I do," I admitted, smirking as I met Az's bored gaze. "You may help him, but remember what I said."

Sadist, Az replied, leaving his post to carry out my orders.

I smiled at his back. *We both know you'll enjoy harnessing his power, Commander. He looks good beneath you.*

Az didn't reply, but I heard his mental agreement. Although, part of him wasn't pleased with me, which I'd anticipated.

Because he was just as lost to this enchantress as Ajax and Melek were. Fortunately, though, my Commander understood his role. He would carry out his task efficiently and effectively; he just might curse me in the process.

Although, I suspected he'd be too busy immobilizing Ajax to worry about me. It was imperative that my Warden accept this punishment with grace, or I would be forced to do something worse.

I couldn't afford to display any favoritism toward him. Not after all the turmoil in the realm these last few weeks.

My fae needed to be reminded that I was in charge, that I was a capable leader, and that I put all their needs above my own.

Which made Camillia De la Croix a problem.

She'd been removed from the bride trials, and my Hell Fae required an explanation as to why. But I couldn't simply say, *It's because she touched my source and I'm evaluating her.* That would inspire panic—panic that would likely lead to a call for her death.

My little prince would suffer if that happened.

So I needed an alternative solution. A way to dismiss her from the trials but still allow her to remain within our realm.

And my Warden had provided me with the perfect option—I could use his infatuation as a reason to disqualify Camillia and also teach my other Hell Fae a lesson in the process.

The sponsoring program was about courtship, but that courtship could only go so far. My Hell Fae were aware of the rules. However, I hadn't extended those rules to Ajax because I'd assumed he wouldn't be interested in any of the brides.

While it was the truth—I truly hadn't anticipated him wanting to be involved since he'd originally come here to avoid emotional entanglements with others—it also served as the perfect excuse to make an example of him.

An example that would distract my Hell Fae from Camillia's disqualification and allow me to keep her in the realm for further observation.

A win-win, apart from the fact that Ajax was likely going to want to kill me for this. But Az would help me tame him.

Or, at the very least, Az would make him understand.

Meanwhile, I would simply enjoy the show.

And test Camillia's resolve in the process, I mused. *How strong are you really, little one? Strong enough to play my games? Or will that courage of yours wilt on the stage?*

Melek might have already claimed her, but I needed to be certain of her worth before I truly accepted their match.

Thus far, I was solely convinced that she had cast a spell over my men. Some sort of enchantment I couldn't see. Maybe because it didn't appeal to me, thereby making me immune to her magic.

As I should be.

I'm the fucking Hell Fae King.

And dear Camillia De la Croix was about to find out exactly what that meant.

My jaw clenched, my eternal energy flowing warmly through my veins. It'd grown more intense recently, something I knew Melek had noticed. Az, too. But neither of them had commented on it, aware that it was my burden to bear.

Creation came at a cost.

It was a high price, one I was willing to pay to protect all those residing within my realm.

This was a safe haven. A utopia for all those discarded and abused by the places they used to call home. And this bar was one of my favorite gifts to them.

I used it as an outlet for my power, my internal inferno flowing freely from my spirit into the various elements of the club—the holographic screens over each booth, the ring of fire in the center of the room, and the stage beyond.

Normally, I kept a throne there.

Instead, I had another item hidden beneath my burning flames, one I'd be revealing shortly.

The sea of Hell Fae parted as the female I had been waiting for approached. They were all salivating at the chance to touch her, but that enchanted coat around her shoulders marked her as off-limits. As did the Warden's palm upon her lower back.

Her expression remained stoic, but I caught the subtle hint of fear in her gray eyes, her irises rolling like untamed storms.

You should be frightened, I thought at her. *You're in my Hell now, little one. And I'm not known for my benevolence.*

"I no longer like that look on your face," Melek

murmured. *Why is she here, Ty?*

To watch the trials with us, of course, I told him.

Although, she was here to be *watched,* too.

My men were restless after the disturbances throughout the realm. They needed something to distract them. Camellia had provided me with an opportunity to take care of that. The Warden, too.

Standing, I met her near the ring of flames.

"Welcome to Purgatory," I told her, my energy heightening with my excitement. A gush of heat filled the air as the fire responded to my amusement, my power burning through the club with renewed vigor. "Are you going to attempt to bow?"

It was a meaningful taunt, one that caused anger to flash in her gaze. "No, I don't think I will." A bold reply, one that had Ajax flinching behind her. But all it did was make me smile.

"Pity," I murmured. "I think some of my Hell Fae would have enjoyed the show. But that's all right. We'll give them something else to watch, hmm?"

Her jaw clenched in reply. She knew exactly what I meant.

Ajax seemed to understand, too. He'd likely seen the chains, thereby causing a dozen or more scenarios to run through his mind. Those scenarios were no doubt echoed within Camillia's thoughts, too.

Which was all part of the fun.

What am I going to do? I pondered, grinning. *How horrible will this become?*

This was part of Ajax's punishment and Camillia's test. Sometimes the victim could conjure worse torment than I could possibly inflict on them.

Although, I would try to match Camillia's fears, and supersede them.

Her eyes narrowed into a glare, her ire stoking the flames of my excitement. It seemed to replace her earlier fear, causing her shoulders to tighten and her stance to strengthen with confidence.

Maybe there is more to you than just your stunning looks, I marveled. *Let's find out how deep that boldness goes, shall we?*

"Today the bride trials resume!" I announced loudly, my words for the Hell Fae but my focus still on Camillia.

A cheer followed my statement as the holograms zoomed in on me, my face appearing throughout the club and the entire Hell Fae Kingdom.

The female before me must have noticed because her eyes widened slightly, but that delicious anger of hers continued to color her features.

Very beautiful indeed, I decided. *But I want to see more.*

Checking the sundial on the fiery wall, I noted that we had about twenty minutes before the first trial began, making this the perfect time to introduce today's *entertainment.*

I shifted my focus to the crowd. "You all have been so incredibly understanding while I've sorted out the mess that Monsters Night has caused, and I truly appreciate you allowing the delays in our much-anticipated trials."

Several of the Hell Fae dipped their chins in reverence, their gratitude at being acknowledged for their patience palpable.

"Therefore, I thought we could all indulge in a little prelude before the trials kick off." I gestured to Camillia. "What do you say, gentlemen? Would you like to see what's under the coat?"

The crowd jeered in response, their eagerness a wave of chants on the air that caused Camillia to take a step backward. Only, Az was waiting for her, his chest blocking her path.

He'd clearly anticipated her reaction, just as he'd apparently anticipated the Warden's reaction, too. Which explained the whip of power lashing out at my senses. He'd already immobilized Ajax, making it impossible for the Midnight Fae to move or speak.

Melek joined me, his curiosity playing through our bond. *What are you hiding under the coat?*

A present, I admitted.

For me?

If you want to unwrap it, I'll allow it.

You'll allow it? he countered, his amusement caressing his words. *Meaning you'll watch?*

Perhaps.

Hmm, he hummed, leaning against me. *I'm intrigued.*

Good.

Although, I think she wants to kill you.

She probably does, I agreed.

Not a great way to court her, Ty.

I'm not courting her.

We'll see, he countered.

I ignored him and met Camillia's stormy gaze. "Remove your jacket, Camillia."

A cheer followed my words, and roars of encouragement rippled around us.

Her knuckles turned white as she clutched the embroidered material tighter around her body. "No fucking way," she bit back, exciting me.

"Hold her," I ordered my Commander.

He complied by grabbing her shoulders, which made her eyes go round. She appeared ready to say something, but Ajax's growl drew my focus to the infuriated Warden.

Other than the subtle vibration of that single sound, he remained silent and still, his body trapped beneath Az's power.

I arched my brow in open challenge.

However, I knew he couldn't respond. And that was entirely the point. The crowd would see his silence as acceptance, which was precisely what needed to happen.

"You touched something that doesn't belong to you, Ajax," I told him, ensuring the whole crowd could hear me. "I warned you not to get distracted. You didn't listen. Now she's tainted and ineligible for the trials. For that, you'll both be punished."

His jaw clenched, his eyes narrowing into slits.

"Do you have anything to add?" I taunted him, aware that Az had Ajax's being wrapped up in an energy-infused chokehold.

Sadist, Az echoed into my mind. *She is wearing something under this jacket, yes?*

Some decorative chains, I told him.

No wonder she's squirming, he replied. *I suspect I know where one of those* decorative chains *is located.*

If she put it on correctly, then you're likely right, I drawled, my attention still on Ajax as I watched the furious black flames circle his pupils.

My Phoenix wants to fuck her on the stage, Az all but growled back at me. *I'm starting to think you're punishing me in this situation, too.*

Because I am. I looked at Az. *You and Ajax chose to indulge in fucking her when you were supposed to be interrogating her. That's not the focused Commander I know.*

He snorted back at me. *Pleasure can be an excellent interrogation tool.*

So that's your excuse?

No. It's merely an explanation. Besides, I don't need an excuse for what we did. She gave us the truth, so I let my Phoenix play. It likes her.

I nearly shook my head in annoyance. *She must have a magic pussy.*

She does, Az replied. *And it's currently wet, thanks to whatever you put on her.*

I didn't reply, aware that all the Hell Fae were watching, awaiting my next move. They would have perceived my pause as giving Ajax time to think.

But he hadn't reacted at all. Because he couldn't.

Time to formally ignite the show, I decided.

"Warden Ajax took his *sponsorship* with Camillia De la Croix a little too far. Not only was he technically ineligible as a non-Hell Fae, but he also didn't follow our preestablished rules. *No. Fucking. The. Candidates.*"

Those last four words whirled around the room on a wave of power, ensuring everyone heard and felt that command.

Several Hell Fae sobered, their expressions turning angry as they looked at Ajax.

"I've said you're allowed to touch and play, so long as the candidate consents. But penetration isn't permitted. That's reserved for mates." I glared at Ajax. "And Camillia De la Croix isn't *your* mate."

She was technically Melek's intended, but I couldn't add that part out loud. Not until I finished testing her worth and deciding if I supported that union.

If Melek wanted to share her with Ajax and Az, so be it. I had no problem with that. I honestly didn't even care that Ajax had fucked the girl.

This was about making a statement for my Hell Fae.

And hiding the real reason for her disqualification.

"As a result, Camillia De la Croix is disqualified from the trials. And, Warden Ajax, you have been temporarily removed from your post while I determine how to handle this situation." I glanced at the crowd. "Meanwhile, all of you deserve to earn some recompense from this situation, yes?"

This time my words were met with snarls and growls more than cheers of excitement, their expressions hungry and underlined with a hint of envy.

Ajax had touched something that didn't really belong to him.

Had he wanted to participate in the trials, I would have allowed it. But he hadn't even asked, instead taking on his Warden role and helping corral bridal candidates. That had left him in an unfair position to seduce, something the Hell Fae would assume he'd taken advantage of with Camillia.

That had to be punished.

And this was my way of acknowledging that.

I met the former candidate's gaze, noting the blazing hatred in her gray eyes. Melek was right—this certainly wasn't going to impress her in the slightest.

But I didn't want to curry favor with her.

I wanted to test her. Make her prove her worth for my men. Find out why they cared so much about this female. Maybe determine if she truly was worth all the fuss.

If that happened, I'd be the first to grovel.

However, I very much doubted she would prove herself to be worth my time.

I stepped closer to her. "If you won't remove the jacket, then I will."

She responded by trying to wrap it more tightly around herself.

"Az," I said softly.

His sigh was loud in my mind, but he didn't outwardly betray his emotions at all as his palms slid down her arms to clasp her wrists.

She wriggled a little, then flinched, likely from the

chains pulling at her sensitive skin. Her lip disappeared between her teeth, her body jolting a little as Az deftly pulled her hands away from her coat.

Her eyes narrowed at me, more of her delicious anger taking over her expression.

But then something strange happened.

The fury lining her shoulders seemed to disappear as a sense of resolve stole over her features. She no longer appeared irate so much as confident, as though she knew something I didn't.

It had me suspicious. *Did she forgo the chains for something else?* I wondered. *Would she defy me in that way?*

My lips nearly curled down at the notion, my mind unclear on how I would proceed if she had.

I slipped my fingers under the edges of her coat, determined to find out if she'd followed my command or not, and paused when a shiver of power rushed between us.

Her flaring nostrils told me she'd felt it, too, but her face remained impassive. Almost as though she was suddenly bored.

What is this? What happened to the emotion in her eyes?

It wasn't dulled, necessarily. Nor was it chased away by dejection or anything depressive.

She was simply staring back at me with a look that said, *Do your worst, Hell Fae King.*

Like she didn't fear me at all.

And I found that oddly... intriguing.

No, *arousing.*

This woman really is enchanting, I realized, her energy shivering over my skin. *Except...* I considered her for a long moment, my gaze narrowing at the subtle shimmer in the air. *Oh, no wonder I'm aroused.*

I brushed my lips over her cheek, my tongue sneaking out for a taste of what I'd just begun to suspect.

Melek. I opened our mate-bond to say, *You dusted her again.*

I did, he admitted.

When?

Two days ago, he replied. *When I kissed her.*

I nearly jolted in surprise. *You kissed her?*

I did, he confirmed. *Thoroughly.*

Hmm, I hummed, intrigued. *I want details later.*

Or you could kiss her yourself, he offered, his voice playful. *Although, I think she might bite you if you try.*

I smiled, pulling back from her. *She absolutely would,* I agreed, catching the flare of her pupils. She was still hiding behind this new mask of self-assurance, but that subtle hint of rage peeked at me now.

No more stalling, I decided, pulling the jacket open.

Camillia didn't make a move to stop me, instead holding my gaze the entire time.

Shouts of approval echoed through the nightclub as the feather-layered jacket fell to the floor.

But Camillia ignored them all, her eyes solely on me, her confidence shining through.

The holograms throughout the Hell Fae Kingdom all showcased her clearly on the screen. Not that she bothered to look. But I could see it in my peripheral vision, just as I could see her right before me.

She was stunning with her hair tied up in ribbons that matched the vibrant red woven through her chains. Her gorgeous breasts were on display, framed perfectly in the chains, while the rest of the garment masterfully accented her lower half while keeping it beautifully hidden.

The heels she'd added were a nice touch, the red lace

matching her outfit as it wound up her shapely legs to her thighs.

That's a cleverly placed knot, my king, Melek mused. I couldn't see his eyes but assumed his gaze was on the secure strand trailing down her abdomen to her pussy.

I thought you might approve of that, I replied.

I do. As well as the red color.

It suits her, I admitted, still holding her gaze. *As does her assertiveness.*

She wasn't quaking or crying or begging me to stop this. Instead, she was staring me down with a look that told me she fully intended to put my balls in a vise and squeeze.

I might just allow that.

If she chose to do it while wearing this outfit.

Clearing my throat, I stepped away from her and sent a trickle of fire to burn her coat. She wouldn't be needing that again.

But I wasn't done.

I allowed the flames around the center of the room to die into smoky tendrils, revealing my gift to the room—a golden cage.

Camillia didn't turn to look at it. She didn't need to because it was now showcased on all the holograms.

At least the Hell Fae can't touch her in that, Az muttered.

I wouldn't admit it, but that was why I'd fashioned it—to protect her. Well, more to please Melek, as I knew he wouldn't enjoy sharing her with all of Hell Fae kind. Just a chosen few.

But watching her in a cage, he would absolutely enjoy doing.

As would I.

"Take her to the stage, Commander," I told Az, solidifying his punishment. "And let today's entertainment begin."

CHAPTER 31

AJAX

I'M GOING to fucking kill you, I thought at Az.

Not that the bastard could hear me. But he could absolutely feel my fury. Because it was his fucking energy holding me captive.

Not unlike Cami in her damn cage.

Except my imprisonment wasn't meant to be a statement. Az's chains were invisible restraints that kept me from doing the one thing my body was screaming at me to do.

To end this.

To free her.

To *claim* her.

If Lucifer was going to punish me for fucking a candidate—*penetration is reserved for mates*—then I might as well bite her. At least then I could communicate mentally with her and apologize profusely for this situation.

Fucking prick.

I'd expected Lucifer to punish me. To torment *me*. Not Cami.

She didn't deserve this. Yes, she'd touched his source

and disappeared for thirty days, but she'd explained that. She'd been honest, even after everything she'd been put through. And she'd been trying to learn how to be a Hell Fae, just like Lucifer had told her to do.

Fuck, all she'd been trying to do was *survive*.

Yet Lucifer punishes her with this?

Forcing her to stand almost naked in front of a crowd of salivating Hell Fae?

Rage seeped through my senses and made every muscle ache. I wanted to break apart the bars with my bare hands and mark Cami with my teeth, declare her as mine, and prove this entire punishment to be a facade.

It was ludicrous.

I'd never felt so possessive in my life. But that female was mine.

Yet, just like in my past, I was being forced to watch her suffer while *frozen*.

A flicker of memory appeared behind my eyes, showing me Emelyn's face frigid with terror on a stage surrounded by chanting Midnight Fae.

It was so similar to this, only the fae here were panting, and Cami wore a goddess-like expression, marking herself as untouchable and above the crowd.

If she was afraid, she wasn't showing it.

Instead, she gazed out at the room with a vacant expression, ignoring all the crude statements and salacious offers being flung her way.

When the trials started, she shifted her focus to the screens and simply watched as though bored.

The only inclination I had of her discomfort was her rigid stance. She acted as though she couldn't move. However, her cage was the size of a small room. There wasn't anywhere to sit other than on the floor, but she had space to pace around.

However, she remained in the corner, her eyes glued to the screen.

I kept testing Az's binds, trying to find a way to break free. He'd yanked me to the side of the stage, essentially positioning me as a fancy guard off to the side. Which allowed me to see Cami but also placed me near all the hungry Hell Fae.

Several of them had approached me with angry comments regarding the rules, saying I wasn't worthy of her and how dare I taint her for the rest of them.

Some asked me how she tasted.

And a few others actually admitted that they couldn't blame me for taking advantage of the situation, their comments crude as they evaluated her flawless form.

I suspected that last group would be going on one of Lucifer's famed lists. He would want to know who thought my behavior was admirable, just to keep a closer eye on them with their sponsored brides.

Az approached in my periphery, his power lashing out at my senses as he seemed to release me from a few of the binds. "Don't make a scene," he said under his breath.

"By doing what?" I met his gaze. "Biting you?" Because he'd only freed my head.

His lips twitched. "Now, we both know I might enjoy that."

"Except it would mate us," I countered. "And I absolutely do not want to be mated to you."

His eyebrows lifted. "Oh? Would I make such a terrible mate?"

I glanced at Cami and back at him. "Yes. You would."

His gaze narrowed. "You think I like this?"

"You put her in that damn cage, Az. So you clearly don't dislike it."

He grunted. "She's fine and she's safe. That's all I care about."

"She's not fine," I gritted out, looking at her again. "She's stiff and uncomfortable."

"So I'll give her a massage later and worship her with my tongue. She'll forgive me then."

I highly doubted that. Something had shifted in her the moment Lucifer had removed her coat. Some sort of fire igniting, a subtle resolution fueling her current state.

She wouldn't be forgiving any of us easily. Including me.

"How does your Phoenix feel about all this?" I asked him, purposely goading him. "Does he like having all these other men staring at *his* Cami?"

Az's lips flattened, his gaze perusing the room. "My Phoenix understands loyalty," he said vaguely.

"To whom?" I wondered aloud. "Because it's clearly not to me or to Cami."

Black flames danced in Az's gaze as he faced me, his Phoenix peeking out from the depths of his eyes. They were quickly squashed by his usual violet.

"I've bound you to protect you," he muttered under his breath. "If you fight this, your punishment will worsen. You have to know that."

Maybe I did.

But that didn't mean I had to like it or accept it.

"Just let him have his fun torturing you, and he'll reward you later," Az added, his voice still pitched low in case the surrounding Hell Fae were trying to listen.

Most of them had returned to their booths, their focus on the trials unfolding via the screens. Only a few were still lingering about, but they were more interested in studying Cami's breasts than listening to me and Az.

"I don't care about my punishment," I hissed at him. "I care about Cami. She didn't do anything wrong."

"Maybe this isn't a punishment for her so much as a test," Az countered. "A way to prove her mettle in an intense situation."

Frowning, I studied Cami and considered Az's suggestion. *A test, not a punishment.*

A test for what?

To see how long she can withstand this humiliation?

She stood with her feet braced and her arms hanging limply at her sides, but the tension in her shoulders told me she wouldn't be able to maintain that position much longer.

It'd been a few hours already, and the trials weren't even close to being done. The brides were still in Unseelie territory, with very few of them having passed the trial. And they had to go to the Naga region of the Marsh Lands next.

Maybe he's testing her endurance, I thought, admiring her confident form. *Or how long she can just take his cruelty without speaking.*

"Why would he test her?" I asked Az. "To see if she's worthy of Melek's intentions?"

Az lifted a shoulder. "I know better than to ask Typhos questions. He'll explain his reasons when he's ready."

I clenched my jaw. Cami's words about jumping off a cliff under Lucifer's orders came rushing through my mind, her accusation one I felt to my very soul.

Because I would follow his orders to the grave.

Yet something about this was different. I wanted to break free of Az's energy chains and release Cami, help her escape this realm, this situation, this *everything*. And say "fuck it all" to Lucifer's games.

For the first time in a very long time, I wanted to put someone else first.

To do what I felt was right instead of just accepting this fate or assuming my superior had a decent motive.

Lucifer had always proved wise, his decisions frequently impacting others in a positive manner rather than a negative one.

But this... I couldn't see anything positive in this situation.

Cami winced, her palms grabbing the fiery bars before yanking them back with a hiss. My body jolted—or tried to —as she fell to her knees, her legs giving out beneath her.

Az glanced up at the stage, obviously having heard her soft cry of pain, but did nothing to help her as she rocked forward, her palms meeting the ground.

The cage wobbled a little, making my brow draw downward.

It seemed the contraption was balancing on a sphere somehow. *Is that why she remained so still?* I wondered. *Because she could feel the balance of it shifting?*

But she hadn't been able to stand anymore, her limbs shaking from the effort, and now she appeared to be panting as her cage rattled and moved.

Several other Hell Fae had ceased watching the screens, their attention on Cami's quivering form. Her breasts hung in full display, but the chains kept her lower half hidden. Although, she seemed to be clenching her thighs, like she was trying to ensure the garment stayed on.

Wait, no... I narrowed my gaze. *I recognize that action.*

She wasn't trying to keep anything on.

She was trying to stop herself from *coming.*

My lips parted. *That's why she couldn't walk earlier,* I realized. *That fucking outfit is stimulating her clit.*

I hadn't taken the time to properly admire her in the

chains, as it had felt wrong to do so, given the situation, but now that I was studying the outfit, I could see where it looped down her center to cover her sex.

Fuck.

The cage moved again, this time resulting in Cami making fists as her entire body trembled.

She was close to the edge. If she had an orgasm while in Lucifer's cage, that would finalize her humiliation.

She couldn't take much more of this. And I couldn't either.

Whatever *test* this might be wasn't worth Cami's pain. This had gone on long enough.

"Release me," I told Az. "*Now.*"

"No," he replied, but he seemed preoccupied with Cami's state, his lips curling downward into a frown. Perhaps because he'd just realized what I had—that Cami was about to come in front of all these panting Hell Fae.

I very much doubted his Phoenix would approve of that.

My gaze went to Melek to find him transfixed on Cami as well, his own expression not showcasing his usual amusement. Which suggested he also wasn't keen on this demonstration.

He leaned in to say something to Lucifer, causing the Hell Fae King to glance at Cami. He shrugged, then went back to a device in his hand.

Is that doing something to Cami? To the cage? I wondered. *Or is he just sending a message to one of his Nightmare Fae Kings?*

"No," I said, the word filled with my rage. "I don't accept this."

Az startled as though he'd forgotten I was beside him.

But his energy held fast, keeping me frozen while I watched Cami bite her lower lip.

"Constantine once held me captive beneath a spell," I

told Az, my voice low. "Forced me to watch all those I cared about lose their will to live just before he cemented them in stone."

I looked up at him, ensuring he could see every ounce of agony I felt when recalling that cruel day.

"Now you're forcing me to observe Cami lose her fight. She may not be my mate, or my family, but she's the first woman to make me feel anything more than death in the last decade. And *you* are forcing me to watch her suffer. Tying me down. Making me powerless. *Just like Constantine.*"

Az winced. "Ajax."

"*No.*" I wouldn't hear his reasoning or his platitudes anymore. "This is wrong." Cami was ours to protect. And we were letting her writhe up on that stage for the entire fucking kingdom to see. "I'll never forgive you for this."

There might be a logical explanation for all of this, one I would have understood a week ago. Fuck, I might have even accepted it hours ago.

But not now.

Not after watching Lucifer put Cami's body on display like some sort of power move.

She's not a statement.

She isn't entertainment.

She's a person. My *person.*

A beautiful warrior and a woman of integrity and strength.

She had honor. Honor that deserved to be defended, not ripped from her in front of an audience.

"Fuck," Az breathed, his power pulsating around me. "Ajax—"

An explosion rocked through the nightclub, sending me sideways to the ground as Az's energy snapped like a rubber band.

I blinked, dazed and startled by the impact, not understanding what had just happened.

Cami was on the floor a few feet away, the cage having dissolved into ash around her. She appeared just as lost as I did, her eyes round as she took in the room around her.

The fires are gone, I realized, noting the dull hum of light coming from the screens and nothing else. Az was on the floor as well, his violet eyes flickering in the dark as he scanned for danger.

Then his focus went straight to Lucifer.

The Hell Fae King stood in the middle of the room, his gaze on the still-glowing hologram. I followed his focus, my lips parting at the sight unfolding before us.

Oh, shit…

The murky waters of the Marsh Lands were swirling in a whirlpool of chaos. Hell Fae Brides rushed out of the way, along with the Unseelie they'd been engaged with, all trying to avoid the spinning vortex at the center of the insanity.

Another portal.

In the Marsh Lands.

And it's sucking in everything and everyone around it.

Like a black hole…

My gaze darted to Cami again, my instinct to go to her overriding all reason.

Except she was nowhere to be seen.

Gone.

Vanished.

The only sign of her that remained was a few red ribbons from her hair.

And the subtle hint of her flowerlike scent.

CHAPTER 32

CAMI

A FEW SECONDS EARLIER

WHAT THE FUCK JUST HAPPENED?

I'd seen something on the screens. A portal, maybe? But it hadn't looked like the one I'd conjured with Vita. It'd... it'd resembled a swirling hole of intensity, threatening to destroy everything around it.

Then I'd been thrown around in my cage like a toy as if the bottom had dropped out of the entire club. I'd been so pissed that it wouldn't have surprised me if the blast had come from me.

But it hadn't, and now everything *hurt*.

I tried to move, then groaned as pain snapped through my ribs. The scent of ash wrapped around me, making me dizzy as I tried to discern what had happened.

I reached out for the cage bars, hoping to stand, only to realize it had incinerated around me.

Maybe it broke open in the blast?

Wait, what about the portal thing?

393

I tried to see through the dust, but it swirled around me like a sandstorm, confusing my senses.

Suddenly it felt as though I were wrapped up in a tornado of ash and embers, pure heat bathing my skin as something tugged at my chains. *What the fuck?*

I coughed, my hands automatically flailing around in an attempt to clear the debris, to be able to *see*.

My stomach heaved, the sensation reminding me of when Melek had taken me to the palace the first time and leaving me uneasy.

I tried saying his name, but the torrent of atmospheric particles made it impossible to speak. I coughed again, burying my face in my hands as I struggled to decipher what was happening.

Then it all stopped, my body seeming to freeze on a murky floor. My nose crinkled as the ash blended with a new smell. Something sour and wet.

Did a water line break?

Do buildings in the Hell Fae Realm even have water lines?

I brushed my nose, wanting to get rid of the acrid stench, but that only made it worse.

Because there was something mossy on my hand.

What the…?

Peering around me, the air cleared enough for me to confirm that I was no longer in my cage. Hell, I wasn't even in the nightclub.

Is that sunlight? It seemed a little sickly as it battled with the dusty air, the dim rays fighting their way through the obscure sky. What few beams made it into the garden around me shattered when they hit an invisible wall, becoming broken rainbows that cast various colors over fairylike statues.

Uh, yeah, definitely not the fiery lights of Purgatory…

My fingers brushed the ground, only instead of

touching something mossy this time, it was stone-like. *No, not a stone. Another statue.*

I blinked up at an Unseelie female, feeling dwarfed by it as I tried to process my current location.

In the Unseelie Court?

Inside their... what was it called? The Bridal Garden?

I frowned. *Did I hit my head in the blast at the club? Am I dreaming?*

Because that would certainly explain my random appearance here.

Yet it... it felt real. *Looks real, too.*

There were vines hanging all around me, their dark green limbs laden with blossoms that helped dispel some of the musky scent around me. This area almost seemed peaceful. Quiet. *Beautiful.*

The book I'd read on this region had claimed it'd once been a forest filled with life, and looking around, I could see that now. However, there were deadly influences here, too. Subtle little black stems indicating where life had ended.

And so much power, I marveled, sensing it all around me.

Lucifer manages all of this.

Every kingdom within his realm.

That's a lot for one fae to maintain.

That didn't make me like him, though. Not after everything he'd done to me today.

So where is he? I wondered. *How did I end up here?*

The statue suddenly buckled as a shock wave rocked the ground, shattering the stones as I scrambled backward on my hands, the chains digging into me as I moved.

"*Fuck,*" I hissed, the outfit strangling my thighs and lower body.

Either this is really happening, or I hit my head and this hideous lingerie followed me into a nightmare.

Fuck this outfit.

Fuck Lucifer.

Fuck all of this bullshit.

I was about to roll to my hands and knees, to see if I could find a way to stand, when strong arms wrapped around my middle and tugged me backward into a hard chest. "Shh, it's me," a deep voice said against my ear.

Ajax.

I opened my mouth to tell him off, when a flash made me blink.

More followed, flickering all around us as a low hum tickled my senses. I couldn't quite place the cause of the sound until I caught a glimpse of a sparkling flutter touching the dull daylight.

Wings. Lots of wings.

Unseelie, I marveled. *Real ones.*

They probably didn't like us here in such a sacred place.

But why is the ground still shaking? I wondered.

Another statue crashed in the distance, sending the mirrorlike stone tumbling across the ground. Bent trees snapped and petals floated in the air, giving the atmosphere an eerie tone as destruction rumbled in the distance.

"Hold the wall!" a male voice shouted when a scream accompanied another explosion.

I strained to see where it had come from. Glimpses of *something* blurred through the air.

"We need to get out of here," Ajax said as his shadows began to unfurl.

But I shook him off. "No. We can't leave." The words tumbled from my mouth unbidden, my instincts rioting at the very thought of fleeing.

Something had pulled me here.

Something that had felt a lot like Lucifer's magic.

Okay, but hold on. I would really rather watch him rot in literal Hell, I thought darkly. *Especially after what he's done to me.*

So maybe leaving would be—

Another scream rent the air, sending a chill down my spine.

That sounded feminine, not masculine.

Because the brides are in this kingdom for their trial, I realized. *Shit.*

We couldn't abandon them. Not with that... that *thing* I'd seen in the feeds. "Was that a portal?" I asked, referring to what I'd witnessed on the screen. "That vortex thing? Was it a portal in the middle of the trial?"

"Yes, which is why we need to get the fuck out of here. It's sucking everything into it," Ajax told me as another statue crumbled a few feet away.

He engaged his magic again, his shadows forming around us.

"*No,*" I snapped at him.

Maybe we weren't supposed to be here, but something had pulled me here for a reason. I could feel it in my soul, the rightness of this moment.

"We can't leave," I said again.

Another blast hit the garden, sending more stones tumbling and crashing to the ground. Shouts echoed through the air as Unseelie burst into view and launched into the dusty sky.

Some of them had Hell Fae Brides with them, while others were holding ropes to keep one of the stone walls from falling.

"Brace yourself!" a voice called out.

It was the only warning we received before half of the barrier ripped apart.

The shock wave rushed through the ground and sent

my braids flying, the strands becoming tousled as the reverberations had me jolting against the mossy floor.

This fucking outfit! I thought, groaning as the chains dug into my skin once more.

The one side snagged, squeezing on my rib to the point of pain and eliciting a sharp gasp from my throat.

Ajax's black shadows swirled around me again, but I forcefully pushed them down with a rush of magic—magic I hadn't even realized I possessed. It just came naturally, my spirit refusing to leave.

Ajax snarled as he replaced his muted magic with his hands, palming my face. "We have to leave," he stressed, his dark eyes filled with concern. "It's not safe."

The intensity in his voice surprised me. "And go back to Purgatory, where I can be a fucking sex puppet on display?"

"No," he snapped. "That's never happening again, Cami. Never."

I stared into his black eyes edged with blue flames.

Did he mean that?

Did he know what he was suggesting? Because Lucifer would do something far worse than just demote him from Warden if he tried to help me escape.

The irony wasn't lost on me. He'd been demoted for *allowing* me to escape. Now he wanted to help me?

Too fucking late, Ajax, I wanted to say, but a cry sliced through the murky atmosphere, clawing at my attention.

I untangled myself from Ajax's grip, my eyes searching for the source.

When it came again, this time with even more agony underlying the sound, I forced myself to my feet. Everything hurt, the outfit doing little to protect me from the elements.

But fuck this.

I had to... had to *help*. It was like this intrinsic need burning through my soul, demanding action. Demanding recourse. Demanding *purpose*.

I hissed through the pain and forced myself to head toward the injured bride. Or I assumed that cry had come from an injured bride, anyway. It was too feminine to be an Unseelie.

My chains seemed to burn with unnatural heat as I moved, but I ignored it, my adrenaline pumping too hard for me to focus on anything other than identifying the source of that sound.

Find the source of that sound, I echoed to myself as I ripped off my shoes and jumped over some of the broken stones.

Ajax called out my name, but I ignored him, focused on the whimpering.

Stepping around one of the statues, I spotted one of the fallen brides—a red-haired female that I recognized from my first trip to the library.

Veronica, I recalled, her name having been engraved on the back of her shirt that first day. *Veronica Scottsdale.*

Her fiery strands clung to her face, going frizzy and limp in this inhospitable land.

Unlike the other brides I'd seen on the feeds earlier, she wore a sheer black dress with gold trim. It was just as revealing as the fitted warrior leathers but definitely not giving her much protection, as evidenced by her cuts and bruises.

"Veronica," I said, kneeling beside her and noting the marble piece trapping her arm. Blood coated the left side of her face, and her eye was swollen shut. There was also something sugary on the other side of her cheek.

I frowned at it. *Is that icing?* I wondered.

Then I shook myself and focused on the marble.

LEXI C. FOSS & J.R. THORN

Her green eyes—or the uninjured one, anyway—seemed unfocused until she blinked. "What the fuck are you wearing?" she asked as she took in my outfit. Then she flinched again, another one of those sad little whimpers leaving her mouth. "*Fuck*, this hurts."

I assumed she meant the debris on her arm.

Ignoring her question about my attire—because I really didn't want to waste time answering that—I focused on the piece holding her down. "I'm going to move this so you can get up."

She glanced at the marble and winced. "Yeah, okay."

"Can you try to roll a little as I push on it?" I asked.

But before she could answer, the piece disappeared into a puff of smoke and Ajax appeared with an exasperated look.

Veronica cringed away from him, then jumped as Az materialized beside him from a cloud of ash. His disheveled hair fell into his violet eyes, his expression one of concern.

He immediately kneeled beside me, his gaze scanning my mostly nude state. "You're hurt?" he asked.

I nearly laughed at the false concern in his voice. Like he fucking cared. He'd put me in a cage a few hours ago while dressed in this ridiculous outfit. "I'm fine," I snapped. "But Veronica is hurt. Get her out of here. *Now*."

I didn't care if this was a Hell Fae trial; something was clearly wrong. And he could spend his time worrying about her, not me.

When he didn't react or say anything, I added, "Unless you want her death on your hands? She's probably suffered internal bleeding and needs medical attention." Because from what I could tell, she was a Halfling like me, not a full-blooded fae.

Az shook his head as though waking from a spell and

looked at Ajax, his eyebrows flying upward. "Why haven't you gotten Cami the fuck out of here yet?"

Ajax merely stared at him. "Oh, now you suddenly care about her well-being?"

"Don't start—"

"Or are you going to freeze me with your fucking restraint magic and force me to watch her suffer again?" Ajax continued.

Wait, what?

"I was doing my job," Az hissed. "And we don't have time for this right now. Get Cami out of here. I'll handle the bride."

Ajax folded his arms. "She doesn't want to leave, and I'm not going to force her, even if it's the right thing to do. She's had enough manhandling for one day."

Now my eyebrows flew upward. *Ajax is taking my side?*

"Fuck this," Az snarled, grabbing both me and Veronica.

I opened my mouth to protest as his ashy magic settled all around me, the world disappearing in a cloud of black.

Only for it to blink back into the dim light as I stumbled backward with a magical jolt. My chains cut into my skin again, stirring an agonized groan from my chest.

At least it wasn't stimulating me anymore.

But it certainly didn't feel good.

Az reappeared in the next blink with a struggling Veronica in his arms, his violet gaze raging as he glared at me. "What the fuck, Cami?"

I brushed him off, unable to even begin to answer him. I hadn't tried to fight his teleport, but my magic had. And my magic had won.

So I was staying here for a purpose I didn't fully understand. Nor did I really feel like discussing it with the man who had put me in that damn cage.

A man I'd started to like, against my best wishes.

A man who had apparently immobilized Ajax to keep him from helping me.

Not that he would have anyway, I thought.

"*Fuck,*" Az said, drawing my attention to him and Veronica's fleeing form.

"I am *not* going back!" she shouted as she bolted with much more speed than I would have expected from her.

She didn't want to return to bridal hell? S*hocking.*

Az cursed. "I'll get her," he said while shoving a finger at Ajax. "But don't let Camillia out of your sight, understand?"

"Just go chase the girl." Ajax sounded exasperated, as if it was a dumb order and he couldn't possibly lose sight of me.

Except I was already halfway across the rubble, and Ajax cursed. "Cami, hold up!"

"I will not hold up. You *keep up,*" I shouted over my shoulder.

Because it was clear that no one knew what the fuck they were doing. Innocent lives were being endangered over a fucking trial, and on top of that, there was a massive portal in the Marsh Lands destroying everything around it.

I'll take care of this myself if I have to, I growled in my head. Not that I had a fucking clue how, but I was over it. The bureaucracy. The male superiority.

All of it.

And it was time for this insanity to come to an end.

CHAPTER 33

CAMI

"CAN you conjure me some shoes? And maybe something more appropriate to wear?" I demanded after stepping on something sharp, making pain radiate up my leg.

If he was going to stick around, he could at least prove useful.

My feet were starting to burn, and I realized I had cuts. Probably more than I cared to admit. The rest of me was painfully exposed, too. Not to mention my aching ribs were making it hard to breathe.

And now my clit is throbbing again because of these fucking chains.

"Some underwear or pants would be nice, too," I grumbled.

Ajax responded by withdrawing his wand, but when a blast of purple magic ricocheted off of me, he winced.

Well, that clearly wasn't going to work.

But his eyebrows simply drew downward in the next breath, determination overtaking his features as he narrowed his gaze. He muttered another spell, this one seeming to slither around me like his pet snakes.

I shivered, worried that I'd just made a terrible mistake when the chains started to move and re-form around me.

Frowning, I looked down to see the lace and metal creating a top that actually covered my breasts.

I jolted as the metallic piece against my mound moved, then sighed with immediate relief as it freed my tender skin. My insides burned, reminding me of the chains against my skin, but a subtle hint of coolness from my necklace helped calm my fiery nerves.

Then Ajax took a step back to evaluate his handiwork. "I can't remove the outfit, but I can apparently manipulate it."

He'd created several layers, the red lace and chains turning into a somewhat functional dress that cupped me from breast to thigh.

Not exactly the best wardrobe for our current situation, but maybe the metal would serve as a shield.

He added a new pair of shoes, similar to the ones I'd discarded, but flat this time.

Then he handed me a set of throwing knives.

My eyebrow rose in surprise.

"I figure I owe you several of these after what happened today," he explained with a shrug. "And probably a thousand apologies."

Hmm. "Maybe you're not an asshole after all."

"Oh, I am," he promised. "But I expected Lucifer to punish me, not you. And had I known what he would do…" He trailed off and shook his head. "I told you a memory with you was worthy of punishment. I meant it. But that…"

I considered him for a long moment, then nodded, understanding what he was trying to say. He'd been okay with everything knowing he would be the one punished, but he hadn't known Lucifer would do what he'd done today.

"Az bound me with magic," he added as the ground started to tremble again. "Otherwise... I would have done something."

"Lucifer made him bind you."

"Yes." Rage filtered across Ajax's expression. "Just like the day Constantine froze me in place while Emelyn and my family were killed."

I swallowed, suddenly realizing just how bad Ajax's punishment had been today.

Except... I hadn't been killed. Just sensually tormented. And I wasn't Emelyn or his parents.

So why is he comparing the two?

I nearly asked, when an Unseelie burst into existence in front of me, staring me down.

Stunned by not only his presence but also his incredible beauty, I dumbly stared as his wings broke into multicolored lights and disappeared.

Leaving a very attractive, powerful fae standing before me.

One that was wearing a crown.

He had a few feet on me, and his long hair reminded me of liquid mercury. It floated around him, making him look both ethereal and dangerous.

I held up my two new daggers in self-defense, but that only seemed to amuse the creature.

He raked his gaze over me as his nostrils flared. "Well, you're certainly a pretty thing, but not who I'm looking for. Have you seen a female pass through? Perhaps one with a penchant for cupcakes?" he asked, his panty-melting accent indecipherable. *Irish, sort of? Maybe a hint of Scottish, too? A mixture of multiple accents?*

His vibrant eyes locked on me with an invisible pull,

407

the sensation reminding me of how Az's Phoenix tended to hypnotize me. I suddenly felt dizzy, my blades falling to my sides.

Only for Ajax to rush forward in a blur of shadows, his back knocking me free of the alluring spell the Unseelie had just cast over me.

"King Erebus, I assume," Ajax greeted.

King? I repeated, peeking around Ajax to evaluate the Unseelie again. *I suppose that explains the crown.*

"Warden," the king purred in response. His expression lit up with a grin that seemed borderline psychopathic, like he was just as likely to hug Ajax as he was to kill him.

My guess was the latter.

Lethality radiated off the Unseelie as the ground trembled around us. I wasn't sure if the quake beneath my feet was because of the portal or the angry Midnight Fae in front of me.

"I mean no disrespect, but I would appreciate you not enchanting my female," Ajax said.

My eyebrows lifted. *Your female?* I wanted to ask. *In what way, shape, or form is that accurate?*

And why do I like the way it sounds?

King Erebus smirked, his gaze flicking over Ajax's shoulder and back to me. "Oh? Is this little creature really *yours*? Because she smells like *Lucifer's*." The sheer wings behind him fluttered back into existence. "If you're looking to return her to the Hell Fae King, he's in the courtyard. Or what *used* to be the courtyard. However, I suggest leaving the grounds immediately. This area has become unstable."

No shit.

And what do you mean, I smell like I belong to Lucifer?

Like hell I would *ever* belong to that monster of a man.

King Erebus's wings began to flutter, moving too fast

for me to see them anymore and leaving the space behind him a multicolor blur.

"I suppose that's not the point," he went on. "I have a particular bride who's already intrigued me. If she went this way, she's in serious danger of attracting my soldiers as well. And if that happens… well. Let's just say that I really should get back to tracking her."

Rather than ask us again if we'd seen her, the light around him broke and he disappeared.

What an asshat. He's more worried about claiming a damn bride than the crumbling state of his kingdom.

But it didn't surprise me that the Unseelie King would be an asshole. What did, though, was what he had said about me.

"Why did he say I smell like I belong to Lucifer?" I asked, not liking the sound of that.

Ajax's Warden mask was securely in place, so I couldn't sense a reaction. I suspected it wasn't because he was trying to bury his feelings, but because he wanted to make sure we made it out of this alive.

"I think it's the chains," he said, looking pointedly at my new dress. "And that probably has something to do with why I can't conjure you out of it. No telling what other sort of effects those things have the longer they're on you."

I snorted. "You're the one who told me I had to wear them just a few hours ago."

"Before I realized what exactly Lucifer had planned," he muttered.

"Seems like it was pretty fucking obvious to me when I saw the outfit," I countered.

He sighed and shook his head. "I'm sorry, Cami. I'll never be able to say it enough."

Well, that much was true, I supposed. And this wasn't

the place to discuss it more. "Which way?" I asked, my instincts demanding that I stay here yet not telling me why or what to do.

He nodded toward the fallen wall. "That way is toward the main courtyard."

The courtyard. As in where Lucifer is, according to King Erebus. "You want me to go *toward* the Hell Fae King?" I asked incredulously.

"Do you have another idea? You're the one who refuses to leave this kingdom."

I stared at him, considering. "Actually, no, I don't." Because something about the direction he'd pointed in had felt right.

What is this weird pull? I wondered. *Why does it feel like I should be here?*

Helping the brides made sense, but deep down, I knew that wasn't the real reason I wanted to stay. There was some intrinsic need inside me driving my actions.

Similar to when I touched the source, I realized.

Then maybe I should leave.

Run away.

Ignore this tugging on my spirit.

But I'd never been one to back down from a challenge.

Which was why I'd faced the one Lucifer had laid out for me earlier with my head held high.

This might be a more dangerous situation, one that made little sense.

But I had to follow my instincts.

I looked at Ajax. "Let's go."

CHAPTER 34

CAMI

APPARENTLY, the half-fallen wall was what had separated the Bridal Garden from the exterior region. The moment we crossed over the center of it, I heard Melek's familiar voice.

"This isn't going to fix things, Ty." He sounded concerned. "Let's take a step back and evaluate the best—"

"There's no *time*," Lucifer interjected.

It was a different tone from that of the smug king who had been in the club.

This was the ruler, the one who was dealing with an active threat in his realm, an attack on his people.

This was the Lucifer who cared.

I'd better memorize it because I doubt I'm going to see this side of him again—assuming I survive the night.

Ignoring that thought, I continued climbing over debris, making my way toward Lucifer's and Melek's voices. Every step I took in their direction felt right, like I was being reeled in by some magical power.

What is this? I wondered. *Why do I feel like I'm on an invisible leash?*

Maybe it's these clothes, I thought, glancing down at the enchanted metal. *Is it trying to find Lucifer?*

I stumbled over one of the rocks, only to be caught by Ajax's arm, his hand immediately going to my hip to help me over the particularly difficult terrain.

"If that vortex starts trying to suck us in, you have to let me shadow you," he said softly. "Please."

"Sure," I agreed, not bothering to argue with that. It was logical and made sense. "But I suspect my magic will just yank me right back here again."

He frowned at that. "You mean you're not doing it intentionally?"

I shook my head. "No. I didn't fight Az, but my magic did."

He hummed in consideration, then paused as the portal came into view.

It was massive, sitting in a sea of destruction amidst the center of a marshy pit.

Damn.

It was so much worse than what I'd seen on the screen. So much larger, too.

"Was it that big before?" I asked slowly, taking in the engorged size of it.

"No, it's grown," Ajax replied, sounding grim.

A rush of murky waters swirled around the opening, the magic seemingly created by the creatures of this world. Or perhaps it was the very essence of this kingdom being drawn into the massive black hole.

The whirlpool seemed to be sucking in everything around it—trees, pieces of the Unseelie palace, Unseelie themselves, a few Nagas...

And brides.

Lucifer floated into the sky as his magic sent heat blazing all around him.

While the chaos had stolen my attention, nothing compared to the fury of the Hell Fae King.

A pair of ashy appendages resembled wings against his back, but they weren't feathery or bright. More like shadows that seemed to carry him higher into the dusky air. A dark substance moved with him and swept up and down like burning feathers threaded with fire.

Beautiful.

Terrifying.

Intense.

My heart thundered in my chest as I dug my fingers into my palms. Another shock wave boomed, causing my knees to buckle.

But Ajax caught me again, his shadows keeping us stable while the ground trembled around us. The power of it all echoed in my chest, making me feel like a living drum.

Lucifer, I realized on a breath. *That's* Lucifer's *power.* It radiated around me, distorting the air and tugging at my insides.

More, I thought dizzily. *Give me more.*

I blinked, confused by the desire.

"I need to be closer," I whispered.

Ajax glanced at me, his brow furrowing. "I think we're close enough."

Lucifer's magic beat at my being as his thunderous voice ordered those below to assist. "More water!" he shouted, his words seeming to be for a group of Nagas who were chanting around a gushing geyser.

A blast of liquid followed, the snakelike beings lifting their hands as it shot up into the sky.

"Lift!" he yelled, this time at the Unseelie who

appeared to be sending air currents up to swirl around the vortex in the opposite direction.

He's trying to close the portal, I realized.

But it wasn't working. His power was one of fire and brute strength, and it beat against the whirlpool, only severing it and making it open wider.

The scent that followed reminded me of an old family trip to the Everglades, making my nose curl as my mind spun the memory behind my eyes.

Hellfire, I thought, picturing my father out in the middle of the swamp, covered in dangerous flames.

"You want to kill those mosquitos, Cami? Just burn them," he'd told me.

He'd made a show of setting several mangroves on fire.

Which had spread to other plants.

Growing all around us.

"The trick now is how to put it out," he'd whispered to me, his expression menacing. "Better figure that out or you won't be coming home."

My mom had tsked then, saying, "At least give the poor girl some spells to try."

Papers had fallen from the sky in the next moment, their white gloss flickering in the flames, reminding me a bit of fiery feathers.

I'd snatched them all up, memorizing each chant.

And had finally found the one I'd needed to dispel the blazing chaos.

Lucifer's Hellfire drew me back to the present, my recollection melting beneath the display above. His magic appeared to be fueling the portal more than dissolving it.

Kind of like the fire in the Everglades, I thought, frowning. Some of the spells I'd used then had strengthened the flames rather than extinguish them.

The swirling edges of the vortex yawned back at

Lucifer, opening up a pitch-black center. The immense ripple against reality gulped in everything around it, quickly devouring another section of the Unseelie palace.

Ancient trees decorated with vines twisted and broke, releasing thunderous snaps that echoed throughout the landscape.

Screams rose up when another wave sucked in a second group of brides. They couldn't do anything to stop the current washing them away.

"No!" Lucifer yelled, his frustration palpable as he thrust out a hand and shot pure Hellfire at the portal.

The hairs on the back of my neck stood on end as intense heat washed over the flattened waves.

"Ty!" Melek yelled as he snapped out a wave of brilliant white power. "You can't do this alone!"

I'd never seen Melek's strength before, not like this.

It blinded the sky, sending out a retaliating shock wave that momentarily broke the clouds and caused blistering sunlight to cascade down onto the marshy waters below.

I flinched. *That's definitely not going to work.*

Melek's power seemed to be too much for this kingdom, his light a brightness the Marsh Lands couldn't accept.

Given what I'd read of this land, it made sense. The Marsh Lands were essentially an unstable mixture of the Underwater Kingdom and the Barren Lands.

Too much water destabilized the atmosphere, just as too much light would alter the chemistry of the land.

Understanding that made me realize that Lucifer and Melek might be the worst candidates to fix this. They were trying to drown a whirlpool with water, Hellfire, and brute force.

This is all wrong, I realized when Lucifer's next blast of raw power only served to burst the water into a layer of

LEXI C. FOSS & J.R. THORN

steam. The portal twisted against it, then seemed to expand even wider.

This time it took a blur of what had to be Unseelie with it. The twinkle of broken light came with a rush of filtered cries of horror before they blipped out as if drowned.

The Nagas thrashed, much more visible in their desperate strokes to get away. Their powerful tails raged against the steamy current, but they were no match for the intensity of the growing vortex.

Ajax hissed, his arm leaving my back.

I glanced at him, confused. Then I found his eyes staring down at the chains around my center.

"Cami?" he asked, uncertainty coloring his tone.

I frowned. "What?"

Then another crash ripped my focus away from him, luring me back toward the blistering portal. *This is bad. So fucking bad.*

"He's not doing this right," I told Ajax. "He's making it worse."

"Cami, you're... glowing," Ajax said, ignoring me entirely. "The chains..."

Lucifer raged in the sky as warmth touched my skin, pulling my attention down to my dress again. Ajax was right—*I am glowing.*

My brow furrowed, realization dawning. *Because this is Lucifer's magic.*

That must have been what had drawn me here.

Just like the source, I thought, my lips parting. *That's why this pull is so familiar—it's just like when I touched the heart of his power.*

Only this time, I was literally wrapped up in it, drawn toward him like a beacon.

But it was more than that.

I could feel his power thrumming through me, almost as though I was a conduit of sorts. Or a siphon.

How is this even possible? I marveled, sensing Lucifer's next strike before he released it. *Why am I so close to his essence?*

My mind raced as I grabbed the talisman still on my chest. Melek's power mingled with the heat of the chains, providing me with a calming balance that allowed me to focus.

Warmth, not uncontrollable fire. That was what had eventually stopped the burning of the Everglades. It'd taken me hours to figure it out. But it'd finally worked.

Would it work here? There's only one way to find out.

"Cami?" Ajax asked again.

I ignored him, too busy recalling the spell I'd used that day.

If I really am a conduit, then I should be able to channel Lucifer's power to help boost this enchantment, I thought, closing my eyes and focusing on the sensations of his energy rippling through me. I called upon that warm power deep within my chest, my lips whispering the words I'd learned long ago.

Wind wound around me as I tugged on the magic encircling me, latching onto that tether I somehow seemed to have anchored deep within my soul.

A darkened strand.

Eternal energy.

Lucifer.

This was a place I didn't understand, a place I didn't want to go. But I had to try.

I continued reciting the spell from those wispy white pages, my mind a mixture of the present and the past as flickers of flames danced behind my closed eyes.

So much power.

So much grace.

A calming wave of warmth swirled inside me, waiting to be unleashed. But I needed more. I needed access.

"Camillia," a deep voice whispered into my mind. One I hated. One I desired. One I *needed.*

"Lucifer," I responded. *Let me in…*

The magic of his chains intimately wound around me, but I would use it instead of letting it use me.

Let me in, I repeated.

His power was too wild. Too intense.

I said the spell again, bolstering my warm wave while also whispering, *Let me in.*

So much vitality. Brightness. *Core strength.*

Let me in, Lucifer. Set me free…

Something inside me flared to life, a natural instinct, an inclination to *tame.* It tugged on Lucifer's rein of power, begging him to give me control, just for a moment.

Whether or not my father had somehow prepared me for this, I intuitively knew what to do.

The Marsh Lands was a place of mirages, subtlety, and delicate touches.

The opposite of what I'd seen of Lucifer.

Let me help, I begged him. *I can do this.*

I wasn't sure if he could hear me, but I hoped he could feel my intentions.

Or maybe the source would heed my call.

He'd warned me not to touch it again. But surely he would understand this purpose. *I can fix this,* I kept thinking at him. *You need a calming wave of warmth.*

Which was growing intensely inside my chest, threatening to break free at any moment. But I needed his ability to amplify the power within this realm, to ensure it would be enough to close the cavern of death in the sky.

Please, I begged. *Let me in…*

A stroke of heat brushed over my skin in response, tentative at first.

Then it grew, the chains around me hardening into diamond-like bits that clawed at my skin.

I winced, the pain increasing with each second.

He's fighting me.

He's pushing me out.

He's going to ensure I fail.

I shoved back, refusing to accept his rejection and needing to do this. *Let me help!*

The chains around me shattered, the pieces sinking into me and dragging an excruciating scream from my lungs.

It burns.

It's killing me.

It's… it's… My eyes flew open as the bright lights of the source surrounded me. *It's accepting me.*

I latched onto it without a second thought, taking the energy I needed and infusing the warmth burning inside me.

In a blink, I was back in the Marsh Lands, my gaze on the portal once more, just in time to see the Hell Fae King coming toward me.

His ashy wings were spread out behind him, Hellfire running over his arms.

I'm definitely a dead fae.

But I had to use this to my advantage, to use my last moments to do something good.

I brushed Melek's talisman with my fingers, finding the star's unique energy. *The conduit*, I reminded myself.

That was how I could do all this—the conduit had allowed me to pull Lucifer's power from the chains and into myself.

Now it was going to allow me to blast that damn portal with my own magic.

A maelstrom built inside of me, the combination of energy unlike anything I'd ever felt. It terrified me, perhaps even more than the approaching King of Hell.

An uncontrollable building of fire and ice whirled within me, combining with the warm wave. I let it grow instead of dousing it, needing to ensure this would be enough.

Just a few more seconds, I thought, aware of Lucifer's nearness.

My fingertips glowed, the water on my skin steaming into mist.

And the air around me grew heavy until I knew I couldn't hold it any longer.

Releasing my breath, I reached out with my hand.

And let it all go.

My ears popped when the ground detonated beneath me, and a shock wave burst out, sending a blast of water and debris flying upward. Lucifer was almost upon me, but now he went tumbling through the air as my explosion of unfettered magic spiraled toward the portal.

It delved inside, instantly solidifying it like glass.

Burning it hadn't been the solution.

It'd needed a delicate balance of *warmth.* Just like the Everglades. It seemed counterproductive to intuition to swelter a fire with warmth, but this hadn't been any ordinary inferno.

Just like the Hellfire my father had unleashed that day, long ago.

It'd been the opposite of what a firefighter would have known how to handle.

"Most magical elements can't be fought with logic," he'd told me after the fact. "Now you know."

Yeah, Dad, I thought now. *I definitely know.*

Deafening silence followed, and the portal fizzled and disappeared, leaving miles of destruction in its wake.

A fine mist followed, one that rained over my bare skin, making me shiver.

Then a thunderous Lucifer appeared before me.

I didn't try to run. I'd lost the useless knives somewhere in the chaos, leaving me completely defenseless and naked before him.

But I didn't bother to apologize.

I merely stared up at him, waiting for his judgment.

Instead, he looked like he didn't know what to do with me.

But oh, he was pissed. The fire in his sapphire eyes raged even hotter than his Hellfire, and the beautiful line of his square jaw was as sharp as a blade.

"Come, Camillia. I think it's time we had a chat."

He grabbed me by the nape, then we vanished into a cloud of fiery ash.

Yep. I'm definitely going to die.

Slowly.

And painfully.

Cami's story continues in *Hell Fae Commander*...

Curious about the Nightmare Fae?

Their Lethal Pet and *Their Blood Queen* are standalone reverse harem romances that follow the events of Monsters Night in the Netherworld and Morpheus Kingdoms.

Their Pixie Mate is a standalone reverse harem romance following Veronica's story as she runs with the Unseelie in the Marsh Lands.

"Mate me or die. Your choice."
The words weren't meant for me, but I felt them resonating in my very soul.
What would I choose? *Death.*

Of course, I would just burn to ash and wake up again with the same damn problem swirling around in my heart and mind.
My inner beast thinks it has imprinted on a Halfling Hell Fae.
Without my permission.

Now all I want to do is hold her. Kiss her. F-ck her.
Claim her.
But I can't.
Not until we solve this mystery going on with the Hell Fae Source and these rogue portals that keep popping up everywhere.

The Hell Fae Realm is in chaos, and my potential mate might be to blame.

Warden Ajax and Prince Melek think she's innocent.
The Hell Fae King is sure she's not.
And I'm too busy dealing with my panting Phoenix to pick a side.

All my animal can think about is biting his intended.
Meanwhile, all I can think about is how to stop him.

Camillia should have a choice.
Only, she doesn't seem to want to choose…

Authors' Note: *Hell Fae Commander* is a dark paranormal romance with four tormented mates and no choosing required. If you like your antiheroes dominant and sexy, you've come to the right realm—the Hell Realm, where the romance is hot and no forgiveness is required. This book ends on a cliffhanger.

About Their Lethal Pet:
A Monsters Night Standalone

Blood. Blades. Bodies.

Just another job. Until three men dressed in black stole me into the night.

I thought they were faceless enforcers from a past assignment, perhaps sent by their master to exact a little revenge.

But then they took off their masks and revealed the true monsters beneath.

Death Fae.
Inhuman.
Dangerous.

Now I'm locked in their golden cage, told that I need to behave to be set free. The problem is, their version of behaving means having me on my knees.

I don't care how gorgeous they are or how well-endowed they seem to be—I kneel for no one. And I have no interest in becoming their lethal little pet.

"Try to tame me," I dare.

"We have no interest in taming you, sweet pet," they say. "We want to make you ours."

"Ours to worship."
"Ours to love."
"Ours to keep."

About Their Blood Queen:
A Monsters Night Standalone

They're coming.
Monsters Three.
It's Monsters Night and they're after me.
One has claws.
One has fangs.
The third is terror incarnate, and it's me he'll claim.

I said the curse.
Three names of Blood.

A dedication. A desecration.

Nemmus. Nefarus. And Nood.

I wanted my enemies dead.
I wanted revenge.
It was Monsters Night and it sounded like a fun game.

Except no one is left laughing—no one except the monsters in my head.

The question is, did I imagine them?

Or perhaps… I'm the one who's dead?

My Monsters Three came for me.

They need my nightmares. They need my rage. They feed on everything that makes me who I am… and now all those who crossed me will pay.

THEIR PIXIE MATE:
A NIGHTMARE FAE STANDALONE

Run, little pixie.
But stay away from my soldiers—they're far worse than me.
And don't believe what you see, because this is my land, little pixie.
I'm the Unseelie King, and you stepped into my fairy circle.
You accepted my gift.
That makes you our queen.

All I did was step into a damn circle that had a cupcake in the center.

I like cupcakes. Does that make me a criminal?
With icing still stuck to my face, he appeared. The gorgeous, incredibly lethal Unseelie King.
But I know the Unseelie. I know the stories.
They're tricksters. They act on a whim and will just as quickly kill you as help you.
They love their pranks and especially misfortune.

Now I'm running for my life because I've attracted the worst Unseelie of them all.

Not just their king, but his elite soldiers, too.

And now they all want a taste.

And I don't think it's the cupcake they're interested in.

It's me.

Want to see more of the Midnight Fae Realm?

Welcome to Midnight Fae Academy.
Home of the Dark Arts.
Vampires.
And cruelly handsome Fae.

A forbidden bite led to my capture and recruitment.
There are no flowers here.
No life.
Only death.

I'm an Earth Fae who doesn't belong here.
They can play their little mind games all they want, but
I'm going to find a way back to my elemental world. Even
if it kills me.

Except Headmaster Zephyrus is one step ahead of my
every move.
Prince Kolstov won't stop cornering me.
And Shadow—the reason I'm in this damn mess to begin
with—haunts my dreams.

My affinity for the earth is dying and being replaced by

something more sinister. Something powerful. Something
deadly.

The Midnight Fae believe this is my fate.
They claim that I was "recruited" for a purpose.
To battle a rising presence.
Or to die trying.

I don't owe them a damn thing. But if I have to pass their
trials to find my way home, then so be it. I survived a
plague and far worse in the Elemental Fae realm. An
ominous energy? Please. What a joke.

Give it your best shot.
I'm waiting.
And don't you dare bite me.
Or I'll make you regret it.

Author Note: This is a dark paranormal reverse harem
trilogy with bully romance (enemies-to-lovers) elements.
Despite Aflora's opinions on the matter, there will definitely
be biting. Shadow, aka Shade, guarantees it. This book
ends on a cliffhanger.

USA Today Bestselling Author Lexi C. Foss loves to play in dark worlds, especially the ones that bite. She lives in Chapel Hill, North Carolina with her husband and their furry children. When not writing, she's busy crossing items off her travel bucket list, or chasing eclipses around the globe. She's quirky, consumes way too much coffee, and loves to swim.

Want access to the most up-to-date information for all of Lexi's books? Sign-up for her newsletter here.

Lexi also likes to hang out with readers on Facebook in her exclusive readers group - Join Here.

Where To Find Lexi:
www.LexiCFoss.com

J.R. Thorn

Reverse Harem Paranormal Romance - Never Choose.

J.R. Thorn is a Reverse Harem Paranormal Romance Author who loves coffee, stormy weather, and heated discussions with her inner muse. She can often be found scribing her steamy stories in her writing cave far away from the prying eyes of her toddler, husband, two vocal cats, and canine pack.

www.AuthorJRThorn.com

facebook.com/BloodStoneSeries

amazon.com/stores/J.R.-Thorn/author/B01LYC5DM9

tiktok.com/@jrthorn_author

WELCOME TO HELL.

MY HELL.